Praise for Maxim Jakubowski and His Books

"An intriguing mixture of past tradition and future-shock dystopia, written by a giant of the genre…highly recommended."

—Lee Childs, author of the Jack Reacher novels

"I have been a fan of Maxim Jakubowski for years. There just is no finer mystery writer and editor anywhere. Find a comfortable chair and a strong drink and prepare to be enthralled."

—Alexander Algren, author of *Out in a Flash: Murder Mystery Flash Fiction*

"*The Book of Extraordinary Historical Mystery Stories* is a stunning collection, simply the best short mystery and crime fiction of the year and a real treat for crime fiction fans. I highly recommend!"

—Leonard Carpenter, author of the Conan the Barbarian books and *Lusitania Lost*

"Maxim Jakubowski is deeply experienced in the field… Sometimes a brief zap of great writing is just what you're in the mood for or have time for. That's when anthologies like his are ideal…intellectually outstanding."

—*New York Journal of Books*

THE BOOK
OF EXTRAORDINARY
IMPOSSIBLE CRIMES
AND PUZZLING
DEATHS

Published by Mango Publishing Group, a division of Mango Media Inc.

Cover Design : Roberto Nuñez
Layout: Jayoung Hong

Mango Publishing Group
2850 S Douglas Road, 2nd Floor
Coral Gables, FL 33134 USA
info@mango.bz

For special orders, quantity sales, course adoptions and corporate sales, please email the publisher at sales@mango.bz. For trade and wholesale sales, please contact Ingram Publisher Services at customer.service@ingramcontent.com or +1.800.509.4887.

The Book of Extraordinary Impossible Crimes and Puzzling Deaths: The Best New Original Stories of the Genre

Library of Congress Cataloging-in-Publication number: 2020933898
ISBN: (p) 978-1-64250-218-3 (e) 978-1-64250-219-0
BISAC category code FIC022050, FICTION / Mystery & Detective / Collections & Anthologies

Printed in the United States of America

THE BOOK OF EXTRAORDINARY IMPOSSIBLE CRIMES AND PUZZLING DEATHS

The Best New Original Stories of the Genre

Maxim Jakubowski

CORAL GABLES

This anthology is dedicated to Paul Barnett, who also wrote as John Grant, whose story in this volume was his last and which he wrote and kindly sent me just forty-eight hours before dying unexpectedly of a heart attack.
R.I.P. Paul...

Table of Contents

Introduction
Maxim Jakubowski

At the heart of most crime stories, there is a mystery: whodunit, whydunit, howdunit? A challenge not only to the investigating character, be he a professional cop or an amateur everyman, but also to the reader, who races along the pages to the end of the novel or story not only to witness that the bad guy (or gal) gets his or her just deserts, but to find out how the sleight of hand is explained—always in the hope they will deduct matters early in their read or to get confirmation of their suspicion. It's a well-worn formula that we never tire of, whether in the context of the civilized crimes of the worlds of Conan Doyle, Agatha Christie, and many of the unforgettable exponents of the Golden Age of crime writing, or amongst the rougher, hardboiled school of writing characterized by Raymond Chandler and Dashiell Hammett, whose practitioners today still thread clever variations with an inventiveness we can only admire.

Within this category, there is also a thriving subgenre which focuses with laser-like precision on what is generally called the impossible crime, often typified by locked room murders. Crimes that, at first appearance, defy all expectation once you banish the supernatural to the wings. There is a body in a room, it is locked from the inside, all exits, windows, and such have not been breached... How in hell did the murderer escape, and if he wasn't actually in the room, how was the crime committed? From Edgar Allen Poe and Sherlock Holmes on to undoubted classics like Gaston Leroux's *Mystery of the Yellow Room*, Hake Talbot's *Rim of the Pit*, and countless others (including the majority of John Dickson Carr's fiendish novels, written as both himself and Carter Dickson), the imagination has been stretched to the limit to come up with logical explanations. There is actually a reference book by Robert Adey, which offers over four hundred pages a surfeit of such quandaries and explains the hundreds of fictional impossible crimes away (a volume not recommended for those who avoid spoilers). The locked room murder genre has always been a challenge to crime mystery writers, and thrives to this day all over the world (the French author Paul Halter writes only such books!), and its success has never wavered. Many of the contemporary and past stars of the genre have, almost as a matter of principle, risen to the task brilliantly, as if it were a personal Everest. It has even birthed several TV series along the same principle, including the recent BBC TV series *Death in Paradise* and *Jonathan Creek.*

To encapsulate an impossible crime in a short story as opposed to a novel is not just a mighty challenge, but also a devious plotting structural engineering feat, and that was the proposal I issued to several handfuls of today's most respected mystery writers. And they most definitely delivered the goods, in this third volume of our anthology series of the best in contemporary crime writing. Not all came up with specific locked room murders, but each death is particularly puzzling, to say the least, and it's a daily wonder to me how, despite the heavy heritage in whose footsteps they follow, they have succeeded in coming up with more imaginative variations and improvisations on the theme and allowed their little gray cells to run riot for your reading pleasure, in a pleasing diversity of settings and timelines. Crime writing is most definitely alive and well…

Enjoy!

The Locked Cabin
MARTIN EDWARDS

T hey make a handsome couple," the man murmured, as the band struck up "The Lullaby of Broadway."

He was addressing a woman in her late thirties, darkly glamorous in a sequined gown. She sat alone at the back of the grand ballroom on the *Queen Mary*. Turning her head, she considered the man's long hair, carelessly knotted bow tie, and soft, almost feminine features. Her red lips pursed in distaste.

"I beg your pardon?" she said, in an accent unmistakably Italian.

He gave an extravagant bow and said, "Please excuse me, *signorina*. I have a dreadful habit of thinking aloud."

"A dangerous habit, perhaps."

The man's mischievous smile suggested he was not easily abashed. "Once again, I must apologize. I was watching Cynthia Wyvern and her charming companion. They dance divinely, don't you agree?"

He spoke with a faint lisp. The woman frowned and said nothing.

"I suppose," he continued, "she is determined to make the most of her freedom while she has the chance. Typical Cynthia. Lovely but headstrong. Mind you, she should have a care. Dancing cheek to cheek with handsome strangers is another dangerous habit. Especially for a young woman in her position."

"I'm afraid you have the advantage of me, sir," the Italian woman said coldly. "I don't know Miss Wyvern, and I have no idea what you are talking about."

"Forgive me! I've always had a weakness for gossip." A waiter glided by and the man snapped his fingers. "Another Hanky Panky, please. What may I offer you, *signorina*, as recompense for interrupting your reverie?"

The woman raised her penciled eyebrows.

"I do not drink cocktails."

"Another—what, lime and soda, then? Splendid." The waiter hurried away. "My name's Breen, by the way. Feargal Breen. Dublin-born, though now domiciled in Mayfair. Delighted to meet you."

He extended his hand and the woman took it with barely disguised reluctance. His handshake was weak, his palm damp.

"My name," she said, "is Sophia Vialli. And if I may say so without giving offence, I am not here in search of company. I yearn for this crossing to reach its end. At Southampton I shall be reunited with my husband."

"He is working there?"

"We are partners"—she hesitated—"in a photographic business. We travel around the world."

Breen contemplated the splendid curves of her ballgown. "You are his model?"

"I am a photographer," she said coldly, "and I prefer to remain behind the camera. As for Miss Wyvern, I know nothing of her."

"Don't worry," Feargal Breen said. "I'm not one of these dreadful wolves who prowl the decks looking out for beautiful women to take advantage of. Whether or not they are happily married."

He tittered, and the woman shook her head.

"I'm sorry, Mr. Breen…"

"Feargal, please. Ah, there's no harm in me, I can assure you. I talk too much, that's all. It amuses me to see young Cynthia clinging on so closely to that good-looking fellow. He's certainly enjoying himself. Not an Englishman, I'd say. His swagger strikes me as distinctly American. Mind if I pull up a chair?"

Sophia Vialli gave a shrug of indifference. As he sat down beside her, Breen nodded toward the dance floor. Now the band was playing "I Get a Kick out of You," while Cynthia Wyvern gazed into her companion's eyes as if hypnotized by his smoothly chiseled features.

"Ah well, my lips are sealed." Breen tapped the side of his nose in a knowing manner. "She's a lovely young thing, and it won't be long before her horizons narrow. Algy Neville-Ferguson is so dull he makes ditchwater look like the clear blue ocean. Just as well his pater is worth a mint. And when Algy comes into the baronetcy…"

He was interrupted by the arrival of their drinks. "Chin-chin!"

She raised her glass. Scorn had given way to a hint of amusement. "You're a friend of this young English rose, Miss Wyvern?"

"We've bumped into each other several times, but these days she tends to give me a wide berth. I used to contribute an occasional paragraph to the society columns, and since her engagement to Algy, she needs to be on her best behavior. Very tedious, but there it is."

Sophia Vialli sipped her lime and soda. "The young lady does not appear to be wearing an engagement ring."

Breen chortled. "You don't miss much, do you? I can see you're a woman of the world. I spotted that omission myself. Quite deliberate, I'm sure. Cynthia knows what she's letting herself in for with Algy, and if you ask me, she's determined to have a whale of a time before sinking into the quicksand of respectability. A little bird told me that she spent the past fortnight swanning around New York City in her glad rags. Heaven only knows what she got up to. Now the party's almost over."

"I'm sure you do her a disservice."

"Oh, my lips are sealed. At least, I'm not planning to spoil things for her by mentioning anything to the press. We all deserve to let our hair down once in a while."

Sophia Vialli finished her drink and gave an ostentatious yawn. "Perhaps you are right, Mr. Breen. Anyway, it is past my bedtime. May I wish you goodnight?"

Without waiting for a reply, she stood up and left the ballroom.

***

"I always like a front-toucher!"

The American gave Cynthia Wyvern a cheeky grin. They were playing deck quoits under a high sun.

Blushing prettily, she tried and failed to suppress a giggle. "Ellis, really!"

He spread muscular arms in a pantomime of mock innocence. "Whaddya mean? It's just a technical term. For when the quoit touches the hob."

"Ah."

"Better than a side-toucher or a back-toucher, take my word."

She laughed. "You really are a very bad influence, Ellis. I'll have you know that I'm a very respectable young woman."

"So you keep saying. Butter wouldn't melt, and all that. Hey, this is warm work. Do you fancy taking a turn around the deck? Or four turns, to make a mile? Then we'll really have earned another gin fizz."

"I mustn't drink too much," she said. "It goes to my head."

"You'll be fine," he assured her. "You can trust me. I'm the son of a senator."

***

"We meet again, *signorina!*"

The first class lounge was the last word in sophistication, with glass and chrome lamps, Art Deco bronzes, and an end wall that converted into a cinema screen. The upper part of the semicircular, split-level space served as an observation deck, the lower part as an ebony-fronted bar, above which hung a large painting that celebrated the Silver Jubilee. This was the hub of social activity on the ship, and as the evening drew to a close, the buzz of conversation filled the air. Sophia Vialli stood apart from the throng, drinking orange juice and studying her fellow passengers.

"Good afternoon, Mr. Breen."

"You remembered my name, Signorina Vialli! I'm flattered. And I see you've got your eye on that young couple again."

He gestured to a corner of the bar, where Cynthia Wyvern and her American admirer were having a *tête-à-tête*. In front of them were two empty cocktail glasses. Cynthia's eyes shone as her companion chattered.

The Italian woman shrugged. "No, no, I only noticed them a moment ago. I recalled our conversation. But—as you say, I mind my own business."

"Not like me, eh?" Breen gave a high-pitched laugh. "He really is a smart-looking chap."

"And the young lady is beautiful," Sophia Vialli said slyly. "Or is she not—well, your *type?*"

With a roguish wink, he drained his cocktail glass. "You do me an injustice. As you can see, I love nothing better than finishing off a White Lady!"

She permitted herself a smile. "I think you like to tease."

"I am a humble fellow, Sophia—may I call you Sophia? I feel that we are becoming friends—but I do claim a talent to amuse. As for dear Cynthia, I agree that she is lovely. No doubt her American swain thinks so too. I'm sure the fellow's well-heeled, but he can't offer a country house or a Rolls-Royce with chauffeur. It's just a passing amusement for both of them. A shipboard romance. Delightful. As long as Algy doesn't find out."

Sophia Vialli wagged a finger. "You said you would…"

"Keep mum?"

"A peculiar phrase."

He handed his empty glass to a passing waiter. "Indeed. Frankly, it's not much of a story. An innocent shipboard flirtation? There's no real whiff of scandal. It's not as if they…"

"And if they did?" Sophia Vialli allowed herself the glimmer of a smile. "This man Algy, he would not turn a blind eye?"

Breen sniggered. "Shocking temper, that fellow. Can't say I'm fond of him. We're both members of the Garrick, and he once said something very rude to me. I'd have asked him to step outside but—well, fisticuffs have never been my way of settling scores."

Cynthia slid her hand across the small table and the handsome American brought it up to his mouth, and kissed her fingers. As Breen and Sophia Vialli watched, he withdrew a cabin key from his pocket and put it down in front of her. Then he stood up abruptly and headed for the door.

***

The first class swimming pool was suitably opulent, with its mother-of-pearl ceiling and gold quartzite floors. The surface of the water was well below the pool deck. It would never do for spectators to be covered with water if the ship had a sudden roll. Ellis Hart hauled his lean frame out of the pool and stood waiting for Cynthia to join him.

"You won!" she gasped. "I thought you said you weren't much of a swimmer."

His grin showed a lot of white teeth, a tribute to American dentistry.

"I guess it's all relative, honey. I did give you half a length start."

Cynthia giggled. "You rotter, you tricked me!"

"All's fair in love and war."

"You're not about to declare war?"

"Maybe I want to make a declaration of love."

She blushed prettily. "Remember, I told you. I'm entirely respectable. Spoken for."

"You took my cabin key yesterday evening."

"And I left it in your door, without going inside to await your arrival."

"You lost your nerve," he chided.

"I'm not what you Yankees call a pushover."

"I guess not. But you lost the race, and that changes everything."

"How so?"

He grinned again. "Didn't I mention that, either? A winner is entitled to claim his spoils."

***

"We really must stop meeting like this," Breen said. "People will talk."

Sophia Vialli sat in a deck chair, reading a novel from the ship's library, while a young couple played tennis nearby. Her glare at the interruption dissolved into amusement. "I'm beginning to suspect you are following me, Mr. Breen."

"The charm of your company is irresistible, *signorina*. I can't deny that I enjoy our little chats."

Breen sat down beside her without so much as a by-your-leave. "It's so refreshing to have a *confidante*. I don't know a soul here other than Cynthia and a dreadful old couple from Holland Park, and there's nothing I like more than a natter." Sophia frowned in bewilderment. "A spot of gossip. Especially as I've made a rather extraordinary discovery about where…well, where Cynthia is sleeping."

"You make it sound," she said, "extremely salacious."

"No, no, on the contrary. It's simply rather…" Breen's pause was theatrical. "I don't know. Macabre."

Sophia Vialli put her book down next to the Kodak camera at her feet. "I am, as you would say, all ears."

Breen leaned toward her. "Cynthia is occupying one of the finest suites on A Deck."

She shrugged. "You told me she is an heiress. No doubt she can afford it."

"Letty Bohannon died in the very same suite."

The Italian woman's eyes widened. "Letty…?"

"Surely you recall the name?"

"I…I'm not sure." She ran a hand through her black hair. "It sounds familiar, but…"

"Let me jog your memory." Breen smiled as a loose return sent a tennis ball bouncing toward him. He caught it in one hand and tossed it to the server. "The Locked Cabin Murder Mystery. Now, does that ring a bell?"

She stared at him. "The Locked Cabin…yes, I read something in the newspapers, but I'm a little confused. Did I hear correctly? You said *murder?*"

Breen nodded. "Yes, the tragedy occurred during the *Queen Mary's* third Atlantic crossing. The story created a minor sensation. I was certain that you'd call it to mind."

"It's coming back to me," she said. "Refresh my memory."

"Letty Bohannon was found dead in her cabin by the steward. She was making the crossing to Southampton unaccompanied, just like Cynthia. Give or take a year or two, they were the same age. Like Cynthia, she had everything to live for, but she was shot through the head."

"How dreadful. I'd forgotten her name. But in the case I'm thinking of, the girl killed herself, didn't she? It was a clear case of suicide. Her cabin door was locked."

"So the authorities claimed," Breen said darkly. "Anything else would have been catastrophic. Imagine the lurid publicity. Murder most foul on board the flagship? Unthinkable! No wonder it was hushed up."

"What you say makes no sense. If nobody else was involved, how could there be murder? And didn't she write a suicide note?"

Breen tutted as the serving tennis player double-faulted for the umpteenth time. Game, set, and match.

"Fred Perry has nothing to fear from our fellow passengers," he murmured. "Shall we take a turn around the deck while I tell you about the ghastly business?"

***

"I'll have you know that I'm highly respectable," Cynthia whispered.

After a game of shuffleboard, she and Ellis were strolling arm in arm in the open air.

"Absolutely," he replied.

"I really can't invite you back to my stateroom. And I'm certainly not going anywhere near yours. What would the stewards think?"

"Aw, honey, you think they aren't used to turning a blind eye?"

"Besides," she said primly. "There's Algy to consider."

"Algy!" He tightened his grip on her arm. "You have the rest of your life to spend with Algy. This is a once in a lifetime opportunity."

His wheedling voice made him sound like a small boy. She shook her head and smiled. "Tell you what. After dinner, we'll take another turn around the deck."

"Under the moonlight," he said enthusiastically. "So romantic."

"Yes," she said, squeezing his fingers. "So romantic."

***

"What makes you so sure that this woman—Letty—was murdered?" Sophia asked as they ambled along the deck.

"I fancy myself," Breen said airily, "an amateur psychologist. The way people's minds work fascinates me."

"Can we ever know what another human being is thinking?" She sounded wistful.

"I knew the Bohannon family. They made a fortune out of shipping, although old George Bohannon was terrified that his son would spend it all on fast cars and even faster women the moment he inherited the estate. A wild and impetuous young fellow, Henry, a daredevil and a gambler. He was called to the Bar, but couldn't stick the law. Fancied himself as a thespian, but he wasn't much of an actor. I've even heard whispers that he's chanced his arm as a gentlemanly cat burglar. A second Raffles, no less."

Sophia's eyes widened. "Extraordinary! He was a criminal?"

"Nothing was ever proved. Poor Letty was devoted to the fellow. She was pretty and charming, if rather highly strung. Good sportswoman. At the time of her death she was engaged to be married to a young banker, dull but decent, you know the sort. Pots of money. Everything to live for."

"So," Sophia said, "it comes to this. You can't accept that a well-favored young woman could ever wish to kill herself."

"Precisely!" Breen exclaimed.

Sophia shook her head. "Your loyalty to her memory does you credit, Mr. Breen. But you said yourself that she was highly strung."

"Yes, but…"

"Strange things happen on sea journeys." She gestured toward the ocean. "Some of us love the roar of rushing waves. For others, it becomes oppressive, perhaps menacing. Even for those cocooned in luxury on A Deck, a private suite can come to resemble a well-appointed prison. If she was a poor sailor and seasick…"

"But she loved sailing! Her death came utterly out of the blue. It made no sense."

"The pistol was her own?"

"Yes," Breen admitted. "It was a birthday present from her brother."

"He has a lot to answer for. Why on earth give her a lethal weapon?"

"Letty was a first-rate shot. She and her pal Winnie would go to Bisley and…"

"At all events, who could want to murder her?" Sophia interrupted. "Did she have enemies? Even if she did, surely it's hardly plausible that they were on board the *Queen Mary*?"

"She was rich," Breen retorted. "And about to become even richer. Where there is money, there is envy. People will stop at nothing, not even murder…"

"Possibly so," Sophia interrupted. "There are enough examples of sordid crime in my own country. But how could someone get into a locked cabin, commit murder, and then escape without leaving a trace? It makes no sense. It is quite impossible."

"I suppose you're right," he said sheepishly. "Perhaps I've been reading too many detective stories."

"Forgive my bluntness, but I'm quite sure the inquest verdict was correct. She must have killed herself. We can only presume that the balance of her mind was temporarily disturbed."

"You think so?" Breen sounded weary, old beyond his years.

"Of course," Sophia said, "what other explanation can there be?"

"I'm…I'm afraid for Cynthia."

"Superstitious nonsense!"

"But don't you see? She occupies the self-same stateroom. It seems like an omen!"

Sophia halted in her tracks. "Shhh…they are coming toward us."

She tugged his sleeve. The couple they had watched on the dance floor were approaching from the other end of the deck. They were smiling fondly at each other, as if neither of them had a care in the world.

***

"You shouldn't be here," Cynthia said. "Clearly you're not a true gentleman."

Ellis Hart laughed. They were sitting together on the settee of the sitting room in her suite. On the small table in front of them stood a champagne bottle in an ice bucket and two glasses, filled to the brim.

"Say, tell me this. All that baloney about being worried that the steward would think you were a hussy. When did you ask him for the bubbly?"

Cynthia giggled. Over dinner, attentive waiters had already plied them with drink, although she hadn't attempted to keep pace with her companion. She handed Ellis a glass and clinked hers against it.

"We need a toast," she said. "*Carpe diem!*"

"*Carpe diem!*" he echoed.

"Like it?" she asked, indicating their surroundings.

The Cunard Line had spared no expense in ensuring that passengers with the deepest pockets enjoyed the last word in luxury. The close carpeting was supplemented by woven rugs, while illumination came from lights concealed in troughs of molded glass. The furniture was quilted maple, the paneling light mahogany. The door to the bedroom was wide open, affording a provocative glimpse of pillows and bedspread of ivory satin, their pink and green ribbon appliqué a perfect match for the sitting room curtains.

He savored his champagne. "Love it. How the other half live, eh?"

"You're no pauper, Ellis." She brushed her fingers along his leg. "Not if you can afford to travel on the *Queen Mary*."

"I can't complain."

"You certainly can't, young man," she said coquettishly. "Invited to the stateroom of a pretty fellow passenger. Plied with champagne. I only hope you have a good head for drink. Perhaps you shouldn't have any more."

"Life is short," he said, draining his glass in a single gulp. Deferential as a chambermaid, she refilled it.

"Would you excuse me for a few moments?" she asked. "I just need to freshen up."

He laughed. "Honey, you're the freshest thing on this whole damn ship."

She stood up and considered him. "I hope this doesn't seem forward, but I may slip into my pajamas. I like to get to bed early, you know."

"Hey, you won't need to wear pajamas tonight, baby."

She wagged a finger in admonition. "Patience, Ellis. You know what we say in London? Everything comes to him who waits."

"I don't care to wait too long," he mumbled. "I'm a…man of action."

She lifted her glass again. "Then let's drink to *action*."

He watched with bleary admiration as Cynthia shimmied into the bedroom and, with a sly glance over her shoulder, shut the door. Hearing a key turn in the lock, he took another drink of champagne.

***

"How much…longer?" Ellis Hart demanded, putting down his glass. His jacket and tie were on the settee. His shirt was unbuttoned, his hair rumpled.

"I've been making myself beautiful for you." From behind the bedroom door, Cynthia's voice was muffled but seductive. "I'm coming out now."

The key turned again and the door swung open, revealing Cynthia in blue Chinese silk pajamas. The black trim of her jacket was embellished with scrolling embroidery, each of the cuffs had an exotic floral motif. Only two of the four closures were fastened, allowing a generous display of pale pink flesh.

"Worth the wait, I hope?" she asked.

For a few seconds Ellis was motionless, as if paralyzed by the sight of her. Then he gave a short whistle.

"Sure…sure is."

He stumbled toward her, and she turned her face up to his. As their lips met, the door of the stateroom was flung open.

"So this is what you get up to when my back is turned!"

Sophia Vialli was standing in the doorway, camera in hand. Taking a step into the room, and kicking the door shut behind her, she took a photograph. As the flashbulb popped, Cynthia screamed.

Ellis pushed her through the open door and onto the ivory bedspread. He slumped down beside her. Cynthia wailed in dismay. Sophia followed them into the bedroom.

Another flashbulb popped.

"Harlot!"

"What…what is happening?" Cynthia sobbed. "Ellis, talk to me!"

He pushed a hand through his hair. "Honey, you shouldn't have led me on the way you did. It's not right…you being all but married, and all."

"You wanted me! You said…"

"Never mind what he said," Sophia snapped. "The camera never lies. And I have the evidence of my own eyes. You have been committing adultery with my husband."

"*Husband?*" Cynthia turned to the American. "Ellis, is this true?"

He dropped down on the bed beside her. "Yeah, it's…"

"Slut!" Sophia hissed. "Wait till the newspapers hear about this. The supposedly respectable Cynthia Wyvern betraying her fiancé by seducing a naïve young American."

"Please!" Cynthia cried. "I'll do anything! Is it money you're after?"

Ellis gave a foggy smile. "Now you're…talking, honey."

"My silence will not come cheaply, you understand," Sophia said.

"How…how much?"

"You are a rich woman." Sophia named a figure. "Where is your checkbook?"

"It's too much! That amount will ruin me."

"What is marriage to your beloved Algernon worth? What price your future happiness?" Sophia bared her teeth in a fierce grin. "Regard it as an investment."

Cynthia opened the drawer of the dressing room table and lifted out a checkbook and pen. She turned to face Ellis. "You tricked me, didn't you? It was all a ploy, so that the pair of you could blackmail me."

He grinned stupidly. "I guess…"

Sophia tried to yank him to his feet. "What's the matter with you, Joel? Don't tell me you're drunk! I thought you had a harder head."

"It wasn't…" he began.

The door of the wardrobe swung open. Standing there, dressed in a cabin steward's white uniform, was Feargal Breen. In his hand was a small black gun.

"The man's right." The Irish accent had vanished and he sounded as if he'd just stepped off the playing fields of Eton. "It wasn't ordinary champagne. I slipped in, if you'll forgive a vulgar phrase, a Mickey Finn."

***

Cynthia reached under a pillow and took out a snub-nosed revolver. "Don't move an inch, either of you."

Sophia blinked. "What is the meaning of this?"

"You've left it too late for a show of dignity," Breen said. "I gave you your chance as we strolled along the deck. If you'd showed a degree of contrition, things might have been different."

On the bed, Ellis groaned. His eyes were shut and he was holding his head.

"What are you talking about?" Sophia demanded.

"I told you. This concerns the murder of Letty Bohannon. My sister." He smiled as the woman absorbed his words. "That's right, I'm Henry, the scapegrace son with a taste for acting. Rather a ham, I'm afraid, but not to worry. I do hope you appreciated my mincing Irish gossip-monger."

"You tricked me!"

"Sauce for the gander. Your lover set out to seduce Letty so that the pair of you could exploit her. You travel the high seas in search of prey. Rich victims with a great deal to lose. On that occasion, however, you went too far. You threatened Letty with ruin and in a fit of panic, she shot herself. Yes, this stateroom was locked, but you killed her, just as surely as if you'd pulled the trigger yourself."

"She was neurotic."

"She was distraught," Henry said. "That was clear from the note she left. Thank the Lord, the coroner didn't make its contents public. Poor Letty had suffered enough humiliation. She didn't know your real names, naturally. The inquiry agent I hired discovered the truth. You believed you were beyond the reach of the law. There was no independent evidence that either of you had committed a crime. The police weren't interested in pursuing you. But we were. I loved my sister."

"And I am Winnie," the girl said. "Her dearest friend."

"So what do you want?" Sophia was defiant. "We have no money to pay you back. The Bohannon girl's check was useless, her death made sure of that."

"We have plenty of money," Henry said. "These staterooms don't come cheap."

"What, then?"

"We want justice."

***

For a few seconds, Sophia was silent. Her brow furrowed. Henry had spent long enough at racecourses to know she was calculating odds. The woman was another gambler. In a tight corner, she'd risk everything if she thought she could get away with it. She couldn't hope for help from the American. He'd lost consciousness while sprawled across the bed.

"What do you mean?"

"We want you to write a confession," Henry said. "Admit to what the two of you did to Letty. You must tell the world everything. And don't try blaming it all on Joel Dyson here, alias Ellis Hurt. You're the brains behind the partnership, aren't you, Sophia? Or should I call you Maria Mancini?"

"Words written under duress," she said with a dismissive gesture. "They are worthless in a court of law."

Her voice was curiously flat, as if her mind was elsewhere.

"Watch her!" Winnie shouted.

At that moment, Maria Mancini sprang forward. Her sharp fingers became talons clawing at Henry's eyes. As he fell back, she leaped upon him, trying to wrench the revolver from his hand.

"Let him go, or I'll shoot," Winnie hissed.

"You won't dare," Maria spat. "You'll hit him, not me."

She was strong and sinewy, and Henry fought to keep hold of his gun. Winnie jumped forward.

In the confines of the bedroom, the noise of the shot seemed deafening.

Maria screamed in horror. In the struggle, her lover had been shot in the chest. Blood oozed over his shirt. Henry seized hold of her wrist, only for the gun to fire again.

The second bullet hit the side of Maria's head at point-blank range.

***

Winnie sobbed as Henry checked the blackmailers' pulses and found no sign of life. He laid a hand on her shoulder.

"You must keep calm. There's work to be done."

Still wearing the steward's uniform he'd bought in London, he strode out into the corridor and headed for the laundry room. It was in darkness, as he'd expected. Hinting that he planned a surreptitious liaison with a fellow passenger, he'd given the steward a lavish tip to make himself scarce.

The wicker basket he'd spotted the previous day stood in an alcove. He lifted the lid to make sure it was still empty before dragging it back to Winnie's suite. She was drying her tears.

"Give me a sheet to keep the blood off the basket," he said.

"What...what will you do?"

He pulled a pair of gloves from his pocket. "I'm taking these bodies back where they belong."

"You can't throw them overboard!"

"I could, but I won't. Tidy up and make a bundle of the bloodstained bedclothes. Chuck it over the side of the ship while I shift the corpses. Thankfully their cabin is only down one flight of stairs and pretty much underneath us. But I'll need two journeys. This wretched basket isn't big enough for both of them."

***

"Are you sure people won't suspect?" Winnie was breathless. The past hour had been a frenzy.

"There's a sporting chance," Henry said. "If we hold our nerve."

"But the angle of the second shot…"

"Is consistent with a self-inflicted wound," he said. "Just about. When their steward finally opens the cabin, he'll discover a macabre tableau. What happened will be obvious. A violent quarrel got out of hand, these Latin women are tempestuous types."

"People have seen me in his company," she said.

"Hence the quarrel."

"They've also seen you talking to her. If the authorities ask the right questions…"

"We have answers." Henry clasped her hand. "After you left the lounge with him, I noticed her following. There was a confrontation in the passageway. Raised voices. You made your excuses and left them to it. Meanwhile, I did my best to cheer you up and refused to let you out of my sight. A perfect alibi."

"Only if they take our word for it."

"Who can contradict us? Thank your lucky stars for good old British reserve. The only two people on board who thought of us as Miss Wyvern and Mr. Breen, rather than Henry and his pal Winnie, will never utter another word."

A thought struck her. "What if someone heard the shots?"

"There's no better-built ship than the *Queen Mary* on the seven seas, remember. The stateroom walls are solid, and I'm your next-door neighbor. Everyone else on A Deck is still waltzing the night away. The band is loud, and if anyone did hear shots, they might easily suppose they came from our friends' cabin. It's almost exactly below us, don't forget."

"Whatever the ship's officers may think, the police…"

"Are likely to take the easy way out," he interrupted. "Legal jurisdiction on the high seas is as clear as sea mist. Or so I recall from my tedious year in chambers."

"You're sure everyone will believe…?"

"That, just like Letty's death, it's a tragedy rather than a mystery?" He gave a dark smile. "People believe what they want to believe. Just as Mancini and Dyson were only too happy to believe in Cynthia Wyvern and the mischief-making Irishman."

She remained quiet for a few moments. "Am I stupid to believe that you intended them to die all along?"

"You could never be stupid, my dear." He paused. "Blackmail was their sport. They reveled in it."

"You planned all this, didn't you?" she murmured. "You love playing for high stakes, whether you're burgling or…that's why you took an impression of his cabin key before I put it back in his door, isn't it?"

"Don't worry. Ten minutes ago I threw my copy of the key into the waves."

"You never meant to use it simply to snoop around for evidence of their crimes."

"Call it poetic justice," he said softly. "The authorities will realize it's impossible that anyone else was involved. A plain case of murder and suicide. Maria shot her faithless lover and then turned the gun on herself. Their bodies were found inside a locked cabin. And to prove it, the key is lying on the floor for all to see."

It's Not What You Know
O'NEIL DE NOUX

The rookie guarding the front door yawns as I open my coat to show him the gold star-and-crescent detective's badge clipped to my belt. He tells me, "The body's inside," as if I thought the body would be outside.

Four people are inside the art gallery when I step in—another rookie I don't know, a heavy-set man with a bad toupee, a thin man with coal-black hair, and an eager-looking cop with reddish-brown hair done up in a bun. Her, I've seen around headquarters. The Revenant Gallery, sandwiched between two antique shops along the 600 block of Royal Street, occupies a typical three-story New Orleans Creole townhouse with arched doorways, a black lace balcony, and fourteen-foot ceilings. The place smells of furniture polish.

The eager-looking cop comes up, extending her hand. "Hi, I'm Sally Gallagher."

I shake her hand. Her palm's damp. I resist the urge to wipe it on my suit pants. "LaStanza. Homicide," I tell her. "Anything new going on in your life?"

"Pardon?" She's taller than me, around five-nine.

I lean closer. "Somebody musta died, or you wouldn't have called me."

"Oh." Sally recovers. "Two victims went to Charity but didn't make it."

I look over at the bad-toupee guy and the guy with the coal-black hair. Both glare at me with distrustful eyes.

"Then where'd they end up?" I ask Sally.

"Pardon?"

"You say that a lot, don't you?" I look into her wide green eyes, a couple shades darker than mine. "If our victims didn't make it to Charity Hospital, where'd they end up?"

"Oh, no. They made it to Charity, but they died."

I keep my face expressionless, as if I'm serious. She shrugs again. Still hasn't figured I'm messing with her. Pulling my notepad and pen from the pocket of my navy blue suit jacket, I jot down the date and time—Friday, September 13, 1985. 10:45 p.m.

"Tell me what happened," I say without looking up.

"I think it was poison. In the punch. It smells funny."

I look over at the small table she's pointing to—marble, with a crystal punch bowl and several crystal glasses on it, one with the same red liquid inside as in the bowl. I move to the table. A couple dozen ice cubes float in the punch.

"Probably cyanide," Sally adds. "It smells funny, like almonds. Smell it." She leans over and takes a sniff.

"Cyanide fumes are deadly," I tell her. "It's what they use in gas chambers."

Sally blanches and I run my hand over my moustache to hide my grin. Okay, I'm messing with her. I need something to keep me jazzed. Almost made it through a long night until this call came in. Should've picked up some coffee-and-chicory on the way.

"The fumes have to be a lot stronger than a simple sniff," I tell her, but she doesn't look reassured. "So, who died?"

She takes a step away from the lethal punch and flips through her notepad.

"Jane Hayes, white female, twenty-four. She was the ex-girlfriend of the skinny man over there. Also dead is Ned Brossard. He was an artist."

I point my chin at the civilians. "What's their names?"

"The heavy one is the gallery owner, Mal Banky. The skinny one, Jane Hayes's ex, is another artist, Pency Andover."

I look back at Sally. "Mal and Pency?"

She nods.

"Mal and Pency," I call out as I move toward the civilians.

I hear Sally following me. Mal, the fat guy in the bad toupee, puts his little fists on his waist and sticks his chin out. Pency, with the coal-black hair, steps forward and points to Mal. "He did it." Pency has a deep New England accent. "He made the punch and didn't drink any."

Mal bounces on his toes, screams, then begins slapping Pency, who slaps back. Sally breaks them up, and I ask her to move Mal to the front of the gallery.

I keep coal-black-haired Pency with me. He straightens his gray turtleneck and tugs up his black pants before folding his arms, making sure I see the gold Rolex watch on his left wrist. I reach to my right side and readjust the canvas holster holding my stainless steel .357 magnum Smith and Wesson model 66.

Looking into his narrow hazel eyes, I ask where he's from.

"Arlington. Suburb of Boston," he pronounces it ""baston,"" with a soft *a*.

"I've been to Arlington."

"Really."

"Not yours."

"Arlington, Virginia?" He looks confused.

"No, Arlington, Texas. Suburb of Dallas. Bet it's bigger than your Arlington."

He's really confused now, so I say, "I understand one of the victims was your girlfriend."

"Ex-girlfriend." He lets out a long sigh, his face sad now. "I drank punch too." He points toward the punch bowl. "That's my glass next to it. Check the fingerprints."

Check the fingerprints? I give him a deadpan look.

"Check the video camera," he adds, pointing to the ceiling. "I drank the punch. Shouldn't I go to the hospital, too?"

"If you'd swallowed cyanide, you'd be dead."

He tilts his head to the side like a puppy does when it hears a strange noise.

"Tell me what happened tonight."

He does, his voice deepening as he explains that the party was for his friend and fellow artist Ned Brossard, because of his success in New York and Chicago. Mal had put together the after-hours gathering of friends.

I watch his eyes as I ask, "Did you know your ex-girlfriend was coming?"

"Nope." He stares right back at me.

"Okay to let in the crime lab?" the rookie cop guarding the door calls out to me in a bored voice.

I wave an okay and watch as Howard Coyle lumbers in with his silver camera case and black crime scene processing kit. Tall and bespectacled, Howie has some hair left around his ears and a mole the size of Rhode Island on his right cheek.

I point to the punch bowl and ask if he has a test for poison.

"Just cyanide and strychnine."

"Good. Check for both."

He puts his cases down and digs into the black one, pulling out a test tube. Carefully, Howie uses an eye-dropper to deposit three drops of punch into the test tube. He swirls it, and the clear liquid inside remains clear.

"Not strychnine."

He pulls out another test tube and puts three drops of punch into it. The clear liquid inside turns bright green.

"Whoa. Cyanide." Howie does a little dance. "That's good detective work."

I wave Sally over. "She gets credit. She sniffed it."

Howie shakes his head and tells Sally she shouldn't do that. She's paler than before.

"I need you to dust the bowl and the cups." I point to the half-filled cup. "Especially that one. And collect the punch as well."

"No shit."

Leaving Sally with Pency, I go over to Mal and get his story, which is essentially the same as Pency's. He's still angry, grinding his teeth as he leers at Pency.

"Did Pency know his old girlfriend was coming?"

"I don't know. I think so."

I point to the video camera and ask where's the tape. He tells me it's in back and I can view it on the little TV in his office. I head there. As I sit in Mal's tan recliner—he has a recliner in his kitchen-office—and watch the beginning of the surveillance tape, Sally peeks in and asks if she can watch. "The rookie's keeping Mal and Pency apart."

"Got any popcorn?"

She freezes until I get up and lean against the chair's arm, pointing to the other arm. She goes over and leans against the far arm of the recliner. I fast-forward the black-and-white videotape until I see Mal come out of the kitchen-office with the punch bowl in his hands. He carefully places it on the marble table, making sure not to spill any punch.

A dark-haired woman comes into the picture.

"That's Jane Hayes," Sally tells me. "The dead ex-girlfriend."

Jane is in a tight-fitting minidress and killer high heels. She wears her hair like Morticia from the Addams Family, parted down the center, down to her hips. A good-looking woman, even on grainy film.

Ol' Pency enters from the kitchen-office. He carries a tray with the punch bowl's matching cups. Mal passes him on his way back into the kitchen-office. Pency says something to Jane, who turns away, giving him the cold shoulder.

She walks toward the front of the gallery, and Pency stares at her until another man enters the gallery. Tall and blond, he wears a baggy, pirate-looking puffy shirt with the collar open to the waist.

"That's Ned Brossard," Sally tells me. "The other victim."

No. Really?

Jane and Ned kiss each other flush on the mouth, a nice long kiss. Pency backs away, passing Mal again as the gallery owner hurries out to greet Brossard. Cheek kissing now, and hugging.

"Your family hug a lot?" I ask Sally.

"Uh, yeah. Does yours?"

"Naw. We're pretty antisocial. Being Sicilian and all."

She looks like she believes everything I'm saying, so I'm trying to think of something even more outrageous when I notice Pency again on the video. He comes out of the kitchen-office with a large plastic bowl. He dumps it into the punch, and I see it's ice.

He dips a cup into the punch and takes a sip. Standing there, holding his cup, he watches the three others laugh and talk. Placing his half-filled cup next to the punch bowl, Pency leaves as the others approach the punch. He goes back into the kitchen-office with the plastic bowl, which, I glance around the kitchen area of the office and see, is over in the sink now.

The three talk next to the punch bowl, Mal doing most of the talking, flapping his chubby little arms around. The conversation goes on a while, at least five minutes, but Pency doesn't come back in.

"When do they die?" I ask Sally.

"I don't know," she answers seriously.

Jane picks up a cup and dips it into the punch, passing it to Ned. She dips another and passes it to Mal, who tries to wave it away, but reluctantly takes it. They stand around for a minute, just holding the cups, until Jane dips a third cup in, raises it in a toast, and the men raise theirs. Jane and Ned take a drink, but Mal doesn't.

Just as Mal puts his drink down on the table, Jane and Ned hit the floor, both flat on their backs. Mal bounces twice and jumps down next to Ned. He shakes him and shakes Jane, but they don't stir. He shouts something to Pency as he steps back in. Pency runs back into the kitchen-office while Mal tries to perform CPR, first on Ned, then on Jane. Pency rushes back in and shoves

Mal off Jane, then takes over with Jane. They continue until the EMTs arrive, but the victims don't stir.

We see EMTs enter the picture as Mal and Pency crawl away to catch their breath. The EMTs have as much success, but don't give up, hauling Jane and Ned away on gurneys. The two rookie patrolmen come into view now, and I watch as no one goes near the bowl until Sally is there.

"Anyone go near the bowl after you got here?"

"Only me."

We continue watching the film until Sally leans over the punch and takes a deep sniff.

"You haven't gotten a headache, have you?" I ask her.

"No." She's pale again.

"Then you should be alright."

"What do you mean should?"

I finally lose it, and tell her I'm kidding. She doesn't believe that either, and wrings her hands. Then she asks the most obvious question.

"If Pency drank the punch too, why didn't he die? I didn't see anyone drop anything into the punch after he drank some."

"And the cups were lying upside down," I point out, rubbing my fingers down across my moustache, which I seem to do when I'm nervous or thinking hard.

"Is there an antidote you can take before ingesting cyanide?"

Not a bad question, but I tell her there's no antidote to cyanide. Then it hits me. I jump up and pull open the nearest drawer. I find a big spoon in the second drawer, grab a different plastic bowl, and run back out into the gallery. I carefully scoop out what's left of the ice and put it in the plastic bowl.

Sally's right behind me now, so I ask her to watch the two civilians, see who's most curious about what I'm doing.

"They're both staring. So's the rookie."

I hurry back into the kitchen and shove the bowl into the freezer.

Howie Coyle peeks in and says, "What's up?"

I point to the ice trays sitting next to the sink. "I need you to test these for cyanide. And the ice in the bowl in the freezer."

Sally gives me that tilted-head, puppy-dog look.

"The poison's in the ice. That's why Pency could drink the punch."

Sally's eyes light up. "The ice hadn't melted yet."

Howie steps in with his vials and thirty seconds later confirms there's cyanide in the trays. I ask Sally to bring Mal in. I listen to their shuffling feet and watch Mal bounce in, all eyes now, little arms dangling at his sides. I pull out my ID folder and slip out the Miranda Warning card and read him his rights. Don't really need the card, but I always read from it, make sure I don't miss anything.

Mal interrupts me twice, but I don't stop until I'm finished reading.

"You understand these rights?"

"Am I under arrest?" His voice squeaks.

"No. But you're a suspect. Do you understand the rights I just read you?"

"Yes." More subdued now.

"Did you make the punch?" I ask.

"Yes." Barely a whisper. He points to the garbage can. I can see large cans of Hawaiian Punch inside. I nod to Howie, who goes out for more test vials.

"Why didn't you drink the punch?"

"I don't like Hawaiian Punch." He shrugs. "Everyone else does."

"Did you make the ice?"

Mal shakes his head dejectedly. "Pency brought the ice. His place is close."

I point to the trays. "Those your trays?"

"No. Pency used his."

It takes another five minutes to get the rest of the story out of Mal, who perks up when he sees I'm asking more questions about Pency than about him. I take careful notes. Pency lives two doors down Royal, above yet another antique shop. I ask about Pency's relationship with Jane and Mal is quick to jump on it, telling me how she dumped him and he's still carrying a torch for her.

Howie catches my attention and points to the cans and shakes his head.

I leave Mal in the kitchen-office with Howie as Sally follows me back into the gallery. Pency sits in a folding chair against the wall, his legs crossed and arms folded. Above his head hangs a painting of an octopus mating with a cow, or maybe it's just an amoeba.

"Did you arrest him?" Pency asks, managing to look down his nose at me while still sitting.

"Why should I?" I watch his eyes. "You're the killer."

He tries to keep from reacting, but his pupils become pinpricks. I read him his rights and he sits there, glaring at me. Putting my ID folder back into my coat pocket, I give him the Sicilian stare, the stiletto-stare that pierces all the way through to the back of the head.

"Do you think we're stupid?" I ask.

"He fixed the punch. I drank the punch. I'm a victim!"

I smile coldly. "But you made the ice."

He looks at Sally, then at the rookie standing next to him, then lunges for Sally's gun. She's too quick, however, covering her gun with her right hand as she falls away, punching him with her left fist. I kick Pency's feet from under him. He rolls over and Sally's on him, with the rookie now, and they have him cuffed behind the back in three seconds. They pat him down, then sit him back in the chair.

He looks up at the ceiling, face red, neck veins bulging, and screams, "She ripped out my heart!"

The sound of someone tapping on the gallery door turns me around. My partner, Detective Jodie Kintyre, in her beige suit, with her blond pageboy and hazel cat eyes, blinks at me as she holds up two paper cups of coffee. We've been so busy bouncing from call to call, it's the first time I've seen her this evening. We'd worked a suicide. I did follow-up on an old case.

I unlock the glass door and Jodie passes me one of the coffees. I don't have to sample it to know she's fixed it the way we both like it, coffee-and-chicory with cream and two sugars.

"So, what do we have here?" she asks.

Pency screams again, "She ripped out my heart!"

"A love story," I tell my partner. "Boy meets girl, boy gets girl, boy loses girl, boy murders girl."

Jodie shakes her head and I catch a whiff of her light perfume. Same perfume my wife wears. They've getting as close as sisters. That's all I need.

Sally steps up and I introduce her to Jodie.

"You should've seen your partner," Sally gushes. "He figured it out right away."

"What'd he figure?" Jodie asks, a sarcastic smirk on her face.

Sally tells her the tragic story of the tainted punch.

I watch Pency drop his chin to his chest, breathing deeply as he sits with his legs apart. As soon as Sally finishes, Jodie grabs a folding chair and sits next to Pency. He raises his eyes and looks at her with a tear-streaked face. She talks softly to him and he's listening, intently.

I lead Sally to the door and watch.

"What's she doing?" Sally asks.

"She's being the good cop. I'm the bad cop tonight. She'll get a confession. The DA loves confessions. Hey. That's not an amoeba. It's Jesus." I point to the painting.

Sally laughs. "It isn't Jesus. It's Abraham Lincoln. That's a Salvador Dali." She turns to me with those wide eyes. "Really, how'd you figure it so quickly? How'd you know?"

"It's not what you know," I tell her. "It's what you can think of in time."

As that sinks in, I tell her the truth. Criminals make mistakes. Using the old poison-in-the-ice trick was a big mistake. His fatal mistake, however, was underestimating me.

Murder in Pelham Wood
JARED CADE

ll I want is a relaxing afternoon—" Hermione Bradbury said.

"We certainly deserve it," Lyle said. "I don't know anyone who works harder than we do."

Hermione was in total agreement with him. She felt the warm autumnal breeze whipping her long red hair back from her pre-Raphaelite face as she pressed her foot down on Casanova's accelerator. It occurred to her that life with Lyle Revel could never be described as dull. Their duties as caretakers of Milsham Castle took up a large chunk of their time, in addition to which they both had careers. Hermione was an accomplished cellist with the Gosfordshire Symphony Orchestra, and Lyle's acting ability, coupled with his blond good looks, had earned him success in the theatre. When Hermione had first met him, Lyle's flair for solving murders had shocked her and, although she was used to his talent by now, she couldn't help thinking it was sometimes nothing short of a miracle that they managed to juggle their busy lives so well and stay together as a couple.

Their destination was the Crown Hotel in the village of Brimhurst. It was a popular venue owing to its first class restaurant. An added attraction for guests, as well as local dog owners and ramblers, was that the hotel was situated across the road from the renowned beauty spot of Pelham Wood. The couple were greeted in the foyer by the attractive, dark-haired receptionist, Abigail Mitchell, who seemed her usual cheerful, bubbly self.

"Your table is ready in the restaurant," she said, smiling flirtatiously at Lyle. "It's a really nice one, by the window overlooking Pelham Wood."

Lyle's eyes twinkled as he replied in his agreeable tenor voice, "It's such a nice day that Hermione and I plan to go for a walk there after lunch."

"Lyle is being polite to spare my feelings." Hermione spoke in a relaxed voice. She was used to women making fools of themselves over Lyle, just as he was used to men falling like ninepins around her. "I've brought a basket with me so I can pilfer as many pine cones as possible. They make excellent kindling in the winter months."

"Pelham Wood is full of pine cones at this time of the year," Abigail said. "One dropped from a tree and almost struck me as I was walking to work yesterday. It gave me a bit of a fright."

"You sound as if you know the wood quite well," Hermione said.

Abigail nodded. "This morning Mum dropped me off here in her car, but I usually walk to work and home again through the wood."

She picked up a menu, and they followed her through an archway into a restaurant which was already half full, though it was not yet midday.

"How are your parents?" Hermione asked.

"Dad's a lot better now that he's had his hip replacement operation," Abigail said. "Mum fusses over him too much like she always has."

"Milsham Castle relies on the kindness of volunteers like your parents to help show tourists around in the summer months," Hermione said smiling. "Give them both our love, won't you?"

By a happy coincidence, Ricardo and Sally Moffatt were sitting at another table in the restaurant. Hermione and Lyle fell in with the couple's suggestion of making a foursome for lunch. The Moffatts were well-known locally because they owned a mill that they had converted into a theatre. They knew the Moffatts quite well because Lyle had acted in a couple of their productions. Ricardo Moffatt was an excellent director, and had an entertaining store of anecdotes from the time he had worked as a stage manager at the National Theatre in London. An enjoyable lunch, punctuated with gossip and laughter, followed, in which the quartet kept their tonsils well lubricated with alcohol.

It was just after three o'clock when Hermione and Lyle parted company with the Moffatts and entered Pelham Wood. The golden, red, and yellow autumnal colors were breathtakingly beautiful and Hermione soon filled her basket with pine cones. The pungent smell of the damp earth, together with the crisp fresh air, was marvelously invigorating. Yet the farther they plunged into the wood, the darker and more oppressive it became. The temperature had dropped, and there was a stillness in the air.

"I expect we ought to turn back," she said uncertainly.

"What is it?" Lyle asked, catching the puzzled expression on her face.

"Are you familiar with 'The Gates of Damascus'?" Hermione asked slowly.

"The James Elroy Flecker poem?" Lyle stared at her in surprise. "I studied it at school."

"*Have you heard that silence where the birds are dead, yet something pipeth like a bird?*" Hermione quoted. "We should be able to hear birdsong and other sounds of the wood, but there aren't any."

"It's probably our imagination," Lyle said with a shiver.

But it was apparent he also felt it now. A subtle feeling of menace hung over the wood.

"Shall we go on to the lake or turn back?" he added.

"It's a shame to waste a nice day," Hermione said, striding determinedly ahead of him.

A recent fall of rain had ensured the earth was soft, and they found themselves unwittingly following a fresh trail of size seven shoes along the otherwise unblemished path.

Hermione rounded a bend in the path and her blood suddenly ran cold. The path broadened into a circular clearing that was about thirty feet wide in circumference. In the middle of the clearing lay the battered body of a girl. Her bloodstained dress had been pulled up around her waist and her pants had been ripped from her body.

"Oh, my God…"" Hermione croaked. "You're not going to believe what's happened."

"What is it?"

She heard the sound of footsteps behind her, then Lyle was by her side, gazing in horror at the scene before them.

"It's Abigail Mitchell—the receptionist from the Crown Hotel…" Hermione spoke with a shudder.

Although they were standing some distance away, they could see the killer had taken the belt from the dead girl's dress and tightened it around her purple, swollen throat.

Lyle's voice hardened with emotion. "It looks as if someone has raped her… She's been strangled…"

"There are two different sets of footprints near the body," Hermione said with a shiver. "The size seven footprints are Abigail's."

"The size ten footprints are obviously the killer's," Lyle said. "He wore Wellingtons."

He spoke with the certainty of someone who owned a pair of Wellington boots himself, and Hermione nodded in agreement.

"Look at the trail of footprints," she said. "Abigail entered the clearing along the same path we did."

Lyle's eyes narrowed. "Whereas the killer came along the path on the opposite side of the clearing."

Hermione's eyes shone in dread. "She must have seen him walking toward her. It's possible she may even have recognized him. After the attack, he left the clearing by going back down the far path that brought him here."

"If she recognized him," Lyle said, "she clearly had no reason to fear him initially. She made no attempt to turn back this way and run away from him."

He pulled out his mobile and dialed the number of the emergency services.

"The trail of footprints is unmistakable," Hermione said. "The police shouldn't have any difficulty matching them to the killer's. Who could have done this?"

"Someone very sick and disturbed."

As Lyle was reporting the discovery of the body to the police, Hermione heard a high-pitched pinging sound that set her nerves on edge. It came from another mobile that lay on the ground near her feet. She picked it up and took the call. It was only then that she remembered her own mobile was in her jacket pocket. She had picked up someone else's mobile by mistake. She immediately recognized the agitated voice that spoke in her ear. It belonged to her friend Hilary Scofield, who was the principal flautist in the Gosfordshire Symphony Orchestra.

"Ted, what's taken you so long to answer? I've been trying to reach you for ages…"

Hermione's throat went dry. "Hilary, this is Hermione Bradbury. I've just found your husband's mobile in Pelham Wood. Do you know where he is?"

"Oh, for goodness sake, what's it doing there? I do wish Ted would be more careful. He must have dropped it."

"Where are you now?" Hermione asked.

"I'm at the Oxfam shop in Brimhurst. I work behind the counter each Saturday. Hermione, you sound upset. What is it?"

"Lyle and I have just discovered a body."

"Tell me it's not Ted's!" Hilary suddenly sounded panic-stricken.

"No, it's not Ted. It's—it's the body of a young girl."

"Oh, thank God… For a moment, I thought you were telling me Ted had been taken ill or something—"

"Where is he?"

"At home, nursing his cold. I was phoning him to remind him to take the lamb chops out of the freezer so they'll defrost in time for dinner."

"Hilary, how often does Ted walk through Pelham Wood?" Hermione asked.

"He sometimes picks mushrooms for my mother. But what's that got to do with the discovery of a girl's body?"

"Does the name of Abigail Mitchell mean anything to you?"

"Are you referring to that brazen nineteen-year-old trollop who works at the Crown Hotel?"

"Yes, do you know her?"

Anger rose in Hilary's voice. "I've seen Abigail around the village. Her parents ought to keep a proper eye on her. She's always flirting with other women's husbands at the pub."

Hermione decided frankness was her best option. "Abigail has been strangled."

"You can't be serious—?"

Hermione heard the incredulity in Hilary Scofield's voice.

"Your husband's mobile has been discovered near her body. The police are going to want to know why it was found here in Pelham Wood."

The police arrived soon afterward, in response to Lyle's mobile call, and the machinery of the law was set firmly in motion. Hermione and Lyle were taken to the Brimhurst police station and given cups of coffee, then questioned at length by the senior officer in charge of the case.

"Have you ever known Ted Scofield to make any threats against Abigail Mitchell?" DI Weatherall asked.

Hermione shook her head. "Ted and Hilary are very much in love. They met in their mid-fifties. I doubt if he's ever looked at another woman in all the time they've been married."

"It's only fair to tell you, Ted Scofield is different from other men," Lyle said. "He's got the mental age of a twelve-year-old. In that respect, he'll never grow any older. He's a gardener at the Brimhurst Horticultural Center. Hermione and I sometimes call in there to buy plants and other garden supplies."

"Ted Scofield may be simple," Hermione added defiantly, "but he's got a heart of gold. He doesn't strike me as the sort of man to go around raping and strangling women."

DI Weatherall was not so easily persuaded. "There's a first time for everything."

***

As Hermione and Lyle were leaving the station, they saw two burly police officers escorting a tall giant of a man in his fifties into the building. He was wearing a pair of size ten Wellington boots. It was Ted Scofield, and a set of handcuffs were around his wrists. He was looking visibly distressed.

"I never hurt Abigail," he cried, with a look of shattered trust in his eyes. "She was as lovely as a sunflower… When I was a child, sunflowers grew in my foster parents' garden. I liked to kiss them because they were so lovely…" He became frantic, trying to break free from the police officers' hold on him. "You've no right to arrest me. I haven't done anything wrong…"

His frightened, childlike manner startled Hermione. He reminded her of a distraught dog who couldn't believe the world had turned against him and treated him so cruelly.

"If Ted Scofield wants to prove his innocence," Lyle murmured, "he'll need to cooperate with the police, rather than antagonize them with angry outbursts and unruly behavior."

Two days later, Hermione was making breakfast beneath the black beams of Nettlebed's kitchen when Lyle returned from his early-morning jog.

"Take a look at this," he said, thrusting a newspaper in front of her. He was breathing hard and sank down on a chair, mopping his brow. "Ted Scofield has been charged with raping and strangling Abigail."

"Oh, my God…" Hermione stared in horror at the headline. "I hoped it wouldn't come to this. Hilary must be devastated."

There was a look of empathy in Lyle's eyes. "She's got a choice of standing by her husband or leaving him," he said grimly. "It's a difficult choice for any woman to make."

Hermione said decisively, "She's the maternal type, so she'll stand by him."

"After what happened to Abigail," Lyle said, "I'm beginning to wonder if a man with the mind of a child isn't the most terrifying thing in the world…"

The case against Ted Scofield grew blacker in the days ahead, and became the number one topic in Gosfordshire. Nettlebed stood by the gates of Lord Milsham's ancestral home, outside the village of Compton Sutton, and in their role as caretakers, Hermione and Lyle were constantly hearing snippets of gossip about the case from tradesmen and others visiting the main house.

"Have you heard the latest news reports about Abigail's murder?" Hermione asked Lyle. "The results of the DNA tests prove conclusively that Ted Scofield killed her."

Lyle released a sigh and said, "It doesn't look good."

"Hilary must be worried sick about Ted," Hermione added with a tremor in her voice.

Lyle's gaze softened with a look of admiration. "A lot of wives wouldn't have stood by him the way Hilary has."

Hermione shook her head in despair. "Hilary must be so confused right now. How's she supposed to cope, knowing she's married to a rapist and a murderer?"

"I really don't know," Lyle replied. "The DNA evidence shouts aloud Ted Scofield's guilt. The idea that someone else killed Abigail and avoided leaving behind any footprints or evidence in the clearing now seems not only ludicrous, but totally impossible. If he's innocent, it's going to require an extraordinary conjuring trick to unmask the real perpetrator."

***

In June the following year, Lyle and Hermione found themselves dining at the Wolseley restaurant in London. Their companion for the evening was one of England's leading barristers, Sir Roland Anstruther.

"What's the matter, Uncle Roly?" Hermione asked. "You seem pensive."

Sir Roland roused himself to reply in his rich, fruity voice, "I'm worried about a case I'm defending. I'm sure you can guess which one."

"Ted Scofield's?" Lyle prompted.

Sir Roland nodded. "Your testimony, along with Hermione's, regarding the discovery of the body was clear and concise. It went down well with the jury."

"You've been awfully secretive about the case, Uncle Roly," Hermione said. "Presumably that's because you didn't want to prejudice our testimony in any way. Why don't you come clean and tell us all the facts, on the off-chance Lyle can pinpoint who the real killer is? That's assuming, of course, the person in question isn't your client."

Charm is an extraordinary thing. Lots of women far more beautiful than Hermione might have uttered the same words, but failed to produce a similar hypnotic effect on their listener. She reminded Sir Roland of the girl playing the harp in Rossetti's masterpiece *La Ghirlandata*. Hermione and Lyle seemed so simpatico, so alike in their youthful blooming good looks, as to resemble bookends, and for a moment Sir Roland felt a startled pang of loss owing to his advancing years.

"I daresay a problem shared is a problem solved," he said with a sigh. "Not that it will likely do Ted Scofield's defense any good."

"The Brimhurst police weren't especially forthcoming when they interviewed us," Lyle continued. "We know very little about the case—apart from what we've read in the newspapers or heard on TV."

"The facts are distressingly banal," Sir Roland said. "Last year on the 28th of September, Ted Scofield attacked Abigail Mitchell after she left the Crown Hotel. Another receptionist saw her cross the road and enter Pelham Wood shortly after two o'clock. That was the last time she was seen alive."

"Hermione and I arrived at the Crown Hotel just before midday," Lyle said, frowning. "Abigail seemed in good spirits as she took us through to our table in the restaurant."

"It was obvious she fancied Lyle," Hermione said dryly. "Did she have a boyfriend?"

"No, but that didn't stop her from inventing silly stories and pretending she'd catalogued Lord Milsham's library for him. He assured the Chief Constable all talk of her being pregnant with his child was utter nonsense. The autopsy confirmed she wasn't pregnant."

"There was no chance of her becoming lady of the manor," Hermione said. "Girls make up stories at that age to satisfy their craving for romance. As you know, Lyle and I left the hotel at three o'clock and spent about fifteen minutes in Pelham Wood foraging for cone pines before we found Abigail's body."

"The exact time by my watch was 3:17," Lyle said. "The ground was soft because it had rained while we were having lunch. Abigail left behind a clear set of size seven footprints that led along the path to the clearing. There were scuff marks on the ground in the middle of the clearing where she struggled with the killer. The set of size ten footprints show he left the crime scene by returning the same way he came—along a path on the opposite side of the clearing from the one we used. There were no other footprints within a fifteen-foot radius of the body."

"It would have been impossible for anyone else to approach Abigail without leaving behind a set of footprints," Hermione concluded. "The killer has got to be Ted Scofield, unless we've overlooked something."

Sir Roland released a sigh. "Abigail Mitchell might still be alive today if she hadn't decided to walk home through Pelham Wood."

"Were there any samples of semen, saliva, skin, or hair left at the crime scene?" Lyle asked.

"None whatsoever," Sir Roland replied. "Ted Scofield must have used a condom. Forensic science has taught us that every single one of us has a unique DNA profile. DNA tests established beyond all doubt that the blood found on Abigail Mitchell's clothes and battered body belonged to Ted Scofield. The absence of any cuts on his body suggests his nose bled during the frenzied attack. Several eyewitnesses recalled seeing him in Pelham Wood that morning. The police questioned him within half an hour of the body being discovered. He had the day off work, and insisted he'd spent the afternoon at home with his wife. Hilary Scofield later admitted his alibi was worthless because she was working at the Oxfam shop in Brimhurst."

"Uncle Roly, why do you suppose Ted Scofield targeted Abigail?"

"The general consensus of opinion," Sir Roland replied, "is that she took pleasure in leading men on and then dashing their hopes. It's possible her rejection pushed my client too far and something in him snapped."

Lyle spoke. "What explanation has Ted Scofield given for his mobile being found near the body?"

"He insists he must have dropped it without noticing while he was out walking that morning or the previous day."

"What line are you taking as his defense counsel?" Hermione asked.

"My client is an epileptic and has suffered memory blackouts from an early age. It's not unreasonable to suppose he attacked Abigail Mitchell during an epileptic seizure without realizing what he was doing. He's dreadfully cut up about the whole business and claims he has no memory of being in Pelham Wood with her."

"It sounds like a classic case of subconscious disavowal," Hermione observed. "By claiming he can't remember, he's seeking to disassociate himself from the immediate violence and outrage of his actions."

Sir Roland nodded in frustration. "Scofield has already made matters worse by telling a number of silly lies on the witness stand in a misguided bid to extricate himself from his difficulties."

"My inner voice is telling me Ted Scofield really loves his wife," Lyle said. "I'd stake my life on it. We'll probably never know what compelled him to commit such a heinous crime. Based on what you've told us, the evidence against him is incontrovertible. It would take a miracle to prove someone else did it."

Sir Roland looked crestfallen. "Lyle, I was hoping you would be able to explain the impossible and reveal how someone else attacked the poor girl. I'm up against Anthony Farringdon, QC. We've been rivals for years. The thought of losing this latest case to him is distinctly galling."

***

The next day, Hermione and Lyle remembered the barrister's words when they read in the afternoon edition of the *Evening Standard* that Ted Scofield had been found guilty of Abigail Mitchell's murder.

"Poor Uncle Roly," Hermione sighed. "He hates losing."

"The occasional failure is good for a barrister," Lyle consoled her. "Otherwise they run the risk of thinking they're invincible and become insufferably smug."

They left London the following morning and returned to Nettlebed, hoping it would not be long before the furor of the case died down and life got back to normal. After lunch, Hermione attended a rehearsal with the Gosfordshire Symphony Orchestra at the Corn Exchange in Brimhurst. Ted Scofield's wife was noticeable by her absence. In all probability, the company would have to hire another flautist for their Spring Festival Concert, because Hilary was unlikely to want to show her face in public for some time.

After the rehearsal was over, Hermione was leaving the Corn Exchange when she ran into Vladislav Nicu in the back passage. The dark-haired Romanian violinist had lived and worked in England for several years. He was young, sulky, and decidedly attractive to women. She was suddenly reminded of the fact that she had seen him on the day of Abigail Mitchell's murder.

"Ted Scofield has been found guilty of killing Abigail Mitchell," she began. "He's expected to be sentenced to life in prison."

Vladislav scowled. "The man was a barbaric monster. Why should I care what happens to him?"

"A lot of people like me feel the same way you do," Hermione said. "As you probably know, Lyle and I found Abigail's body in Pelham Wood. We had lunch before that in the restaurant at the Crown Hotel. I remember seeing you sitting at a table for two by yourself. W—were you stood up?"

Vladislav's eyes clouded with pain. "Love is a fool's game—and I've been burned. What can I say?"

"It might help to talk about it," Hermione said sympathetically. "Am I right in thinking the lady in question is married?"

Vladislav flinched, and said in a voice thick with emotion, "How could you possibly know that?"

"A lucky guess."

"If you must know, she's a former flame. She encouraged me to join the Gosfordshire Symphony Company. Sometimes I think I would have been better off remaining an eco-warrior and saving our dying planet."

"Being hurt by the woman you love must have been very painful."

Anger flared in Vladislav's eyes. "What business is it of yours? You think I took my aggressions out on Abigail Mitchell, is that it?"

"No, I didn't say that."

"You're crazy. I have no time for her or anyone else. I'm through with women—"

***

On the way home, Hermione visited Copthorne Cottage. She was aware that, following Ted Scofield's arrest the previous year, his wife Hilary had moved out of the rented cottage they were sharing in Brimhurst and returned to her childhood home in Compton Sutton, to live with her widowed mother. Hilary was looking devastated by her husband's recent conviction for murder. It required little effort on Hermione's part to persuade her to unburden herself.

"I knew from the beginning Ted was far from perfect," she said in a tearful voice. "He's always been inclined to boast and make himself out to be better than he really is. But he doesn't mean anything by it. An inferiority complex is at the root of his insecurity. But that has never stopped me from loving him unconditionally. His foster parents were elderly and died shortly after we met. I'm the only person left in the world who really cares what happens to him."

"Has Ted ever been violent toward you?" Hermione asked.

Hilary shook her head vigorously. "No, he's always been such a gentle giant. He once fainted when he cut himself with a knife preparing dinner. He's got a morbid horror of blood and death. As a child he fell from a horse and banged his head. It was probably that accident, in my opinion, which led to the onset of his epilepsy."

"Is it true Ted is also dyslexic?"

Hilary's eyes glistened with tears. "Reading and writing have always been a struggle for Ted. But when you love someone, things like that don't matter. The publicity from the trial has been awful. Ted must have blacked out in Pelham Wood. He insists he has no memory of attacking Abigail. I've lost count of the times he's begged me to forgive him. How could he not remember killing her? If I'm perfectly honest, I don't think I'll ever truly understand why he did it…"

Her poignant words tugged at Hermione's heartstrings. There was nothing she could say or do to take away the other's pain. What she was witnessing here, in all its banality, was no less a tragedy than Shakespeare's *Romeo and Juliet*.

Hilary picked up the teapot and poured out their tea. "I'm afraid I forgot the milk."

"I'll go and get it," Hermione offered.

She left the front room and went down the passage to the kitchen, where Millicent Wren, a woman of great natural warmth and empathy, was sliding her feet into a pair of size ten Wellingtons. She turned an amiable face to her visitor.

"Is anything wrong, dear?"

"We need some milk for our tea."

"I'm about to go and milk the cows," Millicent said with a chuckle. "But luckily there's some in the fridge."

She took a jug of milk out of the fridge and passed it to Hermione.

"I appreciate you dropping by and making sure Hilary is alright. She's going through a terrible ordeal just now."

"How is she coping?" Hermione asked simply.

Millicent's eyes softened with compassion. "Hilary's as bereft as a poor lamb that's had its throat slit. I felt the same way after I lost her father. You'd never know it, but Ted and Hilary made such a lovely couple in the early days of their courtship. Everyone knew he was simple, but Hilary insisted she loved him no matter what. Being a possessive mother, I refused to give my blessing at first. If I'd known that dreadful little minx Abigail Mitchell was going to come onto Ted, I'd have found a way to stop her before she went too far."

Hermione saw a bowl of mushrooms on the dresser and shivered.

"What's the matter, dear?" Millicent's pale blue gaze missed nothing. "Are you cold?"

"The mushrooms reminded me of the ones I saw the day after the murder."

Millicent smiled reminiscently. "Many is the time I've gone mushroom picking in Pelham Wood. Ted used to pick mushrooms for me, too. He was a good boy that way."

Hermione said slowly, "I remember there was a basket of mushrooms in your kitchen the day after the murder when I called on you to deliver some eggs. You said the mushrooms had been picked the previous day, and kindly offered me some."

Millicent smiled sweetly at her. "It's entirely possible I was in Pelham Wood, but it's such a long time ago, I can't remember. My memory isn't what it once was." Her smile widened, as if she were humoring a child with learning difficulties. "The layout of Pelham Wood is very familiar to me because there was once talk of it being sold off to give way to a nasty highway. Along with other environmental protesters, I chained myself to a tree and refused to leave. After a three-month standoff, we were entirely successful and the developers went away. It was such a relief, I can tell you."

"It's too bad you can't remember if you were in Pelham Wood on the day of the murder," Hermione said. "It's possible you could have seen something that might help clear Ted's name."

"I very much doubt it." Millicent shook her head in gentle wonder. "From now on, Hilary can rely on me to keep her safe. No one else is ever going to hurt my beautiful daughter again, or take her away from me."

When Hermione left Copthorne Cottage an hour later, she couldn't help feeling incredibly sorry for Hilary Scofield. A curtain twitched at one of the windows, and she wondered if her departure was being observed by her friend or the latter's devoted mother.

Over the next week, Hermione and Lyle were kept busy with their caretaking duties around Milsham Castle. Rehearsals for the Gosfordshire Symphony Orchestra's forthcoming concert also made large demands on Hermione's time.

On Saturday night, the couple dined up at the main house with their employer, Lord Milsham. Taxation was the bane of the elderly peer's life, and his accountants had recently advised him that it was safe for him to leave his tax haven in Switzerland and return temporarily to England. By a curious coincidence, one of Lord Milsham's guests was Anthony Farringdon, QC. The conversation invariably touched on crime, and everyone soon tired of listening to the sleek middle-aged barrister's account of his latest professional triumph.

"There was never any doubt in my mind that Ted Scofield murdered Abigail Mitchell," he reiterated, with the conviction of someone who is in love with the sound of his own mellifluous voice. "The jury only took three hours to return a guilty verdict."

With his coal-black hair and magnetic personality, Anthony Farringdon had a way of making his presence felt—perhaps a little too forcefully, if the faintly bored expression on his wife Laura's delicate, patrician features was any indication.

"It was such a distressing case," Dora Bates bleated. "I do hope we're not going to spend the entire night steeped in crime."

She was a pale, emaciated woman and doted on her gray monochrome husband, Edmund. The couple looked as if they hadn't had a proper nourishing meal in years.

"Dora is very sensitive to the suffering of others," Edmund said in a reed-thin voice. "She has a job as a social worker in Gosford."

"Edmund is an orderly at the St. Francis Xavier Hospital." Dora clearly expected the other guests to be impressed by her husband's credentials. "He shares my dislike of violence."

Lord Milsham had invited the Bateses to dinner as a kindly gesture, because they had recently broken his decade-long reign of success by winning the biggest pumpkin contest at the Brimhurst Flower Show. Dora Bates was preoccupied with the idea of having a baby and had driven everyone, including her hen-pecked husband, nearly mad with frustration by regaling them throughout dinner with the couple's failed attempts to conceive a baby with the help of IVF treatments. It was almost a relief when the subject had turned to crime and the murder of Abigail Mitchell.

Hermione suspected Lyle was taking a much keener interest in the proceedings than he wanted anyone to know. He had the air of an actor standing in the wings, waiting for his cue to step out on stage and deliver his lines. She had the absurd notion—or rather a feeling of conviction—that they were on the brink of finding out something important about Abigail Mitchell's death.

A woman of impeccable breeding and good manners, Laura Farringdon turned to her host and asked, "Have you read any good books lately, Lord Milsham?"

"Hermione has given me a copy of John Dickson Carr's *The Judas Window*," Lord Milsham declared with that air of amiable self-aggrandizement that was his custom after a third glass of claret. "He remains the greatest exponent of the locked room murder mystery. I can't say I ever met him myself. Most writers of the Golden Age were hopelessly out of touch with reality. Not like the realistic school of modern crime writing, eh?"

Hermione said with a sigh, "The Golden Age of crime fiction had enormous charm and ingenuity."

"Charm," Anthony Farringdon snorted derisively. "What on earth has charm got to do with violence? John Dickson Carr and his contemporaries knew nothing about the sordidness of real-life crime."

"Really?" Lyle murmured, with a curious gleam in his eyes. "I would have said the opposite was true. The whole point of being a writer is to shed light on man's humanity and inhumanity to his fellow human beings, is it not?"

"The same is true of actors and musicians," Vladislav Nicu said unexpectedly. "It's their raison d'être."

Lord Milsham was a patron of the arts, but Hermione was still surprised he had invited the sulky violinist to dinner. Beneath Vladislav Nicu's dark Caesar haircut, his deep-set eyes blazed with the fervor of a romantic dreamer. Hermione was convinced her uncle, Sir Roland Anstruther, was not the only man who had lost out in love when Laura Farringdon had married her husband. She remembered her conversation with Vladislav Nicu at the Brimhurst Corn Exchange, and was prepared to bet that he was also deeply in love with Laura Farringdon.

Laura Farringdon interested Hermione a great deal. She suspected Laura wanted for nothing in the way of material possessions, but her restlessness of manner suggested there was something her husband was unable to give her, and that was love. Hermione wondered if Anthony Farringdon realized his wife still had feelings for her former lover. There was an silent chemistry between Laura and Vladislav that spoke volumes. The two understood each other, and shared the same sense of humor. There was something dramatic and arresting about them. They reminded Hermione of tragic lovers in an opera. For one absurd moment, she wondered if Vladislav might have raped and strangled Abigail Mitchell in Pelham Wood out of frustrated longing for Laura, but DNA tests had proved conclusively that the blood on her clothes and battered body was Ted Scofield's.

"Murder is the ultimate form of social ostracism," Lyle said. "The world is a much safer place now that Abigail Mitchell's killer is serving life in prison." He paused to gauge the effect of his words on everyone.

Dora Bates's mouth trembled. "Has everyone heard the latest news about Ted Scofield's wife? Hilary was rushed to the St. Francis Xavier Hospital this morning."

"An attempted overdose," Edmund explained.

Lord Milsham unwittingly knocked over his glass of claret.

"I spoke to Hilary several days ago," Hermione said with a shudder. "She can't understand how someone as kind and timid as Ted could have committed such a terrible crime. She's remained loyal and devoted to him throughout this ghastly nightmare."

"Then why try to kill herself?" Laura Farringdon asked, white-faced with shock.

Lyle's quiet reply reverberated with authority. "She loves her husband to the point of idolatry. The idea of living without him is unbearable for her."

"Hilary Scofield wouldn't be the first married woman to make a mistake in the name of love," Vladislav said bitterly.

Laura Farringdon flushed as she said, "Sometimes women have been known to come to their senses."

"Hilary Scofield isn't a Barbara Cartland heroine," Anthony Farringdon said with a flicker of disdain. "She would be well advised to do a reality check. Her husband is a convicted murderer whose vicious crime has contaminated the lives of countless people, including Abigail Mitchell's bereft parents."

Dinner came to an end on that strained note. Lord Milsham suggested they move to the Great Hall to indulge in brandy and liqueurs. On the way there, Dora Bates fell into conversation with Hermione.

"Often our best intentions don't work out as well as we hoped," she said with a stricken look. "It would have been so much better for everyone if Ted Scofield had died of leukemia."

"Let's not go into the events of twenty years ago," Edmund implored.

"What do you mean?" Hermione asked.

"Edmund's donation of bone marrow saved Ted Scofield's life."

"How was I to know I was saving the life of a future rapist and murderer?" Edmund said, shaking his head in self-reproach. "I thought I was doing the right thing at the time. From an early age, I was taught the importance of helping others out in times of need. Through my job at the St. Francis Xavier Hospital, I heard one of the patients was in urgent need of a bone marrow transplant. My own mother died after waiting in vain for a heart transplant. Her loss made me determined to help others in any way I could."

"Ted Scofield made a full recovery thanks to Edmund."

"If Ted Scofield had died twenty years ago," Edmund said shakily, "he would never have raped and murdered that poor girl Abigail. I—I feel so sorry for her parents."

"Anthony Farringdon is right when he says crime contaminates," Lyle said gravely. "It's imperative there aren't any more suicide attempts on Hilary's part."

Hermione liked the Bateses and wished she could tell them that Ted Scofield had been the victim of a miscarriage of justice. But first she had to find a way to bring the real killer to justice. The truth had dawned on her a few minutes ago in the dining room.

Hermione signaled to Lyle that she wanted to speak to him alone. The Bateses went on ahead of them.

"What's the matter?" Lyle demanded in a hushed voice, once they were alone.

"I think I know who really murdered Abigail," she whispered.

"So do I," Lyle relied. "We need to act fast if we're to save Hilary from taking another overdose."

"Some years ago," Hermione said, expelling her breath nervously, "Millicent Wren was part of a group of eco-warriors who succeeded in thwarting developers' plans to bulldoze Pelham Wood to make way for a highway. Their tactics included chaining themselves to trees and building camouflaged lookout posts in the branches high above the ground. One or two abandoned lookout posts are probably still there. Vladislav Nicu was once an environmental supporter. I think he abseiled down a piece of rope, raped and strangled Abigail Mitchell, then hauled himself back up out of harm's way. The overlapping branches of the adjacent trees would have provided him with an excellent escape route across the wood without leaving any incriminating footprints on the ground near the crime scene. Ted Scofield must have stumbled across the body before we found it."

Lyle said grimly, "I wouldn't be surprised if he cried his eyes out and hugged Abigail like a rag-doll in the mistaken belief it would bring her back to life. The shock may well have induced a nosebleed plus an epileptic seizure."

"That explains why Ted Scofield's blood was on her body," Hermione said, "and why he didn't remember the episode afterward." She added with a spurt of anger, "I only wish we'd realized the truth sooner."

Lyle came to a decision. "We need to move fast if we're to expose the killer."

"How are we going to apprehend Vladislav without any proof?"

"Go back to the party," Lyle said urgently. "I'll phone the police and do my utmost to get them to listen to me…"

Hermione's nerves were on edge as she mingled with the others in the Great Hall. Out of the corner of her eye, she saw Lyle join them unobtrusively a few minutes later. She wasn't fooled by his subdued manner. He knew his actions were about to alter the entire outcome of the drama unfolding before them.

Over the next two hours, Vladislav Nicu encouraged Anthony Farringdon to give them a full résumé of his career. The egotistical barrister, blinded by his own insufferable vanity, fell into the other's trap. His wife Laura remained the epitome of charm and graciousness. Only the haunted look in her eyes and rigid set of her shoulders betrayed her unhappiness. Presently, Farringdon broke off from his self-important narrative with a look of irritation as the sound of wailing sirens approached Milsham Castle.

"What in God's name—?" Lord Milsham began.

He opened the front door to reveal several police officers standing on the threshold. Behind them in the driveway were two police cars with flashing blue and white lights.

"I'm DI McGowan," the senior officer said. "The Chief Constable of Gosfordshire has asked me to reopen the investigation into Abigail Mitchell's murder—"

There was a stunned silence.

"Why are you looking at me like that?" Vladislav Nicu demanded angrily.

Lyle stepped aside so DI McGowan could confront the killer.

"Edmund Bates, I am arresting you on suspicion of murdering Abigail Mitchell…"

"Edmund, what's going on?" his wife demanded.

Laura Farringdon was staring at him. "I thought I recognized your face," she said. "I saw you entering Pelham Wood on the afternoon of the murder—"

Edmund Bates began to scream.

***

A short while later, guided by moonlight, Lyle dashed down the driveway to Nettlebed, followed by Hermione. Once inside the kitchen, he dialed Sir Roland Anstruther's number in London and pressed the hands-free button on the phone so Hermione could join in their conversation.

"Roland, it's Lyle Revel. I want to be the first to congratulate you on proving Ted Scofield's innocence."

The barrister's voice was blurred with sleep. "What are you talking about? Have you taken leave of your senses?"

"Twenty years ago, Ted Scofield was treated at the St. Francis Xavier Hospital in Gosford for leukemia. The chemotherapeutic drugs he was given wiped out all the bone marrow cells in his system. Donated bone marrow from Abigail Mitchell's future killer Edmund Bates was then infused intravenously into Ted Scofield's system. The bone marrow began producing cells that were released into his bloodstream bearing Edmund Bates' DNA."

"Are you saying my client shares the same DNA blood profile as Edmund Bates?" Sir Roland demanded.

"Exactly."

"Why didn't the silly fool tell anyone?"

"Ted Scofield has the mindset of a twelve-year-old," Lyle reminded him. "I doubt if he understands the first thing about the science of DNA profiling. He's also dyslexic and suffers from short-term memory problems. Coupled with his morbid dislike of blood and death, I'm prepared to bet the memory of his former illness slipped his mind. His foster parents died several years ago and weren't in a position to tell anyone. Edmund Bates confessed to Abigail's murder when the police arrested him a short while ago. He and his wife Dora have tried unsuccessfully to have a baby for years. Her constant nagging has chipped away at his masculinity. Abigail made the fatal mistake of rejecting his advances in Pelham Wood, so he raped and killed her."

Sir Roland was euphoric. "Lyle, how on earth did you arrive at the truth?"

"Lyle has me to thank for accepting Lord Milsham's invitation to dinner tonight," Hermione interjected.

"Most crimes go unsolved because investigators fail to think outside the box," Lyle said triumphantly. "Ted Scofield is a gentle soul who has been known to faint at the sight of his own blood. My inner voice told me it was entirely out of character for him to have committed such a violent crime. Justice can only be served when DNA evidence is interpreted correctly. He's been the victim of a botched investigation by the Brimhurst police and deserves his freedom back…"

Presently, they heard the sound of a BMW halting outside Nettlebed, on the gravel drive by the front gates. The Farringdons' voices drifted in through the window.

"You're insufferable," Laura said harshly. "I want a divorce."

Anthony's voice was seared with sarcasm. "So you can go off with Vladislav, I suppose?"

"Yes, I married the wrong man…"

The couple's BMW swung onto the main road and receded into the distance.

Lyle grabbed his car keys and hurried outside to where his silver sports car, Lady Godiva, gleamed serenely in the moonlight.

"Where are we going?" Hermione demanded.

"The St. Francis Xavier Hospital," Lyle said, starting the engine. "I want to be there when Hilary Scofield learns her husband is innocent. She loves him as much for his faults as for his virtues. Now that's what I call a woman in a thousand…"

The Last Thing I Do
AMY MYERS

It is my sad duty as recorder for the King Arthur in Kent Association to report the events that culminated in the death of our newly elected chair, Mr. Thomas Tunstall, at the very moment of his coronation in our village hall. The crown having been set upon his noble head, he raised the golden goblet to his lips and drank the sanctifying nectar within. Within minutes, King Arthur was in mortal agony, fighting for breath. Before our very eyes, he had fallen to the floor and could not be revived.

"La Mort D'Arthur," one of our number murmured at this shocking occurrence.

Strychnine, not the sword, was the cause.

How had this monstrous deed come about? For weeks, a battle had been waged between two of our five committee members. It had rivaled the great conflict on Barendoune—now Barham Downs—where, as recorded in Sir Thomas Malory's great work, King Arthur met his enemy Mordred in battle. Although most of the tales of King Arthur associate him with the west and north of England, we in the southeast consider it our duty to preserve the record of his noble deeds in Kent.

Malory writes of his wars with Sir Lancelot in France, during which time his enemy cousin Mordred decided to seize the kingdom for himself. The noble archbishop of Canterbury refused to crown him, cursing him by bell, book, and candle, but Mordred took his army to the cliffs of Dover to fight Arthur and Sir Gawaine on their return from France. Arthur drove Mordred's troops back along the ridge of the North Downs hills until the two armies clashed again at Barham Down. Once again Arthur was victorious. Our small village of Downham Green nurtures a legend that Arthur died here and is buried on the Kentish downs, but we are an open-minded association and are prepared to grant that this noble king might have driven Mordred back to Glastonbury in the west of our fair isle.

As the scholar on the committee for the King Arthur in Kent Association, I feel it my duty to ensure that everything is done in accordance with strict procedure. This granted to our chair, Mr. Thomas Tunstall, the honor of taking the role of King Arthur, and to his vice chair, Mr. Harry Whistler, merely that of the evil Mordred. Some say this was because Thomas owned the manor house in Downham Green and Harry was the village butcher. Surely that is false. However, it is true that for eleven years our committee had the same occupants, and I fear resentfulness had grown.

"It's a farce," Harry had yelled, after the annual election, held at our round table in the village hall on Wednesday, four days before the tragic coronation. "Every year it's the same. High time we had a new chair; it's my turn to be King Arthur."

"You should be grateful," Patricia Cooper snapped. "It's a very important job being vice chair." Patricia is fortunate in that she has no rivals for Guinevere or for being secretary on our committee.

"We're a democracy," Harry pointed out. "We ought to take it in turns playing Arthur. That's the whole point of having a bloody round table, so we're all treated the same. Anyone else think it's unfair?"

"I do," drawled Thomas languidly, before the other members could pluck up courage to agree, "but that's at odds with the fact that I've just been reelected."

"Shall we proceed and reelect our other members?" Ronald Pagfield, our treasurer and Sir Gawaine, said hastily, knowing his role was quite safe as none of us would want it. Patricia was also duly reelected, and I agreed to continue with my role as recorder and Sir Lancelot, although I should mention that Patricia would not be my first choice as my illicit lover. Her sturdiness resembles Brunnhilde more than the slender charms of King Arthur's wife and consort, and her enthusiastic support for women's rights is disturbing. Fond though she was of Thomas, however, I had the impression that she would not be averse to Guinevere taking the chair, although she was not as vocal in her ambition as Harry. I had sometimes spotted an envious expression on Ronald's face, too.

King Arthur is naturally an important role, and thus Thomas was the star of our annual events, chief of which are the Christmas pantomime and more importantly our summer Battle of the Downs, attended by the whole village. There had been a slight embarrassment on one occasion when Ronald exceeded his script as Sir Gawaine, who died after he arrived back at Dover with King Arthur. Dear Ronald demanded he live long enough to take part in the battle of Barendoune. Ronald pointed out that, as Malory wrote that Sir Gawaine's ghost later appeared to King Arthur, there was no reason he couldn't appear at Barham Downs as well. After all, up to the time of King Henry VIII, his bones were on show nearby, at the chapel next to the Pharos in Dover. Ronald conceded that he would have to make some effort to behave like a ghost and not wield a sword. He had never quite forgiven Thomas for vetoing this plan, and instead he became a regrettably staunch (though secret) fan of Mordred (in the form of Harry Whistler), just as Patricia devoted herself to King Arthur's cause.

Patricia did make a feeble attempt for more prominence on her own behalf too, claiming that, as Guinevere was in a convent at the time of Barendoune, she might play an additional role, either as the damsel who acted as messenger between Lancelot and Arthur, or preferably the beautiful Lady of Farthingloe, who according to legend was Sir Gawaine's love and searched for him in vain on the battlefield. Ronald was not keen on this plan.

Lastly there is myself, Jeremy Mandson, tasked with recording the battle and taking a back seat within it, as Lancelot at the time of the battle was busy ruling his lands in France. His role therefore is not so important as Mordred's, who at the opening of our battle picks his fight with the archbishop of Canterbury for refusing to crown him king.

"We could perhaps consider changes to our system next year," Ronald had suggested at Wednesday's election at our round table in the village hall. The result of the election had proved embarrassing this year, as our membership are allowed a say in the matter. Save for Harry, the committee had all voted for Thomas, but our village members were solidly for Harry, although naturally they do not overrule our decision.

The battle at the round table had continued very unpleasantly indeed as Thomas and Harry fought it out, the rest of us becoming virtually nonplayers.

"You said you were going to retire from the chair," Harry had shouted.

"I changed my mind, old chap. And everyone but you has voted for me anyway," Thomas said blandly.

"But it was my turn," Harry had yowled. "And you watch out, Tom Tunstall, the battle of Barendoune is going to have a different ending this year."

I was shocked, even if Harry did have democracy on his side. That was not the way to speak to our chair.

"My dear sir," Thomas had rejoined. "I do believe you're jealous. I must point out that King Arthur never loses a battle. Next year perhaps you'll be lucky enough to play him yourself."

The chortle he gave made it clear that this was unlikely, to say the least. Harry must have thought the same because he banged his tin goblet on the table and stood up, shaking with rage.

"I'll make sure you don't play Arthur on Sunday, Thomas Tunstall, if it's the last thing I do."

Four days later, our newly crowned King Arthur died of strychnine poisoning. It was not a pleasant death. There was no gentle rocking to sleep in the arms of three fair ladies in a barge bound for Avalon, or, as our village legend has it, to the downs of Kent, where he sleeps in peace under a grassy knoll. I mourned the loss of Thomas greatly.

The police were obviously summoned once our village doctor had given his opinion that this was no natural death. A pleasant young inspector from the Essex and Kent Serious Crime Directorate, whom we had in fact already met, questioned us all. He had been most interested to hear about the King Arthur in Kent Association, and readily offered us his services.

"I'll have a bash myself at your next battle," Inspector Jones told us.

Appositely, his name was Gareth, and we informed him that he, Sir Gareth, would be most welcome. He was provided at his request with the details of our coronation proceedings. They are quite straightforward. After a preliminary ceremony, a procession makes its way through the assembled gathering of as many members as our village hall will hold. It enters to the sound of trumpets, or rather trumpet (the trumpeter is Ronald's teenage son, anxious to be part of the ceremony but distinctly discordant), up through the hall with the audience on either side and led by the archbishop (Patricia's daughter). On the stage, Arthur awaits the procession, attended by two acolytes, Patricia and Ronald. The archbishop hands a scrolled document to Arthur, who swears to rid his country of villains such as Mordred and to protect damsels. The archbishop places the crown on Arthur's noble head, and he is handed a golden goblet from which to drink the coronation mead.

I explained to the inspector that, on this sad occasion, the two acolytes could swear that they had prepared the mead together that very morning and guarded it safely to hand to the newly crowned king. Neither of them had added strychnine, Patricia said, sobbing, and she always disposed of everything afterward in the bin so the hall would be tidy. No one else had had access to the mead. The ingredients were simple enough—water, a small jar of honey, and a small bottle of champagne, both newly opened. Inspector Gareth Jones listened to me attentively and agreed that, unless they acted together, there was little or no chance that they could have poisoned the drink.

In any case, neither Patricia nor Ronald had any motive. Suspicion obviously would have fallen on the one suspect, Harry Whistler, who had vowed that Thomas Tunstall would not play Arthur if it was the last thing he did. Would have fallen?

Harry had died three days earlier.

Harry's death was due an unfortunate accident with Excalibur. The short ceremony before the procession, briefly referred to above, involves King Arthur drawing this sacred sword from a "stone," which in our case is a suitably disguised box of old pieces of rubber. As the village butcher and handyman, the precise details of its extraction were left to Harry, who had a close acquaintance with knives and saws. As our King Arthur has to withdraw Excalibur at the ceremony, much expertise has to go into this maneuver to ensure that it is fixed firmly, but not too firmly—a task left to Harry. He agreed to fix Excalibur up on Thursday morning, the coronation being on Sunday. Alas, this year, Excalibur—which was this year a rather smart long dagger borrowed for the occasion—refused to budge when we arrived.

"This," said Thomas Tunstall, "is your fault, Harry. You're determined to mar my coronation. You know you can't get the better of me by fair means, so you've settled for foul."

Harry had snarled in return, "Fine Arthur you make. Can't even get Excalibur out of a cardboard box. Bad omen. I told you I should be Arthur."

"Nonsense, dear boy, it merely makes your role as Mordred all the more important. The villain of the piece, what?" Thomas gave a hearty laugh. "You're planning to fix the box on coronation day so that I haven't a hope of pulling the sword out. Villain of the piece, eh?"

Thus stymied, Harry had demanded a vote on whether he had a point about not electing a feeble Arthur no longer up to the job. The majority—four of us—decided he didn't. Patricia—always, like Guinevere, the innocent in the background (well, relatively innocent in Guinevere's case)—demanded another rehearsal that evening, as Harry had to fix Excalibur. That was agreed.

Alas, I arrived at the hall before Thomas, Patience, and Ronald, and found the door locked, which struck me as strange, since Harry should already have been there. The village hall is niggardly in handing out keys, although Harry had one as vice chair and so did Thomas, who duly let us in.

We were met by a terrible sight. Harry was lying on his side with Excalibur partly wedged in his chest, his hand bloodied from where he had tried to release it, and his face a truly gruesome sight.

This had been our first meeting with the pleasant Inspector Gareth Jones, who nodded when we said that this seemed to be a most unusual and unfortunate accident. It was clear that Harry might still have been finding difficulties in extracting Excalibur from the "stone" and used a great deal of strength to tug it free, lost his balance, and tumbled backward, and the dagger had somehow landed in his bosom as he fell to the floor.

"Harry was such a nice man," Patricia had sobbed in Thomas's arms.

Thomas had tactfully agreed, as he modestly told us that he was still prepared to go ahead with the coronation and be crowned as King Arthur.

Patricia, Ronald, and I were dubious about the etiquette of this, but were persuaded that Harry was a trooper who would insist that the show went on, so we continued with our plans, which would undoubtedly receive much fine publicity.

However, with Thomas's death on the Sunday, the committee was thus in the awkward position of losing two of its officers, both of whom had ample reason to desire the other's removal, neither of whom could have been responsible for the death of the other, and both of whom were no longer with us for the worst of reasons.

The pleasant Inspector Gareth Jones pointed out that even Merlin had never been in this position, and more than a magic wand would be necessary to solve Thomas's undoubted murder. He would, he said, be grateful for any help the committee could give.

"Let's talk things over, man to man," Ronald suggested after the inspector had departed, although I pointed out (being a stickler for detail) that Patricia

would be with us. At that, he pointed out that I was an old stick in the mud
and I knew what he meant. We had spent several days talking, firstly to the
families of Thomas Tunstall and Harry Whistler, both vastly different in their
social positions—one being to the manor born (or, strictly speaking, to the
manor bought), and the other from the "salt of the earth" brigade.

Secondly, we had talked to the police, doctors, nurses, the press, and
everyone in Downham Green who had an opinion on the matter—or matters,
in the plural, in view of the fact that there were two deaths to gossip about.
It had long been the case that half the village were enthusiastic supporters of
the King Arthur in Kent Association, while the other half thought we were
rubbish and out for our own ends. What those ends were had never been
defined, but the deaths of our two committee members, especially one at his
coronation, gave fresh fuel to the smoldering fire.

There was certainly smoldering within our committee ranks when the word
murder was mentioned. The concept of Arthur and Mordred slain in battle
obviously passed muster, but murder by persons unknown was another matter,
especially when it was disputed.

On the Monday morning, we had retired to a nearby hostelry in the next
village for our discussion, as the Stag and Hound pub in Downham Green had
been too close to home for a committee consultation on its sudden reduction
in numbers. The news had obviously spread, however, courtesy of the local
journalists hovering hopefully, but the village itself didn't seem to be preparing
to take up cudgels against the remaining three of us. Granted, there was an air
of satisfaction, though, as if double suspicious deaths could only be expected
of a village like Downham Green.

"Murder is not possible," declared Ronald. Being an accountant, he tends to
see things in black and white.

"It happened," Patricia moaned. "Does it really matter how?"

Ronald was quite clear that it did. "It was accident on both occasions."

I had to dispute that. "Hardly, Ronald."

"Suicide, then," Ronald said flatly.

At this unexpected approach, Patricia burst into tears. She often did, despite
her insistence on women's rights. "That's horrid of you, Ronald. Darling
Thomas would never commit suicide."

"Did darling Thomas commit murder, though?" I suggested meekly.

Two pairs of horrified eyes gazed at me. "Harry died four days earlier, and by accident," Ronald stated firmly.

"Murder," I corrected him gravely. "It can't have been accident, as the door was locked when we arrived and Thomas had to unlock it. If Harry had been there on his own, then it wouldn't be locked. Thomas was not going to see his role as Arthur wrested from him, and Harry was threatening to do so."

"No, old chap, you've got it wrong," Ronald replied fiercely. "Thomas was murdered himself a few days later. Who murdered him?"

"It's my belief Harry did," I said darkly. "He poisoned him."

"Not possible. How?"

"Somehow," I concluded weakly. I agreed it was difficult to see how Thomas could have been poisoned by anyone, let alone Harry, since the coronation mead drink was only prepared that Sunday morning, with two committee members present to guard it until the ceremony. It was easier to work out how Thomas could have murdered Harry, as he was a keyholder. He could have gone into the hall while Harry was working on Excalibur, killed him, and locked the door on the way out, hoping to make it look like suicide.

"But it's definitely murder," I added, "not suicide."

"I still think it was," Ronald said obstinately. "That's why the door was locked. Dear Harry didn't want to be disturbed. He wanted to die nobly with Excalibur. But now you're telling us there were two murderers amongst us."

There was a certain belligerence in his tone now, which I did not like. "Myself and Patricia?" he continued. "You and Patricia? Me? Did we commit these terrible crimes? We could all have done so."

"I think not," I said, mentally examining the facts. "You and Patricia made the mead, you guarded it until Thomas drank it, and you would certainly have noticed me if I had crept up to poison it."

"That's true," Patricia said eagerly. "The water came from the tap, the champagne from a newly opened bottle, and the honey from an unopened jar. So it had to be suicide. Poor dear Thomas." A moment's reflection as the terrible truth struck her. "But it was me who handed the precious goblet to him. I shall never forgive myself."

"It wasn't your fault, Patricia," I said gently. "Of course you couldn't have killed him, and it wasn't suicide. There had to be some other way he was poisoned. The goblet itself, for instance."

"I washed it before we put the mead into it," Ronald said defensively. "So Harry Whistler couldn't have tampered with it, poor fellow. It had to be suicide."

"Especially as Harry was already dead," I agreed. "But the police won't believe the suicide theory. They'll be looking for someone else."

"A wicked murderer?" Patricia moaned. "A villager?"

"There can't be too many wicked murderers close at hand who had a grudge against Thomas, two of whom acted at the same time," I said. "Or two with a grudge against King Arthur. Or against Mordred, in the case of Harry."

"There were two murderers?" Ronald queried, puzzled.

"Murderers always use the same method of disposal," I pointed out, being an avid reader of detective stories. "No murderer would use both knife and poison."

"So there was only one murderer?" Patricia said, clearly confused.

"No, two," I replied.

Ronald looked even more puzzled. Then he exclaimed, "By George, I've got it! You mean they murdered each other."

I nodded soberly. He was there at last.

Patricia was not, however. "That's just not possible," she said indignantly. "Poor Harry's death had to be suicide. He realized he was never ever going to beat Thomas in an election or get to play King Arthur, and not wanting to face such humiliation, he killed himself."

We were back where we started.

"Not quite," I said. "Remember what Harry yelled at Thomas. 'I'll make sure you don't play Arthur on Sunday if it's the last thing I do.' "

Guinevere and Sir Gawaine gaped at me, much as King Arthur would have gaped at Mordred declaring he'd discovered the whereabouts of the Holy Grail.

"The problem is," Ronald ventured to say at last, "that neither of them could have killed the other, however much they would have liked to do so. Thomas could have killed Harry, but he wouldn't have locked the door after him, and Harry couldn't have dropped poison into Thomas's mead because he was dead. What do you say to that, Jeremy?"

I stared at him. I could have pointed out that Thomas could have locked the door in order for it to look like suicide, but I could not believe that of Harry Whistler, so I had no answer for him.

Thus encouraged, Ronald continued, "Harry knew we were all coming and therefore would have left the door open. If he'd been murdered, Thomas wouldn't incriminate himself by locking the door. Conclusion: suicide."
He beamed.

Sometimes facts don't always add up to a solution. One of those times was now. I decided to go for a walk on the downs and clear my head, wondering if King Arthur did this before taking up arms for battle. Perhaps that's why he visited the old chapel in Dover, if he'd just buried Sir Gawaine there, of whom he was very fond. What a heritage we British have, although I doubt whether Ronald ever truly appreciates his role as Gawaine. Such riches we have inherited. I tried to picture Patricia striding through the battlefields like Lady Farthingloe looking for Sir Gawaine's body and doing the same for Ronald, or even Thomas. I failed.

Instead, I forced myself to consider more alternatives to the scenarios we had been discussing over Harry and Thomas's murders. For I was still sure that murder it was—and in both cases, impossible though it might seem. Suppose, for example, Patricia and Ronald had joined together in a mutual pact to kill Thomas. It was conceivable that Ronald might have been harboring a secret passion to play King Arthur, but not that Patricia would countenance such a deed. Nor did Patricia or Ronald have any real reason to kill Harry, much as they might have disapproved of his mission to depose King Arthur in his own favor. No, the scenario, shocking though it was, that Thomas and Harry had killed each other was the only viable one, however impossible it might seem.

Up here on the downs, with the views all the way out to the Channel, it was all too easy to think of Arthur's men frantically sailing back to England to save it from Mordred's evil machinations, or from the Saxons, if one believes the early historians.

And at last an idea came to me. I walked briskly down the hillside, thinking of the battles that had taken place here in earlier years. Perhaps King Arthur and Mordred had fought bitter duels on the very ground I was walking on. This was heady stuff, and exhilarating. I hurried home, eager to get to my study to check the works of Gildas and Nennius.

I found the pleasant Inspector Jones first, however. He was waiting for me in his car outside my home, so he came with me to my study—to talk things over, he told me.

"How are you getting on, Inspector?" I asked him.

"Thanks to your help, quite well." He looked approvingly at bookshelves, sipping the tea I had provided. "No doubt about it," commented, "This King Arthur stuff is a bit of a puzzle."

I laughed. "Indeed. King Arthur has been a puzzle for many centuries. Why no mention of him for so many years? Because he didn't exist is the usual answer, completely ignoring the fact that in Ireland the name Arthur derives from the word for *bear*, and the triumphant winner of the battle of Barendoune would naturally be referred to as *the bear*."

"Ingenious," Inspector Gareth Jones murmured. "This case of ours is a bit of a puzzle, too. No doubt about that. Harry Whistler was murdered, and so was Thomas Tunstall—two impossible murders, one could say."

"I agree, but were they murders?" I was anxious for him to confirm this.

"Oh yes."

I sighed. "The committee and I came to that conclusion too. They are indeed impossible. Except that I do have one humble idea."

He whistled. "Well done, Mr. Mandson. Tell me about it."

Nothing loth to do so, I plunged into my explanation. "Thomas Tunstall killed Harry Whistler because he knew Harry had the village support behind him even though he'd lost the election again. Thomas Tunstall came to the hall with Harry or shortly after his arrival, killed him with Excalibur—"

"Sacrilege," said Inspector Jones gravely. "True, Excalibur had been wiped clean and no fingerprints remained—not even Whistler's, which should have been on it."

Not suicide, then. So much for that theory. "Any DNA?" I asked.

"Still waiting for the lab results."

"But it must have been murder," I said, glad that was now clear. "And Thomas Tunstall's death? The poison was in the goblet, obviously. But how did it get in?"

"The answer to that's quite simple." The pleasant young inspector smiled. "It was in the honey. We managed to find the empty jar in the bin. We got the results this morning. It might have been a new jar alright, but the question is: who made the honey inside?"

This was an aspect I hadn't thought of, and it set me thinking. "Harry, of course," I said after a little thought. "He has honey for sale in his butcher's shop."

"So he does. So that's that. Perhaps they weren't impossible murders at all," said the inspector. "Harry Whistler had every chance of killing Thomas by providing the two attendants with the honey they'd use in the mead earlier, and Thomas could have killed Harry, given the locked door and the fact that he had a key. I think that about wraps it up, don't you, Mr. Mandson?"

I nodded. "Glad to have been of help."

"Just one question you might be able to help with, though. What happened to the key?"

I stared at him. "Thomas Tunstall had the key with him. He unlocked the door for us."

"No. I mean what happened to Harry's key. We searched. He didn't have it with him, but he'd let himself into the locked village hall earlier."

I froze. I'd taken it from Harry's pocket so that I could lock up as Thomas would have done as he left the hall.

"And," the inspector continued, "you bought a pot of honey from Harry Whistler, fermented it, put some old rat poison in it and resealed it to look new."

He stood up. He didn't look pleasant any longer. "Shall we go?"

He was right, of course. I'd been waiting to play King Arthur for eleven years. I'd vowed I'd do it if it was the last thing I did.

By a Thread
KEITH BROOKE

I wonder how many people in that hall were sorry when they watched Superintendent Brightwell bleed out in front of their eyes? Over a career of more than thirty years on the job, the governor had made a good number of enemies and a lot of them were in that room.

He'd even joked about it earlier. "The only reason you're all here is because you want to be sure I'm really going, isn't it?" he'd said to me.

I'd said nothing. My relationship with Ron Brightwell had been strained for some time, and I wasn't quite sure how I felt about the man who'd mentored and bullied me in equal measure finally heading off into retirement.

Instead, I'd smiled and moved on. In that brief exchange, he hadn't seemed himself: he was edgy and looked as if he would far rather be somewhere else. At the time I'd thought it was only natural not to want to be there, but later I wondered if I'd picked up on a hint that he might have known what was coming.

The force had hired one of the Town Hall's function rooms for Ron's retirement. Close to the station, staggering distance from his home, and large enough for the town's great and good to gather and pay tribute.

It was a pretty grand setting. High ceilings decorated with trompe l'oeil murals, marble columns, and stone floor, all giving it more the feel of a church than a civic function room.

The setting featured in the speech from the Chief Superintendent, Malcolm Thorburn. "We are gathered here today…" A pause for laughter. "Bit of a step up from the local nick, isn't it?" he joked, gesturing around the hall. "I've only ever been here for weddings before, gatherings traditionally focused on celebration and happiness." He paused, milking the crowd as they waited for the inevitable follow-up. "And I'm sure none of us are feeling that way about the fact we're finally seeing the back of Ron Brightwell, eh?"

He paused again for the dutiful laughter, his eyes scanning the room.

"Speaking of Ron, where is the old curmudgeon? I'm under strict instructions to be nice about him—he can't miss that."

That was when it happened.

A murmur arose from a part of the crowded room close to the small lectern where the Chief Superintendent was standing.

Gasps.

A stifled scream.

And then the crowd parted, people backing away to leave just two men. One was on his knees and the other, Ron Brightwell, lay back in the man's arms, his previously white shirt turned almost completely crimson with his own blood.

Even as the gathering seemed frozen into some kind of macabre tableau, I rushed to the governor, dropped to my knees, and reached for his neck to check for a pulse, but it was already too late.

Ron Brightwell was dead, and he lay in the arms of one of the town's most notorious gangsters, Terry Wilson.

***

Sometime later, I leaned against the wall in a Town Hall office commandeered for a makeshift case conference convened by Detective Chief Inspector Sally Ryan, who it seemed would be leading the investigation.

Others in the room included Chief Superintendent Thorburn, Detective Inspector Liza McAdams, and two Detective Sergeants, Omar Shah and Harry Slater.

"Okay," said DCI Ryan, a short woman with pinched features and something strangely intense in her look. "Here's the current status. Superintendent Ronald Brightwell, dead at the scene from an apparent knife wound to the upper abdomen."

I looked away. I'd dealt with some seriously disturbing cases in my time on the job, but nothing had struck home quite like this.

"Our suspect, Terry Wilson, with a rap sheet as long as my arm, is in custody, but denied everything before he clammed up and demanded a lawyer."

"Someone must have seen what happened!" said Thorburn.

"Everyone pleads ignorance," the DCI told him. "Conveniently looking the other way."

"What about the murder weapon?" pressed Thorburn. In theory, he was only in the room because he was the senior officer; it was Sally Ryan's case. But in reality Thorburn was the Chief Superintendent, and when he spoke, everyone else would always dance to his tune.

"No trace," said Ryan. "But we'll find it."

"How can you be sure of that? The place was heaving. One of Wilson's cronies could easily have slipped away to dispose of it."

"The room went on lockdown the instant we saw what had happened," said Ryan. "No one got in or out."

"And you're sure of that?"

"We're coppers," said Ryan. "As soon as things kicked off, there were officers on the doors. Not a guest or a member of the serving staff left that room, I can guarantee you that. Before anyone left tonight—even the Lady Mayoress—they were searched thoroughly."

"Then the weapon is in that room somewhere."

"It is, and we'll find it."

***

Later still. Terry Wilson sat in the interview room at the station with his lawyer, who was also his kid brother Callum, a smug grin on both of their ugly faces as DCI Ryan made for the door. Seconds later she appeared in the adjoining room, where I'd been observing with McAdams and Shah.

I'd had a few run-ins with the Wilson clan early in my career, and I'd been involved when Brightwell had managed to pin a grievous bodily harm charge on Terry that had finally put him away for eighteen months. I knew what we were up against. Even now that Wilson claimed to have found God and rebuilt his life, he'd lost none of the air of gangster intimidation about him.

Brightwell had never believed that Wilson had reformed. Up until now I'd reserved judgment, although my suspension of disbelief was wearing thin after events of this evening.

Ryan was seething. Wilson had just stonewalled through half an hour of questioning, retreating into the old pro's defense of saying nothing at all in the interview.

"Okay," said Ryan. "We have Wilson on the scene, closer to Brightwell than anyone when the act was perpetrated. Motive? Wilson had plenty of reason to want to put one over on his old adversary, and doing so just when the governor was walking away from the job might seem fitting to someone like Wilson."

"But there's no weapon," said Liza McAdams.

Everyone at that gathering, right up to the Lady Mayoress and the Chief Superintendent himself, had been searched. The room had been examined closely from top to bottom, every nook and cranny, every ventilation panel that could be moved, every window, but no knife had been located.

"We'll find it," said Ryan grimly. "What's the simplest explanation? That somehow Wilson exploited those first few seconds of confusion and managed to dispose of the weapon. How long are we looking at? One stab to the abdomen, then, what, ten seconds for Brightwell to collapse, and the people around him to take in what had happened and then cry out and raise the alarm. Another ten or twenty seconds for us to see what was happening? Another thirty seconds for us to swing into action and cover all the doors. That's at least a minute, maybe more. Time enough for Wilson to palm the knife off to one of his associates—a waiter, perhaps—who could then have hurried from the room as the alarm was being raised."

I didn't buy it, and Ryan saw the look on my face immediately. "Okay, Fletch," she said to me, "what's giving you a face like a bulldog licking piss off a thistle?"

"We closed that room down almost instantly," I said. "You know that. You were there. Even before officers had reached the doors, we'd have seen if anyone was rushing out, because we were looking for exactly that."

"We're talking seconds here, I know, but that knife had to be removed from the scene of the crime somehow."

"You say it's the simplest explanation, but is it?" I asked her. "Yes, we're talking seconds here. But something like that would require a lot of planning and coordination. Wilson must have gone there with intent, and he must have placed an accomplice on hand to remove the knife. And he must have waited for exactly the moment when everyone was looking the other way. That's split-second choreography. Do you really think the Wilson boys are that good? And even if they are, the big question is why on earth he'd do it like that. It's almost the opposite of a locked room mystery, because it couldn't have been more public than that, and it would be virtually impossible to avoid being caught. I don't buy it."

"Maybe that's the point," Ryan insisted. "Wilson was making some kind of gesture. Gangster bravado. Do it in public and then sit in the interview room no-commenting everything, until we have to let him walk away scot-free. Talk about sending a message to anyone who's ever crossed him!"

I said nothing. Back in the day, Wilson would have loved to do something exactly like that, but I was still a little swayed by his reformed God-bothering act. And by the look of utter shock on his face when the two of us had knelt there, Brightwell lying slumped in Wilson's arms.

"Okay," said Ryan. "Let's play devil's advocate: what if Wilson is telling the truth? Fletch? You knew the governor better than most. Did he have any enemies?"

Knew… I still couldn't get my head around what had happened.

"I'm not sure anyone knew him that well," I said. "Maybe I thought I did for a while, but there's a reason he was known as the OB around the nick."

Old Bastard.

"Enemies?" I went on. "Plenty. Terry Wilson, obviously, and any of the other Wilson boys. But it's going to take a while to come up with a comprehensive list of crooks who won't be mourning tonight."

"Personal stuff? Any enemies outside the job?"

I shrugged. "I really didn't know him that well these days. I can't think of anyone, though."

"What was your relationship with Brightman?"

I gave her a look. For a moment it sounded as if she was trying to put me in the frame, even though I'd been on the opposite side of the room.

"Our relationship? I knew the governor for, what, fifteen years or so? Back when I came here, he took me under his wing."

"He was your mentor?"

"Maybe. He always said I was a bit like him. He meant it as a compliment. He thought I was destined for great things."

"What changed?"

I realized I didn't know DCI Ryan well at all. She'd only come to this town a few months previously, and wasn't exactly a mixer—which is probably why she'd been given the lead on this case, trying to keep things as nonpersonal as it would be possible to be. Much of this background would be genuinely new to her, and I knew I shouldn't feel defensive.

"I disappointed him," I said. "I had all the wrong priorities. My father was in the job, and I'd seen far too many relationships torn apart by the pressures, my parents' included. Call me naïve, but I decided from the outset that I didn't want to add to those statistics. Brightwell tried to convince me that all that just went with the territory and the personal crap was just another part of the risks that went with the job. He saw me prioritizing my family as settling for less."

"Ironic," said Ryan.

So she did know some of Brightwell's background. A little over two years ago, the governor's wife had died after a short and vicious illness. All of a sudden, Brightwell's priorities flipped, and he was family first and all the rest a distant second. Devoted single father to a teenage daughter—I hadn't seen that coming, at all, but he'd taken to the role with the same fierce commitment he'd given the job before that. It just went to show how things can hang on the finest of threads, and at key points in life it can be easy to flip from one direction to another.

"Didn't all that bring you closer again, though? Him becoming a family man?"

I shook my head. That would have been too much like Brightwell admitting he'd been wrong.

"Where is the daughter?" asked McAdams.

Holly Brightwell had barely been mentioned so far.

"She was heading off on a school trip to Italy," Ryan said. "We just got through to her before the flight was called. She was brought back from the airport an hour ago."

"Is it okay if I go and see her?" I asked. "Holly and I always got on well. I'd like to make sure she's okay."

And that was when I finally saw how it had been: Brightwell had been like a grumpy, over-demanding father to me, and in that case, Holly was like a sister.

God, what a mess. The kid had lost everything.

Ryan nodded. "Do," she said, and I'm not sure how much her decision was founded on compassion and how much it was simply to get me away from the investigation because she'd decided I was too close.

A few minutes later, I headed off.

Callum Wilson was having a smoke in the car park. I almost walked right past him, but he caught my eye and nodded.

"Well, this wasn't how I saw the day going," he said.

I nodded. He wasn't trying to have a dig. If anything he was reaching out, and I remembered the look of shock on his older brother's face when he was kneeling there with Brightwell in his arms.

"Tell me, Callum," I said. "Why isn't your brother defending himself? Why all the 'no comment' responses?"

"Because it's what his lawyer advised," said Callum, the lawyer in question. "If he starts answering questions, you lot will take whatever he says and twist it to suit, won't you? Happens every time. He says nothing and you've got nothing to twist against him, have you? You still can't use a man's choice not to comment against him."

His words rang true. Terry Wilson was an old pro and he knew the score, and his kid brother was a smart and wise lawyer.

Which left the investigation nowhere.

***

Holly Brightwell was staying with her best friend's family while her future was determined by Social Services and what remained of her own family.

I'd walked from the station, and approached the house from a street to the rear. I spotted Holly immediately in the back garden, a painfully thin teenager with dyed black hair that hung in a long fringe over eyes painted goth black that, if anything, made her look panda-like.

She didn't see me, and I said nothing, heading along a neighboring alleyway to the front to ring the doorbell.

A bearded, stooping man of about my age answered. "Mr. Patel? I hope you don't mind. I'm Detective Sergeant Danny Fletcher, I worked with Ron Brightwell. I just wondered if I could say hi to Holly and see how she's doing."

The man gave a sad smile. "Of course," he said, stepping back from the door. "Come on through. She's out back."

"How is she?" I asked as we paused, awkwardly close, in the confined space of the hallway.

"Oh, you know. About what you'd expect. At least she has company. Our daughter Mia was going on the school trip too, but she insisted on coming back with Holly. She's a good girl."

I assumed he was referring to Mia as the good girl. The Holly I knew would never fit that description. She'd always been a wild child, but since her mother's death, she'd gone off the rails for a time.

As if in answer to my line of thought, Mr. Patel went on. "I know Holly has a past, but she's been doing really well since she moved to Mia's school. Holly had been greatly looking forward to this trip to Italy. I drove the girls to the airport this afternoon, and Holly was most polite and considerate. She even got here early so as not to inconvenience me. We've taken her in for a few days while things are sorted out."

I smiled and nodded. The man was nervous, upset by what had happened. "She's out in the back garden?" I prompted, when Patel's flow of nervous chatter hit a slight pause.

He nodded and gestured for me to go through.

"Hey there," I said to Holly when I emerged from the kitchen door.

When she looked up, her features bore such an expression of distraught grief, I felt bad for my earlier assessment: the panda eyes were where her makeup had smudged from rubbing at tears, not a gesture of clumsy adolescent goth rebellion.

"Fletch?" She seemed surprised to see me, and I guessed it was probably a year or so since our paths had crossed.

I sat next to her, breathing in the oddly chemical fruity scent of the e-cig she was smoking. She waved the device at me now, smiled, and said, "It was a compromise with Dad. He let me vape, but no baccy or weed."

Instantly, the smile faltered with a trembling of the lip.

"Oh, Holly," I said. "I'm so sorry. He was a controlling bastard, but that was all part of the charm, wasn't it?"

We sat in silence for a while. I don't normally struggle for words, but nothing can prepare you for something like this.

"Were you there?" she asked eventually.

I nodded.

"Did he...did he say anything? Any last words?"

She was clutching for something to remember him by, I realized. Some kind of epitaph.

"He told me we were all only there just to make sure he was leaving," I said. Not his last words, but the last thing he'd said to me, at least, and typical of Ron Brightwell.

She smiled at that.

"If there's anything, Holly," I told her as I was leaving. "You know how to get in touch? Any time of day or night."

That tremor in the lip again. "Thanks, Fletch." Then: "Will you find out what happened?"

I nodded, finally on solid ground. Because if one thing was certain, we were going to solve the puzzle of Ron Brightwell's death.

I made my excuses and departed, choosing to leave my car at the station and walk home to my flat. As I walked, I dwelled on Holly. The poor kid had lost everything: two years ago her mother, and now her father.

And although my own situation wasn't nearly so tragic, I knew exactly what it was like to lose a family, because despite the choices I'd made to put family before job, I'd suffered the fate of so many in the force, and my own marriage had not survived the pressures.

***

I was at the Town Hall early the next morning, but the forensics team was already there, had probably been working the crime scene right through the night. I knew all the stops would be pulled out for this one.

DCI Ryan was there, also, and I wondered if she'd worked through the night too.

"How's the kid?" she asked, as I pulled paper booties over my shoes in the corridor outside the function room.

"About what you'd expect," I said, unconsciously echoing Mr. Patel's words when I'd asked the same question. Then, remembering to be professional, I furnished her with a few more details. "She's staying with the Patels, the family of her best friend Mia. In shock, clearly. Trying to put a brave face on it and bluster it all out and failing dismally. She didn't have anything to add that we didn't already know. She last saw her father about an hour before the retirement do, then went round to the Patels' for a lift to the airport for her school trip to Italy. She didn't report anything unusual in the events of that day."

Ryan nodded throughout, although she only seemed to be half-listening as she surveyed the hall.

"We've been examining photos from guests' phones last night, but there's nothing of any use. Forensics have been over this place with the proverbial, and there's nothing. The only physical evidence is Brightwell's blood on the floor over there. Terry Wilson's saying nothing still, and we're going to have to let him go today, which is exactly what he wants."

"That's still the lead theory? Gangster braggadocio as some kind of statement to the world? So if they planned it so meticulously, how did they get rid of the knife?"

"Maybe we're overthinking," Ryan said. "You agreed yesterday that we should be looking for the simplest explanation."

"And that is?"

"Human error. Yes, we closed this room down with incredible speed, but the scene was chaotic. What if the simplest explanation is that a mistake was made, and someone managed to slip out, or at least slip the murder weapon out?"

**

I'd never seen the pathology lab so crowded. In the lab itself, gathered around Brightwell's supine form, were the lead pathologist Davy Johnston, his deputy Sue Chappel, and a lab assistant I didn't know, along with DCI Ryan and DS Harry Slater. Standing with me in the lab's small glass-screened viewing gallery were DI Liza McAdams, DS Pat Buchanan, and another of the lab's technicians.

Crowding apart, the scene was a familiar one to me, and yet I couldn't escape an almost déjà vu-like sense of both being somewhere familiar and everything about it being wrong. Seeing Ron Brightwell on the slab, naked apart from a tea-towel-sized cloth across his middle, was surreal, like looking at a waxwork dummy of the man I'd known. Or as if at any moment he might swing his legs around and sit up.

Johnston and Chappel moved around the body, and I struggled to hear their muttered exchanges as Chappel leaned in close to take photographs.

They confirmed the known facts first of all. Body of a man in reasonable health, aged about sixty years, consistent with the identification as Ron Brightwell, aged fifty-eight. No indication of a struggle, no defense wounds or bruising. A single, clean wound to the upper abdomen, immediately below the ribs, inflicted by a narrow, single-edged blade.

"A compact weapon, then," said Ryan. "If the blade was slim, then it was probably small…easy to conceal. And dispose of."

I saw the look on Davy Johnston's face as the DCI said this. He didn't rush in to contradict her, but he clearly didn't agree. Instead, he returned to the methodical examination of Brightwell's wound.

He pressed the wound's sides together so he could examine the shape, and nodded. "Yes, I'd say the blade was about a centimeter across, and you can see from the fishtailing on one side of the incision that it was squared off on one side, sharp on the other. No contusions around the wound."

The pathologist took a slim probe from a tray and carefully inserted it into the wound.

"Depth of the wound approximately a hundred mil," he said. "That was no compact knife."

Johnston started to dissect the wound, meticulously parting and peeling back the layers.

Eventually, he straightened and said to Ryan, "Miraculously, the stab missed all major organs, and if it had only been a couple of millimeters to the side, it would have done no more than superficial harm."

"But…?"

"But it wasn't. The edge of the blade sliced through the wall of the abdominal aorta. Cause of death: catastrophic blood loss from a single stab wound to the aorta. He didn't stand a chance."

"And the knife?"

Always, it came back to the phantom knife.

"The wound is ten centimeters deep, so the blade is at least that long. Single-edged, a slim blade. I'd say it was at least a couple of centimeters longer than that, making it a very distinctive item."

"Why so much longer?"

"No bruising or signs of impact around the entry wound, so there was no impact from the hilt, or from the hand holding it."

"What kind of knife are we looking for, then?"

"I'd say we're looking at some kind of boning knife. That would fit the profile perfectly. Give us a bit longer and we'll be able to build a model of it, and then we can do a search of brands to help narrow it down."

Even from the distance of the viewing gallery, I could see the look of frustration on Ryan's pinched features. For a time there, she'd clung to the hope that the evidence was supporting her theory: if the knife had been compact then it would be easy to conceal, easy to slip out from that chaotic gathering.

But a boning knife? How do you conceal a knife that's maybe twenty centimeters or more in length? You could hardly slip a weapon like that into a pocket and walk away from such a public crime scene.

***

Ryan called another impromptu case conference in an office at the pathology center.

"The knife," she said. "Everything revolves around the knife. Distinctive. Unusual. Isn't one of the Wilson family businesses a chain of butchers? Terry Wilson would know his way around a boning knife, alright."

"It's distinctive, yes," said Davy Johnston, "but it's hardly the preserve of a professional butcher. Anyone with a bit of money who watches *Masterchef* on TV these days is likely to have a decent knife set in the kitchen."

"But we weren't in a kitchen," said Ryan. "Someone didn't just grab it from a knife block and stab him. They concealed it on their person, both to get it into the hall and then to get it back out. Right under the eyes of half the county's police force. How do you do that with a knife that size?"

"It'd be sharp, too," said the pathologist. "Boning knives tend to be phenomenally sharp all the way along one edge of that very long blade. I wouldn't want to tuck one of those beasts down a trouser leg and try to walk normally."

"So how did Wilson conceal it? Inside something, perhaps? Like those sword canes, where the blade's concealed inside a walking stick?"

Not one person in the room even bothered to point out the unlikeliness that someone could have unsheathed such a weapon, stabbed Brightwell, and then concealed the weapon again in full view of the room, let alone the fact that no one at the gathering had a walking stick.

She really was clutching at straws.

I chose to walk back from the lab, much to the disapproval of Ryan, who saw it as a waste of time. It gave me time to think, though, time for my brain to tease away at the puzzle of the missing knife.

Much as I didn't buy any of Ryan's pet theories, I couldn't come up with a better explanation for how such a large weapon could have been smuggled out of the hall.

Which made me wonder if we weren't approaching this from entirely the wrong perspective.

What if the knife hadn't been there in the first place?

***

I didn't return to the station. Instead, I kept walking until I reached my destination a couple of streets away.

I approached from the back again, and sure enough, Holly Brightwell was sitting on the wooden bench in the back garden, smoking her tangy chemical fruit vape.

"Holly."

She looked at me, and knew.

Knew that I knew.

I saw that tremor in the lips, the sudden filling of the eyes.

I reflected then, on the questions she'd asked me the last time I'd seen her.

Did he…did he say anything? Any last words?

Not asking for some kind of epitaph, but to see if he'd given anything away.

Will you find out what happened?

I'd misunderstood that, too. I'd interpreted the question as Holly urging me to find the answers, but instead she'd been asking if I thought I would.

Trying to assess her own risk.

I sat with her, as she struggled not to cry. I was pretty sure she wasn't going anywhere. She was just a kid, tragically out of her depth.

On my way here I'd called the pathologist, Davy Johnston.

"Davy, it's DS Fletcher here."

"Fletch. What can I do for you?"

"The Brightwell postmortem," I said. "I have a couple of questions."

"Go ahead."

"A knife wound to the aorta. That's pretty damned catastrophic, right?"

"Aye, it sure is. The aorta takes blood right from the heart, when it's at its greatest pressure. Rupture the aorta and it's like an explosion in a paint factory."

"And it's instant?"

"Absolutely."

"Every time?" Silence. "Okay, bear with me. A man's hanging from a rope. Cut the rope and the result is catastrophic: the man falls. Right?"

"Ri-i-ight," said Johnston, drawing the word out, clearly wondering where I was heading with this.

"But just cut a few strands of the rope, and it'll probably hold, right?"

"Right."

"So at some point there's a level where enough of the rope is cut and the man's weight ruptures the rest."

"You're asking me if an aorta could be cut but not quite enough to rupture, is that it?"

"I am."

"The pressures are phenomenal, Fletch."

"But if the cut was just superficial enough. It'd be like hanging from the last thread of that rope, wouldn't it? Until finally the pressure became too much, sometime later, and the thread snapped."

"We're talking very unlikely here, Fletch."

"But not impossible?"

"Not impossible, no. Perhaps something comparable is someone suffering from something like Marfan syndrome, a congenital condition that can cause weakening of the aorta and an increased risk of aortic aneurism. In such cases the aorta could rupture at any time, without warning."

"Ron Brightwell didn't have Marfan syndrome, did he, but he did have a knife wound that came within a couple of millimeters of missing altogether. What if that knife didn't rupture the aorta immediately, but left it clinging by that last thread? Possible?"

A long pause, before Johnston said, "Not impossible."

"Then what would the physical evidence be?"

"You're saying that knife wound was inflicted some time before the fatal rupture occurred? Then, depending on how much time had passed, there would be signs of healing, dried blood, at least."

"And did you see that?"

"I wouldn't expect to. As I said, a rupturing aorta is a catastrophic event. The pressure of the blood flow alone would purge the wound of any dried blood. And then, by the time I got to see the body, that more recent flow of blood was drying. It would have been impossible to distinguish the more recently dried blood from any that had dried earlier."

"So where else might traces of the older dried blood show?"

"In his clothing. If the wound was inflicted earlier, then he clearly wasn't wearing a bloodstained shirt when he arrived at the event, was he? He must have changed his shirt. So there will be the other, stabbed, shirt somewhere. But also, the shirt he was wearing… The fresher blood from when the aorta ruptured would have soaked into the fabric of the shirt before it dried. If he'd put the shirt on over a preexisting wound, then flecks of that dried blood might have come loose. If there are flecks of dried blood in his clothing that are loose and not dried into the fabric, then they're not from the fatal event, but from earlier."

"Do me a favor, Davy: check his clothing again."

He'd called back to confirm while I was still walking into town from the pathology center.

And so now, I sat with Holly Brightwell as she struggled not to cry.

"You want to tell me?"

She just shrugged. "We fought," she said simply. "We always fought. It's what we did."

"He loved you. More than anything."

"I know. That's exactly what he said…after."

"After?"

"It was so stupid." She was crying now, interrupting her words every so often to swallow. "It was about nothing at all. About the school trip. About me having to call him to say I'd gotten there safely. How stupid is that? But it got to me. He always wanted to control everything."

Her eyes were smudged black again.

"I just lost it. I started slapping at his chest and he just stood there and let me. That's what did it. The way he stood there like that. The look on his face that he wore when he was humoring me. It was the last straw."

"So you reached for the nearest thing you could."

She nodded.

When I closed my eyes, I could visualize the scene. The look of surprise on her face when the knife had sunk in so deep.

"He said he was fine. Said that it hadn't done any damage. And he said he loved me, he'd take care of it, and I should just go straight away."

I remembered Mr. Patel saying how Holly had turned up for the lift to the airport early, as if that was unexpected.

"He really seemed okay. He said he'd been lucky. And that was when he said he loved me, and I think part of me knew, but I let him persuade me to go."

***

Later, finally.

I stood with DCI Ryan as Holly gave me one last, sad smile from the back of the police car that was about to take her away.

"Johnston's confirmed it," she said. "Two stages of blood-drying, confirming an earlier, lesser, bleed. I have a team over at Brightwell's house now, looking for the knife and any bloodstained clothing."

She shook her head in disbelief. "It's bizarre, isn't it? Such a tiny margin between life and death. Brightwell must have really believed he was going to be okay, mustn't he? That the stab had missed all his vital organs and no serious damage had been done. And he'd put a brave face on it, and sent his daughter off on her trip just to let things cool off."

I stared at her.

Was I the only one who got it?

"No," I told her. "It was the exact opposite of that. Ron understood precisely what had happened. If he thought he'd survived a close call, then he'd have put a dressing on the wound, wouldn't he? A damned Elastoplast, at least! But he hadn't. He must have known that a wound like that—so deep!—would almost certainly prove fatal, and so that fierce protectiveness of his erratic daughter kicked in. Any dressing on that wound would have told us it had been inflicted earlier, and so pointed us toward the true sequence of events. So instead, what he did was put as much time—and distance—between his own ultimate death and Holly."

"I don't know…"

"And what about the stab mark in the shirt?" I said. She stared at me, finally understanding. "Johnston said there was a tiny slit of a centimeter or so over the wound in the shirt he was wearing to the retirement do—he must have prepared that earlier and relied on nobody noticing it under his tie. He could only have made that hole himself, to make it look as if the wound had occurred later. That more than anything demonstrates that he'd known he was already a dead man walking, and all he could hope to do was to misdirect us away from his daughter."

"Everyone I asked about Brightwell said he was one tough bastard," said Ryan.

"He was," I told her. "Right until the end."

Goobers

MICHAEL BRACKEN AND SANDRA MURPHY

etective Second Grade Tom O'Brien waited by the front door as his boss, Detective Brad Daniels, got out of the unmarked car. Daniels took a moment to scan the posh neighborhood and the massive three-story house.

"What have we got, Tom?"

"Mostly a mess, sir." O'Brien shook his head. His notebook only had a few lines written in it.

"Start at the beginning. Who's dead?"

"Well, that's the thing. We're not sure anybody's dead." O'Brien opened the door and the men entered a large foyer. Members of the crime scene unit and the coroner stood around, talking quietly. "Third floor, sir."

As Daniels turned toward the stairs, O'Brien said, "The elevator's this way."

"Why is Homicide on the scene if there's no body?"

Once inside, O'Brien pushed the "close door" button, but not three. "Here's the thing. The housekeeper called 911, said her boss's husband is dead, he's been murdered. We all rush over here and find he's in a secure room, only opens from the inside."

"A panic room?"

"No, sir, the wife says he's a writer and he holes himself up in there when the muse strikes, whatever that means. Sounds fishy to me. There's an intercom but he's not answering, which is what made the housekeeper panic. She says he always asks for breakfast." O'Brien looked at his skimpy notes. "Safeall Security is here now, getting the door open. Wife and her sister are in the formal living room with Officer Watts to keep an eye on them."

"Husband might be dead, suspects together? That's not protocol."

"Nothing about this is. One of the CSIs follows the gossip columns and says the wife, Tonya Allen, forty-eight, married this guy, uh, Josh Deveraux, thirty-five, three years ago, after knowing him for six weeks. Her first marriage; not sure about him." O'Brien grinned. "The sister, Evelyn, also known as Evie, had just gotten married for the third time. Might have something to do with Tonya's quickie romance. Not sure which last name Evie's using currently. The rich do things differently."

"Mandy reads the gossips?"

"No, sir, Pete. Don't say anything, he's embarrassed to admit it. Ready to go up?" He pushed three and the car rose silently. The doors slid open to reveal a team of three men from the security company packing up their gear.

"Just going to call for you, sir. We didn't want to open up until you were here. Coroner's on his way up. Thought you might need him right away." A patrol officer motioned for the other men to move away from the door. "I have their contact information and records. Are they free to go?" Daniels nodded as he pulled on gloves and booties.

"Let's see what we've got. Hopefully, he's sleeping off a night of too much to drink." Daniels paused. "Was someone home the whole time he's been in there?" O'Brien shook his head. "Then draw your weapon, just in case he let someone else in."

"Security records show he was the last one in, door hasn't opened since."

"Just to be sure, O'Brien."

"Yes, sir. Open it up, Officer." O'Brien stood to the side of the door as it opened. The room was quiet. The men moved slowly inside. In the middle of the floor was the body of a man, his right arm outstretched toward the desk, his face flushed a rosy shade. "Doc, looks like he's one for you."

The coroner entered the room and knelt. As he examined the body, Daniels scanned the room. O'Brien made a drawing in his notebook with notations of where the body was in relation to the furniture, the intercom, and the door. He touched a gloved finger to the computer keyboard.

"Is that the book he's working on?" Daniels spoke from the other side of the room.

"No, I recognize this. It's an online game."

"One of those with sword fights or space aliens?" Daniels asked.

"No, this one is cards. Video poker, and he was losing, a lot, playing for real money." O'Brien stood back for Daniels to see. "Been going on for a while, looks like."

"Any sign of his writing? Check this file." Daniels pointed to one labeled Daddy's Girl. Both men stared at the photo that showed first. "Well, that's not what I expected." The photo was of a racehorse, jockey astride, with several men in the foreground. Subsequent files showed the cost of a one-third share in the horse, its track record, veterinary bills, and boarding fees. The horse, it seemed, won at races about as much as Josh won at cards.

"Fellas? Looks like anaphylactic shock. Ask what he was allergic to and see if you can find an EpiPen anywhere in here. As severe as this was, he would have had one." The coroner packed his bag and, at Daniels's nod, motioned for the body to be bagged and removed. "I'll let you know the autopsy results as soon as possible. As cold as it is in here, that'll affect time of death. With this much money, the family will be pressuring you, I'm sure."

"Get CSI up here. We'll go talk to the wife and sister." Daniels started for the door. "And have Sanchez talk to the housekeeper, what's her name?"

"Millie Harris. She told the patrol officer her age was none of his business, that he was here to find out why Josh wasn't answering, although she was sure he'd been murdered. Didn't give a reason, but did make fish eyes at the wife, behind her back." O'Brien looked at his notes again. "What are fish eyes?"

The officer spoke up. "That's when you're trying to give a hint without saying anything. Makes your eyes bug out a bit, like this." He shifted his eyes from the detectives to the desk several times. "My wife does that when she's trying to tell me it's time to leave my mother's house on Sundays." He left without seeing their amusement.

"O'Brien, we're going downstairs. Do not give me the fish eyes hint to use the elevator."

"Yes, sir, never crossed my mind."

***

Daniels motioned for Officer Watts to come into the hallway. "Have they been talking?" The sisters sat quietly on the same sofa.

"No, I told them not to and not a peep out of either of them, except to talk baby talk to the dog. Her name's Mollie," he said. "A Yorkie. Wife's got one. This one's not yappy."

"Go help search the grounds for anything that's out of place. Report back if there's something promising." Daniels took another look into the room. "Put Evie in the dining room and we'll talk to Tonya. Tom, you lead. Give her the news about Josh and I'll watch her reaction. Go easy for now."

The men entered and introduced themselves, refused coffee, and when invited, sat. "Ms. Allen, the security company got the door to your husband's workroom open."

"And what did he have to say for himself? Such a fuss over nothing." Tonya smiled. "I'm sorry Millie panicked and called you."

"Ma'am, it wasn't a wasted call. We found your husband. I'm sorry to tell you, he's dead." O'Brien spoke in a calm voice, to head off hysteria.

"That just can't be. He was fine last night before dinner. I'll call our doctor and have him come check on Josh." She reached for her cell phone.

"Our doctor, the coroner that is, he checked. Josh has been dead for several hours. Was he allergic to anything?"

"What? That's impossible. Yes, he's allergic to nuts, but we are very careful. There's never anything brought into the house that has nuts or has been made in the same factory or kitchen where nuts are used." She stood. "You're just wrong. I'll go see."

O'Brien took her arm and gently shook his head. "He's really dead. I'm sorry."

She stared at him for a moment and then collapsed on the sofa. There were no tears, but she was unable to speak.

"When did your sister arrive?" Sometimes a change of subject helped during questioning.

"Evie? Um, she got here three days ago. We went to dinner at that new place on uh, Hamilton Street." She sat up straight. "Oh, if I'd been here, I could have helped Josh!"

"No, ma'am, it was very quick. You wouldn't have had time." O'Brien made notes. "What time did you see him last? He didn't want to go eat with you?"

"Josh isn't all that fond of Evie." She lowered her voice. "He says marriage is till death do you part but Evie thinks husbands are disposable, like tissues. He wanted to write."

"You didn't see him when you came in?"

"No, I wouldn't have. His bedroom is on the second floor. My suite is here on the first, convenient for taking Mollie out, if needed." She straightened the bow in the dog's topknot. "Evie stayed with me."

"Did you come home after dinner? Which car is yours?"

"The Mercedes is mine. We Ubered to dinner, much easier than using a valet and worrying about how many glasses of wine we each had." She continued to look at the dog as she talked. "We went to a gallery opening close by, the Blue Begonia, do you know it?" O'Brien shook his head. "It was boring, the same splotches of color on a black or white canvas that we've seen a million times. Cheap wine too."

"What did you have for dinner? The reviews have been good."

"I was hungry again by the time we got back, no substance to the food. Evie is vegetarian this week. Maybe gluten-free as well? Something like that. Luckily, Millie leaves snacks in the fridge, so we had those, and I opened another bottle of wine." She looked at O'Brien. "I need to make some phone calls, do you mind? We can continue this in a bit. Millie will fix you something if you like."

"Thank you, ma'am. We'll go talk to Evelyn first."

***

"Josh is dead? Are you serious? Well, doesn't that just take the cake? Now Tonya will be able to catch up with me for number of husbands. Of course, she'll have to hurry. I've got a head start." Evie lit a cigarette. "Hand me that dish, will you? Not an ashtray, but it'll do."

"You don't seem very upset." Daniels had broken the news. "Why is that?"

"It was obvious Josh didn't like me. He hit on me once, not a serious move, more just to test the limits." She looked up at Daniels. "He didn't walk so well after that. It was only a matter of time before Tonya got tired of him. Of course, she'd dump him in some terribly proper way. He wouldn't be able to blackmail her into keeping him. Tonya never does anything improper." She tapped ashes into what Daniels thought was a piece of sculpture.

"If you'd give us an idea of your movements last night so we can determine when Mr. Deveraux was alone, it would help."

She sighed. "Josh had been in the pool house, said he was exercising, but he didn't look the least bit sweaty. I think he was napping. Anyway, we said we were going to dinner, but he said no. He's always afraid to eat out, thinks the kitchen help will lie about ingredients. He opted to go write. Have you read anything he's written? No? Well, neither has anyone else." She stubbed out the cigarette. "Tonya went down for a bottle of wine. We had a drink or two before the driver showed up at seven. Dinner, then a boring opening for a no-talent painter. Mollie could do better."

"And after that?"

"If it had been up to me, we'd have gone dancing, but no, Tonya insisted on coming home. We were here by midnight. She went for another bottle of wine, not that we're drunks, and I raided the fridge. Cheese, olives, that kind of thing. She took Mollie out while the wine breathed. I checked my phone for messages. We ate, in bed by two. Not an exciting night."

O'Brien stepped in. "It was really cold upstairs, but it's comfortable in here. You'd think the third floor would be warmer, especially with all the windows he had."

"Zoned heating and cooling. Josh likes a cold room. Tonya doesn't. One reason why they have separate bedrooms. Also helps with the utility bills, not that Tonya needs the money. We inherited; you know."

"Thank you for talking with us."

She was already lighting another cigarette.

***

"Thank you, ma'am, for your help. Our office will let you know when the body is released so you can make arrangements. We may have more questions for you as information comes in." He hesitated. "Again, we're sorry for your loss." Tonya just nodded.

On the sidewalk, they met a short blond who was carrying a dozen garment bags and struggling not to drop them. "Here, let me help." O'Brien took several bags. "What's all this?"

"Black dresses for the viewing, the funeral, luncheons, dinners, the theatre. Shoes and purses are in the van. There's lingerie too. And a hat." She looked back at the van. "I think that's all. It better be, or she'll have my head. I'm Susie, by the way, personal shopper at Neiman."

The men looked at each other and then at Susie. "When did this happen?"

"Ms. Allen called with a clothing emergency about a half-hour ago. Here I am. Thanks for the help, handsome. I'd better carry them in myself." O'Brien shut the door behind her.

"That was fast. Josh probably just made it to the morgue, and she's getting a new wardrobe already." Daniels stared at the lawn for a moment.

"What is it, boss? You've got that look."

"Do you think Tonya is the type to clean up after her dog or do they hire somebody to do that?"

"I'd say she'd hire somebody, but sometimes rich people surprise you. They buy big-ticket items like I'd say yes to 'do you want fries with that' but skimp on small things. Besides, Mollie is so little, well, anything she did would be kinda hard to find."

"Especially at night. Let's head back to the station house. Get Sanchez to report in before Millie puts him into a food coma. He does have a way with women who love to cook."

"I wish I could do that. I didn't get breakfast before we got the call."

"Sanchez has a baby face. You're more the bad-cop type. Go with your strengths, O'Brien."

"Boss, we should have been born rich instead of good looking." O'Brien started their car.

***

An afternoon of research showed the money was Tonya's and she had plenty of it, although not as much as pre-Josh. They talked to the security company salesman who designed the writing room, the elevator installer, and the other two-thirds owners of Daddy's Girl, who assured them, the horse was just biding her time, ready to win any day now. Apparently, Josh had a strong belief in community property where money was concerned. Each person they talked to said the ideas were his, the money, hers.

"I'm tired of sitting. Let's see if the coroner has any news yet. We can walk over, grab a hot dog." Daniels led the way.

With the hot dog vendor just outside the precinct building and each man having two apiece, conversation was limited.

***

"You guys could have brought a couple of dogs for me, you know."

"How can you work with dead bodies all day and then eat in here?" O'Brien shook his head. "I couldn't do it. And how'd you know we stopped at the wagon first?"

"It takes a manly man to do this work, leaves you out, O'Brien." The coroner smiled. "I know where you've been because you have mustard on your tie."

"Oh, man, the cleaners are gonna charge me extra to get that out." O'Brien groaned.

"To business. Severe allergic reaction, did you find out to what? Peanuts, that would do it, most any kind of nut, peanuts most common. Time of death, last evening, probably between eight o'clock and midnight. Hard to pin down exactly because of the body temp. The boys said the EpiPen was ten feet away, but this guy wouldn't have lived even if he'd reached it. Happened too fast."

"Thanks, doc." O'Brien asked, "What are you having for lunch, since we didn't bring it?"

"My wife, she stopped at Ziggie's for me. Brain sandwich, what else?"

O'Brien made a fast exit, Daniels right behind.

***

The next morning, O'Brien was reading the paper when Daniels came into the office. "The society page? I think Pete's love of gossip is catching. Are you trying to improve your fashion sense?"

"I believe I've peaked as far as fashion goes." O'Brien held up the folded newspaper. "The hat has a veil."

"What hat? You're losing me. It usually takes you until ten o'clock to do that." Daniels laughed. "What are you looking at?"

"I, sir, am studying the photo of Ms. Allen, dressed all in black, including the hat which has a veil. I'm betting it's hiding the fact that she is not grieving the loss of her husband."

"People show grief in different ways. Just because she's not wailing and crying, doesn't mean she's not grieving."

"True, but if you look at how close her lawyer is to her, and the position of his hand on the small of her back, I think you will agree, I have a case for my theory."

"O'Brien, you could be onto something."

Before they could get to work, Officer Watts rushed into the room. "Sir, I think I found a clue. You gotta come down to the lab, right away!"

"Okay, Watts, slow down. What clue, where did you find it? Why are you here?"

"You sent me out to search for clues yesterday and said to report back if I found anything. Just as I got out back, the trash truck was picking up the bin." Watts paused for breath. "I ran over and made him put it down before it got mixed in with everybody else's. And now the lab found a clue! So I'm reporting like you asked."

"Well then, Officer Watts, let's go see your clue."

***

The two detectives gathered the three women and the Yorkshire terrier in the living room. Once the women and Mollie were comfortable, Daniels looked at each of the women in turn.

After nodding to the widow, he began. "It's obvious your husband died from an allergic reaction. His attempt to reach his EpiPen tipped us off about that."

"But how could that happen?" asked Millie. "I keep this place spotless, especially Mr. Deveraux's writing room."

"Did you find something up there?" Evie asked.

"No, not in his office," Daniels said. "Not exactly."

"Then what, exactly?" Tonya demanded, out of patience.

"The HVAC system," Daniels said. "Once we realized this place has zoned heating and cooling, we checked the vents. There's peanut butter powder residue in the vents in your husband's office. The question, though, is how did it get there?" He glanced at his notes. "The wine cellar is in the basement, isn't it?"

Millie Harris confirmed that it was.

"So is the HVAC system," Daniels said. "And someone used it to trigger Deveraux's allergies."

"How?" Evie asked.

"That's where Mollie comes in," the detective continued. "While combing through the trash we discovered a dryer sheet wrapped around her, um, waste, and the dryer sheet is contaminated with peanut butter powder. We think someone put the sheet in the HVAC system and then took it out later and tried to dispose of it."

"So, who are you accusing?" Tonya's voice went down a few temperature levels.

"Only one of you went to the basement that evening, and only one of you walked Mollie."

Tonya leaned forward. "Are you implying that I had something to do with my husband's death?"

"You knew he was spending money like water. He demanded the elevator. He got a writing room where he never wrote, just played online poker for real cash. And that racehorse is never going to win. You realized you should have signed a prenup before you married. But you didn't, and if you divorced, he'd get half of everything. There was only one way out."

"That's nuts."

Daniels smiled as he motioned for O'Brien to put the cuffs on her. "Exactly."

Whatever Remains
ASHLEY LISTER

"Once you eliminate the impossible, whatever remains, no matter how improbable, must be the truth."
—Sherlock Holmes

The dead body lay slumped inside the locked glass receiving booth. According to Scott's crime scene report, the victim had once been a nerdy young man named Connor Fowler. Fowler was—Fowler had been, Scott corrected himself—a promising PhD student working on a thesis relating to quantum mechanics. Connor's bespectacled eyes were glazed and stared accusatorily at Scott, as though challenging him to solve the mystery of his untimely death.

Scott sighed and gave up on the staring contest with the corpse. There didn't seem much likelihood of him solving the crime. In truth, he wasn't fully sure he understood what had happened. He supposed part of his self-doubt came from the fact that the murder had taken place in a university laboratory. Interviewing a series of suspects who demanded to be addressed with honorifics such as "Ms.," "Doctor," and "Professor" made Scott feel painfully aware of his own limited academic credentials.

He watched a young police officer take a step toward the corpse in the booth, and then recoil with stifled horror when she realized she was so close to a dead body. Scott had watched a lot of TV dramas that showed police officers implacably dealing with the dead as though such encounters were of little interest and no importance. The truth, he knew, was surprisingly different. Dead bodies, particularly murdered dead bodies, made most people nervous. He knew he was not the only officer to still squirm with unease whenever he found himself on a murder investigation. And he understood why the police officer had released a small shriek of dismay when her gaze fell on the waxen features of the late Connor Fowler.

Stepping away from the officer, allowing her to regain her composure, Scott walked to the man responsible for the laboratory. "Doctor Bell," he began.

Bell glanced up at him. He was a sharp-faced individual who had mastered the art of intimidating subordinates. He wore a stylish three-piece suit, made informal by a collarless shirt that was open at the throat. Beneath Bell's keen glare, Scott felt inadequate.

"Detective Scott?" Bell barked. He spoke as though he was the one instigating this conversation.

"I need to make sure I've got the sequence of events correct in my mind," Scott told him.

"Of course."

"At 10:00 a.m., Mr. Fowler was standing in that booth over there?"

He used his pen to point at the glass booth marked with the letter A at the far end of the laboratory. There were three similar booths in the laboratory: A, B, and C. An array of cameras, recording equipment, and other pieces of science fiction paraphernalia surrounded Booth A and Booth B. Scott had been told that some of the equipment had names like "oscillator" while others did something about "spectrum analysis" but, to his mind, they were simply magical physics gadgets that did magical physics things.

"That's correct," Bell confirmed. "Young Fowler was calibrating photon measurements."

Scott nodded as though the words didn't sound like the sort of gobbledygook that made him switch channels whenever he found himself confronted by a science fiction program on the television. "Very good, sir. While Mr. Fowler was standing in Booth A, you were standing in Booth C—is that correct?"

"Booth C is the control booth for these experiments," Bell agreed. "It allows me to oversee all procedures and operations. It contains monitoring equipment and—"

"And there was no one in Booth B at 10:00 a.m.," Scott interrupted.

"No," Bell said. The sudden sharp sourness of his expression suggested he was a man who did not like to be interrupted. His eyes narrowed with disapproval. "Booth B is a secure receiving chamber fixed with a single-use tamper-proof lock. None of this school's staff have the key to access Booth B.

That's held by the university's provost. Consequently, Booth B always remains empty unless a transference has taken place."

Scott made notes and tried not to puzzle too long over the spelling or the meaning of the word transference. "Shortly after 10:00 a.m.—"

"10:03 a.m., according to the monitoring equipment," Bell broke in.

"At 10:03 a.m.," Scott repeated, trying not to sound belligerent, "a young woman entered the laboratory, brandishing a pistol."

Bell nodded.

"The young woman has since been identified as Ms. Tiffany Langford."

Bell nodded again.

Scott walked across the room to a bright yellow crime scene marker on the laboratory floor. "Ms. Langford stood on this spot," he told Bell. "She raised her pistol to shoulder height, and then called for Mr. Fowler's attention."

Bell's expression showed absolute agreement. "She said," he started quietly, "*You two-timing piece of shit. You won't fuck behind my back again.*"

Scott shook his head and said nothing about the coarse vocabulary of today's youth. Instead, he asked, "And how did Mr. Fowler respond?"

Bell considered this for a moment. "Would it be easier if I showed you the video recording?"

Without waiting for a response, he walked over to a nearby monitor, tapped a few keys on its keyboard, and then brought up footage from the laboratory's CCTV equipment.

Scott studied the monitor and watched as Bell presented him with an image of the laboratory. The timestamp in the bottom right-hand corner of the screen showed the time at 10:02 a.m. Through the magic of recorded images, it showed Connor Fowler alive and oblivious to the grim fate he was about to suffer.

The monitor was fixed to record what happened in Booth A.

Inside the booth, Connor Fowler looked like the resplendent embodiment of geekiness in his brilliant white lab coat and oversized spectacles. His hair was slicked down with a ruler-straight center part. A small and rather limp bow tie hung from his throat. He worked on some device in the ceiling of the booth, using a piece of calibration equipment that Scott couldn't identify. The timestamp had shifted to 10:03 a.m. when a young woman walked into the scene.

The CCTV's camera angle showed the back of her head. The stiffness in her shoulders suggested she was angry, and this idea was further supported by the fact that she was brandishing a small handgun.

This, Scott assumed, was Ms. Tiffany Langford. He was frustrated that the CCTV footage hadn't captured her face. He could see that she was short, and a little on the broad side. Her figure had been disguised slightly by her wearing an oversized hoodie but, as the less politically-correct officers he worked with were apt to say, she looked like a cake-aholic.

"You two-timing piece of shit," Ms. Langford bellowed. Her voice projected with an almost theatrical power. "You won't fuck behind my back again."

Fowler raised his hands, like some bank teller from an old Western who's been told to stick 'em up. Because he was standing inside the booth, his words weren't picked up by the recording equipment, but his mouth was moving with panicked speed. It was impossible to mistake the expression of terror that crossed his face.

"Enough!" screamed the angry woman.

As she pulled the trigger, the sound on the recording changed. There was a loud explosion, but the sound was dragged out like a poor special effect. The image darkened, color drained and pixelated, and then horizontal lines rolled across the screen.

"What's happening there?" Scott asked.

"That was when I hit the transfer button," Bell explained. "I'd seen the woman pointing the gun at Fowler. I realized what was going to happen. And I thought it would be safer to risk a transfer and teleport him out of the booth so that he was no longer in her line of fire."

"And hitting the transfer button causes the sound to hum and the picture to roll?"

"Teleportation uses a substantial amount of electricity," Bell said. "The lights dim. The CCTV slows. The audio sounds like we've filmed in a corridor. It's all part of the power drain caused by the process."

Scott's gaze never left the monitor. There was a single moment when it looked like Fowler had vanished from the booth. And then the screen went black.

"It's part of the problem with teleportation," Bell explained. "The process uses a lot of electricity. More than we can cope with here."

The words took a moment to seep into Scott's consciousness. He glanced from Booth A to Booth B, and then turned to Bell. "He was teleported into Booth B?"

"Yes."

"So, he's been teleported? Like in *Star Trek*, or…" Scott's voice trailed off as he realized he didn't know of any other TV show that made reference to teleportation. "Or the other *Star Trek?*" he concluded lamely.

Bell was nodding solemnly. "It's something we've been working on for a while," he explained. "And we're on the verge of making a great breakthrough. The financial implications for this institution are enormous because it's something that could be of potential benefit to everyone on the planet, as well as the planet itself."

Scott remained silent, trying to work out if he was being played for a fool, or if Fowler and Bell had genuinely managed to create a machine that could teleport someone from Booth A to Booth B.

"If humanity makes that breakthrough," Bell continued, "there'll be no more need for our reliance on fossil fuels, or any of the other hazardous forms of fuel that are used to support the transport industry."

Scott blinked as he digested this. Bell seemed happy to continue talking, and Scott figured that was because this was the man's area of technical expertise.

"The original thinking was that teleportation would need to be like sending a physical fax of a person from the point of origin to the point of destination. But that meant you were left with two copies: the original and the duplicated version. It's not such a bad solution if you're trying to end a famine, or increase finite resources, because it means you're making limitless copies."

Scott nodded, sure he was listening to the ramblings of a lunatic.

"But the fax-machine model proved to be impossible due to developments in quantum physics back in 1993," Scott went on. "Researchers at IBM realized that, when it's done properly, the act of scanning disrupts the original such that the copy becomes the only surviving original."

"So, he was teleported?" Scott repeated, pointing at Fowler's body in Booth B.

"Yes," Bell said. His tone sounded flat, as though he were inwardly admitting defeat in trying to explain quantum physics to a man who spoke about "*Star Trek*" and "the other *Star Trek*."

"My coroner will need access to the body," Scott told him. "Is there any way you can unlock that booth he's in?"

"Didn't I already say that we're waiting for the provost to arrive?"

"Is he the only one with a key?"

Bell's frown deepened, as though he were frustrated at having to repeat himself. "The provost is a woman," he sighed. "And, as I mentioned before, Booth B is permanently sealed, and the keys aren't left in the custody of research staff."

"They don't trust you?" Scott asked.

"It's a precaution that guards against the production of fabricated data."

Scott nodded, fairly sure that Bell's response was confirmation of his suspicions: Bell and his staff weren't trusted.

"Could Fowler have opened the booth from inside?" Scott asked.

"I doubt it," Bell said. "He was dead."

He looked like he was about to say more when his mobile phone began to ring. Without a word of apology, Bell snatched the phone from his jacket pocket and barked a sharp "Hello."

There was a moment's pause and Scott tried, without success, to hear the voice on the other end of the call.

"That's correct," Bell said. "A full transportation of a human subject."

There was another pause. Scott couldn't hear the other voice. He was only able to watch as Bell shook his head.

"It's a generous offer." Bell paused and corrected himself. "It's a very generous offer," he amended. "But I think there'll be several agencies interested in acquiring this technology, and I'd like to give them each a chance to show their potential generosity."

Another pause. Bell's smile grew cruel.

"I suspect you're accurate in calling me a slimy lowborn brigand," Bell assured him. "And, if you're invited to later negotiations, I'll be sure to remind you of those words."

He pressed his thumb on the screen of the phone and ended the call.

Scott raised an eyebrow. "Was that a threatening call, sir?"

"Developers," Fowler told him. "I expect they'll get worse over the next few days. They'll get more threatening. There'll be more money offers. Now that they know we have working teleportation technology, they'll be desperate to get access to our systems."

Scott nodded as though he understood. "And you've got working teleportation technology?"

"How else would you explain Fowler getting from Booth A to Booth B?"

Scott shrugged. He supposed there was no real reason for anyone moving Fowler's body manually, unless they were trying to help with some pretense that suggested Bell had made a breakthrough in teleportation technology. Even then, it would have to be someone who had access to Booth B's key, and that someone would need to benefit from such a murderous deception to the extent that it counterbalanced the moral and ethical repercussions of their actions.

Bell's phone rang again.

He was taking the call as the young police officer that Scott had noticed before approached. She cast a wary eye in the direction of Fowler's body, and then stepped closer to Scott.

"We're having a problem trying to track down this Tiffany Langford woman," she explained.

"Why's that?"

"She doesn't exist."

Scott frowned. "She must exist. I've just watched her shoot our victim." He used a thumb to gesture toward the man in the locked booth.

"There's no record of a Tiffany Langford on the university's database. None of the victim's friends were aware that he was in a relationship. One of them even said Fowler was more likely to teleport than get laid."

"How charming," Scott muttered.

"And, whether or not that's true," the officer continued "we can't find records indicating anyone called Tiffany Langford living in the immediate area."

Scott rubbed his forehead and glanced in Bell's direction.

The doctor was still on his phone, his head tilted down as though he was staring at a sniveling subordinate while spitting bitterly sharp phrases.

"You've seen the video?" Bell barked. "You understand what's at stake here. I shall await your call when you're prepared to negotiate at an appropriate level."

He broke the connection and glanced toward the doorway in time to see a barrel-shaped woman burst into the room.

"Doctor Bell?" she called.

"Provost?" he smiled. "How good to see you here."

"I heard the news," the barrel-shaped woman said as she approached him. "You've made the breakthrough. You've teleported a human."

"I told you we were on the verge of this achievement."

"The funding implications will be enormous." She grinned.

Bell grinned back. "I know. I'm currently fielding calls from some of the bigger names in industry. They've made some substantial offers already."

Scott coughed.

Bell and the provost turned to glance at him.

"Have you brought the key for this booth?" Scott asked.

The provost nodded. She removed a key ring from her pocket, went to the booth, and unlocked the door. She seemed unimpressed by the presence of the corpse inside the booth. "Is there anything else you require from me?" she asked haughtily.

"Yes," Scott said politely. "I'd like you and Dr. Bell to stay here until my officers have finished with the crime scene and removed the body."

***

Two hours later, Connor Fowler had been removed. Every millimeter of the laboratory had been photographed, mapped, and recorded, and Scott found himself alone with Bell and the provost.

"It's very late," the provost snapped sharply. "The crime scene has been finished with. Is there anything else you require from us?"

Scott nodded. "I'd like you and Dr. Bell to accompany me to the station so I can have you arrested for the murder of Connor Fowler."

The provost studied him skeptically.

Bell smiled uncertainly. The expression stayed on his face like a sneer. "I don't quite understand your sense of humor," he said stiffly. "Why would you think that either myself or the provost would be responsible for Fowler's murder?"

"It's very simple." Scott laughed softly. "It's a truism from the Sherlock Holmes stories that, once you eliminate the impossible, whatever remains, no matter how improbable, must be the truth."

"And what impossible have you eliminated?"

"As I understand it," Scott began, "you were trying to tell me that Fowler was working in Booth A when his girlfriend, Tiffany Langford, burst into the laboratory."

"That is what happened," Bell said stiffly. "You saw the video, didn't you?"

"Langford shot at Fowler," Scott continued. "But, in the same moment she depressed the trigger on her gun, you pressed the button to start Fowler's teleportation."

"Yes," said Bell. "I thought this had already been established. I was trying to get Fowler out of harm's way."

"According to your statement," Scott continued, "Fowler was teleported from Booth A to Booth B, as evidenced by the video footage you've already posted online."

"That's right," Bell agreed.

"And the preliminary reports from the coroner suggest it is more likely Fowler was killed by the gunshot and not by the process of teleportation."

"Okay," Bell agreed. "But I'm not sure why any of this means that you want to arrest me and the provost."

"I'm arresting you two," Scott said. "Because you are the ones who organized this deception."

The pair exchanged a glance.

"There is no Tiffany Langford," Scott explained. "The deceased's colleagues say he didn't have a girlfriend. The university's files have no record of a Tiffany Langford. The only person who knows about this woman is you, Dr. Bell."

Bell sniffed. "Is that your entire argument?"

"The provost here is the exact size and shape of the murderer," Scott went on. "If we were to dress her in an oversized hoodie, she'd be indistinguishable from the woman on the CCTV footage."

"There are lots of people of her size and shape."

"But only one of her size and shape who holds the key to Booth B," Scott observed.

"Are you suggesting we've been colluding for some reason?" asked the provost.

"What possible motive could we have for killing a PhD student?" Bell demanded.

"A reason such as increased funding?" Scott suggested. "A reason such as adding credibility to your unverified claim that you've made a major breakthrough in teleportation technology? A claim like that would have investors throwing substantial amounts of money at you. Enough money to make the murder of one insignificant student seem like a fair price."

"If that's the case," Bell demanded, "how did Fowler's body get into Booth B?"

Scott frowned. "I just explained that, didn't I? The provost here has the key. No doubt, when the CCTV had been overloaded, she unlocked Booth B and the pair of you carried Fowler's body to the booth before locking the door and raising the alarm."

The provost was shaking her head. "The lock on this booth is an antitamper device. When I put the key in, I destroyed the lock."

Scott frowned. "Then, perhaps you installed a new lock?"

The provost was nodding. When she spoke, her voice dripped with sarcasm. "Yes," she agreed. "Not only am I the university's provost, but I also have the ability to install tamper-proof locks after I've carried my latest murder victim into a teleportation booth."

Scott shook his head. "If you didn't unlock the booth, how did he get in there?"

"I've told you repeatedly this evening," Bell said. "Fowler was teleported to Booth B."

"No," Scott insisted. "That sort of technology doesn't exist. It's impossible. That's what I meant when I quoted Sherlock Holmes and said, 'Once you eliminate the impossible, whatever remains, no matter how improbable, must be the truth'. Teleportation is impossible. Therefore you two must be lying. And, if you're lying, you're doing it to cover up your involvement with Fowler's murder."

Bell laughed. "You don't believe we've made a breakthrough? I can give you a demonstration if you want."

"No," the provost said quietly. "I don't think that's wise."

Scott ignored her. "A demonstration?" he asked Bell.

Bell led him to Booth A and got Scott to stand inside. He waved at the provost, urging her to go into Booth C. There was something in the gaze that passed between them that made Scott feel a little uneasy. His unease grew when he realized he was locked inside Booth A. He wasn't sure what the pair were planning, but he didn't like it.

"I'm going to teleport you from here to Booth B," Bell explained.

Scott shook his head. "There's no need for such a demonstration."

"I insist," Bell insisted. "I want you to understand that was how Fowler ended up in his final resting place."

Scott tried the handle on the door, but there was no give. He pressed his shoulder against the glass and realized there was going to be no give. The walls and door of Booth A, just like the walls and door of Booth B, were surprisingly secure.

"Let me out of here," Scott demanded. "This is no longer amusing."

"You were right when you identified the provost as Tiffany Langford," Bell said. "She did play that role."

Scott glared at him.

"And the provost did shoot Fowler," Bell admitted. "Although that wasn't what killed him. Your coroner is likely to revise his verdict once he's had a chance to properly inspect the body."

"If it wasn't the bullet," Scott said softly, "what was it that killed him?"

"We mastered teleportation months ago," Bell explained. "We've been able to teleport inanimate objects repeatedly. The only snag we've hit is when we try to teleport a live subject." He smiled sadly and shook his head. "When we do that, we usually end up with a subject that is no longer alive. I've already been through my year's budget on rabbits and guinea pigs and we're not even through the first semester."

Scott pursed his lips. He remembered reading a report about the close relationship between serial killers and animal abusers and he wondered if there was some similar relationship between those involved with vivisection and those responsible for casual murder.

"If your subjects weren't coming out alive, why did you do it?" Scott asked. He tried the handle again, but the door remained locked. "What advantage did you gain by shooting poor Fowler and then killing him with teleportation?"

"We got video footage of a human subject being teleported," Bell reminded him. "Admittedly, Fowler's dead. But anyone watching the video will assume he died from the gunshot wound, not from the teleportation. It's the sort of compelling video evidence that will have backers urging us to write our own checks. There will be entrepreneurs so desperate to get their hands on this technology that I can literally name my own price."

"And you don't think," Scott asked stiffly, "that your incarceration for murder is going to interrupt your plans to spend all this money you'll be receiving?"

"Well," Bell admitted, "if you survive this teleportation, I'm sure that the provost and I will be in serious trouble."

"And if I don't survive it?" Scott asked. "Surely another dead body in your teleporter is going to make it difficult to sell your ideas to industry?"

Bell shrugged. "We can blame it on issues with calibration or some other uncalculated aspect of the process. We'll say that had an adverse impact on the teleportation."

"And what about the fact that you have a dead police officer in your laboratory?" Scott asked.

Bell shook his head. "I don't see it as having a dead police officer in the lab," he admitted. "I look on it as having two pieces of footage that show I've mastered teleportation."

With that, he nodded for the provost to press the red button.

And the last thing Scott saw was the lights inside the booth dimming.

The Golden Hour
A DI Christy Kennedy Short Story
PAUL CHARLES

etective Inspector Christy Kennedy reckoned each case enjoyed a golden hour.

During those first precious sixty minutes, he and his trusted, innovative team had a precious hourlong window to try to determine all witnesses and suspects in a case. Of course, this didn't mean they had to solve the case in one-twenty-fourth of a day. Not at all, but equally, the leads of the mystical period might just reveal the most crucial information which—when the time came to solve the puzzle of the crime, apprehend the suspect, and, vitally, build a watertight case against the she, or he, or even the they who had committed the crime—could prove invaluable in justice appearing to be done.

The witness, the only witness in fact, in this particular case was a Ms. Alice Rafferty. She was waiting for DI Christy Kennedy and Detective Sergeant Dot King by the entrance to the Guitar Shop on the corner of Delancey Street and Arlington Road, in Camden Town. Ms. Rafferty looked like she was in her later twenties, perfectly (but heavily) made-up, with two-tone red and blond hair. In her purple trouser suit, cream blouse, and spotless white trainers, she looked like she hadn't long since returned from her place of work.

"Goodness, you were quick," she gushed.

"Well, we were quite literally passing your door when the call came in," King offered, through an unintentional sigh, as she and Kennedy presented their warrant cards while standing on the chewing-gum-splattered pavement of Delancey Street. This through road was always ultra-busy because it had become a rat-run, used by traffic bypassing the congested hub of Camden Town, en route to Primrose Hill, Belsize Park, Hampstead, Swiss Cottage, and all points beyond.

"Could you please tell us what you heard?" King asked, taking her pink notebook out of the inside pocket of her dark blue corduroy waisted jacket.

"So…I'd just arrived back from work," Alice started, sounding like she felt she was being interviewed on *Newsnight*. "I was in my kitchen starting to prepare my dinner, and I could hear Mr. MacManus walking about upstairs."

"Does he live by himself?" Kennedy asked, as Ms. Rafferty led them up the stairs and away from the noisy traffic.

"Yes, I believe so. He keeps himself to himself, though. He's a bit of a hermit. He has a teenage daughter who comes to see him from time to time. She's very nice, beautiful actually, but I don't think she knows she is. She's extremely bubbly and, unlike her father, always passes the time of day when you meet her on the stairs. He always seems a bit low when she leaves. His moods have been more noticeable over the last few months. I really don't know if he rents or owns his flat. I do know there are a few tenants who rent. I own my own flat, number 12. He's in 22, which is a similarly configured flat on the second floor," she said, barely pausing for breath. They passed the floor her apartment was on and continued up the stairs.

"You were saying you could hear Mr. MacManus walking about in his flat?" Kennedy prompted.

"I did hear him start to take a shower…"

King's face betrayed her questioning thought.

"So," Alice continued and paused impatiently, "we both have the same type of shower pump, and I recognized the noise it makes. A few minutes later, he finished his shower." She paused again, and turned her head slightly to address King directly. "His pump fell silent. Then, maybe thirty seconds or so later, I heard a very loud gunshot."

"Are you sure it was a gunshot?" Kennedy asked. "I mean, when a fuse blows, it too can give off an extremely loud report. Even a car backfiring on the street can create a similar sound to the report of a gun. It's very busy out there," the Ulster detective continued, nodding through the stairwell window in the direction of Delancey Street.

"So…initially I felt it was a gunshot, but then I convinced myself it just couldn't be, and…" she paused, curling the ends of a few strands of blond hair around her right forefinger as she gave Kennedy a brief, but very definite, patronizing smile. "I so wanted it to be a car misfiring out on the street, but then I realized, because of the double glazing, we barely hear the traffic. I reasoned it was definitely an internal noise. I too wondered if it might have been a fuse blowing. I favored the faulty fuse explanation until I realized all the electrical appliances were working perfectly. I thereby concluded it was a gunshot."

"Did you hear any doors closing after the shot was fired?" Kennedy asked.

"No, definitely not."

"Did you hear anyone coming down the stairs?"

"I don't believe so. Our front door has a strong spring-bolt locking device, which ensures the door slams shut after everyone leaves. It's so noisy we've asked for it to be deactivated. The security firm, Surelock Homes, advised us that for security and insurance reasons, they're not allowed to adjust it."

"Fire exits?" King asked.

"Um…yes," Alice started evasively, "I believe this issue is being worked on… You'd have to ask the Freeholder."

By which point they had reached the door to number 22.

DS Dot King put on a pair of blue-tinted evidence-protecting gloves and offered Kennedy a pair as well. She knocked, rather quietly, on the door.

No reply.

King then knocked louder. "Mr. McManus, this is Detective Sergeant King and Detective Inspector Kennedy from Camden Town CID, may we come in please?"

Just as she started to bang her fist on the door again, Kennedy, now wearing matching gloves, disappeared down the stairs.

He returned a few minutes later with a carpenter he'd spotted working on the refurbishment of the building formerly known as Café Delancey, on the other side of the street. Arnie, the carpenter, essentially looked like Arnie Schwarzenegger, only covered head to toe in thick off-white dust.

Kennedy instructed Arnie to break the door down.

The Ulster detective felt as though he, King, and Alice Rafferty were visibly disappointed when Arnie, instead of busting the door down, or maybe even walking through it—just like the Terminator might have—drew a battery-powered drill from his holster, affixed a steel bit firmly in the chuck, and drilled through the brass cylinder. Ghost-like, Arnie quickly followed this up with a few firm taps of his hammer directly onto the rose of the lock, whereupon they could hear the barrel of the lock fall onto the floor inside the apartment.

From the state of the apartment, Kennedy felt Mr. McManus must have been a very house-proud hermit, as the detective hadn't seen a home as well-kept or as clean since his left his parents' house in Portrush all those years ago. Everything had a place, and there was a place for absolutely everything.

The furniture was dated, yet still classy, although the gold and green striped wallpaper in the hallway was a bit too dark and made the ceiling feel very low.

Kennedy sent Alice Rafferty and Arnie back down the stairs. Both seemed very reluctant to follow the detective's command.

Once again, now while in the apartment, King announced their presence.

As Kennedy and King progressed along the entrance hall, the slightly repulsive aroma of gunpowder lit up the detective's memory bank. It was a very organized area, crammed with sights, sounds, and scents from Portrush's Ramore Head Annual Firework Display, dating back to the days of his youth.

They tentatively opened each door on either side of the hallway in turn. The opening of doors and their footsteps on the natural oak laminate floor created an eerie contrast to the silenced assured by the double-glazed windows. They peered into a tidy and airy room with a double bed; a small bathroom (tiny sink and toilet); a busy, yet organized home office; a linen closet packed to the brim with sheets, blankets, and towels. Next they opened the door to a larger bedroom with an unmade double bed. They saw a pair of dark brown corduroy trousers and a blue-checked flannel shirt (similar to those favored by John Fogerty) with a white t-shirt still on the inside, proving shirt and t-shirt had been removed as one item of clothing. The clothes were lying across a leather easy chair like a deflated, headless human. The door on the opposite side of the hallway, when opened, revealed a fair-sized living room/TV room/dining room, with white walls absolutely crammed with photographs, every one of which told a story.

There was only one door left unopened, and Kennedy had started to feel that this particular call-out had been a false alarm. Then he realized what he was doing was simply wishing with all his might Alice Rafferty's call had been a false alarm.

He felt resistance to his attempts to open this door.

He nodded to King to remain behind him.

"Mr. MacManus, are you in there?" Kennedy called out confidently.

He reacted to the lack of reply by pushing the door handle more aggressively. There was definitely resistance. His efforts were eventually rewarded by the door springing open as though released from whatever had been hindering it.

Simultaneously they heard something solid-sounding shimmying across the white-tiled floor. Kennedy immediately slammed the door shut again and waved King back even farther.

"What the heck was that?" she whispered, glaring at him.

Kennedy jerked his shoulders in an "I haven't a clue" way.

"From the way it slithered across the floor, it sounded to me like a very large, hairy rat," King offered.

Kennedy, for his part, hung onto the door handle as though his life depended on it, and perhaps it did. On reflection, he felt the "hairy rat" part of King's comments had set off his internal alarm bells.

Now, however, he couldn't feel anyone or anything resisting his vise-like grip on the door handle. Without letting go, he pressed his ear to the door and was rewarded with nothing but the blissful sound of silence. He gingerly and ever so slowly opened the bathroom door again, while remaining at the ready to slam it shut at the first peep from inside.

There was the distinctive metallic smell of blood, combined with the residual damp smell found in a bathroom after someone has taken a shower and forgotten to open a window to air the room.

The first thing Kennedy noticed was an Astra semi-automatic handgun lying on the floor, close to the door. His knowledge of firearms did not extend to the various types of weapons, so he was happy the maker's name was conveniently displayed along the base of the barrel. The sight of the weapon responsible for the shot Ms. Rafferty had heard removed one of the main concerns for Kennedy. Kennedy had King use her mobile phone to take a few visually restricted photos of the bathroom, encouraging her to go for a close-up of the gun. The detective picked up the handgun using a pen and deposited it straight into King's waiting plastic evidence bag.

It was at this point that he became distracted by the body of a male slumped over the side of the bathtub at the window side of the completely white bathroom. There were even three foot-square, plain white prints in white wooden frames, symmetrically lined up, directly above the bath. The overall effect was very John Lennon, as in absolutely everything in the bathroom was white. Everything, that was, apart from two bath mats. Kennedy figured the general wear and tear of feet, perhaps sweaty before entry to the shower (or bath) and wet upon departure, meant the sky-blue bath mats had proven to be an artistic, but necessary, blemish.

Kennedy knew he could not delay the inevitable any longer, even though the actual delay had only been a matter of twenty seconds.

McManus's remains were head-down in the empty bath. Kennedy felt this meant the victim had most likely been made to lean over the side of the bath, so most of his body weight was on the tub side. Otherwise, when he was shot, he would have slipped back out onto the bathroom floor.

The first thing to shock the Ulster detective was the lack of blood. There was not a single drop around the body. It appeared the bullet to the temple was both lethal and instantaneous. The brain had been immobilized and the muscles of the vital organ had stopped pumping in literally a heartbeat. The end result was merely a trickle of crimson watery discharge which had run over the clean-shaven head of the victim.

Did this mean the murderer was trying to minimize the impact of blood at the scene?

Kennedy quickly, but carefully, stood up from hunkering down and sped out into the hallway again. DS Dot King was standing by the hall door. He rushed over to her.

"Have you been standing here all the time?"

"Yes, of course," she replied defensively, and then whispered urgently, "Why, what's wrong?"

"I think our murderer is still in the apartment."

"Yes…I kinda worried about that too. Ms. Rafferty did say she didn't hear anyone leaving or any doors closing."

On the grounds that they had secured the weapon, Kennedy, while still cautious, examined all the rooms again. Of all the rooms they'd briefly looked into, he suspected the linen closet, with all its sheets, blankets, and towels, was the most likely hiding place. On their second search they found no one there, or even under the beds in the bedrooms. The window in the home office was open, though, wide open in fact, but when Kennedy looked out the window, he discovered there was quite a drop to ground below. He reasoned an escape by this means would have been all but impossible, unless of course one was desperate. Perhaps the murderer had been in the apartment as King and Kennedy had knocked on the door. He tried to remember if this window had been open when they first checked it. He couldn't swear either way. King was likewise vague. Although it was cold in the home office, Kennedy left the window open so the soon to-arrive-SOCO team could dust the window frame and ironwork handles for prints.

Kennedy returned to the bathroom to continue his search for clues.

The barefoot victim was wearing a pair of red-black-and-green tartan flannel lounge trousers and a very loose-fitting dark blue rugby shirt. He looked to be in his mid-sixties, with a slim build, but, because of the position of the corpse, Kennedy could not get a fix on his height.

It was at this point, twenty-two minutes into the investigation, that the scene-of-crime officers arrived with the portly, theatrically-dressed Dr. Taylor. The pathologist immediately started to examine the body.

Kennedy and King retired to the living room to continue their search.

McManus had been the proud owner of a very expensive-looking stereo system. Kennedy noted that the three CDs absent from the nearby alphabetically arranged shelves and neatly stacked on top of the CD player were Lesley Duncan's *Sing Children Sing,* The Blue Nile's *A Walk Across The Roof Tops,* and *The Songs of Leonard Cohen*; three classic debut albums, all from separate but consecutive decades, yet all sharing a very similar mood.

Kennedy studied the numerous photographs around the lounge. Quite a few featured a girl, the same girl, it appeared, but at various stages in her life. In some of the photos she was with other people, family, friends, and fellow students perhaps. In several of them she was with an older man, a much stouter version of the deceased, Kennedy reasoned. They looked very happy together, totally comfortable with each other, and neither was camera-shy.

King continued examining the lounge while Kennedy visited the home office again. He looked out the window for a second time, but couldn't find what he was looking for: an external pipe, which might have assisted the intruder in dropping to the ground. He started to go through the drawers of the ultra-modern desk. The top central drawer contained nothing but two manila files tidily placed side by side.

Kennedy removed the first one and, without even thinking about it, sat down in the super comfy high-tech desk chair. The few sheets of paper within the file revealed what appeared to be an up-to-date life insurance policy.

Kennedy also discovered McManus's first name was Mark. Mr. Mark Robin McManus's life was insured for £495,000 and the sole beneficiary was his only daughter, Mary Martha McManus.

The remaining file in the drawer held the deeds and paperwork for his flat. One of Alice's mysteries had been solved. Mark McManus was not renting the flat. However, he was mortgaged to the hilt, and he was gravely in arrears, proven by various letters from a local bank threatening to repossess his apartment. Kennedy didn't happen upon any other useful information in the home office.

So far, there were no real clues as to who might have wanted him dead.

Kennedy returned to the bathroom to find the SOCO team and Dr. Taylor busy at work. The detective inspector walked the room, slowly, patiently. He noticed the sky-blue bath mat by the shower door still betrayed McManus's footprints. Two thoughts hit the detective simultaneously: Wasn't it sad that a person's footprints would outlast their owner? And secondly, there was something not right about the footprints. He couldn't work out what it was, but he knew from experience that, if he didn't force the issue, it would eventually come to him.

He dropped slowly to his haunches, if only to be able to study the room from a different perspective.

The white floor tiles had been laid very unevenly, but Kennedy quite liked the undulating terrain it created. It reminded him, on a much larger scale of course, of the similarly gentle rises and falls of the white sands Lawrence of Arabia, in the person of Peter O'Toole, might have ridden across.

For Kennedy, these mental distractions were an absolute necessity when he was in the presence of a victim's corpse.

He remained in this position and thought process for quite a few seconds, maybe even a minute. He thought he spotted a long stray hair in what was otherwise a spotless bathroom. When he moved his head to gain a better view of it, the "hair" had disappeared. The light had changed in the bathroom when someone had opened and quickly closed the bathroom door. Kennedy twisted his head this way and that, but he couldn't bring the single flaw back into focus again, so he dismissed the sighting as an errant eyelash of his own.

Behind the door to the bathroom, just above the white sink, he noticed a mirrored medicine cabinet. Inside he found shaving gear; an electric toothbrush; a comb; morphine tablets; a tube of aloe vera gel; a box of Lemsip; two boxes of black currant Dioralyte; Ultra Dex toothpaste; a bottle of the same brand of mint mouthwash; a traditional toothbrush; a few plastic containers of prescription pills, the names of which he didn't recognize; two unopened dispensers of Baylis and Harding hand wash; a pair of scissors; and a packet of cheese and onion Tayto Crisps. Surprisingly, it wasn't the packet of crisps which caught his attention.

At which point, Dr. Taylor had concluded his initial examination and the corpse was now laid out face-up on the bathroom floor.

"As you know, the body was still warm, so time of death would have been in the last thirty minutes or so."

"At the very most," Kennedy said as he checked his watch, noting it was now just before six o'clock.

"I don't know what else I can tell you until I examine him properly back at base," Taylor continued in a respectful whisper, "but I can tell you our victim recently had a laparoscopy."

Kennedy stared at the good doctor, hoping for more.

"Sorry, I should have said minimally invasive surgery, or keyhole surgery, if you will. I won't know if the procedure was successful until I open him up, but it looks to me like, if the assassin's bullet hadn't felled him, the big C would have."

Kennedy agreed with Taylor's request to remove the remains of Mr. Mark McManus to the morgue. He asked the SOCO team if they could leave the bathroom for now, and he and King went inside and closed the door. Kennedy returned to the position he had been in when he spotted Lawrence of Arabia's undulating "desert." He focused on the position close to the door where he'd spotted what he felt was the original stray hair.

No joy in the search.

King, as requested by Kennedy, opened and shut the door, and then gingerly moved around the bathroom as directed by her superior.

Then, in a flash, the hair returned, just as mysteriously as it had disappeared. It was under the white radiator to the right (as he was looking at it now) of the door. Kennedy sussed that it was only visible when the copper-colored hair caught the light properly. He crawled across the bathroom floor and started to pick up the hair while King stood by with an already opened evidence bag. Then the strangest thing happened. As Kennedy lifted the stray hair, it kept on coming and coming and coming, and when he couldn't lift any more it was only because one end of it was attached to the rubber stop on the inside bottom right-hand corner of the bathroom door. The rubber stop was strategically positioned to prevent the door banging into the expensive-looking sink unit, should the door be opened too far.

Kennedy carefully rolled the hair around his other gloved fingers and placed the coil in the evidence bag. He then checked the other evidence bag in which they'd placed the handgun.

A few seconds later, he broke into a gentle smile.

"Okay," he said, "we're all set to head back to North Bridge House now."

"What? Why? What do you mean?"

"We've worked out who the murderer is," Kennedy admitted.

"We have???? You might have, but I haven't. What did I miss?"

"Let's go, I'll tell you on the way."

A full seventeen minutes of the Golden Hour remained as they hit the pavement on Delancey Street. They were immediately welcomed by the extra strong, invigorating aromas of coffee beans roasting in the Camden Coffee Shop on the opposite side of the road. These warmly welcoming scents overpowered the odors of death which had been lingering in their nostrils.

King was glaring at Kennedy as though he'd lost his marbles.

"So, come on, who's the murderer? How did they do it? Why did they do it? And how did you catch them out?"

"Okay," Kennedy started, "first off, I'll tell you how it was done. That hair we found…"

"The one I thought must belong to a giant, you mean?"

"Yes, that one," Kennedy agreed, "but it wasn't a hair, it was a length of fishing line. And, as you saw, one end was attached to the rubber stop on the inside of the bathroom door. The other end was fed behind the radiator pipe by the wall and then eventually it was tied to…"

"The Astra semi-automatic handgun?" she guessed.

"Also known as "the very large hairy rat," the very same," he confirmed, before continuing. "So the trigger was pulled. The bullet exploded into the brain of Mr. McManus, who died instantly. The gun fell to the floor and the corpse slumped into the bath. We come along, and as we force the bathroom door open, the fishing line attached to the doorstop on the inside of the bathroom door, with the other end attached via the fulcrum of the radiator, acted like a whiplash, propelling the gun away from the feet of the victim."

"But why?"

"So it did not appear to be the scene of a suicide."

"Sorry—the murderer wanted to dress the scene so it wouldn't appear to be a suicide," King said, shaking her head in disbelief as she spoke. "Surely it should be the other way around? Surely the murderer would want to make it appear it was a suicide?"

"Normally, yes, but in this case the murderer and the victim are one and the same person."

"So you're saying it was a suicide?"

"Here's the thing," Kennedy began. "Mr. McManus was dying of cancer. We know this from his demeanor, his medication, and Dr. Taylor's examination. Let's suppose he lost the will to live. He saw no end to his pain and suffering. It would appear the only person in the world he loved was his daughter Martha. So we have to guess he would have wished to have left her something considerable. Now we know the apartment effectively belongs to the banks. So he can't leave her the property. We also know that if he committed suicide, his insurance policy would be declared invalid. I think he figured out a way to get around this."

"He did." King gushed. "I mean, did he?"

"Yes. Mr. McManus staged his death to look like a murder. Some of his plan, of course, is a bit obvious, you know, like leaving a window wide open in this weather as a supposed escape route, or pretending to take a shower so he would draw the attention of his downstairs neighbor, Ms. Alice Rafferty."

"How on earth do you know he faked a shower?" King asked.

"Do you remember what we saw on the bath mat just outside the shower?" Kennedy asked in return.

"Wet footprints?"

"Do you remember the shape of them?"

King shook her head.

Kennedy stopped walking and King followed suit.

He lifted his right foot.

"Okay, if I step into a shower," and Kennedy plonked his right foot down in front of him before continuing, "and I step back out onto the bathmat, the damp print of the sole of my foot will be visible on the bath mat. Okay?"

"Okay," she agreed.

"But how about if, instead of stepping into the shower, I just raise my foot and, keeping it raised, to ensure the rest of my body doesn't get wet, then insert only my foot into the shower, just enough to get it wet, and then take it back out again and place it on the bath mat. And then repeat the process with the other foot. In these instances, the bath mat will get damp all around the outline of my foot, but this time the mat will remain dry where the sole of my foot was placed on the mat. There were such damp and dry patches on Mr. McManus' sky-blue bath mat."

King just nodded slowly, in either an "I'm impressed" kind of way, or a "Now, there's a piece of useless information" kind of way—Kennedy genuinely couldn't be sure which.

"Alice Rafferty told us it was thirty seconds after Mr. McManus had his shower when she heard the fatal shot being fired," Kennedy continued. "Yet when we found the dead body it was bone-dry. There was no way he was going to be able to dry and dress himself in thirty seconds."

"Meaning, as your footprints have already attested, he didn't have a shower?" King offered.

"He didn't have a shower," Kennedy agreed.

"But why go to so much trouble?" she asked, as they continued walking toward North Bridge House, the home of Camden Town CID.

"Two reasons, really. He wanted Alice to think he was just going about his normal daily business when someone broke into his flat, shot him, and disappeared. The second reason was probably more important to McManus: he had to attract the attention of his neighbor. He wanted her paying attention to the shot. He wanted—no, he needed—Alice to raise the alarm. He needed her to call us because…"

"Because he wanted someone other than his daughter to discover his body."

"Correct."

"But what if Alice had missed the single gunshot for whatever reason, I don't know, maybe she had the TV volume up too loud, or there were also gunshots on the TV at the same time?" King asked.

"Well, in any of your scenarios, his fail safe would have kicked in."

"His fail safe?

"If Alice didn't, for whatever reason, raise the alarm, his beloved daughter would not come unexpectedly upon a horrific bloody scene, because McManus had stage-managed his death so that, after he leaned over the side of the bath, put the gun to his head, and shot himself, he would topple over headfirst into the bath. He minimized his daughter's potential trauma even further with his expertly aimed shot."

When King didn't respond, as if considering the lack-of-blood aspect, Kennedy added, "McManus's system for getting the gun as far away as possible from his body post-death was the clever part of his plan."

"As in, if the gun was found so far away from him, then it would look like he couldn't possibly have shot himself, and his life insurance policy would still be valid and his daughter would be in line for a windfall?" King offered.

"Exactly!"

"So do we file it as a suicide?"

"I don't think that would be a good idea," Kennedy said, as much to himself as to King. "I mean, we wouldn't want to be responsible for failing to grant a dying man his final wish."

They had reached Parkway and crossed the road without talking. It would have been a waste of time due to the noise of the traffic at the busy junction; they'd never have heard each other anyway.

Kennedy checked his watch; there were still just over two minutes of their golden hour left. As they walked up the steps into North Bridge House, he paused and said to DS King, "Let's just mark this one up as 'unsolved' and close the file."

Expiration Date

BEV VINCENT

Lorraine was already in a bad mood before she discovered there weren't any bodies at her potential crime scene.

"They died at the hospital," the officer in charge told her. "Looks like some kind of poison."

"Could be accidental," a crime scene investigator collecting and cataloging everything in the refrigerator told her. "A lot of stuff in here is well past its best-by date." The woman, clad in a white protective gown and wearing a face mask and head covering, held up a small glass jar. "Mango chutney." She peered at the label. "Expired in August 2010. That can't be right, can it?"

"Bring me up to speed," Lorraine said to the OIC.

The officer referred to his notepad. "Carrie and Lee Foster," he said. "Both admitted to hospital shortly after four in the morning with severe abdominal cramps, vomiting, the whole shebang. Then they went into rapid organ failure. She died first, then he went about three hours later."

"Toxicology?"

"In the works, but it'll take a while."

The CSI eased open a plastic margarine tub. "No telling how long this has been in there, or what's in it," she said, "but it reeks and there's something gray and fuzzy growing on it." She sealed the tub in an evidence bag.

Even through her protective mask, Lorraine smelled something noxious that reminded her of death. "Any idea what they had for dinner?"

The officer shook his head. "Not sure there's anything left in their systems to analyze, either."

"I get the picture," Lorraine said.

Until they eliminated foul play, the case was hers. She surveyed the kitchen, trying to get a sense of what had happened. The dishwasher's digital display indicated that it had finished its cycle. After confirming that the room had been photographed and videoed, she popped the door open and examined the contents. Half a dozen dinner plates, an equal number of glasses, and plenty of silverware were crammed into it, along with some smaller dishes, pots, and pans. Everything was spotless. There would be no way to tell what food these dishes had once held. Nor, in fact, when they'd been washed.

She instructed the techs to get samples from the in-sink disposal unit. "We'll take the whole thing back to the lab," the CSI said.

Lorraine poked through the garbage can. That, too, would go to the lab. The food wrappers and other detritus might lead them to the lethal culprit.

"I think we have a winner," the CSI said, holding up another jar. "Maple butter from 2008."

"Poisonous?"

"Not likely. But it's older than my kid, and she's in second grade."

On the counter next to the telephone, Lorraine found a day planner adorned with handwritten appointments and reminders. The entry for the previous day caught her attention. "Denim and Diamonds Dinner for six, seven o'clock," it said. This was followed by the letters MwS. She wondered if it was an abbreviation for a restaurant. Similar notes appeared on previous pages, roughly once per month. An internet search for the three letters yielded dozens of hits, none of them illuminating or obviously relevant.

"Anyone know what 'MwS' stands for?" she asked the room. "Small w'?"

No one did. Lorraine photographed the entry with her cell phone and made a note to look into it later. She spent the rest of the morning and most of the afternoon supervising the collection of samples and documenting possible evidence.

She clocked out at six and phoned her husband to let him know her ETA. He assured her he'd have something ready to eat when she got there and did she mind Chinese takeout? Again?

Craig was a former member of the department, but he had put in his years and taken retirement. Now he accepted the odd security job, but mostly he stayed home, where the DIY bug had bitten him. He was renovating their house one room at a time. The kitchen was his current project. He'd taken out their aging dishwasher and range, even though Lorraine had begged him to wait for the replacements to arrive first. He wanted to redo the countertops, he'd said, so the appliances had to go.

Of course, there were delays. Their master bath had been in disarray for weeks after the contractors working on that project mysteriously vanished. Something bigger and more lucrative had come along, so their piddling renovation job had been put on the back burner. For nearly a week, Lorraine had had to traipse across the house to use the bathroom upstairs. Finally, she told Craig she was going to relocate to the spare bedroom permanently if he didn't rectify the situation. That got things moving again. Now there'd been a problem with the delivery of the new appliances. Passing through the gutted kitchen on her way to the car each morning set her teeth on edge, accounting for her bad mood earlier at the crime scene.

When she got home, Lorraine did her best to prevent her annoyance from ruining the evening. She averted her eyes when she retrieved paper plates and disposable cutlery from the cabinet next to where a dishwasher once resided... and hopefully would again soon. Craig must have sensed her mood. After asking about her day, he offered a wry smile that encompassed the takeout cartons. "At least we still have the fridge," he said.

"Not funny."

"I promise—by the end of the week, everything will be back to normal."

Until the next project, she thought but didn't say.

"If you're getting tired of takeout, maybe we can try that Meals with Strangers thing."

Lorraine looked up from her plate. "What's that?"

"Just kidding," Craig said.

"No. Seriously. What is it?"

"It's the latest fad, like Uber for meals. Everyone's talking about it—even on *The View*." Since his retirement, Craig had become a TV and news junkie. He was always telling her about something he'd seen online, which was good because Lorraine didn't have time to read the papers or figure out which parts of the online news were real and what was fake. Craig had a good nose for the facts—a cop's nose.

"Show me," she said.

Craig fetched his tablet and pulled up an article, which led them to several review sites and finally to an app, which had a distinctive MwS logo. Apparently it was pronounced "mee-ews," sort of like "meals" but not quite. The company suggested themes for these dinners. Lorraine scanned the list and found "Denim and Diamonds" between "Cocktails and Caviar" and "Leather and Lace."

The concept set off a host of red flags in Lorraine's mind. A cop's mind, too. Inviting total strangers to your home bearing food might seem adventurous or trendy, but there were so many crazies out there. Did you really want to ask them in? Besides, what if they couldn't cook worth shit? Worse, what if…

What if they poisoned you? Judging by the contents of the Fosters' fridge, they had long been a case of food poisoning waiting to happen.

Her mobile phone chirped. She and her husband tried to avoid electronic gadgets while eating, but her job didn't let her cut the cord completely. Craig understood. In the past it had often been his phone interrupting dinner.

She glanced at the text message. "We might have two more vics."

***

The deceased couple lived in a different part of town from the Fosters, but an alert doctor had deemed their symptoms suspicious and called in law enforcement. Miracle of miracles, someone else had put two and two together and made the connection with Lorraine's case.

"Sounds like the same poison to me," Lorraine told her sergeant when she got to the precinct. "Same symptoms, anyway. We won't know for sure until the toxicology results come in."

"Are we thinking homicide or accidental death?"

"We," she said, emphasizing the word for effect, "don't have an opinion one way or the other yet."

"Can you put the—" he looked at the file Lorraine had handed him—"the Garveys and the Fosters together?"

Lorraine shook her head. "Working on it. They may have been using a meal-sharing app. The day planner at the Foster residence said 'dinner for six', so we might be looking at two more victims. We're still canvassing, and I sent out a citywide alert to hospitals."

"Meal-sharing?"

"Total strangers getting together to have a potluck meal. It's all the rage."

"What could possibly go wrong?"

"Right. An even worse idea than blind dates."

"Poison," her sergeant mused. "Usually a woman's weapon." He raised his eyebrows, as if expecting a response. When he didn't get one, he turned back to his paperwork. "Keep me posted."

"We will."

She made a few phone calls. Their techs hadn't been able to contact anyone at MwS yet who could tell them if the Fosters and the Garveys had eaten dinner together and, if so, who had joined them. Not surprising, given the late hour. They'd have to wait until morning, by which time anyone else who'd been poisoned would be dead. Lorraine sighed and headed to the Garvey residence.

The crime scene techs told her they'd matched Edward and Theresa Garvey's fingerprints with several they'd lifted at the Fosters. A nosy neighbor also recognized the Garveys from a photograph and confirmed the presence of a third couple. After overseeing the collection of evidence, Lorraine was getting ready to go home for a few hours of sleep before she had to report for duty in the morning when she received a response to her alert. Two more people with similar symptoms had turned up in the ER in the Med Center earlier in the day.

"Dead?" Lorraine asked the nurse administrator who took her call.

"Just the wife. We think the husband will make it."

"Can I talk to him?"

"Maybe tomorrow. We're hydrating him to see if we can prevent liver and kidney failure," the nurse said. "It would help if we knew what poisoned them."

"That would help us, too," Lorraine said.

***

A text message woke Lorraine at 6:45 a.m. She'd been home for less than three hours, and it had taken her over an hour to wind down and get to sleep. Squinting at the tiny screen produced nothing intelligible. She fumbled at the bedside for her glasses, and it still took several seconds to bring the words into focus.

CAIN-ME: *Amanita phalloides*, the message read.

She scrunched up her face and used her thumbs to pluck out a response to Dr. Cain's text message.

WTF?

CAIN-ME: Death cap mushroom, the response came a moment later, accompanied by a colorful emoji mushroom that looked like something out of Alice in Wonderland.

Lorraine was about to ask the medical examiner if it was poisonous when she reconsidered. The name pretty much spoke for itself.

Common? she typed instead.

CAIN-ME: Ish.

Rather than continue the terse conversation by text, Lorraine took a quick shower, got dressed, nuked an egg-and-bacon breakfast sandwich from the freezer—yes, she was thankful they still had a fridge and microwave—and picked up a coffee from a drive-through window on her way to the ME's office.

"We found mushrooms in the stomach contents," Dr. Cain said. "The symptoms got me thinking." He was nearly sixty, with curly hair and a moustache modeled after Salvador Dali's. "I read an article a couple of weeks ago about the increasing abundance of the death cap in North America, so I ran a test and…" He flung open his raised hands like a magician. "Boom!"

"So it was an accident?"

"Can't say for sure. If one of your victims was an amateur mycologist who skipped a few classes, it's possible."

"Mycologist. I'm guessing that has something to do with mushrooms?"

The medical examiner nodded. "All it takes is for one bad 'shroom to get mixed in with a batch of edible ones. There are a lot of safe lookalikes out there, but I've never heard of death caps ending up in the commercial supply."

"And cooking doesn't break them down?"

"For some kinds of mushrooms, yes, but not *Amanita*. Lovely name, don't you think, for such a deadly bitch? They're supposed to be delicious. And then, six to twenty-four hours later…boom! In the words of the immortal Terry Pratchett…all mushrooms are edible, but some are only edible once!"

"One of the victims is still alive," Lorraine said. "What are his prospects?"

"Better now that we know what we're dealing with," Cain said. "If he makes it through the honeymoon phase, he'll probably be okay."

Lorraine could figure that expression out on her own. Her next stop was the Med Center, where Jason Ellis was hooked up to a bank of machines that monitored his vitals while his system was flushed to eradicate the poison.

"He doesn't know about his wife yet," the charge nurse told Lorraine. "He's still pretty weak."

Lorraine could see that for herself. There were dark circles under his eyes and his skin was an unhealthy shade of pale that she associated with corpses. The file said he was thirty-eight, but she would have guessed fifty based on his appearance.

"Mr. Ellis? Do you feel up to answering a few questions?" she asked after identifying herself.

"What...hit...me?" he asked.

Lorraine had to lean close to hear him. "We believe you were poisoned," she said. "Something you ate."

"Poisoned? Melanie...sick, too?" he asked.

She had the uncomfortable feeling he was looking down the front of her blouse, so she straightened up. "I don't have any information about that," she said. "Were you together?"

Ellis nodded. He seemed to be having a hard time swallowing, and he fussed at the IV needle in the back of his hand.

"Did you know the people you ate supper with?"

He shook his head. "Used Meals with Strangers. Denim and Diamonds Dinner. Mel liked to wear her fancy jewelry."

Diamonds, Lorraine thought. That's interesting. "You'd never met the other couples before? Carrie and Lee Foster, Edward and Theresa Garvey."

He shook his head again. "They sick, too? This was...Mel's idea. Meet new people."

"What did you eat?"

"Everyone brought something different. Some kind of chicken, Marsala I think they said, and a beef dish. We brought pork chops."

"Did any of the dishes contain mushrooms?"

Ellis made a face. "I hate them. Mel should have told them. They were in everything...except the chops."

"Did you eat any of the other dishes?"

"Little bit. To be polite."

That food aversion probably saved your life, she thought. She remained silent until he looked her in the eyes. "Do you remember who brought which dish?"

Ellis appeared to give it some thought, but he finally shook his head.

A doctor hovered at the door. "That's enough for now," he said.

Lorraine nodded, leaving it to the doctor to deliver the bad news to Ellis about his wife. Over the years, she had been the bearer of similar tidings on more occasions than she cared to recall. She was happy to let someone else do it, lingering outside the room to watch how Ellis responded. He might have been weak, but he still managed to screw up his face and look distraught. Was his reaction genuine? Lorraine had seen grief in all its forms, and it was never the same twice. He looked upset, certainly, but something bothered her. He hadn't seemed surprised to be questioned by the police, even though he supposedly didn't know anyone had died yet. That and the fact that he was the only survivor. She decided to dig deeper into his circumstances.

First, she called the medical examiner. "Interested in last night's menu?"

"I've got pork chops, beef stroganoff, and a chicken dish," Dr. Cain said. "Mashed potatoes, green beans, and wine. Plenty of wine."

"Chicken Marsala," Lorraine said. She resisted the temptation to add "boom!"

"I'd buy that."

"Any way of telling which dish had the bad mushrooms?"

"There wasn't much left in their stomachs. You find any leftovers?"

"I'm about to check with the crime scene unit. Did everyone eat everything?"

"I'll let you know when I'm finished with the tests," Cain responded.

By the time she got to the crime lab, the technician had the evidence on display for her perusal. "Looking for anything in particular?" the tech asked. Brina was around thirty, tall and slim, and had a nose ring that Lorraine found fascinating. It wasn't a look she thought she could pull off herself.

"Trying to figure out who made the dish with the deadly mushrooms," she said. "Chicken Marsala would have mushrooms in it, right?" she asked.

Brina nodded. "I'd use cremini, or maybe porcini."

"Sounds delish," Lorraine said, checking her notes. "Beef stroganoff."

"Not my favorite," Brina said.

"Me neither, but it might have mushrooms in it, too. Ellis said he and his wife brought pork chops. No mushrooms, because he doesn't care for them."

"Lucky for him," Brina said.

"That's what I was thinking. Says he only took a bite of the other dishes to be polite, mostly ate what they brought."

"Would you do that?" Brina asked. "Have dinner at a total stranger's place?"

"Not after this, that's for sure," Lorraine said, with a harsh laugh. She looked at the evidence that had been collected from the three houses, some of which was on dry ice to preserve it. "What's this?" she asked, picking up an unfamiliar bottle in an evidence bag.

"Kosher Marsala wine," Brina said. "I found a bunch of kosher stuff in the evidence collected from the Garveys' kitchen."

Lorraine looked over the other items, then made a couple of phone calls. "Okay. That's interesting."

"What?"

"Teresa Garvey was Jewish. She ate kosher, according to her sister."

"So…no pork chops for her."

"Right," Lorraine said. "If the Garveys brought the chicken, and the Ellises brought the pork chops, that means the Fosters made stroganoff, right?"

"Reminds me of one of those logic puzzles," Brina said, pushing her glasses up with her index finger. "If the Browns live next to the Whites and Andrew has black hair, which family has the aardvark?"

"You're a strange woman," Lorraine said. "Anyone ever tell you that?"

Brina shrugged. "When are you going to ditch that husband of yours and come to your senses? Take a walk on the wild side with me?"

"If he doesn't get the kitchen straightened out—and soon—I just may take you up on that," Lorraine said.

Brina was silent for a moment. "The problem with those logic puzzles is that if you make one bad assumption, the whole thing collapses."

"What do you mean?"

"Do you know for sure the Ellises brought the pork chops?"

Lorraine considered the question. "We only have his word for it. Anything here to back him up?"

"Nope," Brina said. "And you want to know something strange?"

"What?"

"There was nothing in their kitchen garbage can."

Lorraine frowned. "What's odd about that? If I've been cooking—back in the days when I had a fully functioning kitchen, that is—I often took the trash out when I was finished rather than let things get smelly."

"Out where?"

"To the big wheeled bin beside the house. Where else?"

"Right. Except their outdoor garbage can was empty, too."

"Hmmm. What's your theory?"

Brina repositioned her glasses. "Just thinking out loud. You've been cooking, and you clean up. Maybe you put some stuff down the garbage disposal—and let me tell you, theirs is super-duper clean. Pristine. But you have boxes and bags and bottles. What do you do with them? Throw them out, of course. So where are they?"

Where indeed? Lorraine used her phone to look up the waste management schedule for the Ellis neighborhood. Their pickup day was Monday—four days before the fateful dinner. Then she looked up "kosher beef stroganoff" and found several recipes. The Garveys could have prepared that dish.

"I didn't like Ellis. He was checking me out, big time," Lorraine said. "Sick as a dog, but he had wandering eyes."

"I check you out, too, sometimes," Brina said.

"Yeah, but you know how to do it right," Lorraine said. She sat at the computer and paged through photographs taken at the three houses and of the couples' personal effects.

"Are these real, do you know?" she asked, pointing at shots of what looked like diamond rings, brooches, earrings, and necklaces. Diamond and Denim Dinner indeed. At least theft didn't seem to be a motive…assuming there was a crime.

Brina looked over her shoulder. "I haven't seen them yet, but I'll take a closer look. I like that one. People don't wear brooches much anymore."

Lorraine pored over more photographs. One, which showed a grocery store game board affixed to a fridge with magnets, gave her an idea. "I think it's time I paid Mr. Ellis another visit."

"Let me know how it turns out," Brina said, and winked. "And keep that offer in mind."

Lorraine blew her a kiss.

***

Lorraine almost bumped into a pretty woman in her mid-twenties leaving Ellis's hospital room. She was crying. Lorraine noticed a familiar-looking brooch on her lapel. The other woman mumbled an apology and sniffled loudly as she continued toward the elevators.

"Your visitor looked upset," Lorraine said to Ellis by way of greeting.

Ellis managed to look Lorraine in the face for several seconds before his gaze dropped. "Uh, yeah. That was Trudy. My, um, assistant. She's really upset about Melanie."

"About that. My condolences."

"What? Sure. Yup. Thanks."

Lorraine held up a sealed plastic evidence bag. It was a gamble, but Lorraine's instincts rarely let her down.

He frowned.

"It's your wife's phone," Lorraine said.

"I recognize it."

"Would you mind telling me the lock code?"

His frown deepened. "What for?"

Lorraine expelled a huge sigh. "You know how it is. The Department of Health and Public Safety is on my case, trying to figure out if they need to issue an advisory about bad mushrooms. I have to look at everything. I mean everything. Cross every t, etc., etc."

"Yeah?" Ellis said, still frowning.

Lorraine waited him out. After several seconds, he gave her the six-digit code, which she keyed into the lock screen through the plastic bag. "Thanks." She found the MwS app and flipped through it. "Hmmm," she said. "That's interesting."

"What?"

"It's just, well, the profile for the Garveys."

"Profile?"

"In MwS. Says she only eats kosher."

"Oh? I didn't look at that. That was Mel's thing." He tried to look sad, but couldn't quite pull it off.

"Or else you wouldn't have brought pork."

Ellis smirked. "Oh, yeah. Oops. Bad on us. At least we didn't fucking poison anyone."

Lorraine didn't buy his sudden outrage, either. She hit the home button and opened the app for the grocery store chain running the contest she'd seen pinned to the refrigerator in the photo taken in the Ellises' kitchen. "Well, would you look at that."

"What?"

She held the phone out so he could see it, but pulled away when he reached for it. "I shop at the same chain," she said. "I'm collecting these game pieces, just like your wife. That's what gave me the idea."

The screen displayed a grid of digital coupons. "Discounts on items you recently purchased," it said. The third entry was for the same brand of kosher wine she'd seen at the crime lab.

"Looks like your wife knew about Theresa Garvey's dietary restrictions after all. I'm guessing it was the Fosters who blew it and brought the pork chops. Am I right? When I look through their trash, am I going to find an empty pork package?"

Ellis didn't say anything for several seconds. At least he wasn't staring at Lorraine's chest anymore. "I'd like to talk to a lawyer," he said.

Lorraine told him that was a terrific idea, read him his rights, and cuffed his wrist to the bedframe. She waited until an officer arrived to stand guard outside his room, then decided to call it a day. The case wasn't a slam dunk yet, but the pieces were falling into place and she was convinced she had the guilty party in custody. Eventually they would figure out how he got the mushrooms. He didn't strike her as being smart enough to hide his tracks completely.

He might be smart enough, though, to make a deal once the DA explained how a jury would react to someone who killed four strangers to cover up the murder of his wife. She also had a feeling that the crying "assistant" might have something illuminating to say about the situation.

***

She arrived home to a surprise. During the day, her husband had taken delivery of a new stove and dishwasher, and installation was complete. The kitchen looked perfect again.

"You better not do anything else to the house for a while," she said. "Because I have other offers, you know."

Craig hung his head. "Can you stand takeout one more time?" he asked. He produced a huge bag from the local steakhouse.

"I guess I'll keep you," she said, over steak and wine. If he noticed that she avoided the mushrooms, he didn't say anything.

"What made you suspect him?" he asked, after she brought him up to speed on the case.

"He kept saying the Meals with Strangers thing was all his wife's doing, distancing himself from it. Then we figured out he was lying about who brought what," she said. "And the fact that he went to such lengths to get rid of their garbage." She took a sip from her wine. "All things a guilty person would do. Plus he gave his girlfriend the same diamond brooch he gave his wife."

She drained her glass and held it out for a refill. "But mostly I didn't like the way he looked at me," Lorraine said. "Like he wanted to eat me up."

The Window

DERYN LAKE

The predominant smell was wet backpacks. That and trainers that had plowed their way through a rainy afternoon. As each hearty student jostled their way onto the coach, glad to get inside, another followed behind, shouting cheerily. The sound and the whiff blowing down the vehicle's central aisle were enough to announce to somebody short-sighted that the scholars from assorted universities were off on a jolly. And were going to have a good time, come what may.

Alice, slightly overawed by the general bonhomie, climbed aboard and made her quiet way to an empty seat near the front, hoping that the place beside hers would remain vacant so that when darkness descended she would be able to stretch out and get a few hours' sleep. But her hopes were dashed when, ten minutes before they were due to start the thirteen-and-a-half-hour journey, a very fat young man—a large Whopper oozing egg and other unpleasantries clutched in his spare hand—plonked himself heavily beside her. He gave her a genial smile.

"Hello there. Name's Ollie. Please excuse my lunch. Grabbed it on the concourse. Looking forward to this outing. How about you?"

"Yes, very much. Have you been to Glamis Castle before?"

"No. In fact, I've never been farther north than Hendon."

Ollie laughed heartily and bit into his bun, a bit of egg juice running down the side of his mouth. Alice looked away.

"You not eating?" he asked.

"Yes, I've got something in my rucksack."

"Here, let me get it down for you."

He heaved her backpack out of the luggage rack and Alice cautiously opened her bowl of salad and ate a tomato.

"Slimming?" enquired Ollie cheerfully.

"No. I'm just careful about what I eat."

"I see," he answered, nodding his head wisely, before thrusting a plastic spoon into his Mars Bar McFlurry. Alice silently smiled and gazed out the window as the coach bellowed into sudden life and majestically drew out of Victoria Coach Station on its way to the land of mists and mysteries.

She had seen the advertisement for the minibreak on the students' notice board. Dominating the written word had been a photograph of Glamis Castle, brooding and formidable against a range of mighty mountains. Alice, who was studying medicine at St. George's University, had felt compelled to read it, then act upon it, which was quite out of character for her.

She hadn't really wanted to be a doctor, but the enthusiasm of her father, himself in practice in a seedy part of London, had spurred her on. He was bringing her up single-handedly, doing everything in his power to be a good single parent after her mother took off with a younger man who resembled a whippet and was trying to make it in show business. Alice allowed herself another smile at the many memories that came crowding in.

"I'm at Kent Uni doing media studies. Where are you?" Ollie's voice broke the silence.

"St. George's. I'm studying medicine."

"You're too small to be a doctor," he said jovially.

Alice answered, "I may be tiny, but I'm a whiz with a hypodermic."

Ollie guffawed and a bit of Mars bar which he was currently consuming shot out like a miniature bullet. Alice dodged. Oblivious, the fat young man continued to eat until darkness fell, which it did early on that late October evening, then he dozed off. Alice, gazing out the window until she could see no more, felt her eyelids grow heavy and almost immediately started to have a most extraordinary dream.

In her sleeping mind, she was standing on a sweeping green lawn gazing up at Glamis Castle. Though she had never visited the place, she knew that this was indeed true because the building's stark outlines, etched like black engravings against the dying sun, were the same as those in the photograph which had persuaded her to take the trip. She was quite alone and very unsure of what move to make when suddenly two female figures, dressed in clothes of the 1920s, came out of a back door and hastened across the grass.

"Good gracious," one girl said to the other. "Where are the rest of them? We can't be the first to arrive. I mean what about Boo Laine and Binky? They're never late for anything."

"I believe they're just coming. In fact, here are the whole damned shooting match. Oh, and there's Totty Trevelyan. Do you mind if I join him?"

"Not at all. Get in before that beastly Maudie Cavendish. She's full of sudden charm since his brother died and he became the new heir to the Earl of Aberystwyth."

Part of Alice's dreaming brain wondered whether she had wandered into a Twenties Fancy Dress party, including the highfalutin dialogue. But, if so, everyone present—and there were about three dozen people gathered on the lawn by now—had been to the best theatrical costumers in the country. She could hear the high-pitched chatter all around her, though no one had so much as glanced in her direction. Then those present began to quiet down as an imposing figure stepped from the castle in a silver evening gown that sparkled from gems with every move she made.

"It's my aunt," drawled somebody near at hand. "The Countess, you know."

The grande dame held up her hand and there was instant silence.

"My dear friends," she said. "We come to the end of the little quest I set you this afternoon. I notice that you have all been hard at work…" She glanced upward, and Alice saw that from every window dangled something white. "And now it will be my pleasure to join in the fun. Rufus, your arm, if you would be so good."

An effete-looking young man stepped forward and, thus aided, the Countess turned around and stared at the castle's looming exterior. Alice and the rest of the crowd did likewise.

It was an amazing sight. Alice believed it to be one of the largest citadels in the British Isles, excluding the royal palaces. From its looming central fortress, the might of which reared against the night sky, were two further extensions, themselves centuries old. The central edifice was covered with tiny towers, the roofs of which pointed sharply, while high battlements were just visible. But it was to the many windows in the great building that Alice's eyes were drawn. The young guests had been as good as their word—from every windowsill fluttered something white. Towels, scarves, handkerchiefs, even the occasional pair of defiant camiknickers or BVD underpants, had been attached. There was a low indrawing of breath from the onlookers, and then total silence.

Finally, the effete young man standing beside the Countess said, "Look, Aunt Cecilia, up there. A couple of windows have got nothing outside."

Everybody followed his raised pointing finger and a second's quiet was broken by exclamations and shouts.

"By Jingo, he's right."

"Golly, I don't believe it."

"Great Scot! I can see another one."

And it was true. Two windows, tiny and barely noticeable, tucked within the mighty central part of the castle's tower, had nothing at all hanging outside them.

"You must have missed them," said the Countess.

A young man and a girl spoke up. "But that was our special task to leave things there—and jolly creepy it was too—and we went everywhere. I mean everywhere."

Countess Cecilia looked at them, a half-smile on her face. "Well, my dear people, I think it is high time to tell you the legend. Let us go inside to the warm, where drinks and canapes will be served. Then you shall hear more of the missing room which, let me hasten to assure you, I searched for long and hard in my youth, but never could find."

Somebody beside Alice gave a loud grunt and, as she turned to see who it was, she felt the earth beneath her feet rumble and her surroundings shift. She realized then that she had dozed off and that Ollie had shifted his bulk sideways and was snoring into her ear. She was both annoyed and slightly afraid. The dream had been so vivid that she had been able to smell the perfume of the girl close to her, something oriental and spicy, probably Shalimar. But Ollie smelled of stale perspiration and breath biscuits. With none too gentle a shove, Alice pushed him away. He woke up a little.

"Sorry. Was I leaning on you? Must have nodded off."

She forced a smile.

"What's the time?

"Late at night. Go back to sleep. We'll be at Dundee tomorrow morning."

"Good-oh." And producing another Mars bar, he sucked at it before passing once more into the arms of Hypnos.

It was a gray day when they finally arrived in Dundee, yet the Backpackers Hostel immediately exerted its charm. It had once been a building of importance, and had enchanting apartments but no lifts, nothing but winding

stairs and spiral staircases. Up these Alice puffed and found herself sharing
a room with a rather alarming female who was studying physics and was
a member of a women's hockey team. Her name was Hilary, and she was
extremely hearty.

"Will you excuse me?" said Alice after a few minutes of cheery chatter. "I
really must get some rest. I've been sitting next to a man of great girth who
snored all night."

"Bad luck," Hilary answered. "I was next to a student from Belarus who
spoke very little English. He stayed awake reading something in his native
language, but I managed to get a few hours' shut-eye. So you go ahead."

But when Alice closed her eyes, a vision of Glamis Castle—huge,
magnificent yet somehow menacing—came once more before she finally
dropped off to sleep.

By daylight, it didn't look quite so alarming. The fabric of the building had
a warm tone, and the rearing central structure did not seem quite so grim as
it had when she had dreamed of that macabre 1920s party looking for the
missing window. Yet her vision of the place had been darkened further by
something Hilary had said at supper the night before.

"I'm jolly well looking forward to tomorrow. I've always had a bit of a thing
about Glamis Castle, ever since I first heard the story."

"What story?" Alice had asked, but already in her mind's eye she could see
that gathering on the lawn looking up at the two small windows with nothing
marking them.

"About the Monster."

"The Monster?" she had repeated, feeling a chill at her spine.

"Yes. Surely you've heard it?" Alice shook her head, and Hilary continued.
"They say that there's a secret room somewhere in the castle. Oh, it's walled
up and has been for ages. Anyway, it was built to house an heir to the title
who was born so misshapen and hideous that he was removed at birth and
hidden from human eyes. Some while later, a workman on the estate found it
by chance, saw the creature, and was subsequently paid to go to Australia and
start a new life."

"Good God. So who took the Monster's place?"

"Well, the Countess gave birth to another child a year later, and this one was
okay. So the whole ghastly scenario was hushed up. But…"

"Yes?"

"On the heir's twenty-first birthday, he is shown into the room and sees the Monster for himself. Apparently he is subsequently plunged into deep melancholia."

"I'm not surprised. But surely the poor creature must be dead by now."

"Oh yes. This was all the talk in the Victorian times. It's all died down now."

"Do you believe it?" Alice had asked Hilary.

"I always think these stories must have a grain of truth in them."

Alice had slowly nodded, and now she looked up at the ancient central fortress and tried to remember exactly where the windows had been— the windows she had seen in her dreaming state. But amongst all those curious little towers there were many sheets of glistening glass together with proud battlements. It was impossible to tell. Ollie panted up, breaking her reflective mood.

"There you are. I looked for you after we got off the coach, but you were nowhere to be seen."

"Oh, I'm sorry. My roommate—Hilary, a very decent girl—and I went round the corner for a meal and then had an early night."

"Dear me!" Ollie gave his interpretation of a mischievous grin. "I expect my snoring kept you awake on the journey here."

"It most certainly did. But don't worry. I've made up for it now."

"I do apologize. May I buy you lunch by way of saying sorry? They've got a jolly little restaurant place here."

"That would be very kind," Alice answered with as much sincerity as she could muster because, to be honest, she would rather have eaten by herself. "What time shall we meet?"

"When the tour's over. I'll wait for you outside."

"Thanks, Ollie."

She hurried away, the thought of having to do the tour in his hearty company somehow overpowering.

By loitering at the back of the group, she managed to get a feeling of being alone, something she had hankered after ever since childhood. A solitary girl, she had woven a thousand imaginary games in the far corner of the playground, where she was a princess setting off to kill a nasty dragon that held a kindly prince in capture. And though she had almost grown out of it, still that longing to do and see things by herself had never really gone away.

She was very slightly disappointed by the tour, moving slowly through grand and impressive apartments, breathtaking though they were. But it was in the Crypt that she finally became intrigued by something quite ordinary, a heavy curtain made of rough and faded material hanging on the wall. Twitching it to one side, she saw that beyond it lay a stone spiral staircase. Almost of their own volition, her feet led her to slip behind the sheltering drape and stare upward. The spiral went on forever, up into the top of what looked like the old part of the building. It was like staring at a Disney cartoon of a fairy residence, and Alice was terribly tempted to climb up and have a look. From where she was standing she could hear the party of students moving off, Ollie's laugh, muffled by a bar of chocolate, ringing out. That decided her. She was going up.

Halfway there, she wished she hadn't. The confines of the staircase grew smaller and she realized that she was in a tower. Alice knew then that she was indeed in the most ancient part of the building, the stark fortress within whose confines had once stalked the Thane of Glamis, Macbeth himself. She felt afraid and terribly short of breath; even the fittest of individuals would have had difficulty with a climb as ferocious as the one which she had just done. She stopped to rest for a moment, feeling a little dizzy, then the feeling passed off and she heard a baby begin to cry.

Looking up, Alice saw that there was a final rise of the staircase and beyond that lay a door. She hurried upward and then cautiously put her hand on the latch. As she touched it, the crying grew louder. She put her ear to the wooden panel, but there were no signs of the child being attended to or picked up. With sudden curiosity, she pushed the door open and went in.

The room was dark, lit just by four candles in heavy carved holders, set at various points. The window was covered by a floor-length ebony curtain. The only furniture in the room was an old-fashioned cot with sweeping velvet decorations and a heavily embroidered hood. In the midst of all this splendor, quite solitary and howling its head off, lay a baby. Alice may have been a loner, but she was also a medical student. Her professionalism took over. She went to the cot and thrust aside the embroidery, looking down at the naked, crying little creature that lay within. Her eyes widened, and she gave a sudden sharp intake of breath. The poor child was hideously deformed, to the point of being a freak. It had no arms, merely two stumps, and tiny feet were growing out of what should have been its knees. Still, it was a human child and obviously much distressed.

Alice picked it up and rocked it, pulling its shawl round it. Its hair was long and dark, down to its shoulders, its face was screwed up, but as it eased in response to another human being, it was actually quite pleasing facially to look at. She guessed correctly that its hideous deformity had condemned it to being left alone.

"Shush, little fellow, shush now. Don't cry. Somebody will come in a minute."

It stared at her, and then gave a tremulous smile. Alice smiled back, and it was at that moment that she heard heavy footsteps approaching. She put the child down in the crib and went to hide behind the door, so that when a footman in livery appeared and went to the cot, she bolted out and flew down that never-ending spiral as if her life depended on getting clear.

The posse of students had moved on to the dining room, its table laid with fabulous crockery and gleaming glass. They were walking round and round, making small exclamations of wonderment. Yet Alice could take very little of it in, thinking instead of that wretched weeping baby and its horrible deformities. It reminded her in a way of the great artist Alison Lapper, who had been born malformed but who had risen to become such a powerhouse. As soon as she could get her hands on a reference source, she would look at that case and find out the name of the condition. Yet paramount in her thoughts was the way that poor maimed baby had smiled.

She could scarcely concentrate during lunch with Ollie, silently picking at her food until he came out with an extraordinary remark.

"I say, Alice, what do you make of this Monster story?"

She stared at him, slightly surprised. "Oh yes, Hilary was talking about it last night."

"He was kept in a secret room in some impenetrable part of Glamis. And the reason that they hid him away from public gaze was that he was born hideously deformed."

Alice fell down a thousand spiral stairs and felt that her brain had gone walkabout. What had she seen two hours previously? A pathetic scrap of humanity, as misshapen a creature as she had ever set eyes on. Yet other things now came into her consciousness. The four ancient candlesticks; the old-fashioned cradle with its velvet hangings; the footman in livery. Had it been possible that she had experienced a moment in which the writer J. B. Priestley so earnestly believed, that all time ran round and round in a continuous circle and that somewhere dinosaurs were still roaring?

"By golly, are you alright? You've gone white as a ghost."

"Sorry. Yes, I'm fine."

"It wasn't me talking about the Monster that frightened you?"

"No, no, honestly. Please go on."

"Well, it was said that he was really the heir, but as he was born such a ghastly mess they hid him away immediately and put it out that he had died. The Countess had another baby a year later and this one was fine. But they kept the other one in the secret room and nobody knew where it was. He had a couple of keepers who used to exercise him at night on the battlements. And apparently the young heir used to be taken to see him on the heir's twenty-first birthday. It was all very depressing."

"I can imagine."

But Alice was answering automatically, her thoughts back in that dark and dreary room—and with the wreck of humanity who had smiled at her.

During that afternoon, looking as inconspicuous as possible, she managed to shake off Ollie and get on the tail end of a group going around Glamis Castle on the two o'clock tour. And somehow, once again, she opened the door in the Crypt, hidden by the thick covering curtain, and began to climb the spiral. But this time, when she was only halfway up, she was met with a wall of solid stone. The staircase had been closed, shut off from human eyes and ears. With a feeling of dread, Alice made her slow way down again. Had she somehow managed to see the Monster of Glamis when he was only a few weeks old? The idea obsessed her, filled her with a longing to see the child once more and assure his carers that he should be encouraged to fulfill his potential and be allowed out into the world of light.

She looked up Alison Lapper on her mobile and saw that that most courageous woman had been born with a condition called phocomelia, which closely paralleled the handicaps of those babies born to women who had taken the drug thalidomide during their pregnancies. The photographs of Alison herself resembled minutely how that little boy she had held for a miraculous moment would have grown up. Somehow—though Alice knew she was not thinking as a logical medical student of the twenty-first century ought to—she determined to see him again. And to try to persuade those looking after him to give the child a bit of scope. But how to slip through the hidden curtain of time and manage it? With a wry smile, Alice thought of herself as a time hitchhiker.

The last tour of the day left at four thirty and, by spending the afternoon trudging round the great gardens and parkland of the castle, Alison managed to avoid Ollie and all the rest of the gang and book herself on it. This time her efforts at disguising herself were pathetic, for the woman selling the tickets said, "My goodness, you must be keen. This is your third visit, isn't it?"

Alice removed a pair of dark glasses. "Yes, it is. Excuse me asking, but do you know what happened to the Monster of Glamis?"

"Yes and no. Presumably he must have died and been buried somewhere or other."

"Did he live a long time then?"

"Oh yes. About ninety years, we reckon. The legend goes that the new heir was shown the secret room when he came of age. Well, it's a fact that the Queen Mother's father was not initiated in 1876 because there would have been no point. The Monster was dead and gone."

"Gosh," said Alice. "It's quite a story."

"Yes, it certainly is. And what is your particular interest in Glamis?"

"Oh, I just like seeing all the precious things and pottering about generally. I hope I'm not a nuisance."

"Oh no, my dear. We could do with a lot more people like you."

So, as the light imperceptibly changed outside, once again Alice hovered in the ranks of the crowd of sightseers, making suitable noises of wonderment as the glorious artifacts of the castle were revealed. And for the third time she slipped behind the curtain in the Crypt—a suitable title for a gothic horror novel, she thought—and set her foot on the lowest step of the spiral staircase. Glancing up, it seemed to her that she could see all the way upward, and so it was with a vague feeling of excited unease that she began to climb. The stone wall was crumbling away, she could hear it. And when she got to the top of those never-ending spiral stairs, the door led off to the right as it had done before. Yet when she opened it, it was to an entirely different scene.

Gone was the cradle and the candles and the gloom, for light poured in from two windows, one on one side of the circular room, the other opposite. There was no baby, but there was a hideously deformed boy sitting in a high chair, his back to her, looking out on the distant parkland below. Disregarding him and playing a desultory game with a grimy pack of cards were two servants, not in livery, but in the country clothes of another century. One looked up as Alice entered.

"Hello. Are you from the kitchens, because he don't want no tea. He's having a sulk."

"No, I'm visiting. I haven't brought anything. I just came to see how he was." The words came out without actually engaging the brain and Alice was grateful that she just hadn't stood silently gawping. "Can I speak with him?" she went on.

They laughed coarsely. "If you can get anything out of him," one answered. "He's in a regular mope today. Like yesterday—and the day before."

Alice nodded and drew level with the side of the chair, looking at the boy intently. He was now about ten years old. His dark hair had been brushed, after a fashion, but not tied back, so that it hung about his face like a cloud. But what a face it was. If had not been for his tragic misshapen body and his sad little feet, he would have been considered beautiful. A brilliant pair of eyes that gazed on the world that he would never be allowed to know glanced at her quickly before turning away once more.

"Hello. I'm Alice. May I ask your name?"

"You can ask, but you won't get," commented one of the servants.

Again that magnificent pair of eyes turned to look at her. They held a look of utter contempt, of total hatred of the world and all who populated it.

"No," he answered.

"Well, that's more than he's said all day."

She persevered. "I'm called Alice. What are you looking at?"

"Isn't it obvious? What I always look at day in, day out. The parkland."

Alice was overwhelmed by the bitterness in the boy's voice. She tried to imagine his existence, captured within his own useless body, with nothing to do for every waking moment. She turned to the warders.

"Can't he read? 'Cos if not, you should teach him. You could give him books. Otherwise his life will be one unrelenting hell."

The child answered for them. "Yes, I can read. Lucy taught me. She was one of my mother's maids who was sent up here to look after me when she got pregnant. Like me, she was not fit for the world to see in that state. But she taught me how to speak. Do you realize that, until she came, nobody had uttered a single word to me?"

"My God, how could people be so cruel?"

"Because I'm a monster. Deformed. Ugly. Hideous."

The boy turned his face away, and Alice could see that tears were running silently on either side of his nose. She couldn't help herself; she knelt by his chair and applied tissues. He snuffled into them, averting his gaze. Alice felt then that for some strange reason—a reason she could not possibly grasp—she must persuade him that, even confined to this room, there was more to life than he was getting.

"I know a woman," she lied, "who looks just like you. She is very beautiful and popular, and she is also a famous artist. She has no arms, so she holds the paintbrush in her mouth, and her work is sought after and people love it—and they love her."

He looked at her fully, turning his head toward her. His eyes were riveting, full of light and brightness.

"Do you really know such a person? You didn't just make her up to please me?"

"Certainly not. Her name is Alison."

The couple playing cards at the table had stopped and were listening with interest. Alice turned to them.

"If you two showed some concern for this child, gave him some paints and paper and brushes, you could make his life a much happier experience. I think it is disgraceful the way he is being starved intellectually."

It was her doctor voice and she knew that they wouldn't understand a great deal of what she was saying but the boy added pathetically, "Please, if they won't, will you get me some?"

"Yes, alright," one of the servants answered. "I'll ask the butler tomorrow. He'll know the right place to go."

The child clapped his little bare feet together to show that he was pleased and Alice smiled.

"I really must go now. But don't sit there and be miserable. Think of Alison and all that she achieves. And promise yourself that you will do likewise."

The gorgeous eyes gazed up at her. "Will you come back tomorrow? Please come and see me. I want you to."

"I'll try, but sometimes finding you can be a bit difficult."

"If you want to enough, you'll know the way."

"Well, I'll say au revoir then."

"But, Alice, you don't even know my name."

"What is it?"

"Alfred. It goes with yours, I think."

"Yes, you're right, it does."

She was out the door before she became any more involved with the tragic, beautiful child. Once more flying down that never-ending staircase, hoping to God that the two oafs who watched over him would have the good sense to carry out her instructions. Another night lay before her, another night of trying to be normal with a bunch of jolly students enjoying a drink. Alice dreaded it.

She had missed the last bus going back to Dundee and had to ring for a taxi, which cost a great deal more than she could actually afford. She sat in its depths wondering how she was going to explain her long absences, a subject which Ollie and Hilary, who had met in the little bistro round the corner, were already discussing at length.

"She's such a strange girl. I sat next to her on the coach and had a great deal of trouble getting her to speak at all." Which wasn't quite true, but it sounded good.

"Yes, I know what you mean. Perhaps she's just not the talkative type. But it's where she keeps disappearing to that puzzles me."

"She's madly in love with Glamis. Been on a couple of tours of the place. Quite frankly, once you've seen it, you've seen it. Now there was a tour of a whisky distillery this morning. Much more my cup of tea, or should I say glass of scotch?"

He roared with laughter at his own joke, and Hilary managed a faint smile before glancing at her watch.

"I wonder where she is now."

"And I wonder if she's got a man tucked away somewhere, possibly works on the Glamis estate."

"Oh, surely not. She lives in London. It would be most inconvenient."

"You mark my words. Stranger things than that have happened."

But at this point, Ollie's words were cut short as Alice came quietly through the door, looking round to see if anyone she knew were present. She looked lovely, quite transformed from the little shy girl on the coach. His suspicions about her having met a man most definitely took root.

"Alice," he called out at top voice. "Over here. Come and join us."

It was the last thing she needed, but politeness and parental guidance won. She crossed over to the table, sat down, and took off her coat.

"What have you been up to?" asked Ollie, leering slightly.

"Nothing, really. I went back to Glamis. There's so much there, I don't think you can take it all in with one visit."

Ollie nodded solemnly. "Of course. We're all different, I suppose."

Hilary spoke up. "Yes, that's what makes us interesting. Being different. I took myself off to a cinema showing classical films of past eras."

"What did you see?"

"An extraordinary film about time travel."

Alice felt a chill start at the base of her spine and work up to her throat. "What was it called?" she croaked.

"*The Amazing Mr. Blunden.* I think it was really aimed at the junior market, but I thought it quite profound. Diana Dors was in it, playing the part of a ghastly old housekeeper called Mrs. Wickens. I never thought she could act until I saw this."

"What was the theme of it?"

"It was about two children who can step back in time and become friends with the children who lived in the house in another century."

"Do you believe that is possible?" asked Alice.

She was actually asking Hilary, but Ollie decided to answer. "No, I don't. It's all jolly good stuff for writers and filmmakers. But I think when you're dead, you're dead. That's it. End of story."

"But what about people who have seen things?"

"Imaginitis. Or wanting to draw attention to themselves. What do you think, Alice? You've gone very quiet."

"I can't begin to give you an answer because I haven't got one. All I know is that it is probably true that time is sequential. Priestley thought so, and he had studied the subject in depth."

"Oh, rubbish. It was convenient for him to think so because he based his plays on that theme. And that is all there is to it. Now what are we all having to eat? Personally, I fancy a pizza."

Realizing that she had not eaten since breakfast, Alice consumed a salad Niçoise. As she slowly ate, she knew with a dreadful certainty that she must go to see the child once more. Why do it to herself, she asked? But really, it wasn't a question of that. She was hopelessly drawn, like an alcoholic to a drink.

She must be satisfied that the two lumpkins who served him had bought him paints and a brush, had given the boy something to live for. If he was alive in his sphere of time, then it should be as bright as she could possibly make it for him.

"Last day tomorrow," Hilary was saying. "I'm off with a party of Jacobites who have promised to show me some interesting sites and sights in the afternoon." She giggled. "Don't forget to board the coach at six o'clock." She looked fixedly at Alice. "You will be there."

"I hope so."

"What kind of an answer is that?" said Ollie. "Come on, spill the beans. Have you got a man somewhere?"

Alice looked at her plate. "No, not exactly."

"What are you saying, Alice? You're being very mysterious."

"I am interested in a child. That's all I'm going to say."

"Where is this child?"

"In Glamis Castle. No more questions, please."

Ollie, with obvious reluctance, dropped the subject and concentrated instead on ordering another large pizza.

She had kept an eye on the staircase all day, waiting for that great stone wall to crumble away, but without any success. She had not gone on any of the tours this time, but had spent what hours she took away from the steps in the cafeteria or the gardens, occasionally joining the other tourists to go to the Crypt and stand beneath the staircase's ghastly never-ending climb toward the turret. At four o'clock, she had become bored with that and had crept up its shadowy length and sat by the wall, clutching her knees and looking downright dejected, waiting and hoping for something to happen. She realized as the last tour of the day went through that she would miss the coach back to London, and wondered if she had gone slightly insane. Then another thought came to torment her. Had she imagined the whole thing? Had the young boy, so horribly deformed, been a trick of her sleeping mind? Was the whole wretched affair a delusion? Had she never seen the baby in the first place?

As the castle settled down for the night, it became eerily quiet. Alice knew perfectly well that somewhere a family dwelled in a comfortable suite of rooms, the Earl and the Countess and their brood of children, possibly an aged relative or two, all had their own quarters. But in this, the oldest part of the castle, where Macbeth, Thane of Glamis and Cawdor, had stalked about, there was nothing but an ear-shattering silence.

Sitting on the stairs as she was, Alice peered down into the cavernous depths at its foot and nearly had a heart attack when she saw a beam of torchlight. Someone was walking about down there, and at any moment she would be revealed if he pointed the torch upward. She pressed her back into the wall, and as she did so, she felt it give a little. She turned. It was crumbling away, and ahead of her she saw the staircase continue. Standing up and stifling a spontaneous cry of joy, she made her way to the top. And then, just as she reached the final step, she stumbled and fell. She gave a cry of fear, which echoed down and down the echoing corridors of time. Then the door flew open and she was encircled by a short, strong pair of arms which pulled her inward.

She fell backward, hitting her head on each stair, so that by the time the night watchman panted up to her she was as dead as it was possible to be. His heart lurched with the usual response to the demise of any young thing that has gone way before its time. Then he left the corpse where he had found it and went down the spiral staircase to telephone the police.

He had been born without arms, so he used his legs, with his big man's feet growing from where his knees should have been. With these locked securely round her waist, he dragged Alice into the warmth and splendor of his room. These days, it resembled an art studio, with dozens of paintings at various stages of development, some only a quarter completed.

"So you've come back to see if I took your advice," he said, and Alice realized that it was a man speaking to her, that what was only a day to her was more like a decade to him. She looked down at him.

The Monster had grown as handsome as hell. His long black hair was brushed neatly into a ponytail, his nose was gorgeous, his chin shaved clean, but his eyes were the feature that made his face quite outstanding. Only someone who had suffered and triumphed could have eyes like that. Alice stared, dumbfounded.

"I'm not going to let you get away this time," he continued. "You see, you changed my life around for me."

"How?" she asked, too breathless to say any more.

"Because I took up painting as you suggested. And I loved it. Moreover, I sell a great deal of my work—the servants acts on my behalf—and I make my own money, and now I can afford to buy things, which I do. How do you like my wheelchair? I had it specially made."

Alice looked down and could not help but notice that a man's torso had replaced that of the small and withdrawn boy. Her breath came rather rapidly.

"Will you stay with me, Miss Alice? Say you won't go away again."

"Yes, I would like to stay."

"For always?"

"For eternity, if you would want me to."

"Until the end of time," he answered, leaning up to kiss her.

***

The police had been unable to trace any living relative of the girl who had died on the staircase, though they had known of her late father, of course. There had been an inquest, naturally, and several of the students who had shared the coach trip with her had been called. They were able to add very little to the story of the loner who had hung around Glamis all the time. Except for Ollie, who had had a field day.

"I believe she had met a secret child," he announced importantly.

"Why do you say that?" inquired the coroner.

"Because she was talking about it at dinner the night before she died. It might even have been her own."

The coroner answered mildly enough, "This woman had had no children, according to the doctor's report."

"Then it must have been someone she met. Possibly another tourist."

The coroner wearily thought that Ollie's type were always a nuisance at inquests, always coming up with totally irrelevant facts.

"Glamis Castle gets a great multitude of visitors," he answered drily, "many of whom the late young woman could have spoken to. And, of course, there is always the Monster lurking about."

He smiled to himself thinly when there was subdued but prolonged laughter in the court room. And some miles away, two little windows gleamed bright as diamonds in the high tower of Glamis Castle.

Gorilla Tactics
ERIC BROWN

Fifty years ago, my grandfather was killed in very peculiar circumstances. I only discovered the details from my mother earlier this year. All I knew before then was that my grandfather had died at the age of sixty-five, long before I was born. My mother rarely mentioned her father, other than to say he was a kind, loving man who had worked as a solicitor in the local town, five miles from the village of Humble Barton where he'd lived for most of his life.

"I've never told you much about Arthur, have I, Edward?" She indicated the black-and-white photograph of a tall gray-haired man in tennis flannels, a briar pipe clenched in his smiling mouth.

It was the occasion of my weekly visit. I poured my mother a cup of Earl Grey and one for myself.

"No, you haven't," I said. "A solicitor, wasn't he?"

She nodded absently, sucking on a bourbon biscuit. "He worked for forty years in the firm of Shackleton, Vine, and Brooke, right here in Sherborne. Nice man. Salt of the earth, people said. Anyway," she went on, "he was murdered."

I lowered my teacup. "Murdered?"

"By a gorilla."

I stared at her. She was getting on—almost ninety—but until now had always struck me as sound of mind.

"A gorilla?" I echoed.

"That's right, a gorilla riding a unicycle."

Before I could ask her if she was feeling well, she continued.

"I'm serious, Edward. I'd just married your father and we'd moved up to London for his work. I had a phone call from your grandfather's neighbor, saying that Arthur was dead and I had to come down. He'd had an accident while crossing the road. I thought she meant he'd been hit by a car—not that he'd been murdered by a gorilla. Anyway, your father drove me down and we did what we had to do, identified the body, and then a nice young constable gave us a cup of tea—it must have been hard for him, come to think of it—and told us how your grandfather had met his end."

"A gorilla," I said, "on a unicycle?"

"One evening in July. It came around the corner, just across from his cottage, and hit Arthur on the head with a hammer. Then it pedaled off down the lane, past the church, and disappeared along Duck Pond Lane. Little Alfie Rhodes saw it all. He was the only witness."

"And did they catch the gorilla?" I asked.

My mother shook her head. "No, Edward. No, they didn't. That's why I'm telling you now. You see, I want you to investigate."

"Investigate?" I spluttered.

"Well, you *are* a crime writer, aren't you?" she said, nodding toward my ranked titles in the bookcase beside the fireplace.

"I write crime novels," I reminded her. "I don't *investigate* crimes. There's a big difference."

"Still," she said, reaching out and gripping my hand with frail, bony fingers, "you'll do it for me, won't you, Edward?"

***

The day after assuring my mother that I'd look into her father's mysterious death, I motored over to Humble Barton and spoke to a few locals.

The evening before, I'd searched online for any mention of the peculiar murder in the summer of 1965, but found nothing. The only tenuous lead I had was the name of the young lad who'd been the only witness, one Alfie Rhodes. I was working on the assumption that, Humble Barton being a tiny village, someone would know if a family by the name of Rhodes still lived in the area.

As events turned out, I was in luck.

I parked outside the Gardener's Arms, climbed out, and looked across the village green—and there it was. A sign hung above an open-fronted garage: *Alfred J. Rhodes and Sons, Vehicle Repairs.*

I wandered over, entered the workshop, and nodded to a grease-stained youth who'd just emerged from under the bonnet of a Fiat 500.

"I don't suppose I could speak to Alfie?" I asked. "Alfie Rhodes?"

"Dad!" he bellowed over his shoulder. "Chap wants a word."

A portly fellow in a navy blue jumpsuit strolled from an office. He had a bald head and a face like a big toe with its nail removed, all bulging brow and pinched features. He wore a pair of thick-lensed glasses and big, beige hearing aids lodged behind his ears.

"Mornin'," he said.

I decided to cut straight to the quick. "You might think this strange," I said, raising my voice, "but I'm inquiring about the death of my grandfather, Arthur Pearson."

"Ah, old Mr. Pearson," he said in the tone of someone recalling a dear friend. "You know, lad, I haven't thought about him for donkey's years. You must be Mary's son, Edward?"

"She asked me to look into the affair," I said. I indicated the public house across the lane. "If you don't mind chatting, and can spare the time, I'll stand you a pint."

"I don't mind at all," he said, and led the way across to the Gardener's Arms.

***

"The coppers thought I was lying," Alfie said, "or seeing things." He took a gulp of bitter. "But I was telling the truth. I was convinced I'd seen a great big gorilla on a 'circus bike'—that's what I told P.C. Evans when he came to take a statement. A circus bike. Didn't know they were called unicycles, you see. Well, I was only seven."

We were sitting at a table outside the pub. I gestured along the quiet lane to the cottage where my grandfather had lived. "How far away were you when you saw the gorilla?"

"Well, I saw your grandpa first. I was coming home from a mate's house around six that evening. Your grandpa, old Mr. Pearson, he was walking along the lane toward his cottage. I was passing the pub, so I'd be…what, fifty yards away?"

I gazed down the lane at the whitewashed thatched cottage. "And then you saw the gorilla?"

He pointed to the lane that formed a junction with the main street. "It came round the corner at a fair lick, it did."

"And you're sure it was a gorilla?"

"Aye, at the time. A big silverback. You see, I was a nature buff back then. I knew my gorillas. I was sure it was a silverback, pedaling a unicycle."

"And it came up behind my grandfather and…"

"It hit him, bop, right on top of his head, and down he went. I watched the gorilla cycle off around the corner down Duck Pond Lane, then I went to see if I could do anything for Mr. Pearson. I took one look at his head, and all the blood, and ran off home in tears. I told me mum what I'd seen and she rang the coppers."

He shrugged. "After I was interviewed, I didn't hear anything else, though much later P.C. Evans ragged me about it. Still does, if truth be told."

"He's still in the village?"

"Aye, retired and bought Mill Cottage, just along Duck Pond Lane."

I watched Alfie Rhodes as he downed his pint. "And what do you think you really saw, Alfie, all those years ago?"

"What do you think?" He grinned sheepishly. "I thought it was a gorilla back then, but thinking about it now… Stands to reason—it was some chap in a gorilla suit, wasn't it? I mean, gorillas can't ride unicycles, can they?"

***

It was the conclusion I'd reached, too, on hearing about the incident from my mother.

I thanked Alfie Rhodes and made my way to Duck Pond Lane, wondering why someone with a grudge against my grandfather, or at least with a motive to murder him, would dress up in a gorilla suit, approach him from behind on a unicycle, and hit him on the head. Riding one of those things would be difficult at the best of times, but would be considerably more so garbed in such a thick, heavy disguise on a warm summer's evening.

Disguise, I thought. That was the reason. Whoever did the deed didn't want to be recognized.

Mill Cottage was a restored flour mill sitting next to the chuckling stream that ran through the heart of the village. I paused at the gate to admire the building, covered as it was in flowering wisteria, and was about to make my way down the garden path when a voice rang out.

"As I live and breathe, I do believe it's Eddie Pearson!"

A bent old man, with a pair of clippers in one hand and a walking stick in the other, beamed at me from a stand of sweet peas.

I crossed the lawn. "That's right—but how on earth...?" I began.

"Never forget a face. Didn't when I was a bobby, and I still don't. My word, young Eddie! You came every summer and stayed with your grandmother. You don't recall me giving you a ride on my bicycle? You must have been three or four at the time." He stared at me. "And you still have the same smile, you do."

I recalled the idyllic summers I spent at Humble Barton with my parents, visiting my widowed grandmother, but I had no recollection of ever meeting the local bobby.

"Anyway, what can I do for you, young Eddie?"

I mentioned my grandfather, and my mother's request, and he gestured across the lawn to a wrought-iron table and suggested we take the weight off our feet.

"No mystery at all," he said as we took our seats. "A gorilla riding a unicycle? Poppycock! Little Alfie was a romancer—still is, the truth be told. What he saw was a chappie on a motorbike."

"A motorbike?" I echoed. "But surely he would have been able to tell the difference? And what about the noise?"

Mr. Evans pointed a finger at me. "Ah, you may well ask. But back then, you see, little Alfie Rhodes was stone deaf. Couldn't hear a thing. He was in his twenties when he had the operation to give him partial hearing. And also, Eddie, he was nearsighted. Consider these facts, together with a lively imagination, and what do you get? A gorilla on a unicycle, that's what."

I frowned at this. "But if it were a motorcyclist," I said, "the fact remains that he murdered my grandfather with a hammer."

But Mr. Evans was shaking his head. "The conclusion my superiors came to is that your grandfather died jumping out of the path of the speeding motorbike and hit his head on the curb. Villagers reported hearing a motorbike around the time of the accident, and a bike was seen by a farmer ten minutes later, racing up the Sherborne road." He shrugged. "The fellow was never apprehended, more's the pity."

***

I took my leave of the old man and motored into town.

I had one more call to make before visiting my mother, as I wanted to know a little more about my grandfather and his line of work.

The venerable company of Shackleton, Vine, and Brooke still occupied the warped, narrow-fronted Tudor building that had been its premises for the past three hundred years. I'd used the firm myself a few years previously, and knew that old Mr. Shackleton still maintained an iron grip on the practice even though he was now in his eightieth year.

A secretary told me he was seeing a client, but would be free in thirty minutes if I'd care to wait. I did so, leafing through a copy of the *Illustrated London News,* and presently the age-blackened timber door creaked open and a young woman appeared, followed by Mr. Shackleton. He was a tall, ascetic-looking man whose choice of black evening wear enhanced his resemblance to a cormorant.

I explained my business, and he replied rather tetchily that he could afford me fifteen minutes of his precious time. "Though I'm sure I can do nothing to enlighten you, Mr. Pearson. A lot of water has passed under the bridge. It must be what, forty, fifty years ago now?"

"More than fifty," I said, following him into his tiny book-lined chamber.

I assured him that I was satisfied, having spoken to various people about the incident, that it had been nothing more than a tragic accident—and went on to say that I wanted, for curiosity's sake, to ask him about my grandfather. "He died before I was born, you see, and I know very little about either his life or his work."

Mr. Shackleton sat back and steepled his fingers before his beak of a nose.

"Your grandfather was," he said, "a respected member of the firm. My father relied on him to run the place, and accordingly allowed him a long holiday every autumn, which he took in Africa with his good friend Lord Hadleigh."

I said that my grandfather's African trips and his friendship with his lordship were news to me, then asked, "And how did you get on with him?"

"I liked Arthur. I was, at the time, being trained up to take over from my father in due course. But I don't mind admitting that I was footloose and somewhat feckless, an attitude which caused my father no little consternation. It fell to your grandfather, on one or two occasions, to have stern words with me about my conduct. I listened to his wise words with respect. He urged me to pay more attention to my work, and to appreciate the privileged position in which I found myself—or, he said, my father might have second thoughts about passing on the business to me. Your grandfather often joked that if he was in control of the firm, he'd sack me!"

"Do you recall the events surrounding his death?"

"A sad day," he murmured. "A very sad day. We were all devastated when we learned of the accident."

"You had no doubt that it was an accident?"

"We were led to believe so, according to police reports. A car, or it might have been a bicycle, mowed into him one evening, and poor Mr. Pearson died instantly. Your grandfather was well liked and didn't have an enemy in the world. No, it was no more than a sad, tragic accident."

***

Later that day I dropped in to see my mother and recount my findings. "It was an accident," I finished, "despite what young Alfie thought at the time."

"That's what the police told me, Edward, but I didn't believe them. And I still don't."

"Why not?" I said. "What on earth made you think that a gorilla killed your father?"

She chewed on her bourbon biscuit for a time, then said, "He was preoccupied, in the days leading up to his death. On my last visit, I could see there was something on his mind. He wasn't quite himself. And then...and then *that* happened."

"But what exactly makes you think a gorilla was responsible, and not someone on a motorbike?"

She stared into space, pensive. "Because of something he said, the last time I saw him. In fact it was the very last thing he did say to me. I asked him if there was something worrying him, and he laughed and said, 'Only an illegal gorilla, Mary'. "

"An illegal gorilla?"

"I asked him what he was talking about, but I was on my way out of the house—your father was impatient to get back to London—and Arthur said he'd explain the next time I visited. Of course, there never was a next time."

"More's the pity," I said.

She took my hand. "But you won't rest till you find out what really happened, will you, Edward?"

I promised that I wouldn't rest, and would report back the following week if I came up with anything.

In the event, I could not report back, because three days later, my mother passed away peacefully in her sleep.

***

All thoughts of my grandfather's peculiar death, and my abortive investigations, were swept aside during the course of the next couple of weeks as I arranged my mother's funeral and sorted out the various legal aspects of her passing.

On the evening of her funeral, I found myself back at her cottage, going through her many possessions and trying to work out what could be sold and what I might retain as keepsakes.

I came across the journals quite by chance. It was almost midnight, and I was about to make my way home when I wondered whether I should check the attic, as I knew my mother had stored boxes and tea-chests up there over the years.

I found the dozen calf-bound journals, in my grandfather's precise copperplate hand, in the first chest I opened. They covered the last thirty years of his life: his exploits during the second World War in Africa, and his less interesting years as a country solicitor. The final volume contained the briefest of jottings, reminders to do household chores, notes on how the garden was coming along, and even descriptions of the weather.

Then I turned to the very last page he had completed, a couple of days before his death, and read: *Worried about his lordship. I don't want to see him get into trouble. I really must go up to Hadleigh Hall and talk to him about that blessed gorilla!*

I stared at the words in the dim illumination of the forty-watt bulb, hardly able to believe my eyes.

His lordship…Hadleigh Hall…gorilla!

I made my way carefully down the stepladder, locked up the house, and decided that tomorrow I would pay a call on his lordship at Hadleigh Hall.

***

The hall was a moldering early Georgian pile lost amid a jungle of rhododendron and reached along a drive made treacherous by potholes. I left

the car near the gates—themselves hanging off their hinges—and made my
way to the hall on foot.

I knew from local gossip that the place was still inhabited. The reclusive
Lord Hadleigh was now in his eighties and rumored to be as mad as a coot.
He hadn't been seen in the village for thirty years, and was looked after by a
woman who popped in every morning and cooked for him. From the state of
the mullioned windows—many of them smashed, and others cloaked in ivy—I
wondered if the hall was indeed habitable, and wouldn't have been surprised
to find his lordship reduced to a skeleton picked clean by rats.

I hammered on a front door made spongy with woodworm and was
surprised when it was opened. A diminutive old woman with cheeks as
wrinkled as wizened apples peered out at me. "Deliveries at the tradesmen's
entrance, young man."

"Actually, I've come to see his lordship," I said quickly before she slammed
the door. "It's Pearson—Edward Pearson. If I could just—"

Then she did slam the door, and I was left staring at the dragon's head
knocker an inch from my nose. I was contemplating trying again when the
door opened and the old dear said, "Mr. Pearson, you said? His lordship'll see
you. Door at the end of the corridor."

I followed her into a dismal, cobwebbed hallway, and she indicated the
nether regions of a darkened passageway. The carpet was mildewed and mice
scurried along the skirting-boards. The air was redolent of fungus and deadly
bacilli. I breathed shallowly and made my way down the dusky corridor.

I knocked on the door and, hearing a grumble from within which I took as
permission to enter, turned the handle and stepped into a chamber of such
Stygian gloom that it took my vision a good ten seconds to adjust.

The first thing I saw was a jaundiced dwarf standing belligerently in the
middle of the room—belligerently because, clutched in his palsied grip, was an
ancient double-barreled shotgun.

Only then did I see the stuffed silverback gorilla in a taxidermist's cabinet at
the far end of the room.

The dwarf bellowed, "Pearson, eh? Back from the dead, are ye?"

I judged it prudent, first, to raise my arms, and then to reassure his lordship
that I was not the Pearson he thought I was.

"Edward," I said. "I'm Edward Pearson, Arthur's grandson."

He peered at me above his weapon. His eyes were as yellow as his skin and his mouth hung open, revealing more gum than enamel.

"Good God, sir! The very image! The spit. Had me going there for a second. Whisky?"

"A double, if you don't mind," I said, following him to a battered, odiferous sofa and sinking into its velvet depths. He flung aside the rifle and poured two generous measures of scotch.

He passed me a glass and slumped down on the sofa. He stank of mothballs and alcohol, and his slippered feet hung inches shy of the threadbare Persian rug.

"I've come," I began, after sampling the rather fine single malt, "about—"

He stopped me. "I know why you're here, Pearson. Been waiting half a century for someone to cotton on. Took your time, didn't you?"

I glanced across the room at the stuffed gorilla, and I swear he stared back at me with a hostile gleam in his eyes. "Well, that is…" I began.

"I feared the police would be onto me quick sharp, once that little Rhodes brat blabbed. Then I heard on the grapevine that the police thought it was an accident, some chappie on a motorbike." He peered at me. "But you know better, hey?"

"As a matter of fact, I find it impossible to believe—"

"I summoned your grandfather to sound him out." His lordship slurped his whisky. "Needed his advice. Thought I might be in a bit of hot water."

"Hot water?"

"Manner of speaking. Y'see, I imported Bertie without a license."

"Bertie?"

He pointed at the stuffed gorilla. "Found him in Gabon when I was out there in '59. Wanted to start a bit of a zoo. Always liked gorillas. Noble beasts. He was an orphan—his parents had been shot—and was about to be sold to natives for the cooking pot. So I bought him for ten guineas and had him shipped back on the quiet. Only then, when he was resident at the hall, did I wonder if I needed a license. So I called on your grandfather for his advice. Good man, old Arthur."

"And what did he say?"

"Came up here the day he died," Lord Hadleigh said, "and he advised me to keep schtum as I'd be in bother if I admitted to illegally importing a gorilla."

"I see," I said, taking another sip of his exceptional scotch. "But what I can't quite fathom is how Bertie came to kill my grandfather."

"Easily explained, young man: he escaped. Just after Arthur took his leave."

"Escaped?" I shook my head. "But…but was he riding a unicycle?"

"Of course he was. Talented fellow, old Bertie. I taught him to juggle, walk a tightrope, play croquet, and ride a unicycle. And then, that evening just after I'd seen Arthur, he skedaddled, hopped on his bike, and off he shot. I followed him in the Wolseley, or rather tried to. But he lost me on the way to the village. Found him an hour later, taking forty winks under a hedge. I bundled him into the car and drove back here. Didn't know about poor Arthur at the time, though."

"When did you find out?"

"When Mrs. Harper came in the following day and told me what young Alfie Rhodes was claiming. No one knew about Bertie, of course, other than me and Mrs. Harper, and I bribed her to keep mum."

I shook my head, mystified. "But why did Bertie kill…?" I began. "No," I went on, "Bertie didn't kill my grandfather with a hammer, did he? He probably startled him, and Arthur fell and struck his head."

His lordship remained silent, staring at me with melancholy in his jaundiced eyes. He pointed a dithering finger at a thick photograph album on a nearby table. "Be so kind, would you?"

I hauled the album to the sofa and his lordship sat with it on his lap and opened the cover as if it were a trapdoor.

He showed me a dozen photographs of Bertie in various extravagant poses: Bertie juggling, Bertie walking a tightrope in the grounds of the hall, Bertie clutching a croquet mallet, and, of course, Bertie perched improbably atop a silver unicycle.

"I lived in fear of the police finding out," he went on, "so I kept Bertie confined to the house and abandoned any idea of starting a menagerie. I was overcome with guilt, though, over your grandfather's death. He was a fine man, and met an undignified end."

I drank to that, and said, "And Bertie?"

"He took to ruby port in his old age," Lord Hadleigh said. "We spent many a long evening in this very room, listening to Wagner and sharing a bottle. Passed away in his late thirties. Cirrhosis, I suspect."

His lordship was leafing absently through the album, his eyes misty with nostalgia. He stopped when he came to a photograph showing a chap in a pith helmet, his right foot lodged on the carcass of a male lion.

"Who…who's that?" I said, pointing with a tremulous finger.

"Why," he said, "that's your grandfather, Arthur."

I stared at the photograph, incredulous.

"And it was he," I managed at last, "who shot Bertie's parents, right?"

Hadleigh sighed. "As a matter of fact, it was," he said. "That's why I asked Arthur up here. He knew all about Bertie, you see, and I could trust him to be discreet." He shook his head sadly. "How was I to know what would happen…?"

I studied the photograph of the big-game hunter, my grandfather.

I looked up from the album and stared across the room at Bertie. No, I thought, surely not. Even gorillas, I told myself, were not that intelligent. And surely they couldn't bear grudges…*could they?*

Bertie the gorilla stared glassily from his final resting place, and I swore that he was grinning at me with posthumous, primate satisfaction.

The Golden Princess
JANE FINNIS

I got up with the sun as usual. If you're an innkeeper, early rising goes with the job. And on this fresh autumn morning, it was no hardship anyway. In October in Britannia, on the northern fringes of the Empire, the sun rises quite late.

I was loitering outside on our paved forecourt, enjoying the sweet morning air, when a horseman came charging up the road as if the Parthian cavalry were chasing him. Well, that's not the right description really, because this horseman was Valens, an officer from the Ninth Legion, and if the Parthian cavalry were anywhere in our neighborhood, *he'd* be chasing *them*.

Valens was one of our favorites at the Oak Tree. Whenever he was home on leave staying with his father, a retired general who lived near us, he was a regular customer, good company, and a generous spender. But I couldn't imagine why he was heading for our door at full gallop at this hour. Clearly it wasn't a social call. His expression was grim, and he and his horse were sweating.

When he saw me, he pulled up and jumped down even before his horse had stopped moving.

"Aurelia! Thank the gods you're awake!" He hurried over to me. "I came as soon as I heard. What's happened?"

"Morning, Valens. You're an early bird! I don't normally expect customers at this time of day. What's up? Has your father run out of beer again?" This was an old joke between us, but today it wasn't well received.

"If only it was something that simple," he snapped. "What's going on? What's happened to the Golden Princess?"

"The Golden Princess? You mean the statue?"

"Of course, the statue!" he was almost shouting. "Delivered here yesterday for safekeeping, to be collected by my father's people this morning. So what's gone wrong? I repeat, what's happened to it?"

"Nothing, as far as I know. Yes, it was left here as arranged yesterday afternoon, and we've kept it safely locked up. Everything's gone according to plan. All we need now is transportation to take it to your father's villa. You can use one of our carts if you like…"

"Don't play games, Aurelia." His expression had changed from anxious to angry, and he stared at me as he might have stared at an insubordinate young legionary who had fallen asleep on sentry duty. "Just tell me the worst. What's happened to the Golden Princess?" Now he really was shouting.

"Valens, calm down. I don't know what you're talking about. Nothing's gone wrong. The statue is here in a locked room, as I promised your father. I even put a man outside on guard all night. It's quite safe."

"But we both know that isn't true!"

I wasn't going to stand for being called a liar. "Look, I can see you're worried and I'll do my best to help, but you're not making much sense. Just tell me quietly from the beginning what the trouble is. We're not on a parade ground, and I'm not one of your men, to be bawled at for no good reason."

That stopped him dead in his tracks. I suppose he wasn't used to people talking back when he ordered them about. But I'm a centurion's daughter. I'm not afraid of soldiers, even angry ones.

He took a few deep breaths and made an effort to relax. "I'm sorry, Aurelia. It's just that I'm so worried by what's happened to the statue. We got this message and I came straight here. And yet you tell me nothing's wrong?"

"Come with me, I'll show you."

We'd locked the big wooden chest containing the statue in an old tack room with a solid door and a good lock. I'd arranged for my handyman Taurus to stand guard all night outside it. He was still there, a giant of a man, armed with a huge cudgel. He smiled at us as we approached.

"Good morning, Taurus. Everything alright?"

"Morning, Mistress…morning, Tribune. Yes, all's well here. A nice peaceful night. The box is ready for you to take away."

"There," I turned to Valens. "As I said. Tribune Valens was afraid something had gone wrong."

Taurus shook his head. "No, sir, everything's fine."

"Thank the gods. But all the same, can we see inside?"

"Of course." I unlocked the big wooden door and flung it wide.

The bare little room looked just the same, dusty and untidy in the dim light from its small unglazed window. The wooden crate still stood on the earthen floor in the center. But it was empty.

It was wide open, its wooden lid wrenched off and lying alongside it. It contained a few handfuls of straw, presumably packing material for the statue. Nothing else.

Behind me, I heard Taurus gasp. I said some words a lady shouldn't know, let alone utter.

"What did I tell you?" Valens wasn't shouting now, but was still very angry. "It's gone. Stolen. How could you let this happen, Aurelia?"

For a few heartbeats, I was too stunned to answer. In the end, I said the only thing I could say.

"I don't know. I don't understand it."

Taurus looked as shaken as I felt. "Mistress Aurelia, where can it have gone? I was here on guard the whole time, all night long, I promise. And I didn't hear or see nothing."

Taurus may not be the brightest of my slaves, but he's as honest as the day. "I believe you, Taurus." I looked at Valens. "Taurus always tells the truth, Valens. If he says he was here the whole time, then he was."

"Maybe so. But he could have been helping the thieves. Leaving the door unlocked and taking a walk while they came in and emptied the crate. Did you have some arrangement with them, boy? Were you hoping for a share of the proceeds?"

"Of course not!" Taurus appeared close to tears. "Please, sir, you must believe me. I didn't have the key to unlock this room. And anyhow I'd never steal from the mistress, or you, or help someone else to steal. I swear by all the gods…" Suddenly he looked frightened and touched the little amulet, shaped like a bull's head, that he wore on a cord round his neck. "It's something wicked, some kind of sorcery, it must be. To make a golden statue vanish away like this. Could be evil spirits maybe, or perhaps the gods are angry."

Valens paused, then seemed to make up his mind. "Alright, if Aurelia vouches for you, I have to believe you had nothing to do with this. And you're right, it's something wicked, but it's the work of men, not spirits. I knew it. That's why I'm here…because we had a message."

"Who from?" Taurus and I asked together.

"I don't know who they are. But they've stolen the Golden Princess, and they expect us to pay to get it back. Their message is in fact a ransom demand."

"So the statue must be valuable, then?" It was a rhetorical question really. If the rumors that had been flying about lately were even half true, it was worth a small fortune, made of solid gold. Now that I thought about it, I was surprised its delivery had been in the hands of just two men and a boy. Surely it should have had an armed escort?

The tribune interrupted my thoughts. "It's valuable alright. Made by a famous sculptor from Gaul. Father was very proud to have gotten it done by someone so well-known."

And he had boasted about it a little too freely, I thought, but didn't say.

"Is the statue of a real princess?" Taurus asked.

"No, it's of a horse. My mother's favorite mare, Princess. She died last year and Mama was so sad. Father had the statue made for her birthday to try and cheer her up. It will, too, I think, she truly loved that animal. Or should I say it would have done…"

He trailed off, glancing helplessly round the little square room, and I did the same, desperately trying to think what could have happened. It held no furniture, and the walls were festooned with broken bits of old harness hanging on nails. The high small window was the only way in or out apart from the door, and it was too small for a man to get through from the outside, even with help to climb up from the ground.

Valens clenched his fists in frustration. "Gods alive, it doesn't make sense. It's impossible."

A voice behind us said, "What's happening here?" It was my sister Albia, my housekeeper at the Oak Tree in those days. She smiled at Valens, but her smile vanished as she saw our grim faces. "Why, what's the matter? Why are you all looking as if someone has just died? Jupiter, Mars, and Juno, what's happened to the Golden Princess?"

"That's what I'm trying to find out," Valens answered. "It seems to have been stolen last night from under your noses."

"Stolen from here? That's plain impossible, Valens." Her reaction was so like everyone else's that I almost laughed aloud. "Plain impossible" just about summed the situation up.

But her next words were more cheerful. "Look, this needs thinking about carefully and calmly. I don't suppose any of you have had any breakfast yet? I certainly haven't."

We shook our heads.

"Then let's have something to eat and put our heads together. As our grandmother used to say, empty stomachs lead to empty minds. So come into the barroom—you too, Taurus—and we'll sit down and try to work out what's happened."

The atmosphere relaxed as soon as the food and drink arrived. Fresh bread, cheese, and watered wine made a good breakfast, and soon Valens was starting to realize that there was no point in regarding us as enemies. We were on the same side, as shocked as he was, and we all needed to work as allies.

Again I asked him about the message he'd received telling him the statue had been stolen.

He drew a wax note-tablet from his belt pouch. "This was left outside our door sometime in the night. It must have been done quietly, because whoever it was didn't set the dogs off." He handed it to me. "See what you make of it."

The tablet was old and worn. The writing was crude, the spelling atrocious. It had clearly been done by someone not very fluent in Latin. But it wasn't hard to make out the sense of it.

"If you want your golden princess, send one man alone with a bag of fifty silver pieces to the nine pines turnoff at sunset. Leave it under the tallest tree and come back at sunrise. The statue will be there. No tricks, mind, or we'll melt it down."

So it was indeed a straightforward ransom demand. My first thought was, these men must know this area well. The nine pines where two small roads joined were a local landmark, remote yet distinctive among our oak woods, and an ideal spot for secret dealings.

I looked at Valens. "Would your father pay the money, do you think?"

He nodded. "Oh, yes, if he has to. That's to say he'll pretend to pay, but set a trap for the thieves. It shouldn't be too hard; we've enough military experience between us to ambush a bunch of amateurs. But he's not exactly happy, and he blames you for letting the theft happen."

"And you?" I had to ask. "Do you still blame us?"

He paused, then answered firmly. "No. I don't think you could have done more than you did, and I don't believe anyone here was party to it."

"Thank you."

There was an awkward silence, broken by Albia. "They'd melt down a valuable gold statue? How appalling!"

"If they thought it was solid gold, they're in for a disappointment," Valens said drily. "Even my father isn't that rich. It's bronze."

"How big is it?" I asked. "What I mean is…if the thieves didn't take it out through the door, they must have used the window. Could it have gone through such a small opening?"

"It must have done." Valens took a thoughtful sip of his wine. "I've never seen it, of course, none of us have. But I know it was supposed to be nothing like a life-sized horse. I assume that wooden chest it came in was designed for it to fit snugly."

"I don't know about that," Taurus spoke up for the first time. "It's nothing special, that crate, a bit flimsy if you ask me. I'd have expected a much nicer box for something so valuable. But it did the job, I suppose. It looked quite heavy, when I saw the driver and his friend unload it from the carriage. Scruffy old carriage it was, to be making such an important delivery."

Valens said sharply, "It arrived in a carriage? Not an army wagon?"

"That's right, sir. A real old bone-shaker. The driver and his escort were scruffy too, and the mules were scrawny, and never been groomed for days by the looks of them."

"That's odd," Valens commented. "Father arranged for it to be delivered in the usual sort of military transport, attached to one of the army convoys. It was my idea to have it left here, so it would be a surprise for Mama on her birthday."

"The whole setup seemed a bit odd, now I come to think about it. You don't suppose…no, it's too far-fetched."

"What is, Aurelia?"

"It's just something that's been puzzling me. Who knew that the Golden Princess would be here last night? Apart from me and Albia, and we'd told nobody. And your father and you, and a few people at the villa, Valens?"

"Only a couple. Reliable men."

"Otherwise, only the delivery men themselves knew the details. They not only knew it would be here, but they personally inspected where it was to be kept! All sorts of people might have wanted to steal the Princess, but only those two knew exactly when and where to find her."

Valens thumped the table excitedly. "By the gods, I think you've answered one question at least. Who carried out this theft? The delivery men. Yes, it must have been." He glanced round the table at each of us in turn. "So now, all of you, can you cast your minds back to yesterday afternoon and tell me every detail of what happened when they came?"

"They certainly weren't the usual sort of army delivery men," I said. "Nothing to do with the army, I'd say. Native British lads. As my father used to say, 'Typical barbarians, with bad clothes, bad breath, and bad Latin.' "

"All I remember," Albia put in, "is that sweet little boy they had with them. Running and jumping and climbing up the oak tree…And his masters were so horrible to him, when you'd have thought they'd be rather proud."

"A little boy?" Valens echoed. "This delivery sounds stranger and stranger. What time did they get here?"

"About two hours after noon, I think." I searched my memory for details of the day before. I should have paid more attention when the carriage arrived. But it came just when the black-and-white kitten had got itself stuck in our big oak tree. The silly little furball was sitting on a high branch, mewing plaintively, while I and Albia and Taurus and a couple of the barmaids stood beneath, wondering how to rescue it. Calling it had no effect, nor had putting a plate of tempting food on the ground. What else could we try?

I remember how we all turned to watch as a small closed carriage approached, accompanied by a rider on horseback. They trotted onto the forecourt and parked the vehicle in the corner farthest away from the oak tree with its marooned cat.

A closed carriage is unusual, and often contains rich travelers. But this one was a disappointment, scruffy and uncared for, with poor-quality mules and an unkempt native driver and escort. Oh well, not a party of rich Roman holidaymakers then, touring Britannia on a pleasure trip, ordering the best wine and food their money could buy. My attention turned back to the kitten.

Then the carriage door burst open and a small boy jumped out. Another native, about seven or eight years old, with red curly hair and a cheeky grin. He was an attractive child, despite his patched tunic and bare feet, and full of energy. He started running around the forecourt, jumping and doing cartwheels and yelling joyfully, the way children do, just for the love of it.

I glanced inside the carriage, but there weren't any other passengers, just a pile of threadbare cloaks, three army-type water bottles, a basket of apples, and a large wooden crate.

"We're not stopping long, boy," the driver called. "So don't you go running off."

"I won't, Master. But look, that little cat is stuck." The lad ran toward the oak tree and called up to the kitten, "Poor kitty, shall I come up and get you down?" Without waiting for an answer, he began climbing the tree, as quick and agile as a cat himself.

The driver swore at him, but the little scamp took no notice and just climbed higher.

"I mean it, boy. We'll be off in no time at all," the driver shouted. "If you get stuck too, we'll leave you behind, and you'll have a nasty cold dark night up there."

"I expect I'll have a nasty cold dark night anyway," the boy muttered, loud enough for me to hear, but fortunately his master missed the comment. By now he was level with the kitten, and he calmly reached out a hand and gathered it to his chest. The cat, recognizing a rescuer when it saw one, kept still while the lad carried it carefully down. When he'd touched ground and released it, everyone had cheered.

Well, everyone except the driver, who was still angry. He'd advanced on the boy and grabbed him by the tunic. "You little pest, I've told you before I don't want you making a spectacle of yourself!" He caught him a vicious blow on the side of his head. "Now get back in the carriage and stay there."

"But I was only…"

His master gave him another sharp blow, which made him start to cry. "Enough! Get off with you." He dragged the lad partway toward the carriage, and stood watching till he'd gone the rest of the distance and shut himself in.

Beside me, Albia murmured, "Poor little scrap. He deserves better than that."

"He does." But of course I couldn't interfere openly. Customers are always right, even unpleasant ones.

"If you can keep the men distracted," she whispered, "I'll take the child some cakes when nobody's looking."

"Good idea." Wearing my best smile, I turned to face the driver as he and his escort strode up. "Can I help you?"

"You the innkeeper?"

"Yes. Aurelia Marcella, at your service." Though the service wouldn't be anything special, I decided. "Can I get you a drink?"

"No. Got a delivery for the General at Oak Bridges," he said brusquely, but in quite good Latin.

"Ah yes, we're expecting it. He's asked us to keep it safe here tonight, and his men will collect it from us tomorrow."

"That's right. And we're to check out where you're going to store it tonight. Make sure it's secure."

"Fine, if you like. But you can trust us with it, we're quite used to…"

"General's orders," he snapped. "Very valuable this delivery is, we can't take chances. A gold statue of a princess. Present for his wife."

"Right. There's a good lockup in the stable yard. If you'll follow me…"

When we reached the old tack room, they both made a great show of inspecting the door and lock, the wooden walls, and the high unglazed window. "It'll do," the driver said. "I'll drive round so me and my mate can unload it. Weighs a ton, it does."

"It didn't look that heavy," Taurus chipped in. "I offered to help, but they wouldn't let me. I suppose they wanted to be extra careful, with the crate not being all that strong."

And as soon as the box was safely inside and the door was locked, the two men had mounted up and driven off, without another word.

"What about the little boy?" Valens asked.

"Inside the carriage, presumably," Albia said. "But I managed to slip over to see him while the men were with Aurelia, and I gave him a drink of milk and some raisin cakes. He was thrilled, and he was so sweet. He kept calling me 'pretty lady,' and thanking me over and over. He wanted to know if the kitten was alright. I assured him it was, thanks to him." She finished her wine. "I hope when he's older he manages to get away from those horrible masters."

I looked at Valens. "I'd say that it's pretty conclusive, wouldn't you? Those so-called delivery men knew exactly where the statue was, and came back in the night to steal it. That little boy who climbed like a cat must have got through the window into the room, and somehow managed to push the statue out to the men waiting outside."

Valens was jubilant. "It all fits together! And once they'd taken the statue, they drove to Father's villa and left the ransom note. They assumed nobody would work out how they'd done it; they wanted you to get the blame for not guarding the box properly. They hadn't reckoned on you putting a man on guard as extra protection. Your idea, Aurelia, presumably?"

"Yes, it was."

"Didn't do much good though, did I?" Taurus asked. "And we still don't know how they got the Golden Princess out of there. They must have made some noise, the lad climbing into the room, opening the box, and then getting himself and a bronze statue through that little opening. But I didn't hear nothing. Wait, though…" he paused. "I did hear the dogs barking, the ones in the pen near the horse paddocks. Something set them off in the dark. Could just have been a fox, of course."

"You didn't go and investigate?" Valens asked.

"No, sir. I reckoned my job was to stay near the box. If I'd gone over to the paddocks, there'd have been nobody to guard the door."

Valens nodded. "Fair enough. And it's more proof that there were intruders here last night." He got to his feet. "I suggest we all go back to the tack room to see whether there are any signs of them there."

We began outside, underneath the window, but found nothing useful. We'd been hoping for footprints; there were none, because as it happened there were paving stones there, not bare earth. Nor were there any footmarks on the wooden wall showing where someone might have clambered up. The boy must have been hoisted on his master's shoulders. Perhaps there were traces on the dusty floor inside? We were all turning to go and look when Albia pointed at the window itself.

"Here's something!" she exclaimed. "See how all the other windows along this row of buildings are covered in huge cobwebs? Some even have spiders in them. Nobody ever bothers clearing them out. But this one is completely clear." She was right. Something—or somebody—had pushed their way through, dislodging the spiders' webs.

Inside we found scuff marks in the dust below the window, where the boy's feet had landed when he jumped down. I tried to picture what it must have been like for him, literally taking a leap in the dark into a pitch-black room, with nobody to catch him or even soften his landing. I doubted I could have done that, and I found myself thinking that though he was a thief, he was a brave one.

Yet still, none of us could fathom how he'd managed to lift the statue up and out of the window. Perhaps they'd used some clever arrangement of ropes? Maybe the men had lowered a rope through the window from outside, and he'd somehow lashed it to the statue so they could haul it out?

Taurus, who'd been examining the crate, startled us all with a delighted shout. "Hey! I can see how they got this box open without making a noise. When I saw the top with all the nails holding it down, I was thinking they'd make a real din just prizing them out. But look, nearly all of them nails have been lined up wrong, so they aren't holding the lid on at all. They're just dangling down inside. Anyone could easily get the thing open, as quiet as a mouse."

"Well spotted, Taurus," Valens said. "That's why they didn't want you to get too close when they were unloading."

He began rooting through the straw in the crate. "Jupiter, now what's this doing here?" He pulled something out of the straw and held it up for us all to see.

It was a half-eaten raisin cake.

"Gods alive," Valens said. "So that's how it was done. The boy never had to break in here at all. He just had to break out."

Back in the barroom, I poured us out more wine and raised my beaker. "We've solved it! The box was empty when it arrived at the Oak Tree, till one small boy crawled inside it, to wait for darkness."

"I don't want to rain on your triumph," Albia said, "but we've only partly solved it. Where's the statue now?"

"Well...the men have hidden it in the woods to pick it up later."

"But where?"

Valens was smiling as he raised his beaker to me. "We don't need to go looking for it. We'll go through the motions of paying their ransom, and they'll bring it to us." He finished his wine. "So thank you, all of you, for uncovering the secret. Now I must be off home to Father to make arrangements for tonight. Setting up an ambush...that's meat and drink to us."

"I wish I could be there to watch," I said, but of course I knew it wasn't possible. I'd have to wait with as much patience as I could muster till sunrise tomorrow.

"I'll bring you the good news when it's all over," Valens promised as he rode away.

Next day we were all wide awake and waiting on the forecourt when Valens made his second early-morning visit. But this time he wasn't galloping in panic; he was trotting in triumph, and he carried on his saddle a bundle wrapped in a cloak.

"Morning, Valens. Successful night?"

"Completely, Aurelia, thank you. The men brought the statue back and then tried to run for it, but we caught them. They'll make useful slaves in the army."

I pointed at his saddle. "Surely you haven't brought the Golden Princess with you?"

"No, she's safe at the villa, and my mother is delighted. I've brought you..." but he never finished the sentence, because the cloaked bundle came to life and a small boy sprang down from the horse and made straight for Albia.

"Pretty lady! Pretty lady! I want to stay with you. Can I?"

Albia was smiling, but she tried to sound serious. "Well, I'm not sure, you young rascal. Valens, don't you want him? Or your father? He's yours by rights."

He shook his head. "We've no use for him, and we probably couldn't keep him anyway, if he's made up his mind to come and find his pretty lady." He smiled at Albia. "Your admirers get younger and younger. He's all yours if you want him."

Albia gazed at the boy with what was meant to be a stern expression. "If you stay, you must promise to be good. No more stealing, ever again."

"No more, ever again. I promise."

"Aurelia? What do you think?"

"It's alright by me, as long as he's prepared to work. Will you work for us? We won't ever shut you in a box, I can promise you that."

"Yes, I will. And I'll rescue all your kittens whenever they get stuck."

Everyone laughed, and Albia bent and hugged him. "Then of course you can stay. Welcome to the Oak Tree."

The Case of the Impossible Suicides

JOHN GRANT

So what exactly is all this about, er… What did you say your name was?" Sir Basil Derringpole puckered his lips as if the very words of the English language were distasteful to him.

"Chaveney," I said, "Jack Chaveney. I married your niece last year."

"Ah, yes." He dabbed fastidiously at those lips with a spotlessly white handkerchief. "A lovely wedding. Quite lovely."

He hadn't in fact been there, instead sending us a matching set of black Bakelite ashtrays that Cynthia had incorporated into the rockery she was building.

"I've been researching—" I started.

"You're the scribbler, aren'tcha, young man?"

"I write detective stories for a living, yes. You may have read some of them."

"Doubt it. Dashed foolish, detective stories. Nothing like the real thing."

I looked at him dourly, ruefully conceding that, if anyone was qualified to make this judgment, it was Cynthia's Uncle Basil. He was employed by some mysterious department of the Home Office to do work about which he wasn't allowed to talk. In his spare time, of which it seemed he had a plethora, he assisted the police in some of their most intractable criminal investigations. The Case of the Supernumerary Widow. The Incident of the Dog's Ball. The Horrific Affair of the One-Eyed Basilisk. Great titles for novels I'd never write. All of these investigations and more had made the front pages of our lower-browed press, and even some of the higher-browed papers had on occasion deigned to pay heed. Not that Sir Basil's name was ever mentioned publicly in connection with such sensational matters, of course. But his superiors knew, and his family knew, and even I, as the most recent addition to the family bar the newborn Earl of Crumford, knew.

In short, Sir Basil Derringpole was a man of distinction. He was also, as I'd discovered over lunch here in the Runagates Club—badly cooked beef olive embellished with suet pudding, followed by a selection of cheeses, all of them leathery cheddar—a crashing bore. The conversation had been worse than the food.

Now, as he turned his watery blue eyes on me, waiting for my response, I reflected that all his vacuous aristocratic look of condescension needed was the addition of a pince-nez to make his face a *Backpfeifengesicht*, as the Germans say—a face badly in need of a fist.

To be honest, I wasn't altogether sure about the necessity of the pince-nez. My hands had instinctively clenched at first sight of him.

"That may be so," I said grimly. "But the public seems to disagree. My books sell in the kind of numbers that'll ensure your niece should never need for anything."

"Ah, the public," he responded with an airy wave of his hand to show what he thought of the common herd. "Tell me, Mr. Man of Mystery, why is it you were so eager to consult me?"

He looked at me over the silvery reflective brim of a brandy snifter that was about the size of a goldfish bowl.

"Well, you see…" I began.

***

Most of the other successful mystery writers today—my peers—invent their plots out of whole cloth.

Not me. Although I don't base my novels on actual real-life cases, I do in-depth research to make sure my "impossible" crimes bear some resemblance to what could be achieved in reality. Yes, to choose a single example from an old John Dickson Carr novel, you could use a tennis net as an instrument of strangulation, but setting up the circumstances to do so without any footprints appearing on the surface of the clay court is not something that can be credibly explained without resort to what's really fantasy.

The novel I was currently researching—contracted by its publisher on the basis of a surprisingly vague two-page outline and due for delivery in about three months' time—was to be called *The Case of the Impossible Suicides*. As always, it would feature my argumentative series protagonists: feisty Hebridean postmistress Agnes Pibroch and tough Glaswegian cop Archibald "Tosh" Mackintosh. United by a friendship deeper than love, these two had bickered their way through a dozen cases together, were adored by countless readers around the world, and would soon, with luck, be the basis for a TV series from Acorn Entertainment.

I normally write my novels in a couple of months, no more, so the deadline wasn't concerning me. But the research—unusual suicides over the past decade or so—had turned up some questions I hadn't expected.

I took a large manila envelope from the briefcase by the side of my chair. "Let me show you something."

He gave an ostentatiously weary sigh. "If you insist, dear boy. So long as it doesn't threaten to spoil this excellent brandy."

I paused with my hand inside the opening of the envelope. For the first time, I noticed his bow tie. Not the tie itself—it was hard to miss, being large and bright red and floppy—but the fact that it bore, neatly embroidered on each of its wings, the Derringpole family coat of arms.

Sir Basil glanced at me again with what I'm sure he thought was an encouraging smile. "Do show, young fellow."

I pulled forth the first of the printouts I'd brought. "See what you think of this."

He took the stapled sheets of paper from me and rapidly began to scan them, brow furrowed.

COLONEL E.A. HUMBLEBY-DICKENS FOUND DEAD IN BATHTUB BY DAUGHTER

read the headline, which I'd discovered on the website of the *West Marple Times & Gazette*.

> *Colonel Edwin Ashton Humbleby-Dickens, 68, noted local grandee and devotee of the turf, was discovered drowned in his bath on Monday by his daughter, glamorous mother-of-two Belinda Troughton, 39. Mrs. Troughton had to break the locked door down to reveal the bathroom's grisly secret. "Of course it was a shock," she told reporters at her Kensington home. "He'd seemed a little quiet recently, but nothing you could put a finger on." Mrs. Troughton added: "His mind was still as sharp as a tack, if that's what you're trying to suggest. Now I'd beg you to leave his loving family to grieve in peace."*

There was a photo of Belinda Troughton clutching little Ronnie, seven, and even littler Lucy, four, to her side. She was a handsome woman in a firm-jawed sort of way, and they were equally handsome children.

"And this is of interest because?" said Sir Basil, waving the sheets in my direction.

I took another sip of my Perrier. "Read on."

> Colonel Humbleby-Dickens, who retired from the army in 2006 at the end of a distinguished career in Whitehall, had become known as one of the most flamboyant habitués of the track. Rumors have swirled in recent years that "Champagne Eddy's" lavish lifestyle and reckless gambling had led him to amass enormous debts, and that Humbleby Hall has been mortgaged to the hilt. Questioned on these matters, Mrs. Troughton retained a dignified silence. Divisional Chief Inspector Andrew Gillup, 48, told reporters that the police do not suspect foul play, and the verdict at the inquest is expected to be that Colonel Humbleby-Dickens took his own life. "He must have realized the financial walls were closing in," said Inspector Gillup, "and decided to end it all, like so many before him, with a bottle of gin, a hot bath, and a razor blade." As testament to a life spent playing the odds, the colonel died with a poker chip from London's Blazing Saddles Casino in his hand. The chip bore the logo of one of Las Vegas's most notorious casinos, the Blazing Saddles.

"The Blazing Saddles," said Sir Basil ruminatively. "Never heard of it."
"Me neither," I said.

"Believe I once met Humbleby-Dickens, though, now I come to think of it. Not at a racetrack. Or a casino, for that matter. Some diplomatic event or other, as I recall. Ghastly little man. Wore brown brogues. But I don't see why I should be interested in…"

"And then there's this." I passed him another of my printouts.

STRING UP YOURS, MATEY!

Sun Journalist Hanged Self In Barn

Sir Basil sniffed, and pushed his nonexistent pince-nez further up on his nose. "Typical *Daily Mail* error-strewn nonsense," he said.

"It is?"

"They called the man a journalist."

His eyes flicked from side to side as he read on.

Debt-ridden Sun journalist Dwight Gee, 62, decked himself by deliberate suicide, curvaceous coroner Elaine Braithwaite, 43, said Thursday, concluding the inquest into the newspaper's top poker correspondent. "He went into the barn of his Cotswolds farm, locked and bolted all the doors, then hanged himself from an uppermost rafter."

"There again," commented Sir Basil, whom I was reluctantly starting to like. "Newspaper…"

"He must have been dissatisfied with the hand life dealt him," his widow, retired model Beth Gee, 37, said in a Mail EXCLUSIVE. Gee came to fame in August 2015 when convicted of cheating the house at the Horny Donkey casino in pulsating Edgware, and served three months of a six-month sentence. Since then he has made guest appearances on such shows as Strictly Come Dancing. "My Dwight loved the tables," said Beth. Tucked into his shirt pocket, scene-of-crime officers discovered when they cut him down, was a poker chip from the Blazing Saddles Saloon in Las Vegas. "It was his way of saying," Beth Gee told our reporters, " 'So long and thanks for all the chips'. "

"There's more of this?" Sir Basil said gloomily.

"You're beginning to see a pattern?" I countered.

"I'd be very stupid not to. Let me see what you have."

He reached across the table for the rest of the contents of my manila envelope, then settled down to read.

Minutes passed.

I could well imagine the thoughts that were passing through his head.

There was Lady Letitia Teakettle, who'd thrown herself down the well at Brobdingnag Abbey in Yorkshire; when her crumpled corpse was pulled out more than three weeks later, it was discovered she was holding a Blazing Saddles chip between her teeth. CCTV cameras, on their records being finally searched, showed Lady Letitia totally alone as she approached the well, lifted the lid, and took her fatal plunge.

American bullion heir Aloysius T. O'Rourke Jr. smothered himself by thrusting his face into a bowl of tapioca pudding and, with remarkable strength of mind, holding it there until he expired. He was found at the postmortem to have a poker chip in his stomach, alongside the remains of the liver and onions he'd consumed as his last meal.

There were others, many others, and all of them shared two things in common. The suicide victims were without exception living under the yoke of huge gambling debts—the dogs, the horses, the cards, the dice—and all their sorry corpses had been discovered to be holding, in one sense or another, a Blazing Saddles poker chip.

Most had committed suicide under circumstances that precluded murder. Lady Letitia with the CCTV. Colonel Humbleby-Dickens with the locked bathroom door. Dwight Gee with the bolts.

Other than that, there were so many differences between the cases. The methods of suicide varied from one to the next: here a hanging, there a smothering, and there…

"Deuce it!" said Sir Basil, face becoming even paler as he stared at the sheet of paper in his hand. "He allowed himself to bleed out after he'd cas—?"

"Precisely," I said hastily, gulping. "And with rather a blunt knife while in full view of an Easter parade. An Easter parade that included nuns."

"Shameful!"

He swiveled in his seat to demand the waiter bring him another brandy of the same size and potency as the last. I told the wizened figure I'd stick with the Perrier, thank you very much, perhaps this time with a racy slice of lime on the rim of the glass.

"Still and all," said Sir Basil, once he'd settled himself, "there's no convincing proof here of any foul play. All of these deaths, however tragic, are demonstrably suicides. That's what violent deaths usually *are* when it's as plain as the nose on my face—plainer, in fact, because I ain't got a bad-looking nose, all things considered—that no one could possibly have effected those deaths as murders."

"If there'd been just one such death, Sir Basil," I said cautiously, "I'd certainly agree with you. But there are so many macabre similarities here that I think we have to conclude there's a killer on the loose—a killer who's committed a series of murders that he's cunningly disguising as mere suicides."

"And the purpose of the poker chips?" said Sir Basil quietly.

"There you have me," I told him. "Obviously there's a message to be read into them, but what might that message be?"

"Vengeance on the part of the Blazing Saddles?"

"There's no evidence of that. Besides, none of the dead people—the, ah, murder victims—were in debt to the Blazing Saddles at the time of their demise. I tried to hunt that clue down to its source, but I came to the conclusion it was a red herring."

"And there were no suicide notes?"

"So far as I can tell, not in a single instance."

Sir Basil said nothing for thirty seconds or more, just stared into his almighty snifter as if it might be a crystal ball.

At last he jerked himself upright in his overstuffed Runagates Club armchair and blinked at me as if recognizing my existence for the first time.

"You're right, young scribbler," he said, his voice cracking slightly. "There's been murder afoot. Too many suicides, too many suicides. Nothing unusual about gamblers in debt choosing to end it all rather than face up to their creditors, but the poker chips—ah, yes, the poker chips. That's a coincidence too far."

He drew a deep breath and stared at me as if he were an entomologist and me a slightly puzzling aphid. "Locked room murders are two a penny. Locked room suicides attract no attention, on an individual basis, because no one ever thinks there might be anything suspect about them—why should there be? But a *string* of strange suicides…"

***

We parted company on the Strand, he hailing a taxi back to Whitehall and me catching a taxi back to Charing Cross railway station and thence to Cynthia. I knew which destination I preferred.

A few days later, I decided to put all thoughts of my meeting with Sir Basil out of my mind—the chances were, surely, that I'd never hear from him on the matter again—and knuckled down to start writing *The Case of the Constant Suicides*.

Or tried to.

For the first time in my life, I ran straight into a writer's block. Nothing serious—it wasn't that I thought I'd never be able to write again, which I gather is what block feels like at its worst. It was just that the ideas wouldn't come.

I'd get up at seven o'clock each morning, as usual; have breakfast with Cynthia, as usual; kiss my artist wife before she headed off for her morning's work in her studio at the bottom of the garden, as usual; and then head for my own study in the attic, as usual. What wasn't as usual was that, after I'd booted up the computer, progress on the novel would be turgidly slow.

I'd brought Agnes Pibroch ashore to spend a vacation in Glasgow, there being not too many people left alive to deliver mail to on her home island of

Aronsay, what with all the murders. Naturally enough, she'd got together with her old pal Tosh, and over a typical Scottish meal of haggis and single malt whisky he'd told her about the rash of suicides there'd been in and around Glasgow over the past few months.

All this had been easy enough for me. I knew my two characters well enough that their dialogue basically wrote itself.

But, these preliminaries out of the way, I found myself spending long hours staring at the screen, occasionally typing a paragraph or two just to persuade myself I was doing some work, then deleting what I'd written.

I'd been going through this charade for perhaps ten days or more when, one morning, Cynthia knocked at my study door. She was wearing a white tunic covered in colored smears of paint, and there was a very fetching smudge of purple on her cheek. In her hand she held her mobile phone.

"It's Uncle Baz," she told me. "He wants to speak to you."

"How come he phoned your number and not mine?"

"He said he's lost yours."

"Couldn't you have—?"

"He insisted I bring the phone to you."

"Oh."

Sir Basil Derringpole had a reputation for being quirky and cantankerous, so there was no point in my pursuing the issue with her. With an air kiss of thanks, I took the phone and put it to my ear.

"Sir Basil?"

"Who the devil else do you think it might be?"

"I, er." I realized he must have been listening as Cynthia and I talked.

After a few moments' token sputtering, he spoke again.

"I have an answer to that, ahem, little problem of yours."

"You do?" This could be the moment when the wall of my writer's block began to crumble. "Tell me more."

"When can you next come to town?"

"Tomorrow, if you'd like. But can't you tell me over the phone?"

"Phones have ears," he said enigmatically.

I said nothing. Surely that was the whole *point* of phones?

"The Runagates Club suit you again?"

I thought fast. Anywhere but the Runagates Club. "How about the steps of the National Gallery? We could feed the pigeons and then eat quiche at their little cafeteria."

"Is there something wrong with the Runagates? They do a damn' fine beef olive."

"It's just that it's my turn to foot the bill."

"Nonsense, dear boy. Our lunch will be paid for by the grateful taxpayer."

So the Runagates it was. I resolved to pack plenty of antacids in my briefcase.

***

"Our murderer would have got away with it," said Sir Basil, "had it not been for his damn' vanity."

He was still peeved that I'd thwarted him by insisting to the ancient waiter, Walter, that I wanted the smoked mackerel salad rather than the beef olive. All through our meal he'd made a big issue of smacking his lips with relish and telling me how delicious his meal was. I'd tried to hide my gloom as I waded my way through a plateful of limp, browning lettuce, a slab of unidentifiable, bone-plagued fish and three radishes that strongly resembled prunes. Clearly salads were not the Runagates' forte.

As for the vinaigrette? Well, the best you could say for it was that it was hard to tell the difference between it and the wine.

Now, once again, the cheese course having been survived, Sir Basil was addressing the contents of a bucket of brandy while I sipped cautiously at a sparkling mineral water.

"The poker chips, you mean?"

"Correct, young fellow. We'll make a detective of you yet. They were his *signature*, don'tcha see? Just like Renoir or Canaletto or that Rembrandt chappie putting their initials in the corner of one of their daubs, he felt he had to leave his own mark on each of his latest artworks."

"His artworks?"

Sir Basil frowned at me. "The suicides, of course."

"But I thought you said they were murders?"

"They were both."

There was a long silence while I thought that through.

Cynthia's uncle was the one to break it.

"You were perfectly correct, see, when you spotted the clue that all of the victims were gamblers who were deeply in debt. And you were perfectly correct to say that none of them had any involvement with the Blazing Saddles Casino—there's no evidence any of them ever even visited the place, in fact. When I looked at the affair, that indicated only one thing to me."

I sat forward, watching him intently.

"If we took it as our hypothesis that there had to be *some* connection with the Blazing Saddles, and yet it wasn't through any of the victims, there seemed an obvious conclusion."

"That the connection was through the perpetrator, of course," I breathed.

He put his brandy down and clapped his hands gently together. "Bravo! I set one of my assistants, Albert, to the task of investigating that aspect of things. Meanwhile, I myself looked more closely at the individual deaths, and what do you think I found?"

"I—I don't know."

He glanced at his watch. "Do you have the afternoon free?"

"Yes. I'd better phone Cynthia if I'm going to be late, though."

"You do that—Walter will show you where the phone is. There's someone I want you to meet."

***

The house was in the less fashionable part of Kensington, but it must once, a century or more ago, have been a very grand place—the home, perhaps, of a wealthy merchant or a cousin of the queen.

Sir Basil, who had clearly been here before, trotted without hesitation up the steps and, standing between the two stone pillars that framed the door, quickly found the right button among the array on offer. A few moments later there was a loud buzzing noise, and we pushed our way into the house.

He led me up a curving flight of stone stairs to the first floor, where he pressed another doorbell.

Almost immediately, the door opened. I recognized the chin of the woman standing there and swiftly put a name to it.

"Belinda Troughton," I said.

"It is she." Her voice was quite rich and deep. "Have we met?"

"This is the nephew of whom I told you, Mrs. Troughton," said Sir Basil. "Nephew-*in-law*, I should say."

"The scribbler?"

"The very same."

I introduced myself more formally to Mrs. Troughton, and a couple of minutes later we were all sitting in her living room confronting cups of tea and slabs of Dundee cake. Brightly colored toys littered the floor. Sounds of fighting children came from a distant room.

"When I was here the other day," Sir Basil said at last, "you told me something under conditions of strictest confidence. I'm asking you now, Mrs. Troughton, if you'd extend that same confidence to my nephew here."

She turned to stare at me, clearly evaluating my trustworthiness…or lack thereof.

"Do you think it absolutely necessary, Sir Basil?"

He raised a reassuring hand. "Absolutely necessary? No, I shouldn't say so. But, since young Jack here was the one who brought the circumstances of your father's death to my attention, I think the request is reasonable. After all, if it hadn't been for him, we'd never have been able to bring the man responsible for your father's demise to justice."

"Is he trustworthy?"

"My niece seems to think so."

Belinda Troughton gave an empty smile. "Then I suppose I'll have to go along with her judgment."

"Thank you," said Sir Basil. "You see, Jack, what Mrs. Troughton told me was that, just a few days before the suicide of Colonel Humbleby-Dickens, the Troughton children were stolen."

"Ronnie and Lucy," clarified their mother.

"Ronnie and Lucy had been playing on the swings in the park around the corner under the eye of their loving mother," explained Sir Basil.

"I looked away for just a moment," said Mrs. Troughton. "Only a moment, I tell you."

"And when she looked back," he continued smoothly, "it was to discover that both of her little darlings had vanished."

"Lucy's swing was still swinging, but Lucy wasn't on it. There was just her cute little green plastic sandal on the grass beside it."

Mrs. Troughton produced a handkerchief and put it to her eyes.

"Very distressing, I'm sure," said Sir Basil, looking embarrassed by this display of emotion.

"What made it worse," the now openly weeping woman explained, "was that for three days we heard nothing—nothing more than a note stuffed under our door telling us our children would be returned safe and sound so long as we"—she made a pretense of coughing—"we 'kept our pie-holes shut', it said. I'd show you the note, Mr. Chaveney, but my husband in his righteous fury burned it."

"There was no demand for ransom?" I said.

"No. It'd have been easier for us if there had been. We're not rich, Mr. Chaveney—quite the opposite, in fact—but we'd have found the money somehow if we'd been asked for it. Anything to get our children back. The fact that the kidnappers seemed to have no interest in money made the situation seem all the more menacing. We knew something was going on behind the scenes, but *we didn't know what!*"

She wrung her handkerchief in her hands and gazed at me with an expression of recalled torture that pierced me to the core.

"But it's all over now," I said in what I hoped was a soothing tone.

"It could happen *again!*" she wailed.

"I doubt it," said Sir Basil. "Bugsy McCorgan, the man who took your children, will never again trouble loving parents like yourself, Mrs. Troughton. Did I not say he had been brought to justice?"

"He has? What's happened to him? Tell me more!"

Sir Basil gazed at her solemnly. "For your own protection, Mrs. Troughton," he said, "I think I had better not."

***

An hour later we were sitting in the Old Goat and Whistle on Villiers Street. It had taken us some time to get clear of the Troughton flat. Belinda—as she'd eventually told us to call her—had insisted we be introduced to the children, and we'd spent a while listening to their chatter and pretending to be impressed by their Lego constructions (Ronnie) and stuffed Eeyore (Lucy). I could see from the corner of my eye that Sir Basil was finding the whole experience a torment fit for one of the deeper pits of hell, but I enjoyed it.

Before that charming interlude, Belinda had described to me how, less than seventy-two hours after their mysterious disappearance, her two little darlings had suddenly reappeared at the front door none the worse for wear—and indeed rather cock-a-hoop about the great adventure they'd had with "the man with the cauliflower nose," as they'd called him.

"Hardly were they home," Belinda Troughton told us, "than the phone went. I swear I'll hear the voice of the man who spoke to me until my dying day. He told me to go at once to my father's home, Humbleby Hall, in West Marple, just outside London. So I left the kids with my husband, went out, hailed a cab, and…"

And the rest, as they say, had been history—or at least a report in the *West Marple Times & Gazette.*

Now, pints of bitter between us, reveling in the fact that the Old Goat and Whistle has neither TV set nor jukebox, Sir Basil and I were able to relax. The street outside was busy with commuters heading for the station. In an hour or so, things would be much quieter and the train far less jam-packed. I was more than happy to wait here while Sir Basil enlightened me as to what had been going on.

"Are you beginning to put things together yet?" said Sir Basil. He was mellower now than I'd seen him, as if the escape from Belinda's children had broken down a barrier.

"I think so," I said. "I take it the Troughtons weren't the only ones to be persecuted by mysterious abductions?"

"You're sharper than I used to think," said the great detective. "Children, spouses, in one case even a treasured Pekinese dog. Some families brought in the boys in blue; others, like the Troughtons, too terrified of the consequences, 'kept their pie-holes shut.' In every case, the result was the same. The abductees were returned as mysteriously as they vanished, and then the next thing was the discovery of the elderly relative's body."

"So the elderly relative concerned was told some hideously sadistic fate would befall their loved ones unless they cooperatively did themselves in?"

"You have it in a nutshell."

"But why?"

"Let me start," said Sir Basil, "with the part of the tale that you can't possibly know."

"The involvement of the Blazing Saddles?"

He tapped a fingertip on the sticky surface of the pub table. "Exactly."

"It all began there, didn't it?"

"In a way, yes." He took a sip of his Wadworth 6X, then a more forthright gulp. "My assistant Albert spoke with someone he knows in the Federal Bureau of Investigation. That's a sort of police institution our colonial cousins—"

"Yes, I've heard of the FBI," I said impatiently.

"Well, they told him the casino has a rather ruthless way of dealing with the unlucky souls who're unable to cover the debts they've incurred at their, um, crap tables—that's the term Albert used. The bettors who might be able to come up with the money if sufficiently, ah, persuaded just have a few limbs broken. A poor move, if you ask me, because then, under that ghastly healthcare system of theirs, the victims have medical bills to cope with as well as trying to raise the money to pay off their gambling debts. Not that anyone *would* ask me. Anyway…where was I?"

"People getting their limbs broken if they owe money to the Blazing Saddles."

"Ah, yes. That's what happens when the casino's mob bosses think they have a chance of gaining settlement. But there's a worse fate in store for the unfortunates whose addiction has led them to the verge of bankruptcy—the people who're never going to be able to pay."

I stared at him aghast. "They get used as examples?"

"*Pour encourager les autres*, I believe the tactic is called. There's nothing concentrates the mind of a feller trying to raise money to pay the mob like having the reminder of what happened to someone who wasn't able to."

"Disgusting," I said, fortifying myself from my own glass. With luck, the antacids would get the smell of beer off my breath by the time I got home.

"It happens in this country too," said Sir Basil, "although the gangsters here tend to be a little less ostentatious about it." He shrugged. "Certainly, when Bugsy McCorgan, the man in charge of the Blazing Saddles Casino's intimidation division, realized things were becoming too hot for him in his native land and came here to bide his time until the 'heat died down,' as I believe the phrase is, he found plenty of takers for his freelance services. Foremost among them were members of the British gambling underworld— seedy casino owners, dubious bookies, the usual."

I finished my pint and contemplated another. "Let me guess. The reason the police in Vegas got after him was because his murders were so *obvious*. That's the way his employers *wanted* them to be. When he set up his enterprise here in Britain, he realized a different approach was called for."

"Assisted suicide, in a manner of speaking," confirmed Sir Basil. "Everyone in the appropriate circles would know why these people lost their lives, so the deaths would have the desired effect on major players tempted to welch on their debts. No need for crimes that shrieked *Murder!* to the world."

"But if everyone in the gambling fraternity knew—"

Sir Basil stopped me with a glance. "Yes, secrets are hard to keep. The police would soon enough have found out what was going on—they have plenty of informants among the fraternity. But your excellent researches got there first, young Jack, and you've saved a few lives by bringing them to me. Scotland Yard is very grateful to you."

One thing puzzled me. "But why haven't I heard any news of the arrest of this Bugsy person? You told Belinda he'd been brought to justice."

Sir Basil gave a deeply false chuckle. "Did I really say any such thing? Alas, no. Bugsy McCorgan evaded society's retribution at the last. He committed suicide, you see."

***

A gaggle of commuters spilled into the Old Goat and Whistle, and for a few moments their loud chatter made it difficult for Sir Basil and me to hear each other without raising our voices. I took the opportunity to replenish our glasses at the bar.

Once things had settled down a little, I said, "You're joking, of course."

He pursed his lips and rocked his head from side to side. A gleam in his eyes told me he was enjoying this game of half-truths. "His suicide was…not entirely unplanned," he said.

I squinted at him. "Did he bring loved ones here from the States? Did you play his own trick right back on him? He doesn't sound like the kind of person who'd be vulnerable to that sort of blackmail."

"Too true, my young friend. If you'd told Bugsy McCorgan you planned to torture his grandchildren—assuming he has any that he knows about—he'd have just laughed. The man was an outright psychopath who cared for no one except himself. But he wasn't without his weaknesses."

"The police found a weakness they could exploit?"

"Well, actually, that was my own part in this little drama." Modesty didn't sit well on Sir Basil's face. "My assistant Albert found out that this frightful American had a deep-seated phobia of wasps. Some people are irrationally terrified of spiders. Winston Smith in that Orwell thriller was irrationally terrified of rats. It's a matter of primal fear. McCorgan had a primal fear of wasps. He may have been stung by one in infancy—who knows? But the discovery there was a wasp in the room would reduce this hulking, broken-nosed bruiser to a gibbering jelly until the insect had been swatted, or waved out the window.

"So I bought myself a tartan cap and a checked suit so loud an American golfer might have mugged me for the trousers, and, presenting myself as a gentleman of the turf, I contacted Mr. McCorgan. It was easy enough. The police knew the channels I could go through. I phoned him up and arranged to meet him in my suite on the top floor of the Cholmington Hotel in Mayfair.

"When he got there, it was to discover I'd been unavoidably delayed. However, my man Albert—posing as my valet—told him to make himself comfortable, feel free with the television and the minibar, and so on. Hardly had Albert left the room than McCorgan burst open the minibar and poured three or four miniatures of Scotch into the glass that Albert had thoughtfully provided. On a table near the open window was a big plastic ice bucket. McCorgan eagerly pulled off the lid and…"

"…revealed a large, active wasps' nest," I finished for him.

"If ever you decide to give up the scribbling and decide you'd like a *real* job," said Sir Basil, giving me an evaluatory look, "the Home Office might have a vacancy for you.

"Anyway. Picture the scene. A cloud of angry wasps rises from captivity. McCorgan staggers back in panic, his arms raised in front of his face. The door's on the far side of the room. The air between him and it is becoming thick with black-and-yellow buzzing insects. But right next to him there's a means of escape."

"The open window," I said.

"Yes. Without thinking, he leaps for it and…"

"…plummets to his doom."

Sir Basil nodded and made a great point of savoring his beer.

"You're a ruthless man, Sir Basil, even if you *are* my wife's uncle."

"It's part of my job specification. And now"—he drained his pint—"I must be on my way. I have a briefing at Number Ten I must attend. And you, you presumably have a home you should go to."

***

Outside on Villiers Street, as I turned to go downhill toward the station and Sir Basil made to climb toward the Strand, he put a hand on my shoulder.

"One more thing, young Jack."

"Yes?"

"Not a word of this must ever appear in one of those scurrilous penny-dreadfuls of yours. You'll have to think up another plot entirely for your—what did you call it?—*The Case of the Impossible Suicides*. Understood? Otherwise I'll bring the full might of the Official Secrets Act down upon you."

"Oh," I said, wondering if this would be legally possible, and in the same moment deciding it wasn't worth the gamble of finding out the hard way.

"Give my love to Clarissa," he said with a farewell flip of his hand. "She's my favorite niece, you know."

"Cynthia," I said to his besuited back. "Not Clarissa. Cynthia."

But, if he heard me, he gave no sign.

The Fire Inside
DAVID QUANTICK

"There is no longer any need, in explaining the phenomena of combustion,
to suppose that there exists an immense quantity of
fixed fire in all bodies."
—Antoine Lavoisier, Memoir on Combustion in General, 1777

She was sitting in my office before I'd even stepped through the door.
I must have left the door unlocked: it was a mercy she didn't find me
sleeping at my own desk, an empty bourbon bottle in front of me. It had
happened before; once, a prospective client walked in and found me with my
face stuck to a case file with my own drool. He was an enormous man who'd
lost a tiny dog, and he walked out after I suggested he search his own clothes
before hiring me.

But this time I'd at least made it to my car before passing out and waking
up just in time to drive home, pass out on the bed, shower, and come back in
to work again. To myself, at least, I looked like the shine on an apple. To her, I
guess, not so much, judging by the look she gave me as I walked in.

"Relax," I told her, "this is my office."

"You're P. D. Jackson?" she asked.

I shook my head.

"Pete died," I told her. "I took over from him and I haven't had time to get
the sign changed." I didn't tell her Pete had been dead six years—you need to
inspire your client with confidence whenever possible.

She was still looking at me in an odd way. At first I thought it was the tie,
a painted horror with a green parrot on that had not been improved when I
spilled mustard on it. Then I realized her gaze was directed an inch or two
above the tie, and she was looking at my face. I had caught a look at it myself

earlier and I could see her point of view: it was blotchy, and badly shaved, and looked like I'd peeled it off a dead guy.

"I've had influenza," I told her, and sat behind the desk. With something big and heavy between us, she relaxed a little.

"Well," she said. "Now I'm here, I suppose I'd better get to it."

For the first time, I got a good look at her. She was what my ex-wife would have called second-glance beautiful—at first glance she was just another city girl, worn down by work and life, but at second glance you saw the beauty, like a piece of music you never cared for that suddenly makes you cry.

"What's your name?" I asked her.

"What's yours?" she said, still suspicious.

I showed her the hunk of wood I'd had made with my name on it. It cost twice what it was worth, and the guy who'd made it spelled my name wrong in two different places, but it would do. It wasn't my real name anyway—I'd left that in the dust that spawned me.

"My name is Melissa," she said eventually, like it was an admission of guilt. Maybe it was.

"So what brings you here, Melissa?" I said, trying to sound like a pal and failing. "Lost cat? Lost husband?"

She shook her head. "I'm allergic to cats," she said. "Husbands, too."

It was a joke. We were moving closer, like two armies in the night.

"I'll try and remember that," I said. "About the cats, that is."

She gave me a look that said *back off, mister*. It wasn't hard to figure out—it was a look I was seeing a lot these days.

"Tell me then," I began again. "What brings you to me?"

That was when she lost it. Her face was a mess of tears.

"I'm dead," she said, finally choking the words out through sobs like punches.

"Dead?" I replied. "Why, what did you do? Who's after you?"

"No," she said, "you don't understand."

"Make me understand," I said.

"When I say I'm dead," said Melissa, "I mean I'm dead."

I must have looked puzzled. I was puzzled.

"I'm dead," she repeated. "I died. Someone killed me."

She looked me in the eye. She might have been crazy, but she believed what she was saying alright.

"I was murdered," Melissa said. "And I want you to find the man who did it."

I sat back in my chair. For once I was glad of my hangover: it was a cloud to hide inside, a shield against a reality that had suddenly lost its mind and was now running round my office like a cartoon animal, cross-eyed and blowing raspberries at the whole notion of sanity. I took a moment to digest her words.

"If you're dead," I said, "how come you're here, walking and talking? You seem pretty alive to me. Unless this is all a dream or something like that."

She shook her head.

"This is no dream," she said. "I'm dead alright."

And she began to unbutton her blouse.

"Stop right there," I said. "I don't mean to be rude, but it's a little early in the morning and besides, we hardly know each other."

She gave me a look that would have withered the roses on my desk, if I'd had any.

"Relax," she said. "You're safe from my feminine wiles. Like I told you, I'm dead."

She undid her blouse, right down to the waist, and pulled the fabric away from her throat. I started back in my seat so hard that I nearly kicked the desk over.

There was a hole right in the middle of her rib cage. A big one, big enough for a child to put its fist into.

"It goes all the way through," she said. "You can see daylight out the back. Wanna?"

"Thanks but no thanks," I answered. Curiosity overcame revulsion, and I stood up and peered at her front. It was a deep hole alright, black and misshapen inside, like someone had taken a flaming torch and thrust it into her.

"Can I—?" I asked.

"No," she said. "Nobody's poking me."

I looked her in the eye.

"I have to," I said. "I've been taken in before."

She sighed, and buttoned up as far as she could. I took a deep breath, and stuck my finger in the hole.

"Jesus!" I yelled, pulling out my finger. "That's hot!"

"Believe me now?" she asked, doing up her blouse.

"Maybe," I said. I frowned. "I don't get it. How can it be so hot?"

She shrugged. "I haven't really given it any thought. What with being dead and all."

"That again."

"Feel my pulse."

Now it was my turn to shrug. I put my finger on her wrist. It was warm enough to the touch, but I couldn't find a pulse. I tried a different finger, the other wrist, her neck: nothing.

"I don't get it," I said.

"How many more times?" she fired back. "I'm dead. Do I have to call a priest?"

I shook my head. I needed a drink, but all the drink I had was still inside me, stale and resentful.

"You got any money?" I asked her.

She agreed to my usual terms and paid up front, which meant I was able to buy her lunch. We went to Hank's, where I had coffee and a ham sandwich because hangovers make me hungry, and she had nothing because she was dead.

I wiped away the last fragment of ham from my chin, took out a pad and pencil and wrote *Melissa* at the top of the page, like a real pro.

"Shaky handwriting," she noted. "Guess I know where that fee's going."

"I get results," I retorted. "Although normally the client and the corpse have the decency to stay two different people."

"Maybe I'm the killer too," Melissa said. "That was a joke, by the way."

"Yeah, I could tell by the way you smiled when you told it," I replied. "That was a joke too."

"I don't have a lot to smile about right now," she said, and I felt sorry for her. I didn't believe she was dead, not for a second, but whatever was really going on, she was in a bad way.

"I'm sorry," I said, and I was. This time she really did smile, a smile that made my heart ache, and my loins too. I'm just a guy, after all. "How about you start at the beginning?" I added, pencil at the ready.

So she did.

Her full name was Melissa May Isinglass. She was thirty-four years old, spoke French and Spanish, and had trained as a dancer and a stenographer ("Not at the same time," she reassured me). She wasn't from California, but she'd been here about seven years, just long enough to realize that waitressing doesn't always lead to meetings with big Hollywood producers. She took the steno course and within a month, she had a job with some guy called Andrew Isinglass.

"Same name as you," I said.

She shot me a dry look.

"Reader, I married him," she said.

Isinglass was a professor up at the university, a historian. I pictured some elderly baldhead with spectacles draped over his beaky nose, but Melissa showed me a photograph and I had to revise my opinion. He was handsome, chisel-jawed, and only some of his hair had fallen out. Maybe it was love or just constant proximity, but either way, after eight months Melissa and Isinglass were married.

"At first we were very happy," she began.

"Those five words should be the motto of the American Divorce Society," I interrupted.

"It wasn't like that," said Melissa. "What came between us wasn't us, it was his work."

"I guess some guys prefer old books to beautiful girls," I said.

She smiled as if to say thanks, but it was a pinched smile, as if to say but no thanks.

"He was a nice man," she said. "He was kind, attentive, he made me happy. And then—"

And then he went nuts, is basically how it went, according to her. Nights in the library, days in the lab—for some reason he had a lab, which is not how they did history in my day, but there he was, reading books and making notes and—

"Making experiments," Melissa said.

"I thought you said he was a historian?"

"He was," she agreed. "He said he was researching hypotheses and he couldn't take them at face value, so he had to test them himself."

"Hypotheses"—I managed to get the word out without biting my tongue off—"from old books?"

"Yes."

"I'm no scientist," I said (I noticed she didn't contradict me), "but these hypotheses, if they were old, then—wouldn't they have been tested already? So the people writing the books would have been able to say, hey this hypothesis is a crock?" I had never said the word "hypothesis" so much in my entire life. I was hoping I never would again.

"That's what I said, more or less," Melissa agreed. "But Andrew said a true historian takes nothing for granted. And then he said—"

Melissa frowned at the oddness of the memory.

"He said he had to find a way in."

"A way in to what?"

She shook her head.

"A way in to the future."

I looked at her.

"These notebooks cost money," I said. "I'm not just going to fill it with nonsense."

Melissa took a deep breath.

"Okay," she said. "But first I need some fresh air. All these cooking smells are making me ill, and jealous."

We took a walk.

"Andrew wasn't being entirely honest when he said he was an historian," said Melissa as we strolled up La Cienega like a young, half-dead couple. "He'd studied a lot of things, but mostly he was a chemist. Or a physicist. Same difference."

I was about to explain the difference when I saw the tiny smile playing on her lips.

"Either way," she said, "Andrew was working a lot of different rackets. I soon realized he was plowing through those old books in search of—"

She turned to me.

"He once said to me that history is 1 percent progress and 99 percent debris. Know what he meant by that?"

I shook my head, to save time.

"He meant that all we know from history is the successes. The battles won, the diseases conquered, the problems solved. Everything else goes into the trash. We don't care who lost the wars, who didn't find the vaccine, or who failed to solve the mysteries of the universe."

"You're pretty eloquent for a dead girl," I said.

"Oh, you should have heard me when I was alive," Melissa replied. "I could charm the professors from the trees."

A sad smile crossed her face, and I realized she must have really loved him, once. Then it was gone, and she went on.

"I said before that Andrew was looking for a way into the future. I didn't know what he meant, but he told me he could only find that way in by looking in the trash. He said everyone else had failed because they'd stuck to the usual paths. They'd mistaken the passage of time for progress."

"Quite a talker."

"That he was. He certainly convinced me," said Melissa. "Andrew said he was going through all the discarded ideas of history—the trash—to find something the olden days people had missed. Like a…"

"Like a private dick looking for clues at a crime scene after the flatfoots have trampled all over it?" I asked.

"You got it," she said.

"I don't understand—well, any of this," I said. "But especially the part about the way to the future. Was he trying to build a…?" I could scarcely say it.

"A time machine?" finished Melissa. "Not in so many words. He didn't want to travel in time, he just wanted to stand at the crossroads and look down the paths. The different roads history might have taken."

"The Devil's at the crossroads," I said. It was an old song that just came into my head.

"It was for Andrew," said Melissa.

She sat on a bench and I sat next to her.

"One day I went into his lab with some papers," she said. "And he was gone."

"You mean he'd left you?"

"I mean he was gone," she said. "You ever walk into a room and you can tell someone just left? Like there's no one there, but you can feel their presence?"

I nodded. "I had a wife like that once," I said.

Melissa ignored me. "I was sure he had just gone outside for a cigarette," she went on. "He wouldn't let anyone smoke in the lab. I was just reaching for the door handle when I heard him say my name. I turned around, and there was nobody there."

She had her purse open, looking for her own cigarettes. Then she shook her head.

"Oh, that's right, I'm dead," she said.

"The dead can't smoke?" I asked.

"No breath to inhale," she explained. "Don't interrupt me."

"Sorry."

"There was nobody there," she continued. "I looked around and said his name. Nothing. Then once more, my name, out of thin air. Almost like it was inside my head. I sat down. My heart was beating like crazy. 'Stop it,' I told him. But he didn't listen. He just kept saying my name. I was getting more and more scared. Every time he said my name and I couldn't see him saying it, my pulse sped up. I was getting warmer, too."

"Warmer?"

"That's what I said. I was burning up inside. Like fear had caught fire inside me. There was this terrible heat," she said, gesturing to her breast. "A rod of pain, white hot like a poker, right through me. I could feel my bones melting, I could feel my flesh burning. I started to black out. I knew I was dying. And then I saw him."

"Andrew?"

"Andrew." She nodded, her face pale. "He was looking right at me. He wasn't sad, or angry, or worried, or anything. He was just…studying me. That was the worst part. Much worse than dying. The look on his face, like I was a specimen."

There were tears in her eyes.

"That was the last thing I saw before I died."

I've met some people in my time. Killers, liars, weepers, laughers, the whole shebang. Every kind of crazy and every shade of nuts. They always have one thing in common. It could be in the eyes, it could be in the voice, but it's always a tiny sliver of doubt that their version of reality is really the right one. Even the confident ones, the guys who think they should be running the world and we're all squashed insects on their boot soles, have that moment when the eyes flicker and some tiny corner of their brain is trying to say, wait a minute here.

But Melissa, who said she was dead and had apparently been killed by her invisible husband literally burning her heart out, sounded as normal as whoever the last sane person I'd met was. She was scared and tired and upset and angry in all the ways people who aren't crazy are, and not once did I detect a sudden twitch of uncertainty in the way she looked or spoke.

How do you believe someone who insists that the impossible is true?

You trust them, that's how.

I dropped the notebook in the nearest trash can and took Melissa's hand.

"I believe you," I said.

She looked me right in the eyes.

"I should hope so," she said. "Now, please, I need you to find Andrew."

She yawned.

"I have to sleep," she said. "Let's hope I wake up, right?"

I didn't think that was funny.

"You can't go home," I said.

"I'm not staying at yours," she said, indignantly. "I'm a lady. Besides, if your place smells anything like your clothes, I will definitely die if I sleep there."

I still wasn't laughing. I peeled off a slice of the money she'd given me and gave her the address of a half-decent motel. Then I hailed a cab.

"I'll call you tonight," I said as she got in.

"Be careful," said Melissa. "He's already killed me, and I'm his wife."

I said nothing to that. There's a time for comedy and a time to be serious.

I stepped into a telephone kiosk and fanned open the phone book. Isinglass was hardly a common name. There were two listed—one was a dry cleaners' and the other was up in the Hills. I took a crazy gamble and wrote down the address in the Hills.

Half an hour later, I was in a bar, waiting for night to fall. An hour after that, full to the gills with lime soda, I drove up to the house. It was a huge mansion, the kind of place that wanted to be a lunatic asylum when it grew up, but for now, had to settle for being cheerlessly imposing. A long gravel drive led up to a front door so imposing that I felt bad knocking on it without a mob of angry peasants behind me with flaming torches. Instead, I rang the doorbell. Nobody answered. The door was locked, so I walked around the place. No dogs attacked me and no burly henchmen ran out and clubbed me to the ground. After a couple of minutes, I found a half-open ground-floor window, raised it, and climbed inside the house.

The room I was in was some kind of library, which figured. In the darkness it was hard to make out the names of the books, but they were all pretty old and had gold writing on the spines, so I guessed they weren't any fun. I left the room and made my way into the entrance hall. An enormous stuffed bear, arms outstretched like it had been pushing a trolley when it was killed, stood next to a huge wooden staircase, apparently made for giants. I climbed the stairs half a step at a time and found myself on a landing whose walls were studded with portraits of people who by the look of it had all been painted with pickles up their backsides. Down the landing, I could see a door, surrounded by thin lines of light. I slid along the wall like I was my own shadow, hesitated for a moment, and swung into the room.

And then I felt it. The exact same sensation that Melissa had described to me. Like someone had just left the room. An absence that was equally a presence. Pointlessly, I looked around for evidence of whoever it might be—a cigarette still smoking in an ashtray, maybe—but there was nothing, only a feeling. There was something else too, something Melissa might not have noticed because she was used to it. A smell, the scent of strong aftershave, astringent rather than perfumed: the kind of thing a man might buy who didn't really care for such things. An absent-minded professor type of guy.

"Andrew," I said. "I know you're here. Show yourself."

For a moment there was nothing, and I felt foolish for addressing an empty room. Then—with, I swear, an audible pop!—he was there in front of me. Professor Andrew Isinglass, hair unkempt, manly chin jutting, lab coat done up wrong.

"How did you know I was here?" he asked.

"When you've been jumped from behind in dark alleyways as often as I have—" I began. Isinglass held up a hand to interrupt me. I guessed he was the rhetorical kind of professor.

"I have work to do," he said. "Important work. What do you want?"

"I'm taking you in for murder," I said. "Melissa May Isinglass."

He looked at me like I'd lost my mind. I could see his point. I was arresting him for killing someone I'd just sent away in a cab.

"Melissa isn't dead," he said. "She's still walking around and talking. And I mean talking. The chewing-out she gave me after—"

Now it was my turn to interrupt him. "After you killed her?" I asked.

Isinglass said nothing. He was fiddling with something on his wrist. I picked up a large book—*An Experiment In Time*, or some such—and threw it at his hand. The something fell off and I caught it.

"What's this?" I said.

He looked pale and furious all at the same time.

"Give me that," he said.

"Not until you answer my questions," I retorted.

His shoulders sagged.

"You're not taking me in?"

"Like you said, Melissa's still walking and talking. You can't have habeas corpus when the corpus is still paying your expenses."

"Melissa hired you to investigate her own—" He wouldn't say the word.

"Death, that's right. Which is what I'm doing right now. So what say you clear this up for me, before I accidentally break this thing you value so highly?"

His eyes fell on the object I had taken from him. It was a large ugly bracelet made of metal and porcelain, with two pocket watches crudely soldered onto it.

"Alright," he sighed.

"That's better," I said. "Now pull up a lab stool and let's get cozy."

"I'm an historian by profession but, unlike my colleagues who get all of their satisfaction from raking over the ashes of the past, I like my research to have a practical application. People are always talking about learning from history, but they never mean it. They just like to catalogue the past and stick it up in the attic like bundles of old newspapers, never to be read again. Whereas I'm more like someone who actually does read those old newspapers, scanning them from front page to back page, looking for stories the attic-fillers missed.

"History is full of roads not taken, and ideas not taken up. I wanted to go back and see if I could find those ideas. What if someone had found a way to build an internal combustion engine way back when, but they hadn't been taken seriously because they were a religious crank or a woman? What if there was a lost cure for the common cold, or a cheaper form of electricity? Some people thought Tesla had found that, but Edison beat him to the punch. Imagine if we could live in Tesla's world, not Edison's.

"Gradually I began to assemble a case history of inventions, ideas, and discoveries that should have been well-known years ago but at the time were suppressed, or ignored, or just laughed at. At that time my ambitions were narrow. I would publish them all in a book and maybe it would change things, maybe not."

He took a cigarette from a pack but didn't offer me one. These great men, eh?

"But the more I came to think about it," said Isinglass, "the more I realized it was too late. The big corporations would block any ideas that challenged them. And I hadn't found any olden-days cures for the common cold. I hadn't even found a good way of removing warts. I needed to think bigger. I needed to forget the specific inventions and discoveries, and focus on the ideas."

He looked at me. I looked at his cigarette. He got the idea and offered me the pack.

"You know the story of the jet engine?" he asked.

"I know what a jet engine is," I replied. "I read about it in a girlie magazine, I think."

"The jet engine is a comparatively new invention," Isinglass said. "But it wasn't something that a single guy dreamed up one day. It was more a possibility that occurred to engineers and scientists all around the world at the same time. The British thought of it about the same time the Germans did, and so did we, and the French."

"That's nice," I said, not taking his point.

"Because it wasn't just an invention," said Isinglass. "It was an idea. An idea whose time had come. And that's how things happen. Inventions don't come along because some guy is messing about in his workshop one afternoon and decides to stick some pipes on an aero engine. It's because there was an idea in the air, just hanging there.

"That's when it came to me," Isinglass said, a glassy look in his eye. "If I wanted to change anything, I had to change the idea."

"You've lost me," I said. Isinglass didn't look surprised. He just carried on talking.

"If I could change the way people thought about things," he said, "if I could go back in time and change the prevailing ideas, then I could influence the development of the world."

"If I could go back in time," I said, humoring him, "I'd kill that bastard Hitler. I lost too many good friends in that war."

Now Isinglass's eyes were glistening.

"But why kill Hitler when you could kill fascism?" he asked. "Why murder a man when you could root out the idea that perverted the minds of that man's followers?"

I nodded.

"Great idea," I said. "I mean if you had a—"

I looked at the metal bracelet I was holding, the one with the two pocket watches.

"Exactly," said Isinglass. "Exactly."

"I don't believe you," I said.

"I told you, I'm a researcher," Isinglass replied. "I found an essay here, a pamphlet there, and even some diagrams. People have been trying to do this for years. They just never pulled it all together."

"You're so public-spirited," I said. "Why not give the information to the government? Or Ford?"

As the words left my mouth, I already knew the answer.

"Because they'd bury it," said Isinglass. "Or sell it, or give it to the military. No, the only way I could do this was by myself."

The way he told it, he spent months building the bracelet while his marriage went to hell.

"I was trying to be a husband and to save the world," he said, a sentence which would drive any woman away. "And I was trying to find the answer. Something I could use to change the negative patterns of history."

"Did you find it?" I asked, casually.

He smiled. It was a sad smile, but also superior.

"Do you know what phlogiston is?" he asked.

I shook my head. "The Congressman for Maine?" I asked. "An Italian tenor? No, wait, I have it. That old Greek barber on Sunset."

He practically sneered at me.

"Phlogiston's not a person," he said. "It's an idea. There was a time when it was the biggest idea of them all."

I won't bore you with the details, not like he bored me with them, but it seems that once upon a time, what passed for scientists in the eighteenth century were trying to find some explanation for, essentially, everything. And they came up with the dumbest idea ever: a substance that you couldn't see, or smell, or touch, or hear, that was everywhere. It was called—yes, you're ahead of me—phlogiston, and it was the mysterious element that explained how we breathe and how we live. You couldn't see it, like I say, but it was there. It was the Emperor's New Ingredient X. But it was the big cheese among ideas for years, until someone discovered oxygen, which had the distinct advantage over phlogiston of being actually real.

"So what?" I said.

"So what if they were wrong?" said Isinglass. "What if modern science—because Lavoisier's interpolations on Priestley's discoveries are arguably the first building blocks of science today—was built on a lie?"

"What if it wasn't?" I shot back, but he didn't seem to hear me.

"All I had to do was move things around a little," said Isinglass. "Make sure phlogiston stayed the dominant idea in science, and bingo—save the world."

"Just like that," I said.

"Just like that," he agreed.

I stared at him.

"So you went back in time, destroyed all the evidence that said oxygen's our man, and that was it?" I asked.

"That was the plan," he said.

"What went wrong?"

For the first time since we'd met, Isinglass looked ashamed.

"Lavoisier's work, his notes and books, were all in French," he said.

"Don't tell me," I replied. "You don't speak French."

Fortunately, Isinglass knew someone who did: his wife, Melissa. Without explaining what he was doing, he gave her a second bracelet, told her to hang on, and—just like that—dropped them both off at the corner of Paris and Eighteenth.

"The shock nearly killed her," he said, a little too matter-of-factly for my liking. "And she wouldn't cooperate at first. She just stood there, shaking."

"Do you blame her?" I asked, angrily.

"I had no choice," he said. "Besides, when I did...persuade her to find the books I needed to destroy, something went wrong. The room was flickering, in and out of vision. Then it was two rooms. Then one, then two."

"You been at the brandy?" I asked.

He shook his head impatiently.

"Changing history is fine, unless you're at the point of change," he said. "We were at the crossroads of two worlds—the one where phlogiston was an outmoded theory, and the one where it was real. History was changing, it was unstable, and it was fighting back."

"Then what?"

"Then Melissa started to burn."

I stared at him.

"You mean the room caught fire?"

"No," he said. "Phlogiston—one of its properties is that it contains fire. They called it 'fixed fire.' The idea was that it's in everything, so when something catches fire, it's just the fire inside it being released.

"Don't you see?" he said, cold fury in his voice. "The changes I caused made phlogiston real. And the distortion of the two worlds…"

"It made the fire burn," I said.

"Melissa screamed and tried to beat it out, but it was inside her," said Isinglass. "I waited for her to die, or something, but she was trapped between two worlds. All I could think of was maybe, if I pushed her back to this world and this time…"

"That's what she saw," I said. "She saw you looking at her from the other place. But how come she didn't mention the other stuff? The books and room?"

"The shock," said Isinglass. "It removed her memories. I came back as soon as I could. I put the books back, restored time. The plan had failed, for now, but at least I'd made everything okay again."

"Everything apart from Melissa," I said, and launched a punch at him. Isinglass caught my fist. He was surprisingly strong for a professor.

"Put her out of her misery," he said. "She's neither dead nor alive, a creature of two worlds."

"She's more alive than you'll ever be," I said. Then I stopped. I had an idea.

"Enough of this," I said. "I'm calling the cops."

"What? But I've committed no crime."

"All I have to say is your wife came to see me, said you'd been threatening her, and when you can't produce her, you'll be the first suspect."

"What about the body? Besides, I'll just say she walked out on me."

"Without packing a single bag?"

He gave me a searching look.

"What do you want?"

I told him. He didn't like it.

"No."

"Yes."

"No."

"Is that a phone over there?"

He didn't look happy, but I didn't care. I had him and he knew it.

"Alright," he snapped.

"Great," I said. "I've always wanted to see Paris."

He gave me the second bracelet he'd made for Melissa, made some adjustments, and then we were there. A room full of books. And even though there was no one there, no footmen in periwigs or women in voluminous frocks, I could tell that I was in the past. Maybe it was the light, maybe the smell, maybe just the sound of carts and horses in the distance, but I knew. I was in Paris, in the eighteenth century.

"This is the exact spot?" I asked.

"Five minutes before it happened," he said.

"Alright," I said. "When they get there—when you and Melissa get here, I mean—"

"I know," he said, "I explain what happened, and I tell them to get the hell out of here."

"Good boy," I said.

"Not quite," he replied, and pulled a knife on me.

I looked at it.

"I'm surprised you didn't bring a gun," I said.

"I couldn't risk destroying books," Isinglass replied.

"Nice priorities," I said, and kicked him in the crotch. He shot backward like a burst zeppelin. I punched him in the face three times for luck and once more for fun. Then I pulled off his bracelet, jabbed at mine, and I was gone.

I'm finding it harder and harder to remember what happened. I know there was a guy, and a library. I have some books on my desk, but I don't know where they came from. One is called *Some Curious Trials Of Yore*, and there's a folded corner of paper on a chapter about some poor guy in Paris, way back when. He couldn't speak French, but he'd been caught red-handed stealing books in some aristo's library, so that was that.

I put the book in my desk drawer. There was a bottle of bourbon there too, but for some reason I didn't feel now was the time.

There was a knock at the door. I closed the drawer and a woman came in. She looked worried and tired, but she was beautiful.

"My name is Melissa Isinglass," she said. "My husband is missing."

"You want me to find him?" I asked.

She looked me right in the eye and smiled. It was the kind of smile a sunny morning might be jealous of.

"I thought I did," she said. "But now I'm not so sure."

The Menace in Venice
RHYS HUGHES

The Reconstruction Club was due to meet, and Pollard hurried to arrive on time. He had heard some very interesting news on the radio and wondered if any of his friends had also been listening. It concerned the discovery of a body in Venice that turned out to be completely desiccated. The victim, whoever he was, had died from dehydration. But what a place to succumb to such a condition! Venice, as everyone knows, is a city where the streets are made of water. To drown there would be an understandable fate, but to turn into a shriveled dry mummy?

Incredible, simply unbelievable, and Pollard was already hoping it wasn't a freak accident but a murder, and one that his club might take on as a case to be solved. He turned the corner into Livingstone Street and opened the door of the house that Rufus owned, the house that was their headquarters, a very modest building with almost no furniture inside it. Rufus was there, so was Jaspers, both of them injured from recent reconstructions that had been successful but drastic, and they were sitting on the sofa in the front room. Pollard gave them a cheerful wave before poking his head into the kitchen to see who might be brewing tea.

"You seem perky," said Gertie as he swirled the teapot.

"Oh, I am," Pollard agreed. He thrust his hands deep into his trouser pockets and waited for the general attention to refocus itself on him. Chunder and Beastly were in the kitchen too, and the little room was crammed to bursting. It was clear they all had a mild horror of sharing the bigger room with two men still swathed in bandages, but this was a situation that couldn't last much longer. At last Gertie bore the teapot and a selection of cups on a wooden tray out of the kitchen, and the others followed him in a line, like ducklings on a pungent pond.

Pollard found himself listening for the arrival of Diggs, the only missing member of the club. Every member had his own key to the front door, and he was expecting Diggs to come in at any moment. He believed that his news was significant enough to warrant the full attendance of the club, but as the minutes passed and the cups were drained through repeated sipping, he started to lose patience. "And Diggs is?" he asked of the air, elevating his eyebrows.

"Not coming," stated Gertie.

"Spot of bother at his bakery, I gather," said Chunder.

"Well now," muttered Pollard.

"There has rarely been a full attendance at any of our gatherings," croaked Rufus from the sofa, the exposed skin of his face blue with bruises, his unfilled pipe jutting from one side of his mouth like a broken tusk. "It doesn't matter." And Pollard had to nod, and he kept nodding until every eye was on him. He was standing in the middle of the room now, teacup empty, heart full.

"It's a shame, that's all, because this morning… Well, did anyone else hear it? The story isn't in the newspapers yet… Just on the radio. Impossible. An impossible crime, if it *is* a crime, which maybe it isn't…"

"Calm yourself. Take it slowly, friend." The voice of Rufus whistled faintly as it emerged from the bowl of his empty pipe.

Pollard laughed. "From the beginning, then," he said. "It appears to have happened on the Grand Canal in Venice. Two nights ago, a gondola slid out of the shadows not long after midnight. A gondolier was standing at the rear, absolutely still, with an oar in his hands, but it wasn't the traditional *rèmo* used by the famous boatmen of Venice. It was just an ordinary paddle, but with another length of wood glued onto the handle to make it long enough to reach the water."

"Anomalies are always useful," remarked Rufus approvingly.

Pollard nodded. "Quite so."

He sipped his tea and the others followed his example.

"That wasn't the main oddity."

"Continue," prompted Rufus, and Pollard smiled.

"Yes. The gondola was about to collide with one of the mooring poles, and this is why some witnesses who happened to be strolling along the embankment that night called out to him to watch where he was going. But he ignored them and the collision happened. The impact must have damaged the vessel because, when a witness jumped into the gondola to check whether the gondolier needed assistance, he found the fellow not only dead but up to his ankles in water."

"How many witnesses in total?" Rufus inquired.

Pollard shrugged. "That information wasn't given. The gondolier was lifted out of the vessel by two of them and carried onto dry land. He was completely stiff, a husk, a mummified personage, a desiccated shell. The police were called. They have asked the public for help in identifying the man. The gondola had no distinguishing marks on it. Everyone is bewildered, and so…"

Rufus leaned forward on the sagging sofa. "You did the right thing bringing this news to us. I vote we take on the case."

Pollard relaxed. He was happy. There was a brief discussion, and unanimously the club decided to attempt the solving of this mystery. Whether a crime had occurred or not was unclear. That was one of the questions they intended to settle. Yet it was best to proceed as if the unknown gondolier was a murder victim, for the reconstruction of mere accidents wasn't something they were interested in. No, there had to be malice involved, else the incident was superfluous to their aims and concerns. The next step was to consider how best to proceed. There was very little to go on, but that was quite enough. The main thing was that they were now all thinking about Venice, a city that none of them had ever visited in person.

They knew about it, of course, from books and paintings. It was a vision, a dream, an ideal perhaps. The city with streets of water. A romantic utopia, a place of moonlit serenades, of rich coffee and masked balls, of wealth and duels, of dungeons, bridges, intrigue, and treachery. They pictured it in their minds at night, filled with vapors, an endless lapping of the waters on old stones. The creak of oars in oarlocks as the black gondolas returned to their mooring posts.

Their souls soared and sang with this fantastic mirage, as their bodies continued to occupy this small house in an insignificant street in Norwich, a city bounded by fields flatter than any others in England, fields bordered with channels down which the cold waters of the marshlands flowed. And there were canals inside Norwich too. Despite vast dissimilarities between the cities, there were sufficient convergences to give the Reconstruction Club hope for a convincing reconstruction. Imagination would fill in the remaining gaps, blur the incongruities.

Chunder abruptly said, "The first thing I intend to do is locate a map of Venice, all the canals marked on it, the lagoons too."

Rufus nodded. "Good idea."

"We need a boat. Will a canoe do?"

"A little small, but that shouldn't be a problem. Do you know anyone who might be willing to lend us such a thing?"

Chunder frowned. He didn't, but he was resourceful, as were the other members. It would work out fine, even if they had to build their own from wooden crates. As for an oar, Diggs was a baker and used a large wooden shovel to remove loaves from his ovens. That would be perfectly suitable to propel the hypothetical craft along. Then Beastly spoke. "I'm going to research mummification techniques," he said dryly, and Rufus nodded again, wincing as he did so. His injuries were healing well, but he was still prone to sudden aches and pains.

The club members were already assigning tasks to themselves. This was nearly always a positive sign. The cases they reconstructed most profitably were those in which enthusiasm for results was close to fanaticism.

It was often true that ebullience proved more important than attention to detail. As Gertie returned to the kitchen to brew more tea, Jaspers shifted his weight on the sofa and sighed. Swaddled in white bandages after his fall from the apex of the fountain in Plantation Garden, he resembled a mummy himself. "Dehydration in a city where no water shortage has ever been recorded," he wheezed. "Yes, on the face of it, that's a mighty strange occurrence, but I don't regard it quite as impossible. Men have died of thirst at sea, on lost ships or drifting rafts…"

"Because sea water is poisonous," asserted Pollard.

"Death from drinking sea water is worse than death from thirst? I'm asking only because I've never considered the matter before," Jaspers said, and he gestured at the room for someone to take up the subject. Beastly was game. His morbid nature was a carefully cultivated quirk. The truth was that he was squeamish and had set himself the task of conquering his aversion to blood, pain, and death by deliberately moving into their proximity whenever he had a chance.

"I will find out all the necessary facts," he announced.

Gertie returned with more tea.

"Are the canals of Venice freshwater or saltwater?"

"This is an important point, I feel."

"I'll research the question," volunteered Chunder.

And so the first stage was done.

One by one, they drained their cups and left the house until only Jaspers and Rufus remained, sunk into that decrepit sofa that was slowly becoming more vegetable-like as the years passed. Although able to walk with difficulty, these two members felt too much at home on the sagging cushions and rarely left them. One day, of course, they would have to accept the truth of their recovery and return to work, but it wasn't time to do that yet. They had become the strategic voices of the club, directing others from this comfortable lair. At least that was the idea.

Rufus said, "I'm not surprised that Pollard takes his news from the radio. He has always been interested in newfangled things."

"To be fair, the BBC have been broadcasting for two weeks now. Pollard has been messing about with radio sets for years."

"A radio ham, I believe is the term for one such as he."

"Yet he loves newspapers too."

"I suppose," said Rufus carefully, "that there's no law against a man listening to a radio bulletin *and* reading written reports."

Jaspers remained silent.

His mind drifted away from the topic under discussion to his budding relationship with Mrs. Busker, the toyshop widow. He hadn't visited her for a long time and it was probable she now assumed he'd lost interest in her. It was unlikely she would attribute his absence to an accident and an injury.

Rufus also found his attention slipping away from the room in which he sat, but it was to an imaginary Venice that it went. The details of the case were too slight for his deductive powers to burrow into. Everything was speculation and nothing more. The city unfolded before his inner eye like a parody of itself, a network of waterways and islands joined by bridges, inhabited entirely by gondoliers who rowed their vessels in complex patterns through the wet sprawl.

It was dusk in his daydream and the mists were curling.

"That map of Venice," he said.

"Yes?" Jaspers blinked.

"I need it. My memory is trying to tell me something. I'm sure that there's a large lagoon that surrounds the city. One big enough to be out of sight of land, I mean. For some reason I'm struck by the fact the dead man didn't have a proper oar. There's an idiosyncratic technique the gondoliers have for ensuring that the vessels are propelled in a straight line. But I just don't know…"

Rufus was a shipping clerk in his day job, and he had arranged the transportation of cargoes to Venice, but it hadn't been essential for him to know about the geography of the city. Nor had the plays he'd read set in that city been of any use in this regard. A secret theatre enthusiast, Rufus knew most of *Othello* and *The Merchant of Venice* by heart, and he had a good knowledge of authors who had actually lived there, Goldoni and Ruzante for example, but how much help was this? No help at all. He pouted and his briar pipe fell from between his teeth.

In the meantime, Pollard was walking to his own house in Wensum Street. It was a fair distance, down Dereham Road and past the old city wall, and over the river on the bridge of Coslany Street. As he crossed this bridge, he stopped and leaned on the iron railings. The river was generally narrow, but right here it widened out for a very short stretch. He rubbed his chin in deep contemplation, deeper by far than the depth of the greenish water at this point. Norwich was hardly like Venice, and yet only the roughest similarity was needed for a good reconstruction. The club had learned this simple truth the hard and dangerous way.

Soon enough he would visit Diggs at his place of work.

"To ask to borrow his shovel…"

Diggs wouldn't refuse. Club business came before everything. And while Pollard was standing on the bridge, Beastly was taking a shortcut through Earlham Cemetery, an enormous expanse of overgrown graves and funeral monuments, many crumbling, some toppled, all grimy and dour. It was very satisfying to Beastly that his own route home lay through the largest graveyard in Norwich. Very few people ever came here and no flowers adorned any grave. It was a sour spot, one that palpitated with a damp atmosphere, as if the ground was breathing.

As the leaves of the twisted bushes dripped with the rain that had fallen overnight and the spider webs glistened, Beastly thought about death from thirst, and death from drinking sea water, and he wondered how to contrast and compare them. A cousin of his had gone missing in the Mesopotamian desert during the Great War. Surely he had succumbed to thirst, but what horrors had he gone through on the way to his death? It was difficult to work them out intellectually. Was his body now a desiccated mummy under the sun, a coriaceous husk, a crispy shell?

Meanwhile, Chunder and Gertie walked together northward up Burges Road and discussed topics tangential to the issue of a mummified man on a gondola. What did they know about gondolas? They had no idea if a collision with a mooring post would cause such a boat to spring a leak in the bottom of its hull. How fast would one sink anyway? There was only one way to find out, of course. Reconstruction! And as this idea rose and fell in their minds, they also speculated on Venetian wines and food, on the climate there, and on whether the windows of the tall houses were covered with those slatted blinds named after that unique city.

Sunday wore on, the sun went down somewhere behind the mass of gray clouds, it rained all night again. Then the working week began and the four healthy members dealt with the business of earning a living. Gertie found time in the evenings to bring food to Livingstone Street, but Jaspers and Rufus had to cook it themselves. They had run out of salt in the kitchen and the meals were bland, almost repulsive. "Sorry, but I keep forgetting!" said Gertie. The following evening, he brought them a ruined paper bag of salt. He had been caught in the rain and the sodden bag had ripped, spilling half its contents. Only by cradling the bag close to his chest was he able to preserve any salt for domestic use. He set it down on the table in the kitchen and Rufus spoke from the sofa in a pensive voice. "Salt is the answer."

"To what exactly? Tastier food?" Gertie called back.

"Dehydration," declared Rufus.

"As opposed to a thorough baking in the sun, you mean?"

"Yes, precisely so... Because..."

"Because what?" Jaspers was fully involved now. "The temperature in Venice can be sweltering. The sun does often beat down with tremendous force. This deduction I make simply through an awareness of lines of latitude. The further south toward the equator we go, the hotter the days are."

"Not always true," said Rufus, "but it doesn't matter."

"Why doesn't it? Please explain."

"A man who is in the actual process of dehydration, who is still alive while all the dreadful physical changes are taking place, wouldn't allow himself to remain standing in the sun until it parched him into a lifeless manikin. He would jump in the water to cool off, splash his tortured body with liquid."

"Unless he was held in place by manacles," said Jaspers.

Gertie came into the front room.

"Or nailed to the bottom of the gondola," he offered.

Rufus gestured impatiently.

"The simplest explanation is usually the best. Salt is connected in some way. Has Chunder reported anything to you yet?"

"No," said Gertie, "I haven't seen him since our last meeting here. I am sure he is at the library right now doing his research."

"Salt draws out moisture."

"But not when there's more water than salt, and in Venice water is by far the most plentiful substance," commented Gertie.

"I wonder what Pollard is up to?" mused Jaspers.

"Who knows?" said Rufus.

Nestled amid the soothing hum of vacuum tubes, Pollard was in his attic, in one hand a soldering iron, an invention made commercially available the previous year. He was repairing the radio set he had constructed himself, increasing its amplifying power as he did so, in order to begin receiving broadcasts from distant regions. This hobby of his consumed a large part of his income, but he didn't regard the sacrifice as a vain one. The future was about to open, like the petals of a monstrous flower, and he needed to anticipate everything it might bring in order to survive it. Thus was he determined to be relentlessly modern.

When the set was ready, he flooded the triodes with power and turned the variable capacitor dial. He had already erected a tall aerial on the roof of his house. Listening intently through headphones, he scanned the airwaves. At last he found what he was hoping for, the faint warble of a baritone singer. The song was unfamiliar to Pollard, but it was certainly in Italian, and the transmission clearly originated in Venice itself. The signal had bounced off the ionosphere and, despite the curve of the world's surface, was reaching him in his Norwich abode.

Pollard drank in the music, absorbed it, until his soul was full.

He was connected with a distant realm.

With Venice, that tidal paradise.

He listened for a few minutes, then removed his headphones and went down to his kitchen to pour himself a glass of whisky. That was his reward for his success. He had moved the investigation another notch further along. What was the next step? Getting Diggs involved was probably necessary.

The following day he rose early and went to visit Diggs at his bakery. He knocked on the window and Diggs opened the door, plucked at Pollard's sleeve, and pulled him over the threshold. His hands were white with flour and dust swirled around his head and his exhilaration was boyish but noble.

"Come and see what I've been doing."

Diggs led Pollard into a back room where a table stood with an enormous loaf on a tray. The loaf was embossed with the equals sign that was the Reconstruction Club's adopted symbol. "Charming," said Pollard.

"I thought you'd be impressed. It's for our next meeting."

"Rufus and Jaspers will be grateful."

"What's the matter, old fellow? You seem agitated."

"It's just very hot in here."

"The ovens, of course. You are sweating heavily. Take care not to dehydrate." And as Diggs wiped his own brow with a napkin, Pollard seized the opportunity to tell the ruddy baker about the mummified gondolier and to solicit his help. It was almost as if the brief exchange had been scripted.

"By all means, but what can I do?" Diggs panted.

"We need your bread shovel for an oar, and maybe yourself as a volunteer. When we reconstruct the incident there must be one to paddle the boat. It's your shovel and your arms are strong. Will you do it?"

Diggs smiled. Asking was a formality. He couldn't refuse. The club had strict rules that were unwritten but inviolable.

The newspapers contributed no further information about the strange case. All the members bought a paper every day and devoured it. Venice was too far away, a dead man in a leaking gondola too unimportant. The week ended, and on Sunday morning the club reconvened to discuss progress.

"I have managed to pick up a radio station in Venice," Pollard informed them, his facial muscles twitching in excitement. "It broadcasts mostly music, but I think there are news bulletins too, and surely those bulletins are concerned with local affairs. The problem is that I don't speak any Italian."

None of the club members knew that language. But Gertie said, "There's a college of modern language studies in Norwich, isn't there? Maybe we could hire one of the students to listen and translate for us."

"I'll arrange that," offered Chunder.

Now it was Beastly's turn. "Death from thirst and death from drinking sea water are identical things," he said, "for the drinking of sea water encourages the body to lose more liquid than it absorbs. Dehydration is the result in both cases and all the stages of the process are the same. The tongue swells up, the blood thickens, then the brain shrinks and even tears away from the inside of the skull. The saltier the water, the faster the death, but it is still painful."

"And the waters of Venice are brackish," Chunder added. "A mix of salt and fresh. They can be drunk in small quantities, I suppose, but they are hardly the cleanest on the planet. Disease would probably be the result, even if dehydration wasn't. A thirsty man, a man driven to extremes by thirst, would surely cup them to his lips and drink. He wouldn't care about the risk of bugs."

"Did you obtain a map of the city?" asked Rufus.

Chunder nodded and spread a map on the bare floor. There were no carpets in any room of this house. They examined the map, the injured men on the sofa straining to lean forward with a popping of rusty springs. The smallness of Venice, the scattering of tiny islands that formed the city in the lagoon around it, was striking. It looked as if Venice had been dropped from a height and had fractured into thousands of shards. It was a full five minutes before Rufus said:

"You can fold it away now. I am getting a clear picture."

The others exchanged glances.

"I don't suppose you'll tell us anything yet?" ventured Gertie.

"No. I may be very wrong."

More information was needed. Chunder paid a visit to a professor he was distantly related to at the College of Modern Languages, and the professor arranged for one of his most promising students to visit Pollard and listen to the broadcasts from Venice. She was a young woman, much to everyone's surprise, and Pollard was nervous as he answered the door to her and led her to his attic. She sat primly on a stool next to his own with a notebook and pencil. She listened through the headphones with an ironic smile and jotted down words as they came.

"You are translating in your head," said Pollard.

"Sorry?" She was unable to hear him, and so she removed the headphones, gazing at him with big brown eyes. "You said?"

Pollard dropped his eyes, saw flesh between her shoe and the hem of her skirt and before he quite knew what he was doing, blurted, "You have a very nice ankle, Miss Worthington. Yes, it simply must be stated."

"I have two of them, a pair. And call me Laura, please."

"Oh really, two of them?"

"I'm afraid so. Now then, the news bulletin is over and the station is broadcasting music again. Do you require me to remain?"

He did, for personal reasons, but was unable to bring himself to admit it, so with a shake of the head he led her back down the stairs and to the front door. "Tomorrow at the same time, Miss Worthington…?"

"Of course," Laura said.

And Pollard experienced the most awkward week of bliss he had ever known, but when he came to read the notes she had taken, he was rather disappointed. There was nothing at all about the mummy in the gondola. The news was mostly political, and it was plain that the country of Italy was going through some momentous changes. The government had been replaced by some fellow named Mussolini who had aggressive supporters and equally forceful opponents. A plot against the Venetian authorities had been uncovered and the police had taken preemptive action to defeat it. Infiltrators had been prevented from entering the city. Pollard wondered what use this might be to Rufus. He would find out in due course.

And he did find out. Rufus was delighted by the news.

"All the pieces are in place now."

"I don't even know what the pieces are," grumbled Gertie.

Rufus sucked gently on his pipe.

"Four infiltrators, let us say saboteurs, were expected to arrive in Venice. It seems certain they would have chosen to do so at night. And from the sea. One of the many modern playwrights I was keen on reading before my injury was a chap by the name of Gabriele D'Annunzio. After the Great War, he put together a private army, invaded and took over the town of Fiume in Croatia, declaring it an independent state. Many of the troops under his command were former members of the *Arditi*, the elite storm troopers of the Italian army, devoted to him but also to the principles of force, death, war, and the eternal inequality of people."

"And the fellow who has just come to power in Italy, Mussolini, seems to embody that type perfectly," commented Pollard.

"Exactly! And to the best of my knowledge, Venice is not a socialist-inclined city. The authorities there must welcome what has happened. But not everyone in Italy has the same sensibility on this question…"

He asked for the notes Laura Worthington had made and received them in his still bandaged hands. He read them carefully.

"The news bulletin mentions the *Arditi del Popolo*, who were a breakaway group devoted to socialism, communism, and anarchism. They were the deadly enemies of D'Annunzio and now will be equally opposed to Mussolini. It is four members of this organization who planned to sneak into Venice undetected in order to cause chaos in the city. My friends, the time has come!"

They knew what that meant. They were almost ready for a reconstruction. No one doubted the competence of Rufus, but they were bemused as he gave instructions for them to assemble next Sunday on the Coslany Street bridge that Pollard had crossed on his way home. "We require a boat," he added, "and salt, lots and lots of it. Do you know where a ton of salt might be obtained?"

"You use salt in your baking, don't you?" Gertie asked Diggs. "I mean, as well as flour, sugar, and yeast. Bread contains salt."

"But not a ton of the stuff."

"Will you provide it?"

Diggs nodded. "I will purchase some more. I will bring it. But I don't know where we might buy or borrow a boat from."

Rufus coughed. "Why don't we use this sofa?"

"Won't it sink?"

"Not immediately, no."

Slowly they chewed the special loaf Diggs had brought them. It was a little stale, but no one protested. Gertie went to brew tea. Jaspers sank deeper into the sofa, as if acutely aware that soon he would have to sit on the floor instead. The house needed a few chairs, but would it ever get them? Probably not. The Reconstruction Club had a formal disdain for luxury. The only comfort they allowed themselves was the comfort that came from solving crimes, especially those so-called impossible cases. The sofa had been requisitioned. It was doomed.

Pollard wanted to see Miss Worthington again before the day of the reconstruction, but he lacked the nerve, and so a possible romance was finished before it had begun. Jaspers pined helplessly for Mrs. Busker. What romantic daydreams, if any, Rufus had would remain a mystery. As for the others, they were too busy with their wives, jobs, and habits to yearn for anything they did not already have. The fateful day dawned at last. Beastly and Gertie came to pick up the sofa and load it into a van that belonged to Chunder's brother, who was a housepainter. Rufus and Jaspers did not stir from the cushions and grimly rode all the way from Livingstone Street to Coslany Street like thrill seekers on a damaged roller coaster.

Pollard, Chunder, and Diggs were waiting for them. The sacks of rock salt were in place, lined up against the bridge railings. Jaspers and Rufus dismounted. It took four of them to hurl the sofa over the side. It landed with a powerful splash that sprayed a weedy water over them. Then it bobbed and settled among its own concentric ripples and Rufus pointed imperiously at Diggs.

"Take the paddle and climb down onto the boat."

There was a flight of stone steps leading to the river. Norwich was a place where boating was a normal pursuit. Diggs hurried and reached the bottom step just as the sofa floated past. It was less than a yard away. He leaped and landed squarely in the middle, keeping his balance by executing a peculiar set of body gyrations. The sofa sank lower in the water, but it bore his weight, and the other club members burst into applause. Diggs grinned back up at them.

"Maintain an erect posture," said Rufus, "and start paddling."

"Yes, I will," replied Diggs.

This was the spot where the river widened a little. He dipped his oar into the oily green depths and pushed with all his strength. The sodden sofa began moving against the slow current, but not quite in a straight line. It described a gentle curve. Diggs was alarmed by this, but Rufus called to him:

"Keep paddling! Don't stop. Just keep paddling…"

Diggs obeyed diligently.

"He's going around in circles," said Gertie.

"Open the sacks of salt."

Pollard did so with a penknife. The salt was in blocks the size of a human fist and it was extremely hard. To crumble it, two blocks had to be bashed together. Even so, this was not the sort of salt one sprinkles on a dinner. Pollard was reminded of a book he once read about the legendary city of Timbuktu with houses made from blocks of salt in a land where it never rained.

Rufus called down, "Are you perspiring yet?"

"Yes, yes I am," puffed Diggs.

"Then keep paddling. Don't stop. Whatever happens, don't stop. We have faith in you, my friend. We *trust* you utterly."

Diggs nodded and that was when the first salt rock struck him on the nape of the neck. Rufus had thrown it, wincing as he did so, for his own body was still painful. A deep sigh escaped the mouth of Diggs, but he said nothing in protest. Rufus looked at his colleagues and said, "It's necessary."

One by one they selected a piece of salt and cast it at Diggs on the river below. As the missiles rained down, some missing, some on target, Diggs uttered muffled cries of pain that seemed to encourage the other club members to greater efforts. Soon the sofa was littered with chunks of salt that glistened. But Diggs kept paddling and his improvised boat went around in circles.

"It is daylight, so he can see where's he is going," pointed out Rufus, "but imagine if he was paddling at *night*. He might think he was going in a perfectly straight line. I can see the sweat pouring off him. He looks like a squeezed sponge!" And he hurled a jagged piece of salt that struck the baker in the chest and made him exhale his breath and sprang huge drops of perspiration on his brow. His head was covered in shards of salt that drank up this moisture instantly.

"Keep bombarding him. Forget he's our friend," said Rufus.

Then Pollard seized the last unopened sack and lifted it with both arms above his head. It was the size of a small boulder, and when the sofa on its circular path passed near the bridge he hurled it brutally down.

It struck Diggs full in the face, smashing his nose flat and knocking several of his teeth out. His lower jaw hung open unnaturally. He dropped the paddle and clutched at his mangled mouth. The whites of his eyes were bright red and a dark fluid thinner than blood flowed out of both his ears.

The rain of lesser missiles ceased.

"What now?" asked Beastly.

"Watch closely and see," said Rufus, and he pointed.

Diggs sank to his knees.

"Try to remain standing upright," shouted Rufus.

Diggs stood erect but wavered.

The blood streamed down the lower half of his face and poured onto the sofa, but the sofa was already covered in blocks, splinters and crumbs of salt which drank the fluid thirstily. Every droplet that fell from him, whether blood, sweat, tears, or saliva, vanished into the salt within moments.

Then Diggs fell into the river and spluttered there.

"Go and fetch him," said Rufus.

Gertie and Pollard looked at each other. Chunder took an indecisive step forward. There was a pause and then all three of them set off together, scuttled down the stone steps and managed to snatch Diggs as he floated past. They dragged him to the bridge and set him down before Rufus, who said:

"We ought to take him to a hospital, I guess."

They lifted him into the back of the van, and everyone else clambered aboard. The sofa sank with a panoply of bubbles as they drove away. They deposited Diggs in the nearest hospital before returning to Livingstone Street. Without a sofa the front room seemed alarmingly bigger and also unfriendly. They sat on the floor and Rufus spoke at length about the conclusions he had drawn from the reconstruction. It had been an outstanding success, he said, and he thanked them. And as he spoke, he evoked very forcefully a strange world of intrigue.

The government of Italy had fallen into the hands of radical nationalists. And the opponents of the new regime had decided to move quickly. They arranged for agents to enter those cities that had most closely aligned themselves with Mussolini and do damage there, to sabotage machinery, kidnap politicians, rouse the mob to fury, the usual revolutionary stuff. Four members of the *Arditi del Popolo* had been selected to enter Venice stealthily in the middle of the night. A coastal vessel had sailed into the lagoon surrounding the city and a gondola had been lowered over the side. Three of the saboteurs were passengers and the fourth acted the part of the gondolier. This was the safest way to enter Venice undetected.

But on that coastal steamer was a double agent, a man who secretly supported the nationalists and was against the plot. He decided to ruin the four saboteurs. First he killed three of them; exactly how is unknown and unimportant. But he was unable to kill the fourth. If a gondola wasn't lowered into the lagoon with four people on it, his own counterplot would be detected by those on board who opposed Mussolini and he would certainly be executed himself. Then he had a bold and ingenious idea. The ship was a trading vessel and it happened to be carrying salt from the Sečovlje salt works, which are just across the Adriatic Sea from Venice, down the Italian coast to Ravenna or Rimini or some other port. The cunning fellow carved three large blocks into the shapes of men and covered them with blankets, then he placed them in the gondola. The fourth man later joined them and assumed they were living people. The gondola was lowered and he rowed toward Venice.

But he was no professional gondolier and had no idea that the oar he should have been given had been switched for an improvised one. The oars of Venetian gondolas are specially designed to rest in the oarlock in such a way that the slight drag of each return stroke pulls the bow back to a forward position. That is how the craft are able to maintain a straight course. But the oar used on this adventure was a simple paddle that had been extended in length. The inexperienced saboteur set off into the darkness and never knew he was propelling the gondola in large circles on the lagoon. As the coastal steamer sailed away, it unwittingly abandoned him to a terrible fate. He rowed and rowed and the effort was immense. He sweated copiously and his sweat dripped onto the four statues carved roughly from salt.

Of course he never expected his passengers to say anything. This mission was a secret one and caution was a prerequisite. He never suspected the trick. He just kept paddling all night. At some point he was so dehydrated that he dipped his hands into the lagoon and drank the cupped liquid, not knowing that this brackish water would hasten the drying out process of his flesh.

At last every last drop of moisture in his body had come out and the passengers had dissolved. He was a dry husk, but in the bottom of the gondola sloshed the very salty water that had once been inside him. He stopped paddling because he was dead and the currents pushed him by chance across the lagoon and into the city, where the gondola collided with a mooring pole. The collision caused no leak, but when it was noted that he was ankle deep in water it was assumed by the witnesses that a leak had indeed occurred. In fact he was standing in his own life juices. This might seem too elaborate a way to kill a man, but the murderer, whoever he was, had no other choice. The gondola mission simply *had* to go ahead.

Rufus stopped speaking and Chunder went to brew tea.

"Highly speculative," said Gertie.

"Of course! But the crime was an impossible one, so what else do you expect? I'm probably wrong on certain details, but…"

"It's a good enough explanation," declared Jaspers.

Rufus smiled, but not with his eyes.

A few days later, Chunder and Beastly carried Diggs into the house. The hospital had discharged him one evening. He was wrapped in bandages, his jaw encased in a peculiar half-mask of wire and plaster. They gently lowered him between Rufus and Jaspers, who were sitting on the floor with their legs stuck out before them. The three rested against the wall and began laughing. The laughter caused pain and they yowled and this set off a deeper and longer bout of laughter, and so on. Slowly the lagoon of night enclosed the room in hilarious darkness.

The House by the Thames
CHRISTINE POULSON

It was one of those chance meetings that happen now and then on the London Underground. Frank was on the down escalator at Piccadilly Circus and Stella was coming up. His eyes slid over her and then he did a double-take. Surely it wasn't—but yes, it was!—and he saw the moment when recognition dawned for her, too. As they floated past one another, she said, "Frank! See you at the top?"

At the bottom he got straight back on the up escalator.

They hugged and he said, "You look great," and she did, better than when he had first known her all those years ago. She had aged well, and being in her fifties suited her. And that scent that she was wearing—something a little musky…

She said, "So what are you doing in London, Frank?"

"Down here for a conference on family law."

"Funnily enough, I was thinking about you just yesterday. What luck, meeting like this!"

He couldn't help but be absurdly flattered.

She went on, "I remembered that you used to love all those old crime novels and stories about impossible crimes. Well, how would you like to solve a real-life locked room mystery?"

"Are you serious?"

"Come round for dinner and I'll tell you all about it. No time like the present. Are you free tonight?"

"Nothing I can't duck out of."

In fact it was the end-of-conference gala dinner, but he wasn't going to pass up this chance. They'd gone out together for a month or two when they'd been undergraduates. He'd been crazy about her, but she'd dumped him for the man she was later to marry. Much later, he too had married someone else. But now he was divorced. And so was she. He had heard that through mutual friends.

She gave him her address. "I'm in Bermondsey now," she said. "My aunt died and left me her house. That's part of the story actually, but I'll save that for tonight."

The taxi wound through narrow streets that ended in a cobbled cul-de-sac right down by the river. The little enclave had somehow survived the bombing by the Luftwaffe and the predations of postwar planners. The street must have looked much like this in Dickens's day, Frank reflected, as he paid the taxi driver. Stella's house, Pear Tree Cottage, was at the end. An elegant red brick building with sash windows and a cobweb fanlight over the door, it was set at right angles to the river. The rooms on that side must look directly onto the water. At the other end of the house was a high wall with a door set in it, the entrance to a walled garden, probably. He guessed at a date in the early 1800s. The place must be worth a fortune.

It was already dusk and a huge full moon, so orange that it was almost red, hung over the rooftops. It was a strangely sultry evening, more like August than September.

He hesitated on the doorstep, clutching a bottle of wine and a bunch of flowers. He couldn't believe how nervous he was. It was like being a teenager again.

He had thought of Stella so often over the years. It was one of those what-ifs that can haunt you for a lifetime. In the last few months he had been tempted to get in touch with her, and yet he had held back. He had done alright for himself—he lectured in law at a university in the north—but Stella inhabited a different, more glamorous world. She was a theatrical costume designer and belonged, he imagined, to a London scene of famous actors and arty types. Perhaps she would see him as someone dull and provincial.

A speedboat roared past on the river and the swell slapped against the wall only yards away. He wondered if there was a flood risk so close to the river and recognized the thought as the delaying tactic that it was.

He rang the doorbell.

It was after dinner, and Frank was sitting opposite Stella and her friend Mary in an upstairs sitting room, drinking coffee. The women were drinking herb tea. The windows looked down on the walled garden that Frank had seen from the street. The sun had set and yet, if anything, the heat seemed to be building. Perhaps there was going to be a storm. Stella had opened the window and left the door ajar in the hope of getting a through draft.

Frank had been disappointed to find that it wasn't to be dinner a deux, though in other circumstances he would have been pleased to see Mary. She had been one of their undergraduate gang, and she had matured into a striking woman with cropped white hair and vibrant red lipstick. She was a historian and, like him, had become an academic. He'd even read one of her books on the Victorian family.

At least there didn't seem to be a man around. And the children were away, one still at university, the other having a gap year abroad. Perhaps Mary would go before he did, leaving him alone with Stella…

But meanwhile, he was curious to hear the locked room story.

"I couldn't have planned it better. A historian and a lawyer," Stella said. "If you two can't work it out between you… Or maybe I ought to make it a competition and offer a prize to the winner. Anyway, the first thing you need to know is that this house has been in the family for a couple of hundred years. I inherited it from my aunt, who was childless. She got a bit eccentric in her old age, became something of a hoarder. And she got obsessed with a murder that took place here. She did a lot of research, looked at original documents, and put together a narrative of what happened. I've got it here." She gestured to an archive box by the side of her chair. "In 1838 the house was occupied by my great, great, great, great-grandparents. Celia had been married to Hubert for six years, and they had two small children. Hubert was older—twenty years older—and wealthy. He had made his money as a ship's chandler, and he'd done well enough to have a housekeeper and maids, and for Celia to have a companion, Margaret. Margaret was some kind of distant cousin."

"It was common enough for a well-to-do middle-class family to have a relative to live with them in that way," Mary remarked.

"Those two watercolor portraits are of Celia and Hubert." Stella got up and led Frank and Mary to where two small framed pictures hung on the wall.

They were half-length portraits. One was of a young woman wearing an off-the-shoulder dress. She had long hair parted smoothly in the center and cascading in ringlets on either side of her face.

Stella said, "You can see that the dress is made of brocaded silk. The pointed waistline and the boned bodice and full, pleated skirt—they were all the height of fashion in the late 1830s."

Mary laughed. 'There speaks the costume designer. You can date the portrait from what she's wearing, I expect."

"Yes, both must have been done shortly before Hubert died. Celia was a trophy wife, that's my reading of the situation. She was actually the second wife. There were grown-up children from a first marriage. By now Hubert had made his pile and he wanted everyone to know it."

Frank was staring at the portrait, fascinated. "Do you know," he said, "if you took away those ringlets, she'd look a lot like you."

Stella smiled. "You're not the first person to say that. Funny how these things come down through the generations. I think I've inherited her skill at needlework. She was a good businesswoman, too. She was the one who established the family firm of theatrical costumers. It was only wound up in the fifties."

"And this is Hubert," Mary said, examining the other portrait. "He looks like a pretty tough customer."

The picture was of a thickset man of about fifty in a double-breasted frock coat worn over an embroidered waistcoat. He was clean-shaven and balding. And Mary was right, Frank thought. There was something about the set of his mouth that suggested he might drive a hard bargain.

Stella said, "Okay, you've seen the principal characters."

They sat down and Stella said, "I want to take you back to an evening in September 1838. It was unseasonably warm—rather like today, in fact. You need to know that because it explains why the window in the first-floor drawing room was open and also why the curtains weren't closed even though it was dark. Those are important parts of the story."

"Wait," said Frank. "You mean—it happened here? This is the locked room?"

"Well, strictly speaking, not actually locked—but as good as. Let me tell you what happened." Stella took a sheaf of papers out of the box. "The three of them, Celia, Hubert, and Margaret, were sitting in this room, taking tea after dinner. It was dark by then. This is Celia's account as it was given at the inquest—and I'll tell you now that Margaret's account tallied with it in every detail."

The tea had been brought in and I had poured it out. Hubert was reading aloud to us— it was Mr. Boz's Pickwick Papers and Margaret and I were sewing. We were laughing at the droll remarks of Sam Weller, when all of a sudden there was a clattering at the window and a creature appeared on the sill. It had the appearance of a man, but like no other I had ever seen, tall and thin with eyes like burning coals, and wrapped in a black cloak. We were all three of us struck dumb with amazement. Then with a single bound—as if he was on springs—the creature leaped into the room. He seized Hubert by the hair. He raised a hand and I saw with horror that he had claws like daggers for fingers. With one sweeping stroke he cut my poor husband's throat. The next moment the creature had bounded back on the windowsill and, jumping out, disappeared into the night.

"My God!" Mary said, her hands to her mouth.

Frank stared at Stella. He hadn't been expecting anything so outlandish. "She claimed that this creature jumped in through an upstairs window?"

"And then left the same way. Drops of blood on the carpet and the windowsill seemed to confirm that part of the story. There's more. Two witnesses testified that no one had entered either before or after the women began screaming. Down in the hall at the foot of the stairs—with the door of the sitting room in full view—were the housekeeper and a local doctor who had been called in to see a sick maid. This is the housekeeper's testimony. Again, I'm reading verbatim from the report of the inquest."

I was in the hall with Dr. Jenkins in conversation concerning the indisposition of the maidservant, Hannah, when of a sudden there was a scream from the upper sitting room where I knew my master and the mistress were taking tea. Yes, the door was in my sight and had been for some ten minutes or so. Why had the conversation taken so long? Must I say? Well, then, the doctor was explaining to me that Hannah, foolish wench, was in the family way and was refusing to say who the father was. At any rate, I can testify that no one went in or out of the room while I was standing in the hall. Dr. Jenkins was taking his leave when the screaming started.

"Then there's no doubt about it. It must have been one of the women," Frank said. "Surely no one believed a trumped-up story like that."

"There were two things that swung things in their favor. Have you ever heard of Spring-heeled Jack?"

Mary frowned. "Spring-heeled Jack? Yes, of course, it was about that time, wasn't it, the late 1830s?"

"The first sighting was in 1837," Stella said. She flicked through the pages. "Here we are. A maid servant claimed that she was walking home at night across Clapham Common when a strange figure jumped out, gripped her in his arms, ripped her clothes and touched her with claws that were 'as cold and clammy as those of a corpse.' She screamed and people came rushing out of their houses, but the creature had disappeared. The next day someone or something answering the same description rushed in front of a carriage, causing the coachman to crash. Witnesses claimed that the man—if it was a man—escaped by jumping over a nine-foot wall. There were more and more sightings around the end of that year and early in 1838. One witness even claimed that the creature had leaped twelve feet, leaving no tracks in the snow. And so the legend of Spring-heeled Jack was born."

Mary sighed. "And a legend was just what it was. He's generally agreed to be a folkloric figure. There were reported sightings all over the country. It went on for years and years—right through the century. One explanation—and I think it's a likely one—is that some of the original sightings were pranks played by a group of aristocratic young men. After that, well, people were primed to see what they expected to see."

Frank agreed. "Eyewitness accounts are notoriously unreliable and people love a mystery, whether it's aliens making crop circles, or big cat sightings, or the Loch Ness Monster. Stella, you said that there were two things that persuaded people that the two women hadn't done the deed. What was the other one? I hope it was more compelling than that."

"Far more compelling, Frank, as I think even you will have to admit. I'll go on reading from the housekeeper's testimony."

We ran up the stairs and into the sitting room, where our eyes were met by a most horrid sight. My poor master was lying back in his chair with his throat cut. For a few moments I came over faint and the room spun round and all the time the mistress was screeching like a banshee. Miss Margaret was trying to help the master and there was blood all over her. James, our indoor man, heard the commotion and came running and the doctor sent him first for brandy and then for the constable. When the mistress and Miss Margaret could speak, they both told the same story about a monstrous fellow coming in through the open window and attacking the master… Yes, it was the doctor's idea that we should search the two ladies. So yes, I searched them—right down to the skin with the doctor looking on. As God is my witness, I could find no knife or blade of any kind concealed about them.

Mary was about to speak, but Stella raised a hand. "Wait, that's not all. Two constables then searched the room from top to bottom—took the room apart, in fact—and found no weapon. There was nothing bigger than a needle and a pair of miniature scissors hanging from the chatelaine belt at Margaret's waist. Neither of them could possibly have caused those terrible gashes like the raking of claws. There was nothing in that room that could have inflicted those wounds."

Frank said, "Then they must have thrown the knife—or the dagger or whatever it was—out of the window?"

"They could only have thrown it into the garden below. That too was searched by the constables."

Frank was sitting facing the open window. There was a flicker of light in the night sky.

"I think that was lightning," he said.

They waited. It was a while before there was a distant rumble of thunder.

"It's a long way off," Stella said,

A sound came from somewhere below in the house.

"What was that?" Mary said.

Another sound. Then light footsteps came tip-tapping rapidly up the stairs. The hairs went up on the back of Frank's neck.

The door opened slowly. A large black-and-white cat appeared and stood there, blinking benignly at them.

Mary let out her breath in a sigh. "I thought that was—well, I don't know what I thought."

"I've never heard that the house was haunted," Stella said, "though it wouldn't be any wonder if it was." She patted her knee. "Come on, Freddy." The cat hurried over, as if the offer might be withdrawn at any moment, and sprang onto her lap.

Mary said, "I suppose it did all really happen, did it, Stella? Why've you never mentioned it before, in all the years I've known you?"

"I didn't know myself. I'm guessing that my ancestors weren't exactly thrilled to have something like this in their family tree. They were a bourgeois lot. My aunt only discovered it when she got interested in genealogy a year or two before she died. And the solution only came to light when—" She broke off. "No, I won't say yet. Let's hear what you two think."

Frank said, "The housekeeper or the doctor, maybe both, could have been in cahoots with the women."

Stella shook her head. "No. The housekeeper was devoted to her master, she had been with the family when the first wife was alive. She was no friend of Celia's and was a reluctant witness. She had to admit that no one could have come into or out of the room—after all, the doctor was a witness too—and that she hadn't been able to find a weapon. But all the same, she believed that her mistress had done it and she went around saying so. She left the family shortly after the murder and she was actually taken before the magistrates for spreading calumny. As for the doctor, it was the first time he had attended the house and it couldn't be proved that he had met any member of the household before. He too was skeptical about Spring-heeled Jack, but equally, he couldn't explain what had happened in that room."

"I've been assuming from what you've said that the two women got away with it?" Frank said.

"Yep. My aunt was sure that Celia or Margaret were killers and that—in the melodramatic words of the time—they had cheated the gallows. But the question was—how did they pull it off?"

"And why," Mary said.

"That's not so difficult," Frank said. "Let me guess. After a discreet interval, she married again—this time to a younger man that she'd been in love with all along?"

"No, she never married again, even though she lived to a ripe old age."

"Alone?"

"Accompanied to the end by her faithful companion."

"The companion never married either?"

"That's right."

"And that was the same woman that was in the room when her husband died?"

"It was."

There was a thoughtful silence.

Frank said, "Celia had two small children, didn't she? And the year was
1838. That was before the Custody of Infants Act. If a marriage broke down,
a woman had very few rights over her children. In the majority of cases,
custody was awarded to the husband. Even babies and small children could be
removed from their mother."

Mary nodded in agreement. "And there were precious few ways of getting
rid of an inconvenient or even an abusive husband—at least for the middling
classes. Divorce as we know it didn't exist. Then as now, those with sufficient
money and privilege could usually find a way, but even so the advantage was
all on the husband's side."

"Okay," Frank said. "Let's assume that the one or other of the two women
did the deed. How could a weapon like that just vanish from a room?"

"Over to you, Frank," Stella said, and there was a challenge in her voice.

He thought about it.

There was another flash of light and a clap of thunder, a little closer this
time. The weather was breaking and a good thing, too. It was so humid. His
shirt was sticking to his back.

At last he said, "Well, there's that staple of locked room stories, the dagger
that's made of ice and then melts. But there wouldn't have been time for that,
even if it was a warm evening—and I can see from the expression on your face
that it's not the answer. Alright then. How about this? The dagger was made
of glass, and it was concealed in a jug of water or in a vase containing flowers?
I read a story recently in which that was the solution."

Stella laughed. "Great idea, but it doesn't happen to be right."

Frank sighed. "I wish I could have searched that room."

"Well, here's the next best thing. They made an inventory. I've got a copy for
each of you." She fished them out of the archive box and handed them over.

Frank studied it. The inventory certainly seemed comprehensive. Even the
individual contents of a sewing basket were listed. And yet nothing suggested a
solution to him.

Mary reached the same conclusion. She shrugged. "Nothing you wouldn't
expect to see in an ordinary well-to-do middle-class household. And nothing
here that could inflict the kind of wound that you've described."

"I'll give you a clue. Look for what wasn't in the room and should
have been."

Frank looked again. "Nope. Can't see anything."

"Look at the contents of the sewing basket."

After a few moments, Mary said, "Wait, Celia was sewing, yes? There should have been a pair of scissors?"

"That's right. As I said, there was only a miniature pair attached to a chatelaine belt that Celia wore."

Frank said, "They made sure that there was nothing in the room that could be seen as a weapon."

In spite of the warmth of the evening, he felt a chill. The outline of a monstrous crime was becoming clearer. How carefully the women must have planned it!

Mary said, "Did your aunt work out what had happened?"

"Sadly not. Ironically, the final piece of the jigsaw fell into my hands only after she died. Just a couple of days ago, in fact." Stella paused for dramatic effect. "It was here all the time, in this very house. Though I can't take much credit," she added. "It was quite by chance that I found the murder weapon."

She took from the archive box a narrow, slender object made of some hard, white material like ivory, not much thicker than a knitting needle.

She gave it to Frank. "Careful how you handle that."

He saw that one side had been sharpened to a fine blade.

"Yes, that would have done the job alright," he said. "But how on earth did they manage to conceal it?"

"Let me see." Mary took the object from him. She examined it, and a curious expression appeared on her face. "Is it whalebone?" she asked.

Stella nodded.

Mary shook her head. "So that was how they did it..."

Frank stared at them, baffled...and uneasy. He didn't understand. But then something stirred in the back of his mind. The portrait with the nipped-in waist... Celia's skill as a needlewoman...

And then he also knew. "You mean, that—that was—"

"Yes," Stella said. "It was sewn into her dress. No, that's not quite right. It was actually part of her dress. Whalebone would have been used as boning in her bodice. You can see it in the portrait. She must have been wearing this very dress. Celia or Margaret must have undone the stitching, removed the bone, sharpened it, and put it back in the bodice. And then this is what must have happened that evening. Celia took the sharpened whalebone out of her bodice. Margaret clapped her hand over Hubert's mouth while Celia did the deed. He wouldn't have realized what was happening until it was too late. They cleaned the knife by wiping it on Margaret's dress. That would be covered in blood anyway, to be explained away by her cradling the dying man. They inserted the whalebone back into the bodice and Celia sewed it in, a matter of a minute or two for an expert needlewoman. Only then did they start screaming."

"But where did you find it?" Mary asked.

"I told you my aunt was a hoarder, and it clearly ran in the family. There was stuff in the attic that had been there for generations. When I started clearing it out, I found a trunk full of old clothes, including this dress. It was just what I needed for that adaptation of Mrs. Gaskell's *Wives and Daughters*. I took it apart to make a pattern from it—and found that." She pointed to the sharpened whalebone.

"Why didn't they dispose of the evidence?" Mary wanted to know.

"It wouldn't be so easy to get rid of the dress without people wondering why. In those days, clothes like that were valuable. It couldn't just be thrown out, and she couldn't have given the dress to someone else—they might have wanted to alter it and undo the stitching. Better to quietly pack it up and store it in the attic."

"Do you think they were in love, those two, Celia and Margaret?" Mary asked.

"That's my guess," Stella admitted. "And I've wondered too about that pregnant maid. Could that perhaps have been laid at Hubert's door? But I guess we'll never know what drove them to do what they did."

Frank listened in silence. Yes, in those days, it had been hard if not impossible for a woman to escape from a marriage, no matter how bad. And who knew what lay beneath the bland, respectable exterior of the paterfamilias of the portrait? Hubert might have been an adulterer, a brute, a sadist. But all the same: to do what those two women had done, to commit such a cold-blooded murder, so breathtaking in its sheer inventiveness and audacity...

What had Hubert thought and felt in those last few moments, when his wife—or was it her companion?—had grabbed his hair and pulled his head back? Frank felt nauseous. But even worse was the thought of Celia calmly wiping the blade clean and sewing it back into the bodice with meticulous little stitches. And all in this very room. It wasn't just a puzzle, like something out of a John Dickson Carr novel. It had really happened.

The heat was humid, stifling. Mary and Stella were sitting opposite, as those other two women had sat here so long ago. It seemed that they were looking at him strangely.

"Are you alright?" Mary asked. "You've gone pale."

Frank said, "I'm fine, really, it's just—it's getting late. I've got an early start in the morning. I'd better ring for an Uber." All thoughts of outstaying Mary had gone. Politeness compelled him to ask if he could give her a lift.

Stella said, "Mary's staying over." She smiled at her and Mary smiled back.

And with that, Frank saw that there wasn't a chance for him and there never had been. He had totally misread the situation. He only hoped Stella hadn't guessed what had been in his mind—but he felt sure she had. He couldn't wait to get away.

Luckily the taxi came quickly. The two women came down to see him off. He said his thank-yous and how interesting it had been.

Stella said, "Now that we've met up again, we must keep in touch." Of course he said he would, all the while thinking that wild horses wouldn't get him back to this house.

Stella opened the door and cool air flowed in. The temperature was falling and the weather was breaking at last. Forked lighting zig-zagged across the sky, followed closely by a clap of thunder. Any moment now, there would be a deluge.

The taxi had parked at the end of the cul-de-sac. Frank ran toward it. He looked back and waved. The two women were still standing in the doorway. Mary had her arm round Stella's shoulders.

He opened the door of the taxi just as the first fat drops of rain began to fall.

Black's Last Case
L.C. TYLER

Carter had waited a long time to meet Harry Black. It was unfortunate for both of them that, when it finally happened, one of them was lying on the floor with a bullet through his head. It was a nice day for it, though.

***

The wheels of the car had crunched on the hard snow as Carter and I turned off the main road and onto the long, straight carriage drive. The previous day's billowing, bruise-colored clouds had been replaced by blue skies and a warming sun, but it would still take a while for the drifts to melt. It had been quite a storm. We had long vistas across sparkling white tree-spattered parkland—the sort of countryside that estate agents describe as gently rolling, containing the sort of properties that I might have been able to afford if they'd had one or two fewer zeroes in the price.

"Do you think we'll make it all the way to the house?" asked Carter, shielding his eyes for a moment from the dazzling reflection. "The road was dodgy, but that has at least been gritted. This looks pretty deep to me."

"One car's been down here since the snow fell," I said. "You can see the tracks."

"So you can," he said. "One car leaving the house—or traveling there. Could be a four-by-four, of course."

"The tires are too narrow," I said.

"Quite right. Sorry. I wasn't thinking."

"Well, I was, and that's probably why I'm a detective inspector and you're merely a sergeant," I said. "Stop worrying and drive. If we get stuck, I'll take over at the wheel and you can get out and push."

"Could I drive and you push?"

"No," I said. "That's not the way it's done. And, from the way the crime's been reported to us, today's going to be a day for traditional, old-fashioned police work."

Carter proceeded cautiously, as he usually did. The distance to the mansion at the far end of the drive lessened bit by bit. Our speed at least allowed me all the time I needed to admire the view. It was a classic Christmas scene. The undulating snow. The manor house, a perfect cube of pink Queen Anne brick, with a white Portland stone portico set into it. The green of the firs beyond, where the ground started to rise more steeply. And, beyond them, the slender spire of a parish church, blue-gray in the distance. It would have been idyllic, if we hadn't known about the body that was lying in the library, on a blood-soaked carpet.

"Well, Black must have been doing alright for himself," I said. "You can't buy a joint like that on a policeman's salary."

"He made his money in IT," said Carter. "Then he retired early to do what he does now—happy is the man who can turn his hobby into his day job, eh? But I doubt he currently makes enough from it to pay his gardener."

"If you knew him that well, are you sure you should be investigating his death?" I asked.

"Of course, I've never actually met him or spoken to him," said Carter. He turned, somewhat riskily, and looked at me rather than at the road. His disappointment was plain to see, but that was his problem, not mine. I just had to work out how Black had been killed and who had killed him. That was plenty to be going on with.

"Just focus on the job at hand, Sergeant," I said. "And change up a gear, while you're at it. You'll be less likely to skid."

We swung onto the pristine snow outside the front portico. Nobody had come or gone this way since last night. The departing vehicle, whose tracks we'd seen, had left from somewhere at the back of the house, where the garages might conceivably be, not from the front door. It was a big place—no doubt about that. There might be almost anything hiding in the grounds—stables, garages, barns, dairies, servants' quarters—who could say? I got out of the car and felt my feet sink, almost up to my ankles, in icy whiteness. I hadn't packed boots. A rookie error. I hoped we wouldn't be searching the grounds too much.

A maid in a black dress, white apron, and little lace cap opened the great mahogany door before I'd even rung the bell. We must have been visible for a while, inching our way down the drive. There wouldn't have been any doubt where we were going or what our business was.

I showed her my warrant card and Carter did the same.

"Was it you who phoned us?" I asked.

"Yes, sir, it was. Shall I take you gentlemen to the library? I assume you'd like to see the body straight away?"

"I should have a brief word with the victim's wife first," I said. "Could you tell her we're here?"

"Mrs. Black drove into town after breakfast," she said. "We've tried to contact her, but she seems to have her phone switched off—or there's no signal where she is. Do you want to wait for her?"

"No, in that case, we can talk to her when she returns."

"Of course, Inspector," she said. "I'll show you to the library, then."

It was the sort of library most people get to see only by paying their ten quid (plus gift aid) at the door of some crumbling stately home. There were books, floor to ceiling, on all four walls. I'd have said five or six thousand of them. And, unlike a lot of libraries in country houses, this one wasn't just moldering old leather-bound volumes of unmissed dead authors. At my elbow, I noticed much of this year's Booker Prize shortlist and, stretching away into the distance, a lot of crime novels. On the vast stretches of carpet there were some substantial leather armchairs, a leather-covered desk, and a huge globe on a brass stand. All very traditional. It wasn't a warm room—distinctly chilly, in fact—then I noticed the half-open sash. So that was how the killer had got in? I walked over to the window. There was a book on the floor, suggesting that Black might have been standing there, reading, shortly before he was shot. I noticed a confused mass of footprints outside in the snow. What had been a drift under the window had been comprehensively trampled. Very straightforward so far.

Black was currently spread, face up, arms flung outward, across the Persian carpet, right by the fireplace, twenty feet or so from the window. A deep, rich red stain was darkening as we watched. There was a single bullet hole drilled in his forehead.

"It would seem," I said, "that he was shot through the window, which he had left open in spite of the coldness of the day. The killer was outside in the snow. Black had been reading at the window, so his assassin knew he was in the room. The killer crept up and, choosing his moment, took aim. Black, who was now by the fireplace, heard something and turned to face the garden. The shot was fired. Black collapsed where he had been standing. The murderer then made off across the lawn."

"No," said the maid. "That simply isn't possible."

"The many footprints outside are strongly suggestive of my theory," I pointed out.

"The footprints are mine and the butler's," said the maid. "We had to gain access to the room that way, since the only internal door was locked. Entering via the garden, through the open sash window, seemed the best plan. You will see, if you lean out, that the footprints come from the side door over there. There are two distinct sets—my own small feet and the butler's larger ones. There are no others. Neither set continues across the garden in any direction that the murderer might have used to make his escape."

I walked across the room and looked out at the vast swaths of unmarked snow. I recalled how deeply my feet had sunk into it by the front entrance. You couldn't cross it without leaving obvious tracks.

"So when you and the butler arrived…"

"The snow was pure and unsullied. Nobody could have entered or left that way."

"Didn't you realize that you were tramping through a crime scene?" I asked.

"Not at that precise moment, no. Later, yes, of course. But a lot had happened before that."

"Okay, maybe you can just tell us the whole story from the beginning, then," I said.

"It would be my pleasure, sir. Well, I served Dr. Black and Mrs. Black their breakfast at eight o'clock."

"Where?" I asked.

"In the breakfast room, of course. Everything here is done in the traditional way. Everything. I cannot stress that too strongly."

"How many staff work here?"

"Just the butler and I live in. There is also a gardener and an under-gardener, but they are both on leave until the New Year. Anyway, after breakfast, the mistress said she was driving into town to do some last-minute Christmas shopping. She was also going to buy me some new work shoes, which was easy for her to do, her shoe size being coincidentally the same as mine. I think that she and Dr. Black may have had some sort of disagreement over breakfast, because he retired almost immediately to the library in a huff and locked the door, saying he had work he needed to do. We heard the sound of Mrs. Black's sports car leaving the garage at nine, just as the clocks were striking. Then, for about half an hour, nothing happened."

She paused and looked at us.

"You are sure that Mrs. Black had really left?" said Carter. "You say they argued. She couldn't have secretly returned, persuaded her husband to unlock the door and let her into the library, then—"

The maid held up her hand like a traffic cop stopping a convertible with particularly dodgy tires. Her smile was a bit like that, too. "No, sir, she could not. Mrs. Black was driving very slowly because of the conditions. I happened to glance out of the window briefly when she was halfway down the drive. We heard the car's engine fade gradually into the distance. Then there was silence. There could be no doubt she had gone. Those were the only tracks on the drive until your own car arrived—she couldn't have driven back again. The butler and I got on with the clearing away and the washing-up. Then, half an hour after Mrs. Black had left, the butler said to me: 'Was that a shot I heard?' "

"Was it?" I asked.

"With hindsight, yes. At the time, we were uncertain."

"So Dr. Black was killed at nine thirty?" I said.

"No, sir, at least I don't think so. As I say, we weren't at all sure that it was a gunshot—it actually seemed a bit improbable in a comfortable country house in a peaceful English village—so we just carried on putting things away. Then, twenty minutes later, there was another sound, just like the first. We looked at each other and wondered if Dr. Black had just gone to the library to watch some detective program on television."

"Does he often do that?" I asked.

"Yes. Anything by Agatha Christie. Or *Midsomer Murders*. Or *Death in Paradise*. Or *Jonathan Creek*. That sort of thing."

"I saw a lot of Golden Age mysteries on the bookshelves," I said.

"He had an extensive collection."

"Chandler? Hammett? Macdonald?"

"Not so much, sir."

"He was missing some good stuff," I said. "Anyway, after the second shot, you still didn't go and investigate?"

"No, sir. Not until what seemed to be a third shot, another twenty minutes after the second. That was when we both went to the library and found the door firmly locked against us. We could see the key was clearly in the lock on the other side. We knocked, of course, but there was no reply. We knocked harder, then listened. The room was as silent as the grave, if you'll excuse the slightly unfortunate expression. The butler suggested that we use the side door to get outside and look in through the window. We walked across the snow—the completely unmarked snow—until we reached the window. We were surprised to find it open. The butler gave me a leg up and I was inside in a jiffy. And that's what I found."

She pointed to Dr. Black's body. It was an incongruous addition to a scene of time-honored comfort. The leather of the armchairs looked soft and inviting. On a small table were a pipe, tobacco, and matches. It could have been any library in any English country house over the past sixty or seventy years. Only the open laptop on the desk struck a jarring modern note. Though this was clearly a room for serious work, a number of concessions had been made to the coming festive season. There were Christmas cards arranged on a table. Large bunches of holly hung on either side of the mirror. On the mantelpiece was one of those decorations where four candles cause metal angels to spin round and round when the wicks are lit. The candles had burned down completely. The angels were stationary. For some reason, something that looked a bit like thin fishing line had been wrapped round the spindle, quite a lot of it.

"He must have lit that this morning," said the maid. "I can't think why. He said he was getting straight down to work."

"Well, he clearly didn't," I said. "You say the door was still locked from the inside when you found him?"

"Yes, sir."

"Could he have shot himself? asked Carter.

"No sign of the gun," I said. "And you can see there are no contact wounds. He was shot from a distance of several feet at the very least. It doesn't look as if he was shot from outside the window. But if the killer was inside the room, how did he get out again? Not via the window—no footprints. And not via the door—that was locked and the key in it."

"I suppose there are no secret passages?" Carter asked the maid hopefully.

"Absolutely not," she said. "Dr. Black could never abide secret passages of any sort. He said there ought to be a law against them."

"A law against them?" I asked.

"Don't worry—I understand what he meant," said Carter. "A rule—yes, a law if you want to put it that way. I agree with him completely."

I went over to the window again. "How far was this open when you first looked through it?" I asked the maid.

"About two feet, I'd have said."

I examined the windowsill. The melting snow lay there in irregular mounds, unlike the smooth, even covering of the other sills.

"You disturbed the snow as you climbed in?" I said.

"Probably, sir. Both on the windowsill and under the window. But, now I think of it, the snow on the sill was piled up in a funny sort of way even when we arrived—as if Dr. Black had been building a snowman or something there."

"A snowman?" I said.

"I know, it's odd."

I looked from the angel ornament on the mantelpiece to the window and back again.

"If he had so much work to do, why was he messing around with candles and snowmen—very small snowmen admittedly, but all the same. It wasn't as if he had to amuse some children."

"Do the Blacks have children?" Carter asked the maid.

"No, sir. I understand that Dr. Black has a twin brother in Australia."

"Estranged?" asked Carter. "Jealous of Dr. Black's success?"

"Not that I know of, sir. In fact, I believe Dr. Black's brother was planning to visit England very shortly."

"Was he indeed?" Carter looked at me significantly.

I said nothing, but squinted at the sun shining off the snow-covered lawn. "I suppose the killer could have hidden in the bushes over there," I said, "and used a rifle with telescopic sights, so that the shot passed cleanly through the opening without breaking any glass."

"The angle would be tricky," said Carter. "But it would be possible."

"Yes, it would be possible," I said. "But why did Black open the window in the first place on such a cold day?"

"Just a thought," said Carter to the maid, "was the estranged twin brother by any chance a crack shot with a rifle?"

"I think he used to do some shooting," said the maid. "Dr. Black once told me he'd won a medal of some sort."

I shook my head and examined the angle again, then turned to view the wall behind me. "Even if it was an Olympic gold," I said, "I'm afraid it still doesn't work, Carter. Do you see that mark on the top shelf of the bookcase?"

"Looks like a bullet hole," said Carter. He whistled through his teeth.

"Right through the spine of that volume of John Dickson Carr. And there's another down there in the skirting board, just below *The Murder of Roger Ackroyd*. The angle for those two really would be impossible from the bushes, even if somebody could have got one shot neatly under the sash window and into Dr. Black."

"So there were three shots," said the maid. "Just as we thought." She seemed pleased.

"Exactly," I said, "not one shot but three. And that presents other problems. Not only does the killer need to have stood either inside the library or just outside the window in order to hit all three spots—and we agreed both of those things are impossible—but we are now also saying that the killer fired the first shot at John Dickson Carr, then, twenty minutes later, a second at the skirting board just below Agatha Christie, then, twenty minutes after that, one straight through Dr. Black's forehead. And Black apparently just stayed put in the library while the bullets were being sprayed around, neither making a run for it nor calling for help."

"Maybe the killer shot Black first?" said Carter.

"Then remained here for forty minutes, firing random shots at the wall while he waited to be caught?"

"I agree that's not usual," said Carter. "The accepted thing to do is to get the hell out."

I turned back to the maid. "Do you know what Dr. Black and his wife argued about at breakfast?" I asked her.

"No, sir. I just heard her say that something was not possible and Dr. Black say it certainly was."

"It doesn't help us much," said Carter.

"Or maybe it does," I said. "I agree that, on the face of it, we're left with an impossible murder. A dead body in a locked room—the only possible exit across virgin snow and no footprints in it. And a window opened for no good reason I can see. No contact wound and no gun, strongly suggestive of it not being suicide. But he's dead and there must be a rational cause."

"A helicopter!" said Carter. "The killer is lowered on a rope, onto the windowsill. He opens the window, climbs in and shoots Dr. Black, then leaves the same way."

"You say you heard the car leaving very clearly," I said to the maid. "Did you, by any chance, also hear a helicopter?"

"No, sir," she said. "Anyway, that wouldn't explain the three shots, the pile of snow on the ledge, and the angel-candle thingy."

"True," I said. "Especially the angel-candle thingy. Everything in the room looks normal enough, but a fishing line wound round a Christmas decoration is odd, isn't it?"

I continued my examination of the room. There was absolutely no sign of the murder weapon. No clue as to how the killer might have left the locked library. Then, just above the angel-candle thingy, I noticed a staple in the wall. It was a simple bent piece of wire, securely hammered home. Higher up, there was another. Eventually I traced six of them between the fireplace and the window opposite. The final one was in the wood of the sill itself.

"They look fresh and untarnished," I said. "A recent addition to the decor?"

"I'm sure they are," said the maid. "I dust in here once a week. A staple like that would snag in the duster something terrible. I'm certain I would have noticed them. I dusted here on Monday, so I'd say somebody had put them in over the last couple of days."

"The line round the angel-candle thingy," I asked. "How long is it?"

Carter and I unraveled the line. When passed through each staple in turn, it just reached the window. Indeed, there was no more than six inches to spare. Once in place it was almost invisible.

"When the spindle turns, it winds in the line," I said. "The line passes through the staples, which hold it all in place."

"And raises the window?" asked Carter.

"I doubt it would be strong enough," I said. "The line's quite thin. Black, or somebody, must have raised the window himself."

"Well, there's nothing else over here now that you could attach the line to," said Carter. "Maybe there was something that the line was supposed to drag with it, and Black later removed it? What about the book on the floor below the window?"

"Sorry," said the maid. "I think I must have knocked it off the sill as I climbed in. It was sort of propped up there."

I looked at the book more closely. There was a dusting of gray powder on one side.

"Gunshot residue?" asked Carter.

"I'd have said so. So, if the book was on the sill, that suggests the killer stood just outside in the garden—which we've already said was impossible."

Carter frowned, but even his fertile imagination offered no solution.

"Who has access to the room?" I asked the maid.

"Normally? Pretty much everyone. The master locks it only when he has a particularly difficult problem to work on and doesn't want to be disturbed. Well, if that's all, would you gentleman like tea in the drawing room?"

"We may as well," I said. "We're done here. Then I'd like to talk to Mrs. Black."

"Not so fast," said Carter, addressing the maid. "We're relying on everything you've told us being the truth—that the door really was locked from the inside and that the mess of footprints outside is just you and the butler. Of course, the convention is that the evidence of servants is to be relied upon, because they are considered too stupid to be devious."

"Dr. Black frequently said the same thing, sir."

"But not always. You might, for example, have had a secret relationship with the long-lost twin brother in Australia, who could well have been left a substantial bequest in his brother's will. You waited until Mrs. Black had left. You arranged for a recording of gunshots to be played, somewhere in the house, for the butler's benefit, to disguise the timing of the murder. Then you knocked on the library door, knowing that Dr. Black, already annoyed and now in the middle of his work, would not reply. You went round the side, getting the butler to let you into the room first. You took a small pistol with a silencer from your apron pocket and shot Dr. Black through the head, fired two more shots at the wall, then called to the butler that you had stumbled on the body. Then you phoned me, saying that Dr. Black had been murdered. That's exactly what happened, wasn't it?"

"Do you in fact possess a small pistol?" I asked the maid.

"No," she said. "Dr. Black never allowed the servants to keep live ammunition in the house. Just in case he was wrong about the lack-of-deviousness thing. Anyway, why would I fire two shots at the wall?"

"Okay," said Carter. "Fair enough. Just thought I'd run it past you both anyway."

The door behind us opened. A tall, elegantly dressed lady, still wearing a snow-speckled fur coat, swept into the room. She looked at Dr. Black's body.

"Idiot," she observed. "I knew this would happen sooner or later."

"You must be Dr. Black's wife," I said.

"Dr. Black's widow," she said. She fitted a cigarette into a long ivory holder, lit it, and drew in a lungful of smoke. "Hudson told me that Harry was dead in his study. I just wanted to check he'd got it right. Traditionally, you can rely on statements from servants, but... Well, that's that, then. Have you been offered tea, by the way?"

"I think this is probably a good time to have some," I said.

"Not so fast," said Carter to Mrs. Black. "You claim to have driven into town to get some Christmas shopping. The servants heard the car's engine fading away, but you could have got somebody else to drive the car— possibly Dr. Black's long-lost twin brother—making them think you'd gone. Meanwhile, everyone's attention being distracted by the artificially slow departure of the car, you quickly ran ahead of your husband, getting to the library first. You shot him, then hid behind the sofa. Nobody came, so you fired twice more to attract attention. After the maid had discovered the body and had gone to make the phone call to the police, you climbed out of the window, onto the now very conveniently disturbed snow, your shoe size being, as the maid had already told us, coincidentally, exactly the same size as hers. You made you way back into the house via the side door. Then you waited until you heard us arrive. Finally, you appeared here, as if you had really been into town."

"Hudson is currently unloading the car," she said. "I have credit card receipts from half the shops in town, all timed and dated, together with a pair of black work shoes in the right size for the maid."

"Thank you," said the maid. "Very kind of you, I'm sure."

"My pleasure. You will appreciate, Inspector, that I couldn't have both shopped and killed my husband. Since it was so close to Christmas, I, like any woman in my position, had to prioritize shopping. You can see that, surely?"

"Then," said Carter, "I am completely stumped. Do you have Earl Grey? With lemon—no sugar?"

"Earl Grey would be excellent," I said, "but I think we have now enough evidence to know what happened. Strangely it was the book on the floor that was the final clue. A seemingly unimportant detail, but it had to be there for a reason."

"Did it?" said Carter. He was not pleased.

"Of course. It's obvious how my husband was killed," said Mrs. Black. "I assume the maid told you about our argument?"

"A little," said Carter.

"And didn't you spot the almost invisible fishing line and the angel-candle thingy?"

"Yes. We did," said Carter.

"And the pile of the snow by the window?" she said. "And the gunshot residue on the book?"

"Yes. We got all that," he said. "What about the twin brother in Australia, though?"

"Were you really taken in by that obvious red herring?"

Carter shuffled his feet and said nothing.

"And you doubtless found the gun?" she asked.

"No, I said, "we didn't. Was that critical?"

"No. Not critical, just mildly surprising. So, with all that and my husband's profession, it should have been obvious. You both know what my husband did, of course?"

"Carter explained on the way here," I said. "Your husband wrote crime novels. Carter is a bit of a fan of his, aren't you, Sergeant?"

"I've read them all," said Carter.

"Locked room mysteries mainly," said Mrs. Black despondently. "Very traditional, fair-play plots that stuck to the rules. He wouldn't have stooped to resorting to a secret passage as the solution or to an estranged twin brother merely mentioned in passing. It didn't earn him much, but it kept him amused after he sold the IT business."

"And the argument this morning…?" Carter asked.

"He'd come up with particularly implausible plot. He thought you could commit a murder by attaching some fishing line to a candle ornament like that one. When the victim lights the candles, the spinning movement winds the line in. The far end of the line is connected to the trigger of a pistol, which is propped in the open window by packing a heap of snow round the handle to keep it in place and concealed behind a book artfully placed on the sill. The spinning angels activate the trigger, and the shot is fired directly at the spot in which the victim would be standing. The sun outside melts the snow and the gun falls backward out of the window into the snowdrift, unnoticed, where it can be collected later by the killer."

"Ingenious," Carter said. "It would have been one of his best plots."

"Or, to put it another way, another load of total crap," she said. "I mean, really? The fishing line would snag. You couldn't possibly aim the gun that accurately. You couldn't depend on the line detaching itself from the trigger after firing the fatal shot and then reeling all the way in. And the gun would be quickly discovered in the snowdrift—unless, of course, people trampled over the snow soon after it fell, disguising the obvious hole it would have made. I told him it was impossible. He said he'd prove me wrong. He went off to the library to work on it. From the bullet holes in the top row of books and the skirting board, the first time he failed to use enough snow and the gun tipped backward too soon. The second time he overcompensated, and the bullet went much too low. But the third time…"

"Third time, he struck lucky," said Carter. "Shame he didn't move fast enough to get out of the way of the shot, but well done him, I say."

We looked at the body again and, for the first time, I noticed on the face of the corpse a look of smug satisfaction.

Mrs. Black nodded thoughtfully. "It was the way he'd have wanted to go," she said.

Killing Kiss
LAVIE TIDHAR

Beyond the ghetto walls the trains pass in the night. They whistle greetings. Their wheels screech on the tracks. And Shomer's boy so loves the trains. Shomer and Avrom stand by the walls and listen. Shomer holds his boy's hand. There are rumors of the deportations to the East. Resettlement, some say. Others speak in hushed voices of more terrible things. The trains go full, but they return empty. And more and more they go.

There is nothing in fiction as terrible as that which can be found in the real world, Shomer thinks. Before the war he used to be a writer of shund *or* pulp*. Now his mind keeps desperately trying to escape.*

"Daddy, Daddy," Avrom says. "Can we go on the trains, one day?"

And Shomer doesn't have the words to say what can't be said. He hoists his boy up in his arms and holds him tight, and his mind shies from the glare. A story, then, another one. A simple, easy tale of mystery and murder in which order still prevails.

There's hope even in stories, still. As futile as they are.

And so:

1

His name was Edward Kiss, but despite the name he was as German as a liverwurst sandwich. He paced round my office above the Jew baker's shop and glared at me mournfully.

"You see, Herr Hitler, I fear someone wishes to murder me."

I couldn't blame them if they would, I thought, but didn't say. I rubbed the bridge of my nose. The man was already giving me a headache and it wasn't even lunchtime.

"You must help me, Herr Hitler!"

"It's Wolf now," I said tiredly. "Just Wolf."

It was a cold and dismal London spring and I had not seen the sun for days. I stared at this unwelcome specimen who had intruded into my office and wondered how I could get rid of him. Maybe with some lead aspirin, if I got lucky.

"What is it you do again?"

He puffed up all importantly. "I'm an archaeologist," he said.

"I see," I said. I didn't.

"I am in London for a conference," he said. "Of the *Ahnenerbe*. We are a loosely-affiliated group of like-minded free thinkers on the origins of the Aryan race, racial theory, Glacial Cosmology, phrenology, and the like. Important, real science. Not like that corrupted Jewish rot people subscribe to nowadays, that awful nonsense of relativity and suchlike."

I was very fond of *Glazial-Kosmogonie* myself, though I didn't tell him that.

"So why would anyone want to murder you?"

He shrugged. "I'm sure I don't know."

"Do you owe anyone money?"

"I say, Herr Wolf!"

Which meant he probably did.

"Been rolling in the hay with the wrong *fräulein*, have you?"

"I say!"

Which meant he probably had.

"So what?" I said. "What did you do?"

"Nothing, Herr Wolf. I am the victim here!"

"Prospective victim," I said.

"There have been two attempts so far," he said. "A highly poisonous spider—a Chilean Recluse Spider, in fact"—he said it almost proudly—"was on my pillow two nights ago on the ferry to England. I squashed it to a sludge. And yesterday afternoon while taking tea, I distinctly smelled the scent of garlic in my drink. Someone must have spiked it with arsenic. I spilt it immediately, of course."

"These seem rather ridiculous ways of killing a man," I said. "I myself have always favored the bullet to the head as the simplest solution."

"Well," he said. "It is probably one of my colleagues. In our line of work we do sometimes tend to the theatrical."

"A rival?"

"Perhaps. I am very highly regarded, you see. My research into the ancient Aryan-Atlantean culture of Tihuanaku was groundbreaking!"

"Was it really?"

"You *must* help me, Herr Wolf. Or next time they might succeed."

"What is it you wish me to do, Herr Kiss?"

"Accompany me. Ensure my safety. I can pay you handsomely. Perhaps I did not mention I have a rather successful sideline as a novelist. You must have heard of *The Queen of Atlantis*? Royalties from that and my other novels are robust."

I myself had written one book, though it was nonfiction. It was about my struggle. Nowadays it was out of print, as National Socialism was no longer *de rigueur* in Europe. This was a source of some not inconsiderable pain to me.

"I'm afraid I am more of a Karl May reader," I said. "Though I have recently become very fond of Agatha Christie."

He huffed as though I'd offended him. "Pish posh," he said. "My books explore the true heritage of the Aryan race as directly descended from the great civilization of Atlantis. It is a knowledge that will change everything we think we know about history!"

It sounded like the sort of shit my old comrade Himmler was always so fond of. But those days were gone forever. Once I was great, a leader of men. Now I worked cases out of a drafty office in Soho and I was lucky if I could pay the rent.

"So?" he said. "Will you help me?"

I sighed and stared out the window. I missed the sun, and my old summer pad in the Alps, and the dog I used to have.

"I will need the cash in advance," I said.

2

A small banner inside the lobby of the Midland Grand announced The First Annual Ahnenerbe Conference on Race Science. I noted with interest that the keynote speaker was to be none other than Hans F. K. Günther, the well-known eugenicist, whose books on the origin of race had formed much of my early thinking about the fate of the Fatherland and the problem of the Jewish

Question. I would have liked to see him speak, but slapped across his face was the legend *Cancelled*.

Oh, well.

A much bigger sign above us said the conference was *Sponsored by IG Farben, purveyors of fine aspirin, heroin, toothpaste, and pesticides.*

The hotel was next to King's Cross Station, where they say that savage queen of theirs, Boudicca, lies buried. There was a woman who liked a bit of mass murder, I thought almost fondly. But she was nowhere to be seen. The hotel had a grand staircase with steps that looked threadbare, an army of servants that looked even worse, and dirty spittoons everywhere. Clearly it had seen better days and, it occurred to me then, so had I. Edward Kiss marched up to a reception desk set up in the lobby and announced his own arrival.

"Yes, yes, I am registered," he said irritably to the woman in charge of handing out attendee badges. "Kiss, Edward Kiss, surely you are familiar with my work on Tihuanaku—"

I heard the click of a cigarette lighter and smelled that foul smell of tobacco smoke. A cool, amused voice said, "Ah, Herr Kiss."

I turned and saw a hook-nosed blond with a full crown of hair, a deep tan, and a satisfied smirk wrapped around his cigarette holder.

My client stared at him in loathing.

"Beger," he said.

"It is I. I have only recently returned from Tibet, you know. We did valuable work there, me and Schäfer."

Kiss smirked right back at him. "Measuring skulls? Counting bones? Fiddling with skeletons?"

"Valuable scientific work," Beger said. "Not something you'd know anything about, Kiss."

"Fuck you, Beger!"

"No thanks."

The blond laughed. He too turned to the reception desk. "Beger," he said. "But you know me, darling."

The woman handing out badges almost blushed. Kiss fumed silently beside me.

But I had no eyes just then for either. Instead I stared appreciatively at Beger's companion. She stood there cool as a *gurkensalat* in winter, taking it all in and not giving anything back. She had dark hair, full breasts, a deep tan, and the sort of eyes that would make a *Schäferhund* shit itself and get an erection at the same time.

"Who are you?" I said.

She gazed back at me coolly.

"Who the hell are *you?*" she said.

"Name's Wolf. I'm a private eye."

"Like William Powell in *The Thin Man?*" She looked at me with amusement. "Do you solve murders, too, Mr. Wolf?"

"There is seldom any real mystery in murder," I told her stiffly. "I am far more curious to investigate *you*, Miss...?"

"Trautmann, if you must know," she said. "Erika Trautmann. I'm—"

"Let me guess. An archaeologist?"

"I study petroglyphs and rock runes, particularly in relation to the superior Aryan civilizations of prehistory."

"Of course you do."

"You do not believe we Aryans descended from a superior race that first brought civilization to this world?"

"On the contrary," I said, giving her my best smile. "I believe it explicitly."

"Good, then," she said. Then she looked at me curiously. "You remind me of someone," she said. "But I can't tell who."

"I just have that kind of face," I told her. "I like yours more."

She laughed. "You think you're charming, don't you?" she said. But I could see that she liked it. I always could tell, you know.

"You will excuse us," Beger said coolly. I doffed my hat to Erika Trautmann as the two of them headed toward the hotel's ballroom. By the desk, my client had finally gotten a name badge and turned to me with a scowl.

"Here," he said. "Your lanyard."

"Oh."

I put it on. It looked ridiculous.

"Well?" Kiss said. "Shall we?"

I shrugged. "It's your party."

"It's my *life* that's at stake here!" he said.

"Don't worry," I said as I followed him to the conference hall. "You'll be as safe as Hildegard of Bingen's maidenhood."

In that, of course, I was wrong.

3

A man from IG Farben opened the proceedings. I supposed he had every
right—they had paid for it, after all. His name was Wilhelm Mann and he was
a brutish looking c—t with close-cropped hair and the cold eyes of a pesticide
salesman. He was the sort of guy who marries his cousin.

He spoke a few words—to scattered applause—then left the stage to
the scientists.

The lectures were as boring as one could expect from a bunch of Germans
who have fingered too many skulls in dark caves.

The material itself, though, was fascinating.

How the superior Aryan race evolved out of the ancient civilization of
Atlantis, for which there was definitive proof in cave paintings uncovered by
Altheim and Trautmann in France, for instance.

An old boy, Herbert Jankuhn, gave a rousing lecture on the mass execution
of homosexuals in the ancient bogs of Tollund, of which he was very
approving, and for which there was a loud round of applause.

Beger discussed his expedition to Tibet with the noted explorer, Ernst
Schäfer, where they had indeed measured the skulls of the native Tibetans for
comparison with modern-day Aryans, and also took samples of seeds.

It went on and on and I gorged myself on *spitzbuben* and butter cookies, of
which I am very fond.

Then the conference finished for the day and the good Aryan professors
and their assistants retired to the hotel bar, where they proceeded to get
uproariously and disgustingly drunk. Watching them like this, you could
have thought the good old times of Weimar never ended, that we had never
fought the good fight and lost to the Communists in '33, that I had never
fallen from grace and been imprisoned, and that National Socialism was still
alive and well.

I hated them for that. For the truth was we *had* lost, and I had barely fled the
Fatherland with my life, and the Communists ruled Germany now. And I, who
all of Germany knew and feared and loved at one time—I was a nobody now.

I hated them for that.

A flushed Erika Trautmann came up to me at some point and leaned in
close. I could feel her heat, and smell the alcohol on her breath.

"You do not drink?" she said, only slightly slurring her words.

"I never drink," I told her. "It is a filthy habit."

"A girl can be filthy," she said, and gave me a leer. I felt my throat constrict.

"And you are so pure…" she said. "Are you my Galahad?"

"Listen, Toots," I said, "all the knights are dead."

Instead of an answer, she reached quite boldly and grabbed me by the *fleischklößchen* without so much as a how-do-you-do. I gave a little yelp.

Sometimes this job was hard.

Something was getting hard, at any rate.

Her smile grew wider.

"Is that the Grail in your pocket," she asked, "or are you just glad to see me?"

"Take your hands off of me!" I croaked. "I do not like hussies, and besides I'm on the job."

"F—k you, then!" she screamed in sudden fury, and tossed her olive martini in my face, the b—ch.

She stalked off. I massaged my groin and stared after her. It was funny, but I didn't think she was as drunk as she made herself out to be.

The man from IG Farben—Mann, I remembered his name was—circulated. I saw him speak to Kiss at some point, but they spoke quietly and only for a moment. At some point this Mann made to come up to me, but I avoided him easily. I do not like salesmen.

I kept an eye on Herr Doktor Kiss. He seemed to be having a marvelous time, though one incident did occur. At some point I noticed Kiss arguing loudly with a mustachioed man in his fifties.

"I have conclusively proven Atlantis, the cradle of Aryan civilization, was in the North Atlantic!" the man shouted, poking his finger in Kiss' chest.

"You fraud! You utter buffoon!" Kiss yelled, all but spitting in the other man's face in his passion. "Your theory of the matriarchal society of ancient Atlantis is nothing but degenerate fetishism! Men ruled Atlantis, good Aryan men!"

"You imbecile!"

"Hack!"

"Gentlemen, enough!" I said, stepping between them. "Herr Kiss, it is time to go."

"Fuck you, Wirth!" Kiss yelled, ignoring me as he tried to drunkenly launch himself at the other man. I held him back.

"Come," I said, not entirely gently.

At last he relented. Last orders had anyway been called. Still yelling insults at this Wirth, he let me lead him away to his room.

I went in first and checked the room thoroughly, ensuring there were no silent assassins, exotic snakes, or poisonous spiders under the pillows. The windows were closed and locked and there was no one in the room.

"Alright?" I said.

"Alright, Wolf," he said.

I waited until he shut the door and locked it from the inside. I listened as he staggered round the room for a while, cursing Wirth and Beger and muttering about Atlantis. Then he finally plonked himself into his bed and, moments later, began to snore.

Satisfied that I had done my job correctly, I went to the adjacent room which Kiss had booked for me. I fell asleep quickly, and was only woken up in the early dawn with heavy knocks on my door, to find two irate police constables who informed me Kiss had been murdered.

4

"What the bloody hell do you mean, murdered?" I said. "He was sleeping like a baby last I checked."

"Baby's dead," Constable Marsh said.

"Bye-bye, baby," Constable Carr said mournfully.

"Know anything about that?" Constable Marsh said.

"Me?" I said. "I didn't do it! He hired me to protect him!"

"Good at your job, then, are you?" Constable Carr said.

"Look," I said, "what is all this about? Are you sure he's dead? It makes no sense."

"See for yourself."

"Yeah."

"Come along then, Wolf, or whatever you call yourself."

"Yeah."

I followed them out to the corridor. The door to Kiss's room was open, broken by the police from the outside. I stepped into the room and saw him curled on the armchair in a frozen pose, his nails torn and his face caught in a frightening rictus, as though whatever he'd seen in his last ever dream so spooked him that he died there and then.

Oh, he was *dead*, there was no doubt about it. He was dead as a doorknob. He was dead as a dodo. He was dead as whatever stupid f—king expression the English have for this sort of thing, in that filthy inbred tongue of theirs.

He was very f—king dead, is what I'm saying.

The only thing I couldn't work out was *how*.

"The door was locked," I said dumbly. "From the *inside*."

"Yes, yes," Carr said. "It's a real mystery."

"Quite a conundrum," Marsh said.

"The windows are closed!" I said. I sniffed the air. He'd shat himself in death. It smelled disgusting. Something else, too, very faint now. Something like vanilla or almonds.

"Maybe he killed *himself*," Carr said.

"Suicide, for sure," Marsh said, nodding sagely. "Looks like a clear suicide to me."

"Either way, who gives a s—t for one dead kraut," Carr said, and glared at me as though hoping I'd be next.

"What?" I said. "You can't just *leave* it!"

"The hotel wants the room," Marsh said.

"They'd like the corpse *out*," Carr said.

"And *we'd* like a bacon sandwich and a hot cuppa," Marsh said.

"You're s—t for protection," Carr said.

"S—t," Marsh said, nodding.

"Now f—k off," Carr said. "Or we'll book you for murder, or obstruction, or for being a German in the wrong place at the wrong time."

"Yeah," Marsh said, "the wrong place being England, and the wrong time being right now."

"F—" I started, then stopped when I saw them reaching for their batons.

I stared at my former client. Kiss was dead and that was that. I'd done my best for him, but sometimes your best is not enough.

"Scram," Carr said.

So I scrammed.

5

"What is the meaning of this?" Herman Wirth said. He was the mustachioed man I had seen arguing with my client the night before.

"Kiss is dead," I said. "One of you lot must have murdered him."

"Murdered!" He stared at me in wounded surprise. His moustache quivered. "That's absurd."

They were gathered in the lobby, these scientists of the fallen Reich that never came to be, these eugenicists and race theorists and archaeologists of ancient Mu or Atlantis, or wherever it was they said the Aryan stock came from. They looked up to me, I realized at that moment. It had been a long time since anyone had looked at me that way. Once, I had been their leader. Back then, I still had my moustache. Then came the Fall; the Communists took power; the Reichstag burned and I was tossed into a concentration camp, and barely escaped with my life; to England; to this dismal s—thole of a place.

Now they no longer even remembered me. I, who was once their master!

"Anyway," I said, "it's none of my business, and the police are sure it's suicide."

They visibly relaxed. And I knew then that one or more of them had killed him. I just didn't know how—or why.

A familiar fury took hold of me then. Back when I was a leader of men, all of Germany marched to the beat of my drum. I would stand on the podium and preach National Socialism and they lapped it all up—they loved me for it. I could not *abide* to be dismissed!

It came down to *order*. There had to be order, above all things.

"But it was not," I said then. "One of you *is* guilty. I can smell it on you, like a bad sweat. And I *will* find you."

"You're not even a guest here," Wirth said. "I demand you leave immediately!"

"Actually…" This from Beger, the tanned blond. "Herr Wolf is a registered member of the conference." He smirked at the assembly. "I believe he has just as much right to be here as any of us."

I realized he was right, of course. But still. I was a foreigner in this country where they did not like foreigners, and while these scientists would leave London in a matter of days, I would remain behind, and I knew how the police here treated the German refugees. We were little more than rats to them. The sensible thing was to depart, and keep the client's money...

"I would like to speak to each of you in person," I said.

"Who does he think he is, Hercule Poirot?" I heard someone mutter. I ignored it. I would not be compared to a f—king *Belgian!*

"Beginning with *you*, my dear," I said.

Erika Trautmann turned and gave me an icy smile. "You'd have to buy me a drink first," she said.

"That could be arranged."

"Then lead the way, Herr Wolf. And I will have the *expensive* champagne."

I thought of poor old Kiss's money in my pocket and just shrugged as I led her to the bar.

6

"Did you know him well?"

She sipped from her coupe glass. "Everyone knew Edward. He was a pompous s—t but, you know. We're all one big happy family."

"The *Ahnenerbe*," I said.

"Yes. There has been talk of establishing a permanent institution, you see, but that rather fell by the wayside when the Communists took over. Some of us still believe in Nazism, though. Science proves it. Germans are pure of blood, Jews and Gypsies are inferior races. It's there in the runes on the cave walls, if you know where to look. Besides, Kiss was always happy to buy a girl a drink." She downed her glass and waved it at the bartender for another.

"So you had no reason to dislike him?"

She shrugged. "I'm just a girl," she said. "Listen, Wolf, or whatever you call yourself. Kiss was a passable novelist and a mediocre archaeologist. If that's a reason to kill someone, half the people here would be dead already."

"I saw him shouting at that fellow, Wirth, last night," I said.

"Ah, Herman," she said. "He is our cofounder. Joined the Party early, you know. Big admirer of Hitler—that's who you remind me of! Only he had a moustache... Anyhow, Herman's paper on 'The Prehistory of the Atlantic Nordic Race' was very important work. But he and Kiss did not see eye to eye."

"Oh?"

She shrugged again. The bartender poured her another glass of overpriced champagne. "Herman thought the ancient Atlantids worshipped a single god, and were ruled by women. Kiss has—had, I mean—other ideas. But people don't die over scientific arguments, Herr Wolf."

"No," I said. "They die over a lot less."

I stared at her over her glass. Something rang false about Miss Trautmann.

"Where are you based?" I said.

"The Netherlands, nowadays. Most of us had to leave Germany, you see. But we carry on the work."

"You travel much?"

She smiled. "It is my work. We all do. I had only recently come back from the Middle East, as it happens."

"Alone?"

"With Franz Altheim." She looked at me coolly. "He is one of my lovers. Do I shock you?"

"Lady," I said, "very little shocks me."

She sipped her drink. "Are we done here?"

"What were you doing in the Middle East?"

"Studied the pyramids and inscriptions in Abu Simbel. That sort of thing."

"And did you arrive at any conclusions?"

"Yes," she said. "It's too hot there and the food's unbearable." She laughed throatily and pushed closer into me. Her knee pushed between my legs and rubbed against me. "Can't find a decent bratwurst *anywhere*, if you know what I mean."

The woman was insufferable!

"Thank you, Miss Trautmann," I said stiffly (in more ways than one), and got up. "That will be all for now."

"I'm in room 405, if you need to ask me any more...questions," she said.

"But that's the room next to Kiss's!" I said, surprised. "Did you hear anything in the night?"

"I'm afraid not," she said. "I'm a heavy sleeper."

She downed the second glass and sauntered away, glancing back at me only once. She didn't look like a killer, but then, those kind of dames never do.

7

"Kiss?" Herman Wirth said. "The man was a fool, but I didn't kill him. If I went around blithely murdering every idiot who called himself an archaeologist, there'd be no one left at the *Ahnenerbe*." He grimaced a smile at me and helped himself to some nuts on the bar.

"What did you disagree about?"

"What didn't we," he said, chewing loudly. The man was a pig. "You can come hear my talk on ancient Atlantis and make up your own mind. It is most illuminating."

"I'm sure it is."

"Listen, my friend," he said, leaning close and spitting bits of nuts in my face. "*Cherchez la femme*, do you get my meaning?"

"I'm not sure that I do."

"Kiss had a thing for the Trautmann woman. Well, you saw her. She's quite the piece. My colleagues all f—k each other like dogs in heat, you know."

"I didn't. Are you suggesting Kiss and Trautmann had an affair?"

"I'm sure I couldn't say."

"Why would she kill him?"

"Listen, man," he said. "What does it matter who killed him, when you don't even know *how* it was done? I understand the room was locked from the inside."

"It's a mystery," I admitted. I hated mysteries.

"Must have killed himself, then," Wirth said. "And good riddance."

"You just suggested Trautmann killed him."

"Did I?" He wiped his lips with a napkin and stood up. "Well, you're the detective, Herr Wolf. You figure it out. Pip-pip, tra la la!" He saluted me and sauntered off.

I was trying to figure out my next move when the man from IG Farben—the one who looked like he married his cousin—came up to me. Today he was in a conservative gray suit. He shook my hand and looked at me gravely.

"Wilhelm Rudolf Mann," he said. "International sales. At your service."

"Are you?" I said. "At my service?"

"Not really," he said. "Herr Wolf, we at IG Farben do not like a spectacle. Slow and steady and respectable, that's more us. So as regrettable as Herr…

Kiss, was it? Kiss's death is, the case is closed. There *is* no investigation. And we'd much rather you just…moved on. Do you get my meaning?"

"Scram?" I said.

He looked at me dubiously. "Yes, that," he said.

"I'm afraid I cannot. I still have principles."

"You are a buffoon!" he said. "I know who you are, who you once were, at any rate. I believed in the cause. I'd joined the Party back in '31, you know. I was a Brownshirt, too. I was as good a Nazi as anyone here."

"Mazel tov," I said.

He looked at me in anger. "But you are being bad for *business*," he said. "Walk away, Herr…*Wolf*. Go back to your office in Berwick Street—"

He made a point of telling me he knew where I lived.

"And find some other employment. A juicy divorce, perhaps?"

"I don't work divorces," I told him, angry. Though of course he was right. You had to pay the rent *some*how.

"Word to the wise, Herr Wolf. Walk away."

And with that he turned and left me there, full of thought.

8

"You're barking up the wrong tree, Wolf, old boy," Bruno Beger said. He looked at me pleasantly and drank his beer. "Kiss wasn't anybody."

"He was your rival."

"Hardly! He was a fantasist and his best days were behind him. Must be why he topped himself."

"It was murder."

"Not what the police are saying."

"Listen, Beger. British cops don't give two f—ks about a dead German. Not these days. What surprises me is that neither do any of you."

"What can I tell you, Wolf? He wasn't the most popular guy."

"Did you kill him?"

He laughed in my face. "Are you that inept?" he said. "*This* is how you go about solving crime, randomly accusing people?"

I shrugged. Truth was I just wanted to see his reaction. I said, "Where were you last night?"

"I had a few drinks, then went back to my room."

"Were you alone?"

He smirked and didn't answer.

"Who do you work for, really?" I said.

"I'm just an anthropologist."

I let him go at that. They were all liars; scam artists who preached Aryan superiority and Atlantis while doing…what?

It had not escaped me that these people, in the guise of harmless scientists, could travel freely—and did so. That they could go places others could not. And, moreover, could gather information while doing so.

There was a word for that, and the word was *spies*.

They were all former Nazis—devoted ones. But National Socialism had collapsed with my fall. My former comrades had dispersed to all corners. I knew Hess was in London, though I had not seen him in over two years. Goering had wormed his way into the good graces of the Communists and now served in some function back in Germany—the fat c—t always knew how to sail with the wind. The others I knew little about and cared even less. They had betrayed me—they had all betrayed me!

I should have ruled Germany—I should have ruled the *world*!

But anyway.

If these people were spies—then who did they work for?

I settled my by now considerable bar tab and made my way back up the stairs to Kiss's room. The police had come and gone and the broken door remained hanging open, so I stepped in. The corpse had been removed, but no attempt had been made to clean up the room.

I looked around. There were signs of a struggle, but I knew Kiss was alone. Something had spooked him, inside the room. I saw the expression on his face in death. He must have moved around, tried to escape his fate somehow. The chair was broken and he had thrashed and flailed before death took him.

How did he die?

I searched the room—

There.

Some fine powder on the floor under the air vents. I didn't touch it. I knelt down, though my knees creaked, and sniffed. Kiss had been right. The killer or killers were theatrical. I did not like the theatre, myself.

You see, this is what these f—kers never understand. Murder is not an elaborate *show*. It takes no costumes, sleight of hand, exotic reptiles, or fireworks. Murder is utilitarian and simple and brutal and it's too f—king *easy*. You don't need brains to kill a man. You just need to be willing.

Murder, truly, is the triumph of the will.

I looked around some more. I noted someone had gone through the stuff before me. Kiss's suitcase, previously closed, was open on the bed. It had been tossed. It did not surprise me.

Very few things did, these days.

Kiss had flashed his cash around. I did know that—the man paid me fully in advance.

He said he had independent income from his novels.

But in my experience no one earned as badly as a writer. You may as well try to sell Scotch eggs to the French or good wine to the English. There's just no future in it.

So had Kiss lied to me?

And if so, where did he get his money?

9

"You may be wondering why I've gathered you all here," I said.

Erika Trautmann took a sip of wine and smiled at me sweetly. "Not really," she said.

Beside her were Bruno Beger, the blond anthropologist; Herman Wirth, the mustachioed Atlantis aficionado; and Wilhelm Rudolf Mann, the sales agent from IG Farben.

"Get on with it, then," Wirth muttered. He lit a cigar.

Beger smiled as he lit a slim cigarette. "Let the man speak, Herman," he said.

Mann said nothing, just glared.

I sighed.

"Very well," I said. "One of your comrades, Edward Kiss, has been murdered in this very hotel. None of you seem concerned in the slightest."

"He was a s—t," Wirth said.

"He was not a very good archaeologist, I'm afraid," Beger said, almost apologetically.

"He was an inadequate lover," Erika Trautmann said. Then: "What?" into our expectant faces.

I sighed again. I could feel a headache coming on.

"Yet one of you felt strongly enough about the man to commit murder."

"Absurd, man!" Wirth said.

Beger just laughed. The Trautmann woman sipped her wine. The man from IG Farben glared wordlessly.

"The problem with amateurs," I said, "is that they make things needlessly complicated. In this case, a real locked room mystery. How *did* they do it? Was it the snake on the bell cord? Was it bullets made of ice? Was some sort of specially-trained pygmy assassin hidden behind the curtains? This is all nonsense."

"I told you it is," the man from IG Farben said. "So why are you still here?"

"You!" I said, pointing. "What does IG Farben sell, Herr Mann? Fine toothpaste, for sure. Aspirin, and heroin of the highest quality, indubitably. But something else, too."

"Yes?"

"Yes," I said. "Pesticide. Zyklon B, to be exact. Hydrogen cyanide, which comes conveniently prepared in capsule form. The very poison gas that *your* company manufactures!"

"So? Anyone could buy that at their convenience," he said. "I hardly carry pesticide around with me, Herr Wolf."

But I had already dismissed him.

"You!" I said, pointing to Erika Trautmann. "It was *your* room that was directly adjacent to Herr Kiss's. The poison was administered through the connecting air vents. The pellets were simply dropped through. On exposure to air the gas was released. Herr Kiss had less than two minutes to live. He died in agony upon inhaling the gas."

I looked at them triumphantly.

They stared back at me with indifference. Beger took a drag on his cigarette. Trautmann sipped her wine. Mann and Wirth scowled.

"Are you accusing me?" Trautmann said.

"You!" I said, pointing to Beger. I was beginning to enjoy myself. "You said you had spent the night in your room, with company. I suggest to you that the reason you were not alone was that you spent the night with Miss Trautmann!"

"So?" Beger said. Trautmann smirked. "I am very fond of Erika and, besides, she's a tiger in the sack."

"You're not too bad yourself," she murmured.

"If Miss Trautmann wasn't in her room, it was easy enough for someone else to gain entrance and administer the poison across," I said.

"So I'm not guilty?" She turned those innocent eyes on me and pouted, almost as though I'd disappointed her.

"Which leaves *you*," I said softly.

"I beg your pardon?" Herman Wirth said, looking startled, and not at all pleased.

"This is *your* little operation, is it not?" I said. "The *Ahnenerbe*. A think tank, I believe you call it. An odd assortment of Nazi-sympathetic scientists, archaeologists and the like. You could have been a real something, if the Party had won in '33. But with the Communists in charge, you are diminished. The world laughs at your science. They embrace *Jew* science—Freud and Einstein! Relativity, psychoanalysis! They laugh at your stories of Atlantis! It must hurt, Herr Wirth. It must hurt so bad, to lose."

"Why would I kill Kiss?" he said. "You are being ridiculous."

"My guess is he was blackmailing you," I said. "He had too much money for an archaeologist. What he had on you I don't know. It's always something grubby and sordid, though. Proof of an affair or embezzlement, maybe a compromising photograph or two. This is what you people never understand. Murder is a *simple* art."

"Stay back," he said. I saw then the gun he had in his lap. It was pointing at me. "You can't prove any of this, Wolf, or whatever you call yourself. You're a nobody."

"Take it easy with that gun," I said.

"The man was a fool! His research was laughable. It threatened the integrity of my work."

"Is that why you killed him?"

He all but gloated. "It was simple enough," he said. "Zyklon B, why had no one else thought of this? I gassed the f—ker and didn't feel a thing. You know, we could have got rid of the Jews this way, and IG Farben would have made a fortune in the process selling the stuff."

"Why did you kill him?"

"There was a night in Tangier, we both got very drunk and spent the night with some Moroccan houris. You know how it is. The man must have had a camera on him. When I came to, he had all he needed. I am not a rich man, Herr Wolf. The goal of my life is science, not filthy lucre. I had no choice. You *must* see that."

Beger tapped out his cigarette. "Put the gun away already, Herman," he said irritably. "Herr Wolf was just leaving."

"Was I?" I said.

"Yes. This charade has gone on long enough. What do you expect to happen now, Wolf? The case is closed and the police aren't interested. No one gives a s—t."

"Yeah," Erika Trautmann said, and drained the last of her drink. She stared me at through the glass. "You're boring us," she complained.

I stared pleadingly at the man from IG Farben, but he seemed lost in thought.

"Mass gassing?" he said. "How would that work? You'd have to brick the windows and lock the doors, drop the pellets in through the air vents... Yes, it could work, I suppose, on an industrial scale. But you'd need the infrastructure! Camps, trains to bring them all there... Crematoriums for after..."

He was lost in what must have been, for him, a pleasant daydream.

"Well?" Wirth said. The gun was still pointing at me.

I stared at him in loathing.

I had found the killer and solved the crime.

And it had made no difference at all.

That's the thing about crime. Bad deeds often go unpunished. The guilty walk free. It doesn't matter if you find the killer if there is no one left to keep the law. All that bull the Dickson Carrs and Allinghams of the world try to sell you don't mean s—t in the final count.

Murder's just another dirty business.

"Tons of Zyklon B..." Mann said, dreamily.

Wirth smiled at me nastily. The gun was pointing at my abdomen.

"Well?" he said. "Scram."

So I scrammed.

***

They return home and Shomer tucks Avrom into bed, beside his sister. He sits there by the window and watches his children sleep. Beyond the ghetto walls the trains pass, whistling, going east. The night's as quiet as it ever can be, here. The single candle's light ebbs against the walls. And Shomer closes his eyes, and wishes he could sleep. How softly do the children breathe.

They have that, he thinks. For as long as they have breath, they will—

Historical Afterword

IG Farben—purveyors, indeed, of fine aspirin, heroin (trademarked 1895), toothpaste, and, yes, pesticides—were the largest chemical and pharmaceutical manufacturer in Nazi Germany. Amongst their many profitable enterprises were the extensive use of Jewish slave labor, and the wholesale provision of Zyklon B for Auschwitz-Birkenau's gas chambers.

Wilhelm Rudolf Mann (who really did marry his cousin, proving Wolf right) had indeed joined the Nazi Party early. He was a board member of IG Farben, in charge of the pesticides department, and was behind financing the grotesque experiments of Josef Mengele in Auschwitz. He was captured by the Allies and put on trial for war crimes alongside his colleagues at IG Farben, but was acquitted. He died peacefully of very old age in Bavaria, long after the war.

The curious reader may wish to pursue Diarmuid Jeffreys's *Hell's Cartel: IG Farben and the Making of Hitler's War Machine* (2008) for more on this subject.

The *Ahnenerbe* was formally established by Heinrich Himmler in 1935. Herman Wirth was its first president. The institute gathered the worst of the Nazis' pseudoscientists, eugenicists, and believers in Atlantis, "glacial cosmology," and, of course, the superiority of the Aryan race. As ludicrous as their work may seem, it was real, and had real-world and deadly consequences. The *Ahnenerbe* served to justify and provide a scientific rationale for the Holocaust. Bruno Beger personally was in charge of selecting prisoners to be murdered by gas simply in order for the *Ahnenerbe* to have a skeleton collection. Edmund Kiss joined the Waffen SS toward the end of the war, but never stood trial. Erika Trautmann's Middle East trip involved spying for Nazi intelligence.

For more on the *Ahnenerbe*, the reader may wish to seek out Heather Pringle's *The Master Plan: Himmler's Scholars and the Holocaust* (2006).

As for Wolf, he appears in my 2014 novel, *A Man Lies Dreaming*, and has been haunting me ever since. I hope and pray this is his last outing—but somehow I doubt it.

About the Authors

MICHAEL BRACKEN and SANDRA MURPHY. Michael Bracken is the author of several books and more than 1,200 short stories, including crime fiction published in *Alfred Hitchcock's Mystery Magazine*, *Ellery Queen's Mystery Magazine*, and *The Best American Mystery Stories 2018*. Sandra Murphy is an extensively published nonfiction writer, the author of several short stories (including crime fiction collected in *From Hay to Eternity: Ten Tales of Crime and Deception*), and the editor of *A Murder of Crows* (Darkhouse Books). www. crimefictionwriter.com.

KEITH BROOKE's first novel, *Keepers of the Peace*, appeared in 1990, since when he has published eight more adult novels, six collections, and more than seventy short stories. His novel *Genetopia* was published by Pyr in February 2006 and was their first title to receive a starred review in *Publishers Weekly*; *The Accord*, published by Solaris in 2009, received another starred *PW* review and was optioned for film. His most recent SF novel, *Harmony* (published in the UK as *alt.human*), was shortlisted for the Philip K Dick Award. Writing as Nick Gifford, his teen fiction is published by Puffin, with one novel also optioned for the movies by Andy Serkis and Jonathan Cavendish's Caveman Films. He writes reviews for the *Guardian*, teaches creative writing at the University of Essex, and lives with his wife Debbie in Wivenhoe, Essex.

Born in Haworth, West Yorkshire, ERIC BROWN has lived in Australia, India, and Greece. He has won the British Science Fiction Award twice for his short stories, and his novel *Helix Wars* was shortlisted for the 2012 Philip K. Dick award. He's published over seventy books and his latest include the sixth crime novel in the Langham and Dupré series, set in the 1950s, *Murder Served Cold*, and the Sherlock Holmes novel, *The Martian Menace*. He lives near Dunbar in Scotland, and his website is ericbrown.co.uk.

JARED CADE is an acknowledged authority on Agatha Christie. His biography *Agatha Christie and the Eleven Missing Days* is officially endorsed by relatives from the Watts side of the family who gave him exclusive access to their family papers, memories, and photo albums. He recently turned to crime fiction with the publication of his first full-length novel *Murder on London Underground* in which he utilizes his insider's knowledge of the transport system to produce a race against the clock, high body count thriller featuring Lyle Revel and Hermione Bradbury. The couple make their short story debut in "Murder in Pelham Wood."

PAUL CHARLES was born and raised in the Northern Irish countryside. He is the author of the critically acclaimed Detective Inspector Christy Kennedy series which is set in Camden Town and Primrose Hill. *Departing Shadows*, the eleventh full-length Kennedy murder mystery, has just been published by Dufour. He has also written three Inspector Starrett mysteries set in Donegal, a couple of McCusker mysteries set in Belfast, and four stand-alone Castlemartin novels set in rural Northern Ireland in the 1960s. The short story in this collection features Inspector Kennedy at work in the heart of his patch in Camden Town.

O'NEIL DE NOUX is a New Orleans writer with forty-one books published, four hundred short story sales, and a screenplay produced. He writes crime fiction, historical fiction, children's fiction, mainstream fiction, science fiction, suspense, fantasy, horror, Western, literary, young adult, religious, romance, humor, and erotica. His fiction has received several awards, including the Shamus Award for Best Short Story, the Derringer Award for Best Novelette and the 2011 Police Book of the Year. Two of his stories have appeared in The Best American Mystery Stories anthology (2013 and 2007). He is a past vice president of the Private Eye Writers of America.

MARTIN EDWARDS' latest novel, *Gallows Court*, was nominated for both the 2019 eDunnit award for best crime novel and the CWA Historical Dagger. He was recently honored with the CWA Dagger in the Library for his body of work and has received the Edgar, Agatha, H.R.F. Keating and Poirot awards, two Macavity awards, and the CWA Short Story Dagger. He is consultant to the British Library's Crime Classics and president of the Detection Club.

He has published eighteen novels (including the Harry Devlin series and the Lake District Mysteries), nine nonfiction books, and sixty short stories and has edited forty anthologies.

JANE FINNIS lives in Yorkshire and has been fascinated by ancient Roman history ever since, as a child, she walked the straight Roman roads that still cross the countryside there and saw the historic remains in cities like York. Her mysteries are set there in Roman times when Britain was a raw frontier province of a mighty Empire. Her amateur and rather reluctant sleuth is Aurelia Marcella, who runs the Oak Tree Inn on the road to York, where she receives all sorts of visitors bringing all sorts of problems. Aurelia appears in several short stories and also in a series of novels: *Shadows in the Night, A Bitter Chill, Buried Too Deep*, and *Danger in the Wind*.

JOHN GRANT is the author of over eighty books, including *A Comprehensive Encyclopedia of Film Noir* (2013), the largest of its kind in the English language. His stories have been collected in (so far) *Take No Prisoners* (2004) and *Tell No Lies* (2014). He's the author of a loose series of books on science issues, including *Discarded Science* (2006), *Corrupted Science* (2007; revised 2018) and *Denying Science* (2011). For his work editing the Paper Tiger imprint of fantasy/ sf art books, he received a Chesley Award. For his own nonfiction, he has received two Hugos, a World Fantasy Award and others.

RHYS HUGHES has written many short stories in the past thirty years, including numerous crime stories. He is currently working on a set of "Reconstruction Club" tales of which "The Menace in Venice" is the third in sequence. The idea is that each individual story works as a stand-alone tale but is also part of a carefully linked series of yarns, all featuring the same characters. He lives in Wales when not traveling the world and Africa.

DERYN LAKE started to write stories at the age of five, then graduated to novels but destroyed all her early work because, she says, it was hopeless. A chance meeting with one of the Getty family took her to Sutton Place and her first serious novel was born. Deryn was married to a journalist and writer, the late L.F. Lampitt, then to a Sussex farmer, Zak Packham. She has two grown-up children, four beautiful and talented grandchildren, and one rather large cat. Deryn lives near the famous battlefield of 1066.

ASHLEY LISTER is a prolific writer, having written more than fifty full-length books and over a hundred short stories. Aside from regularly blogging about poetry and writing in general, Ashley also lectures in creative writing. His most recent title is *How to Write Short Stories and Get Them Published*. He lives in the North of England.

AMY MYERS, born in Kent, UK, is the author of several series of crime novels and many short stories, most of which appear in *Ellery Queen Mystery Magazine*. She began her working life as a publisher, and, after marrying her American husband, she hopped over the fence to the greener grass (she hoped) of writing full time. Her current series stars a 1920s chef Nell Drury and periodically she revisits former series, such as the wheelchair-bound ex-cop and offspring Marsh & Daughter, Victorian chimney sweep Tom Wasp, classic car sleuth Jack Colby and Victorian master chef Auguste Didier. She loves them all dearly.

Before CHRISTINE POULSON turned to crime, she was an academic with a PhD in the history of art. Her Cassandra James mysteries are set in Cambridge in the UK. Her short stories have been published in *Ellery Queen Mystery Magazine*, Crime Writers' Association anthologies, the *Mammoth Book of Best British Mysteries*, and elsewhere. In 2018 she was shortlisted for both the Margery Allingham Prize and the CWA Short Story Dagger. Her latest novel, *An Air That Kills*, the third in a series of medical mysteries featuring scientist Katie Flanagan, came out in November 2019.

DAVID QUANTICK began his writing career with a short story in *City Limits* magazine and then wrote music journalism for the NME and others as well as comedy for *Spitting Image*. After failing to write several novels, he continued his television and radio career, writing on *The Thick Of It*, *TV Burp*, *Brass Eye* and *Veep* (for which he won an Emmy) and began to publish novels in the twenty-first century—*All My Colors*, *The Mule*, and the forthcoming *Night Train*. He puts a new short story every month on his website, www.davidquantick.com.

LAVIE TIDHAR's most recent novels are *By Force Alone* and *The Escapement*, both out in 2020. He is a winner of the World Fantasy Award among many other prizes, as well as a CWA Dagger Award nominee. Born in Israel, he has also lived in South Africa but now resides in London.

L C (Len) TYLER is a former cultural attaché and chief executive of a medical royal college. He writes two crime series: the Herring Mysteries and a historical series featuring seventeenth century lawyer and spy John Grey. He has had short stories published in a number of magazines and anthologies. He has won the Goldsboro Last Laugh Award (twice), the Ian St James Awards, and the 2017 CWA Short Story Dagger. Len has also been twice nominated for an Edgar Allan Poe award in the US. He has lived and worked all over the world but has more recently been based in London and West Sussex.

BEV VINCENT is the author of over ninety short stories, including appearances in *Alfred Hitchcock's* and *Ellery Queen's Mystery Magazines*, *Cemetery Dance* magazine and two MWA anthologies. His books include *The Road to the Dark Tower* and *The Stephen King Illustrated Companion*. He recently coedited the anthology *Flight or Fright* with Stephen King. His work has been nominated for the Edgar, the Stoker (twice), and the ITW Thriller Awards, and he is the 2010 winner of the Al Blanchard Award. He lives in Texas, where he is working on a novel. Learn more at bevvincent.com.

About the Editor

MAXIM JAKUBOWSKI is a London-based former publisher, editor, and translator. He has compiled over one hundred anthologies in a variety of genres, many of which have garnered awards. He is a past winner of the Karel and Anthony awards. He broadcasts regularly on radio and TV, reviews for diverse newspapers and magazines, and has been a judge for several literary prizes. He is the author of twenty novels, including *The Louisiana Republic* (2018), and a series of *Sunday Times* bestselling novels under a pseudonym. He has just completed his twenty-first novel, *The Piper's Dance*. He has also published five collections of his own short stories. He is currently honorary vice chair of the British Crime Writers' Association. www. maximjakubowski.co.uk.

Mango Publishing, established in 2014, publishes an eclectic list of books by diverse authors—both new and established voices—on topics ranging from business, personal growth, women's empowerment, LGBTQ studies, health, and spirituality to history, popular culture, time management, decluttering, lifestyle, mental wellness, aging, and sustainable living.

We were recently named 2019's #1 fastest growing independent publisher by *Publishers Weekly*. Our success is driven by our main goal, which is to publish high quality books that will entertain readers as well as make a positive difference in their lives.

Our readers are our most important resource; we value your input, suggestions, and ideas. We'd love to hear from you—after all, we are publishing books for you!

Please stay in touch with us and follow us at:

Facebook: Mango Publishing
Twitter: @MangoPublishing
Instagram: @MangoPublishing
LinkedIn: Mango Publishing
Pinterest: Mango Publishing

Sign up for our newsletter at www.mango.bz and receive a free book!

Join us on Mango's journey to reinvent publishing, one book at a time.

9 781642 502183